King of Ruin

The Wicked Wonderland Duet

Lee Jacquot

KING OF RUIN

THE WICKED WONDERLAND DUET

LEE JACQUOT

Cover Design: Cat at TRC Designs

Editing & Proofreading: Ellie & Rosa at My Brother's editor

A Note From The Author

King of Ruin is the second in the Wicked Wonderland Duet. Its predecessor, Queen of Madness, must be read in its entirety before beginning book two.

This is a dark, steamy read intended for mature audiences of legal adulthood age. Please visit https://www.leejacquot.com/content-warnings for possible trigger and content warnings.

While it is NOT a retelling of Alice in Wonderland nor Through the Looking Glass, I hope you enjoy the many Easter eggs, and nods to the original story.

Reader discretion is advised.

You cannot change the past, but I dare say, you might learn something from it.

-Time, Through the Looking Glass

EZEKIEL

AGE 6

PROLOGUE

"And when all was said and done, the little boy knew what the old man said to be true. 'No matter how small you are. No matter how insignificant you think yourself to be. You have the power to save the world, you just have to believe it.'" The skin on my mom's eyes wrinkles in the corner as she smiles at me, closing the old book.

It's her favorite bedtime story, and even though she reads it to me every night, I still don't believe anything in it.

It's kind of like listening to a story about mermaids and unicorns, or wizards and dragons. It would be so cool if it were real, but some stuff is better left between the pages of the crumpled book we found at Goodwill.

Still, when she reads it to me, patting her big, round belly, it's the only time she seems happy. Like the shadows that always follow behind her finally disappear, even if just for the ten minutes it takes for her to fill my head with all the dreams she wants me to believe in.

And they are just dreams.

My father spent the summer making sure of it. It was on my seventh birthday that he showed up and taught me a thing or two about *reality*.

The word is hard for me to say, and I don't know exactly what it means, but I understand how it feels. And it feels like pain. Hot, scary, and dark.

The man with the shiny head comes to get me every Wednesday at the same time. The first time it happened, my heart nearly exploded. I was so excited. The long, black car with dark windows and glossy seats made me feel like one of those movie stars I see on TV. I thought maybe my dad had lots of money and was going to give me some as a birthday gift so I could buy Mommy that footrest she whispers about wanting.

She's always on her feet. Working and working and working until it's way past my bedtime. But I always stay up and wait for her to come home no matter how heavy my eyelids get. I want to tell her how many steps baby Fi walked that day. Or the funny faces she made when I gave her broccoli. Fi hates broccoli.

But on Wednesdays, I don't get to tell her. The nice lady who lives two doors down has to instead because the shiny-headed man comes and gets me.

He takes me to the man with a belly bigger than my mommy, and cheeks pinker than Santa. For a while, I thought he *was* Santa. His house is giant, bigger than ten of my schools stacked on top of each other. He has men running in and out of the place, always asking what they can do for him, just like elves.

When he opens his big arms and laughs, his whole body shakes with joy. I thought maybe that's why he couldn't be around to help me and Mommy. Because he had the whole world to worry about and presents to deliver.

And for a moment, a small moment, I thought maybe the stories were real. Maybe it meant that dragons and unicorns were too. And if that were true, then maybe someone small like me could be enough to change the world.

In those moments, I was the happiest seven-year-old that ever lived. And in the next, *reality* covered me in complete darkness. Like a storm that moved over the perfect picnic. And with the first smack of his hand, the sky cracked open and flooded over me, stealing whatever dreams of happiness I had.

He taught me that I was nothing more than a tool he would shape with fire, just like the Play-Doh I mold when playing with Fi. He taught me who I am, and that I will *never* be able to save the world.

My name is Ezekiel Liam Kane. I am the son of Lucy Kane, and the don, Phineas Murphy. I am to tell no one of who I am or where I go on Wednesday nights. I am to wait, watch, and learn.

And one day, my father will call on me to do something that will set my mother and sisters free. Free from the cracked walls that let spiders in when the weather gets too cold. From the four buckets we have to put on the Xs my mommy drew in marker, so it catches the rain that drips from the ceiling.

Free from the men that come around late at night when I'm supposed to be in bed sleeping and yell bad things at my mommy before hitting her.

And I'll do anything to set us free.

So I say yes.

Yes to the pain.

Yes to the fear.

To the dark closets, and horrible sounds.

To learning to lie to my second-grade teacher, Mrs. Whim, about the dark colors on my arms and under my eyes. And about why on Thursday mornings I don't do too good on spelling tests.

Even though almost a year has passed since my first yes, I know one day, when Wednesday comes, it won't be cloudy anymore.

Baby Fiona coos from her small crib, drawing both me and Mommy's attention. Mom is due to have my new baby sister tomorrow, so she came home early from work today. It will be the first time she's here when the bald man comes.

She worries so much when I'm gone, that when I come back, she inspects my body three times over, treats any wounds, and then cries before taking a short nap. I don't think she sleeps while I'm gone.

Lifting Fi on her hip, she pushes her long brown hair over her shoulder so Fi can't grab it. "Did you like that story, baby girl?"

Fi giggles and waves her hand. "Yah, yah. Gin, gin."

My mommy laughs, the sweet sound filling the tiny room and making me smile even though the bright clock on the wall says it's almost time. "Alright, I'll read it again. But first, let's get you a nighttime bottle."

We all walk to the small kitchen, where Mommy makes a quick bottle and hums as she twirls around the kitchen. Her belly narrowly misses bumping into the counter four times, and each time she giggles.

"Drop those tight shoulders, Zeky. I'm not going to hit Bunny."

I blow out the air I'm holding in my cheeks and do as I'm told, letting my shoulders fall, but keep my eyes on baby B. We call her Bunny because when I put my hand on her tummy, it always seems like she's kicking both feet out at the same time.

After Fi finishes her bottle, her eyes become droopy. We head back to the room for Mommy to read the story again and put her to sleep, but stop short when the sound of a car door shutting rings in the air. The hair on my neck stands up and my skin feels like a thousand ants are marching around, nipping at me every few steps.

A few seconds later, two heavy knocks echo through the

small house, and the light sound of splitting wood tells me that the man is mad I'm not standing at the door waiting for him.

My mom's brows bunch together, the worry in her features making my heart squeeze tight. Even baby Fi hides her face in Mommy's neck.

"It's okay, Mommy. I'll be back at the same time tomorrow. Not a minute later." I try to keep my voice light and happy. I don't want her to be sad when she needs to think about the new baby.

She lifts a sleepy Fi higher on her hip before nodding. "I love you, Zeky."

"I love you, too."

I slip out of my room and rush to the front door, grabbing my jacket that's slung over the couch. When I unlock the bolt, the wood swings open to reveal the bald man and his grumpy stare.

"I don't like waiting, kid."

I clamp my teeth down on my bottom lip to keep from apologizing and nod. One of the first lessons my dad ever taught me was to never say sorry. *Ever*. It means weakness and tells the world you made a mistake.

The Murphys *never* make mistakes.

I brush past him to the long, black car that used to remind me of a celebrity's, but now looks more like the thing that carries dead people.

Maybe it is.

But tonight, no matter what happens, tomorrow won't be so bad because when I get home, I'll get to meet Bunny in the afternoon.

And protecting the three of them will make everything worth it.

Nothing and no one will ever change that.

CHAPTER ONE

Fool. *noun.* A person who acts unwisely or imprudently. A silly person. Synonyms include idiot, dunce, and ignorant.

I am many things, but a fool, I have never been.

Since my parents' murder, I've moved quietly, been meticulous, and acted carefully in order to bring my plan of vengeance—no, of *justice*—to fruition. Even with the persistent theft and murder of my guards, I never acted impulsively, or made a misstep that would potentially put my plan in jeopardy.

Yet, here I am.

My head is pounding, my wrists are chafed and raw from the metal cuffs affixed to my flesh, and the sticky blood that's soaked through my corset and slacks is beginning to make my skin itch. I'm covered in darkness, with only myself, the sounds of faraway footsteps, and an incessant drip of water on the cement floor, as company. Judging by the dryness in my mouth and the contorted growl of my stomach, it's been at least ten to twelve hours since my capture.

I need to figure out where I am, but the tempo of the leaking pipes is near maddening, so I let my mind wander to keep me grounded.

Grounded. Such a simple idea, yet a hard feat to accomplish when my mind is riddled with images of Kilo's mangled legs, my butler's shattered body, and of Kane.

Kane.

My chest tightens at the same time a horrific cackle erupts from my cracked lips, reminding me that I allowed a *man* to make me appear to be a fool after all.

I *knew* what he was. The moment I saw him, I knew he would be my undoing if I let him. Granted, I never once thought he was the *son* of the man who ordered my parents to be slaughtered, but I was well aware that he would somehow be the reason I fell from my throne.

I should have followed my gut, kept him at arm's length, and killed him when the job was done. But I let his shadows encroach around me, hindering my ability to see anything but him. I began to rely on the relief he granted me when he took control of the things I held on to so tightly my hands bled.

He was an illusion of solace. A glimmer of light when all I had known for the past decade is darkness. And he knew that.

He examined my armor for the hint of a weak spot, and when he found it, he embedded himself beneath and exploited it, breaking it from within.

A job well done, even I can admit that.

A slight burn radiates behind my eyes as I reject the sliver of doubt still flickering in the back of my mind. The memory of his rough hands coasting over my body, controlling everything while allowing me to let go, plays on repeat.

He could have killed me a dozen times over, but he didn't. And I can't seem to curb the desire to know why.

No. It doesn't matter why he chose to prolong my death sentence. What matters now is that my estate is nothing more than a pile of rubble, left unguarded to the filthy vermin, and I'm here, unable to protect my family.

I have no idea of their whereabouts or if they're even alive. After Phineas knocked Kane unconscious, he didn't waste any time on a monologue and merely stuck a needle in my neck, damning me to sleep while his goons did who knows what to my home.

When I came to, I found myself in what appears to be a cellar, not too unlike my own. Its floor and walls consist of nothing but concrete and rusted plumbing running along the ceiling. The one overhead light is turned off, leaving the glow from under the lone door as the only way for me to discern any of my surroundings.

Every sixty minutes or so, someone stands in front of it, blocking the fragment of light, but then they do nothing for a full minute before shuffling away. They're checking to see if I'm awake, and in those sixty seconds, I feign steady breaths and the soft hums of someone still unconscious.

They say time is a thief. A villain. But my uncle taught me that it's my best friend in situations such as these. It allows me the necessary duration to listen to my surroundings and take in any sounds that may give me insight as to where I am. It lets any lingering drugs wear out of my system and gives me time to construct an escape plan.

The only con is that with each passing second, my body is without food, without water, and left to rot under the weight of fear.

Only, that's something I'll never have to worry about. Fear left me the day my mother's head rolled on the pristine, white sidewalk. It left when I watched the light leave my father's eyes just before the machete pierced his chest. And the final bit of fear I had about my life after vengeance was completely disintegrated in the flames of Kane's betrayal.

All that remains of me now is an animal. One made from blood, fangs, and hunger.

I don't plan to die here, at least not without taking as many heads as I can, Kane's included.

The thick clunk of a dead bolt unlocking resounds in the small, dark space. Light from the hall floods inside, forcing me to narrow my eyes to keep from being blinded.

I will my heart rate to remain steady as I take in Phineas filling the threshold. His dark suit is ill-fitted, the pant legs pooling at his ankles over buffed loafers. The button on his jacket is barely holding in his rotund belly, and the smug look on his weathered, scruffy face is equivalent to an arrogant villain's before being overtaken due to his negligence.

My body reacts of its own accord, a fury working through my veins and burning my limbs with the need to move. To kill. My wrists twist behind me in the chains binding me to the wooden chair in the middle of the room.

Wooden. Idiots. I'm not sure what irks me more. The fact they call themselves an elite crime family while making mediocre mistakes, like giving me enough time to recover. Or the fact they allowed someone to tie me to a chair, which I broke the second I woke up.

Keeping my hands behind my back, I tighten my grasp on the broken, jagged end of a support bar as I straighten my spine. "To what do I owe this pleasure, Phineas?"

His thick brows draw together as he takes a wide step into the room. Three men with holstered guns follow closely behind, their eyes round as they take me in.

One flips on the dim light but keeps behind Phineas as he

nears me. He's not within arm's reach, but a quick leap will fix that.

My heart hums in my chest, an idea formulating as I examine him and the soldiers' positions. I can have them all dead within six strikes and use their weapons to shoot my way out. Then I'll find the one with the voice I still hear in my dreams before they take me out. I'm owed at least that.

"I see your mind whirling, Onyx. But let me assure you. You won't make it from this building alive."

Building.

My eyes flash back to his. They're dark, unlike his son, and they reek of unease. He knows I am nothing like my parents. I have nothing he can take, which means death is simply a means to an end for me. As long as I take him and the man, *Sam*, with me, I will gladly pay the price. And without any concern of my ultimate death, he won't be able to keep me complacent. He has to know I'll be more trouble than I'm worth.

Phineas clears his throat, the sound of phlegm thick in his esophagus. "It is lovely to finally make your acquaintance. You've grown so much since the last time I saw you."

I drag my dry bottom lip through my teeth before smirking. "How many do you station here? More than eighteen?"

Phineas' head twitches to the side, while the three men behind him exchange sideways glances.

I smile. "Yes, I'd say much less."

"Why does that matter? You have three armed men and myself between you and the door. What gives you the impression you'd make it out of your seat, let alone this room?" His voice is much too high to be intimidating. For a second, I wonder where Kane got the huskiness in his.

Again, I'm thinking of the one who betrayed me to the very man I've been planning to kill.

My tangled insides pull tighter, and my muscles clench around the phantom pain.

I crack my neck to either side and take in each guard behind Murphy. The first one is young—no older than twenty. His face has yet to sprout hair and the way he keeps adjusting his weight on the balls of his feet tells me he's rightfully scared. He's smart.

The second is much more seasoned, also young, but the scars—both old and new—decorating his tan face show he's not afraid to get his hands dirty. His blond strands are long, perfect for holding when I need to steady his face and pierce through his throat.

The last is the only one I have reservations about. He's much older, and his unwavering hand hovering over his holstered gun could either be from nerves or preparedness, though I'm unsure which. He isn't watching me, but instead, his eyes are trained on Phineas' back. He's not the strongest of the trio, that much I know, so I decide to kill him second.

"I'll make it from this room with no problem, Phineas. That, you don't have to worry about."

This turns his amused smirk into a sneer, the face I've studied from afar making its grand appearance. I thought he'd be more intimidating than disgusting. "Tell me how you think you'll manage such a feat, girl. I know they call you a ghost, a legend even. But looking at you now, I must say, I'm rather unimpressed."

"As am I," I counter, my gaze dragging down the lump of flesh in front of me.

Like all other Murphys, it looks as if he hasn't picked up a weight in years, relying on his lackeys to do his heavy lifting. I can almost guarantee he'd be out of breath before he reached the door if he tried to run.

Phineas clears his throat, but his arrogance doesn't waver.

"Tell me, Queen of Hearts, how do you plan to get through me and my men? Entertain me."

Ignoring his latter comment, I tell him the truth, twisting the wood piece in my fingers as I let my eyes drift to each person I plan to kill. "Once I render you unconscious, I'll use that man's gun to kill the other two. Then I'll stab him in the throat with this piece of wood I have in my hand. Once that's done, I'll close the door and have my way with—"

Heavy footsteps stop my words. The sound of thick boots hitting the concrete in a steady interval I know all too well.

The air leaves me the moment Kane walks in the room.

A lump forms in my throat immediately, forcing me to swallow my remaining words as I watch him stand next to his father. My lashes flutter, closing a few times as though he is merely a mirage from lack of nutrients. But when his dark gaze settles over me like a tidal wave, I'm jolted awake and forced to acknowledge his excruciatingly painful presence.

I feel my molars crack as I take in the man responsible for stealing the last piece of my light. It was dim and fleeting, but it was there, and now, a desire to have his head removed from his neck courses through me, retraining my focus. My heart hammers against my rib cage. The visceral need to act *now*, makes my body tremble in anticipation.

It's clear more than anything now that *this* is his authentic self, a don, more so than the man over his shoulder, and I was an imbecile for not seeing it sooner. The shadows that lingered over him have now overtaken him. He somehow stands taller than before, his shoulders square and strong under his tailored midnight suit. A subtle prickling shadow decorates his sharp jawline, and a fresh, bright cut splits his right eyebrow in half.

While most would say he's comparable to Hades, they underestimate the overwhelming power radiating through him.

This man is Zeus. The all-consuming, selfish, angry god. The strongest of them all.

And he knows it.

Kane's eyes rake over my body before sliding to one side of my hip. As though he can see through me and spies the weapon in my hand, he shakes his head slightly in a warning.

A warning?

I fight the urge to laugh and instead feed on the anger vibrating through my core. If I focus on the hint of something else buried deep inside my chest, I'll lose focus, and I refuse to be made a fool of twice in my life.

There were many exercises my uncle taught me while being restrained. First, free my feet. They are more important to have loose, so if all else fails, I can at least escape. Then, naturally, my arms and hands. For this, I'm grateful my genetics include flexible joints because he always forced me to pull bound hands over my head rather than under my feet. He said it was a quicker method if I was seated. While true, every time I moved too quickly, my shoulder always popped out of socket. And right now, I won't have the luxury of moving slowly.

I turn my attention to victim number one, the man in the middle. "Don't throw caution to the wind, boys. Leave me with your boss, or your head is mine. You decide."

Kane huffs, stepping to the side at the same time the men exchange a look and Phineas grins. But the moment is a moment wasted, and their fate has been decided.

I'm already up, and my stick is in the soldier's throat.

CHAPTER TWO

I knew I should have watched for the older guard. Turns out, he wasn't nervous, but ready. His gun is drawn and aimed at my forehead. His chest is moving steadily, but quicker than before, his eyes unwavering as they take in his bleeding comrade.

Even with how quickly I moved, he still could've gotten a shot off, which only serves to irritate me as it must mean Phineas wants to keep me alive. Perhaps it's also the reason Kane never killed me.

My back is open to the younger guard since my hands are still cuffed and currently around the dying man's neck. As he fumbles to get his own weapon, I pull out the wood sticking in his friend's jugular and swing around, pushing the body into the gun trained on me and use the young man as a shield. My right arm singes in pain, a tingle and numbness radiating down the limb. I didn't completely rip the joint from its socket but it hurts like hell, and I can tell if I do too much, it *will* pop out.

Massive tremors rack down the younger one's body, distracting my mind from the discomfort and instead have me delightfully entertained. It's a visual reminder that Murphy's men are made of nothing more than the shit beneath my heels.

With my eyes still on the others—who seem far too calm—my teeth find the guard's earlobe. He jerks violently in my hold when I nip into the soft skin, but when the wood embeds into his neck, he stops, sobs falling from his blubbering lips.

"Such a waste of a pretty face," I whisper in his ear, my gaze flashing to Kane's. "I'd have liked to sit on it just once before I kill you."

His whimpers grow, but they seem far away as I examine Kane. His demeanor hasn't changed, his hands are shoved casually in his dress pants pocket, and his head is tilted to the side as though he's bored. But the flash of fire that passes over his eyes when I lick the shell of the guard's ear doesn't go unnoticed.

Jealousy. Interesting, considering I was nothing more than a tool. It could be seconds or minutes that pass but neither of us blinks, too busy trying to read the other in what could be our last minutes breathing.

The real waste is him. What could have—

"Let him go, bitch, or I'll put two in your head."

Kane and I break our staring contest at the same time, turning our attention to the next corpse in the room.

My adrenaline spikes, blood rushing through my ears so loudly, I have to strain to hear my own words. "Let's make it a race. I say I can kill you before you get the second shot off."

I drop my hands, latching on to the hostage guard's gun at the precise moment the crack of another gun splits the air. An *oomph* leaves the soldier's mouth before he falls from my hold, collapsing on the cement, blood instantly pooling around his head.

But it isn't the fact the man killed a fellow soldier that has my funny bone tingling and shivers drifting down my spine. It's Kane. His own gun is out, pressing lazily into the temple of the killer guard.

It should surprise me, and though it partially does, it also does something more. It pulls at the tender edges of my sanity, filling me with more doubt.

Before I can dwell on what I think I see, Phineas finally takes a step forward, careful not to put himself directly between us. His eyes bounce back and forth between me and his son until confusion and irritation knot his bushy brows.

He looks to his guard. "I hate to break up this little love triangle, but I do need her alive for a bit, Jonas. And you." Phineas looks back at me, igniting a fury that turns my blood into molten fire.

I blame my numb arm for my slow reflexes, so when his hand flicks out faster than I can catch it, I hiss at the sharp pain of a needle burrowing into my neck. Pulling the foreign object out, I realize it's a dart, a pungent, sweet smell coming from the coated tip.

It takes too long for my head to turn and find the three men standing together now, staring at me. They're much taller than they were two seconds ago. Too unfocused. I try to bend and reach for the gun, but when I lean down, I notice my knees are already on the ground.

When did I get here?

The sound of retreating steps and something heavy being dragged across the concrete force my eyes up. The seasoned guard is pulling the one I killed by his collar.

They're leaving. I can't let them leave.

I put my steady hand out to support myself so I can rise, but it connects with the floor. I can't lift it. It's far too much weight.

I can't...

I can't see.

A dark veil of shadows covers my eyes, and I relent, turning onto my back to allow some of the overhead light in. It doesn't work. I can only see a silhouette of someone now.

The familiar warmth of Kane hovers over me, and I swear I

feel the burn of his thumb as it coasts along my jaw. I try to force my face away, but instead, I think I lean into his touch. It's as though my body knows that despite everything, I'm safest with him. What idiocy.

"Tie her back up. This time to the pipes," Phineas commands.

Kane doesn't respond but his hand disappears from my face and snakes around my back. He lifts me as though I weigh nothing, while I can't even muster enough strength to open my eyes.

He cradles my body as he carries me, and my thoughts begin to blur. Images of white roses covered in blood fill my mind until things shift, and one white and one black cat walks through a field of colorful daisies. I try to focus on them. To find something that will ground me. But the stability is fleeting, as the images are replaced by another.

This time, a younger version of myself steals my vision. She's hovering over the graves of my parents, enormous tears falling down her face, filling the empty holes. The blue ribbon in her hair blows behind her in the wind, the ends whipping back and forth as her small body shakes uncontrollably.

I want to reach out to myself. Tell her to get the fuck up and not let them see her weak. But the moment my hand lifts, the blue ribbon lashes out and snaps back, the color fading and shifting into a deep black.

Chills radiate through my arms, traveling toward my tight chest. The air thins as my younger self turns to lock eyes with me. The emptiness in them speaks to the depths of my barren soul, and for a moment we are one and the same.

Angry.

Alone.

Broken.

With the acknowledgment, a mirror I hadn't realized I was looking through, shatters, falling into a thousand pieces. It allows the darkness that took me from my concrete confines to creep into my dreams and drown everything in the same inky shadows.

The last thing I hear before I'm swallowed completely is the deep, husky voice I once allowed to bring me peace.

"Down the rabbit hole you go."

Two Weeks Ago

"Now, Onyx. *Again.*"

"Trigger." I drop my arms, which are nothing more than meek noodles at this point in our training and take a small shuffle back. "You'd have me break my knuckles?"

I curse at the slight whimper soiling my voice but it's too late for recourse because Trigger hears it, and shoves the pads at me harder than necessary, ignoring the way my gaze narrows. "Now. No breaks."

Every muscle in my body burns from his drills, and the repetition of the same fists hitting against the hard surface has left one hand bleeding. I understand his reasoning, but still, even I can admit when I'm nearing my limits.

With a heavy sigh, I bounce on the balls of my feet, shaking my limbs in hopes of regaining some type of moxie.

"Mind if I join you?" Kane's husky voice is somehow simultaneously a shot of adrenaline and Xanax—my heart beats wildly while my muscles relax. A conundrum I haven't figured out if I enjoy or despise.

Trigger, one of the most guarded men I know, looks almost

relieved and drops the padding while nodding. "Please. I need to check on something."

"So *you're* allowed to take a break?" I hiss, stripping my hands free of the thin gloves, annoyance evident in my scowl.

"Do you see how you didn't know I was tired until I *let* you see?"

I bite my tongue to keep from sticking it out as he walks toward Kane. He pauses in the doorway and whispers something to him I can't quite make out before shooting a wide smile over his shoulder. "Promise I'll be back to whoop your ass in a second."

When he closes the door behind him, Kane smirks, his dimples making a brief appearance.

He shoves his hands in his jeans pockets and takes a step farther inside, his eyes focusing on my hand. "Let me see it."

My brows furrow together. "See what?"

He takes a bigger step and I find my stomach fluttering with butterflies.

Yesterday, in my office, Kane took everything—my body, control, my first kiss... It sounds juvenile knowing I'm well into my twenties and have yet to let anyone claim my mouth, but the act has always been far too intimate for me to entertain. Reminds me too much of my parents and the thick love that oozed from them anytime their lips touched.

A love that was their downfall.

The familiar ache echoes across my chest as I think of them, but the squishy sound of the mat sinking under Kane's heavy feet draws my gaze up to his. "Today is your day off. You should be home."

The curve in his lips expands as he holds out a hand for mine. "Do you want me to leave?"

The wings flapping in my belly become heavy, the sensation moving lower. The feelings he is stirring in me are both foreign and curious. I dare say I'm somewhere between a prepubescent teen who is experiencing a crush for the first time and a woman who is addicted to an orgasm she never thought possible.

Both sides of a candle I'd rather not burn.

"I'm not paying you overtime if that's what you're hinting at."

This produces a deep laugh from him which only worsens the dampness between my thighs. "I *was* leaving, but noticed you needed a break."

I scoff, shoving my uninjured hand on my hip. "I don't need you to save me."

"I didn't say you did."

"You're implying it. And just so we are crystal clear, I will never need yo—"

Kane closes the space between us, snatching my sore hand from my side, and holds it up to inspect it. He ignores my hiss and turns it over, running his thumb over my knuckles so lightly, I barely even feel him.

My breathing comes out faster than I intend it to, courtesy of my increased heart rate, but I keep my face passive, brows rising in annoyance.

He disregards that too. "I know. Just like I know you don't need anyone to ever save you. You are the master of this universe. But I want you to understand there will never come a time where I won't protect you."

"Even at the expense of yourself?"

His eyes flash to mine. The golds and greens in them are a work of art I don't think I'll ever tire of looking at. His gaze darkens as he contemplates his words, and a sincere seriousness takes over his face.

His raspy voice deepens. "Yes."

The distinct taste of copper coats my tongue, prompting me

to let go of the inside of my lip I must have bitten down on. Before he lets me form a response, he tugs on my wrist to spin me, one of his heavy hands finding the small of my back to guide me to the sink.

I watch quietly as he turns on the faucet and finds a small first aid kit and a fresh hand towel in the cabinet underneath. He slowly cleans my hand before pouring antiseptic wash over the busted skin. Lifting my hand to the light, he examines his work before drying the surrounding skin and wrapping it in gauze.

He tears the little white tape with his teeth and secures it. When I think he's done, he presses a soft kiss over my knuckles and lowers my hand slowly.

On all the occasions in which the twins nursed my wounds after training with my uncle, never were the injuries so small and insignificant. But the way Kane delicately works over my trivial cut, one would assume I need stitches.

It should vex me, or perhaps entertain me, that he's so diligent in his care. But instead, I think of the time I was cut by a rose and my mother nursed it in the same way.

A sharp burn spreads from my nose to behind my eyes, and before I can form words to either thank or chastise Kane, he tips my chin up with his thumb and forefinger. His eyes scan my face for a moment, stealing my breath under his intense, yet soft gaze.

"I will always protect what's mine," he whispers in my ear, sprouting goose bumps along my exposed flesh as he moves in to press a soft kiss on my cheek.

Then he turns, waving a hand over his shoulder as he passes Trigger, who's been leaning against the door for who knows how long. "See you both tomorrow."

Trigger smirks, but I ignore him, grabbing my discarded gloves and shoving them back on my hands.

A tremor works down my spine as I replay his words, and the absurd thing is, I believe him. The emotions he's stirred and brought forward have me considering what it would mean to allow him in.

And that alone means I'm one step closer to death's door.

Maddy

CHAPTER THREE

For the fourteenth time, I call Harlow, but the results are the same.

No answer. Voice mail full.

I knew she couldn't have made it off the property before Murphy's goons showed up, and when I found her car abandoned near the gate, it was clear they took her. Still, despite my heart ripping in pieces, I keep calling. I *have* to.

All I've done is watch the boys bark orders through their phones, Shi nurse the fresh stitches on her forearm, and listen to the constant beep of Kilo's heart monitor. I need something to do. Something to keep my mind busy instead of acknowledging the constant ticking in my head that's signaling my nearing mental collapse.

Anything to not dwell on the fact that we lost her. We fucking lost her.

I was in the next room, helping one of the guards pick a horse for Saturday's race when it happened. The explosion was deafening, shaking the estate violently, knocking both of us off our stools and onto the marble floor. The ringing in my ears was piercing, but the panic that swelled in my sternum forced me to my feet and propelled me into what was left of the foyer.

It didn't feel as though more than a few seconds had passed from the moment everything happened, but it must have been minutes because Onyx was already gone, and Cat was hovering over a mangled Kilo. And the butler... pieces of him were strung everywhere—entrails hanging from the banister like a Christmas garland, and his blood painted every surface that wasn't buried under rubble.

Before I could make out Cat's screams, a barrage of gunfire filled the air, drawing both of our attention to the hole where the front doors once were.

I bolted outside and joined a bleeding Shi behind a turned-over limo. She tossed a gun at me, a vicious smile curling her lips before twisting and shooting from around the hood.

Our estate guards were everywhere, dropping the pieces of vermin quicker than they could shoot us. But it still wasn't fast enough. The Murphys must have planned for us to overtake them because it was clear these soldiers were left as a buffer. Something to buy Phineas enough time to get away.

And it worked.

When we'd killed enough to jump in the jeep and get to the gate, he was long gone. And while every nerve in my body was burning with the desire to drive to his mansion, we knew they wouldn't be there. Hell, even if they were, they'd be ready, and we didn't have enough able-bodied men to take with us. Quite a few of ours were injured, and with Kilo on the brink of death and the discovery of Z missing as well, we wouldn't make it up their driveway.

After returning, we tried to piece things together with the surveillance, but everything was gone—wiped remotely—leaving us with nothing but the obvious.

We lost.

The shatter of glass against the cold hospital wall jolts me from my thoughts and gives less than a second warning before tiny fragments embed into my exposed thigh. Trick turns to apologize for his moment of frustration but I wave him off. The bites of pain don't bother me. They don't bother any of us. Not when we're barely hanging on.

Trigger throws Trick a halfhearted scowl before checking over Kilo's frame. He was in surgery for twelve hours and has been in a medically induced coma for over twenty. The amputation of the rest of his legs went great thanks to Cat's tourniquet, but scans show he also endured a concussion. We won't know the extent of how much his brain is damaged until he wakes up.

Which might not even happen once they stop the drugs.

"He'll be fine," Shi whispers as if she can hear the doubt sweeping through my mind.

"What if he isn't?" Trick snaps, more to himself than to her, eyeing us over his shoulder. Being head of security, he blames himself for the entire thing. And with Shi being hurt, he's been a touch moody.

Before anyone can answer him, a nurse barges through the door. Her light-blue eyes scan over all of us before settling on the mess Trick made with the glass. Her blonde brows nearly touch in the middle as she steps over the shards and around the bed. "I understand you all may be upset, but for the safety of the patient, pleas—"

"We paid for this entire floor. We paid every nurse and doctor's annual salary to house our people on said floor. We aren't going to fucking hur—"

"Trick." Shi's voice is soft but firm, her eyes trained on her knotted fingers. She shifts in her seat before smiling widely at the nurse. "We will be more careful. Thank you."

The woman's pupils dilate, the soft-blue color becoming a thin outline. She seems to be more taken aback by Shi's eerily calm demeanor than Trick's outburst. But she doesn't respond and simply nods, mumbles about getting a janitor, and walks to the door, four pairs of eyes tracking her out.

We aren't going to get anywhere sitting around, and this small incident will be one of many if we don't get out of this room. Each second, the walls grow smaller with our lack of a response to what happened. We killed over two dozen of his men. They're just as wounded as we are and maybe now is the time to act while they're nursing their own wounds, and we've had time to gather our people.

I slap my hands on my bruised knees, standing with a sigh. "Well, this has been fun. You ready, Trick?"

"Hell, yes. Fuck, I've been waiting for you."

"Wait. We can't—"

"Brother." Trick holds up a hand and the fire in his eyes is enough to burn down the entire city. It lights my insides up like fireworks, the affirmation sending sparks down my limbs. "They came to our fucking *home*. They blew it up and captured Onyx under *our* fucking watch. You'd rather have me sit here and wait for who the fuck knows how long while they could be doing anything to her?"

My stomach twists, the deeply buried memories of my stay with the Murphys surfacing like a body I forgot to weigh down in the river. The dark rooms, the drip from the bad plumbing, the twisted laughter of the men—all of it surges into my throat, stained with hot bile.

Death is a mercy where the Murphys are concerned, and something tells me that's the last thing they plan to offer her.

"Maddy." Shi's sudden touch makes me jump, her cold fingers sending shivers up my arm. "We've talked about this. We can't just barge in there. Phineas knows that's what we'd do, which is why we didn't do it the other night. He expects us to react with our emotions rather than logic. What good are you to her if you're dead?" She pauses, her eyes unfocusing for a moment before welling with tears. I know she's imagining her own life before the boys saved her because I damn sure am.

We are one and the same right now, infected with identical venom left idle in our bloodstream. Without Onyx to damper the effects, it surges through us, robbing us of the women we've become under her care. I won't let the same thing happen to her.

"I can't sit here and do nothing." My voice is a borderline plea and my gaze flashes to Trick. His short blond strands are disheveled, his light eyes quivering back and forth with a mix of anger and desperation flickering through them.

Do I really care if I die to save Onyx? Absolutely not. And the fact I've wasted nearly forty-eight hours with my tail between my legs seems absurd now. Disrespectful, really. Bonkers, but in the worst way.

I may be utterly mad to think I can face them with only Trick in tow, but I never once claimed to have even an ounce of sanity.

A bubble in my chest pops, a string of high laughter spilling from my lips. Trick turns, a smile on his face matching mine. He holds a hand out to which I grab, threading my fingers between his.

He tugs me toward the door as Trigger and Shi stand in unison.

"What if you get *her* killed?" Shi's words shoot straight into my core, wrapping around my spine and yanking me back.

Trick's hand tightens around mine. "If they wanted her dead, she would be."

"Not necessarily," Trigger says, moving in front of us. He's a mirror image of his brother, reflecting the same frustration and fear. The blond tips on the top of his head are mussed, while the ones on the side are matted from sweat and lingering dried blood.

While all of us took quick showers, it's clear spots were missed; everyone far too worried about relocating, getting our wounded men to the hospital, and attempting to find out what the hell happened.

In that time, I can admit rational thought has dwindled, stolen with every strained breath under the enclosing walls of this room. I just want to get out. *Do* something. And blowing up the entire fucking Murphy mansion sounded perfect.

Still does. Because although I'm overwhelmed and confused, I know one thing. "She's not at the mansion. They aren't that stupid."

"Correct, but who's to say they *aren't* holding her there so we don't bomb it?" Shi brushes back the pink strands from her shoulder and I watch as they disappear under the forest of black ends. "In the event of her..."

She trails off and my heart squeezes, the once unthinkable now so fucking tangible, it's taken us all by the throats.

"If something were to happen, everything is given to you and me." She sighs. "We would own it all. And I'm almost certain the phone call will soon be coming with their demands."

"Why wouldn't they do to her what was done to her parents?" Trick asks, his voice much more somber now that adrenaline has faded into waves of reality.

"Because." I unlock my hand from his and collapse into the nearby chair to recount a story we all know. "When they killed the Embros', they thought they had won. They came for Antonio, foolish in their assumption that he wouldn't be ready. But he was. He took out their second-in-command and two dozen soldiers, some of which were actually family members. Not to mention, the local government belongs to Embros. With our people, and the law enforcement, they knew they'd never get through the gates and would have to catch Antonio off the property line to finish the job."

"Things are no different now. Though I suspect the Murphys will want to make an example out of her. Force her to sign over land, and concede, so our suppliers jump ship, and join them. They won't have to strong-arm anyone when they show Onyx on a bent knee." Trigger runs shaky hands over his face, forcing a heavy breath out of his lungs.

We're all tired, and near our wits' end, but to imagine Onyx succumbing to Phineas erupts a horrific type of anguish in my soul. My body aches down to my bones. We stand in silence for a beat, the realization settling heavy in an already stifling room. But just as my mouth pops open, the soft sounds of birds chirping echo in the space.

All eyes flash to me, the mixture of the birds and the beat of the monitor amplifying as I slip a hand into my pocket and draw out my phone. I stare at the screen for a moment too long, watching as the unknown number scrolls across the top. An array of thoughts soar into my mind, all of which are terrible. But before I can fully grab on to a singular guess as to who's on the other end, Trick leans over and taps the green button for me.

Somehow, I find my voice. "H-hello?"

"Is this Maddy?" The feminine voice is new to me.

I nod my head, though I know she can't see me. "Yes."

"My name is Fiona Kane. My brother is Ezekiel and..." There's a brief pause before a shuffle of what seems to be her shifting in her chair. "He told me to call you about his father, Phineas. Do you have a moment?"

CHAPTER FOUR

This time when I wake, I feel like a real captive. My arms are stretched painfully high above my head, held in place by the same pair of cuffs. Only now, a thick chain is securing the restraints to the overhead pipes, guaranteeing I won't be escaping as easily as before.

My feet are on the ground but just barely. I'm suspended in a way that keeps me from being able to move without risking my wrists being sliced by the sharp metal. They were smart this time, tying me high enough that I'm unable to get enough leverage to pick the lock.

My shoulder cracks as I adjust, careful not to pull against my already tender skin. Judging from the ache and the glistening wet blood on the cement, it's only been a few minutes since my encounter with Phineas. But the quiet surrounding me indicates anyone that was here in the building before, is now long gone.

Like the girl from my brief loss of consciousness, I'm alone yet again. Alone and hurt. Something I haven't felt in a long time winds around my heart, squeezing it slightly, and it makes me think of not only my family, but of *him*. Kane.

The man meant to protect me. To guard me with his life.

The one I knew would ruin everything but whom I still let fuck me. He burrowed his way into a minuscule crack in my sternum I hadn't been aware existed until now.

It's my fault, really. Even though I was blissfully unaware of his parentage, I knew we were two feathers of the same bird. Hindsight is always twenty-twenty and dwelling on what I should have done won't alleviate the very real ache in my chest at what he did. Because even though he committed the deepest betrayal, I can't ignore whatever we had twisting in between our tangled limbs.

It was small but powerful. Enough to give me a glimmer of a possible life after destroying Phineas.

Enough to give me hope.

I sigh, forcing my thoughts from the now irrelevant, to my escape. There's plenty of time to plan Kane's death later.

The cuffs are tight, not leaving much space for me to do anything other than keep myself balanced. Long metal pipes run down the center of the room, but naturally the ones I'm attached to look brand new with not a touch of rust or a weak point visible. And with how little slack the chains give me, it would be fairly difficult to walk myself to the wall. Even if I could, joints block me from getting too close, preventing me from being able to get any type of leverage to try and break them.

Vexed, I draw in a shallow breath, rotating my head in a complete circle. That's when I smell him. The deep woodsy scent, equivalent to a drug, sails into my chest, filling it up and coating my lungs. It's as though any breath I'd taken before this one was enough to sustain consciousness, but now they're overflowing with fresh air.

The notion stirs up more feelings than I can identify individually. All except one.

Hunger.

I know exactly where he is before I look over, the same overwhelming presence he always carries suddenly engulfing me. When my eyes find Kane, he's leaning against the far wall, hidden in the shadows with his hands casually tucked in his dark pockets.

"Good morning." His voice is low, rough, and stained with something dangerously close to caution.

An array of unwelcome emotions flutter through me. The relief I once felt when seeing him is now poisoned with everything that's happened, clogging my throat with the urge to do things I haven't done since my parents' death. It yanks at my weak grasp on my control, tempting me to lose focus and lash out.

But viewing me without my shield is the one thing he will never get again. I quell my shaking voice though I'm sure if he looks hard enough, he'll see my pulse thumping in my neck. "So, this is who you are. Ezekiel Murphy."

Saying it tastes vile, and his brows furrow as if he himself is also disgusted.

"Kane," he corrects, his voice one octave below lethal. "My name is Ezekiel Kane."

"I find that rather interesting because I could have sworn Phineas called you his son."

A combination of fury and sadness flashes over his eyes before he narrows them. He kicks off the wall, and eats the space up between us in seconds, stopping just under the overhead light. It washes over him, casting shadows over his face and painting the picture of an angry god.

"By blood, yes. He's my father."

Even though it's a fact I'm already well acquainted with, having it explicitly confirmed by him makes my insides curdle. "So you lied when I asked about your parents."

It's not a question, but Kane responds anyway. "I didn't lie to you. I haven't..."

I scoff, annoyed with him and myself for not exploring the hint of emotion he gave me when I asked him before at the farmers' market. He'd said nonexistent—which could mean a plethora of things—but the way his jaw worked as he answered... I should have dug deeper.

"So this is who you are."

His head tilts to the side as he runs a thumb under his bottom lip. "I'm the same person now as I was two days ago, *mo bhanríon*."

"Don't patronize me, Kane."

"I wouldn't dare."

My teeth snap together audibly as I adjust myself under my restraints. "Why are you here? To gloat? I'm afraid I'm not in the mood to entertain you."

"Before I say anything, I need to ask you something." His gaze falls as he swallows and corrects himself. "I need to *know* something..."

He trails off and I find myself more annoyed than I should be. This man is washed from my system, anything he says *shouldn't* affect me. Yet, sharing the same space is starting to fill me with a burning sense of murderous rage. "Come now, Kane. You've never been shy with words before."

He looks back up to me, and I see the worry before he's able to blink it away. "If I'd told you who I was, would you have killed me or let me explain?"

I pause. The answer's easy but why he's asking it confuses me. He's a rat. Why would he think I'd willingly let him in my home?

"You'd be dead before your next word."

He nods as though he already knew the answer but

inquires further. "Even if I told you I wasn't against you? That I wouldn't hurt you."

"I wouldn't have cared, nor would I have believed you."

"If I said it was to save someone?"

I sigh, ignoring the slight crack in his voice. "Again. I wouldn't care. You are the child of the man who slaughtered my parents. A man who's sold hundreds of women as though they were nothing more than objects he had the right to sell. The moment you opened your mouth and said you were a Murphy, noth—"

"You'd condemn me for what he did? Even if I had no intention of seeing things through at the possible expense of who I had a duty to save?" His voice is rising now, guilt and anger mangling this calm exterior.

"You are one and the same to me now. You bear his sins as if you committed them yourself." Even though I mean it, something about saying it feels wrong—misplaced.

"I am not my father!" he roars, the tender gold flakes in his eyes gone under the dark waves of green. A storm rages in them and for a moment I wish I believed him. "I had no choice."

My laugh is bitter. "We always have a choice, Kane."

"Because the people I want to save mean nothing to you, you wouldn't have even heard me out. You're a fucking hypocrite."

"Step six inches closer and repeat yourself."

The corner of his lip curls, exposing the dimple in his left cheek. Whatever fury was there just moments ago is gone, replaced by something darker. "So I'm within striking distance? Come on, Boss, I know you too well."

"You know *nothing* about me." If my words could carry venom, they would kill him ten times over with the amount I let drip into my words.

"I know more than you'd like me to. For example." He takes

a wide step to the side of me, maintaining his distance while keeping his hands casually tucked in his pockets. He makes a full circle around me as he speaks. "I know *why* you take your breakfast exactly the same each day. How your inability to enjoy a cloudless sky has increased your struggle with acceptance. Why you wear black every day. How you parade yourself as some fearless woman and yet know exactly what you planned once Phineas is dead but couldn't even tell your family."

Does it surprise me that he can read me as though I've written it down myself? No. But it does grate against every last nerve I have.

Running my tongue over my teeth, I curb the rising fire brewing behind my rib cage. This is what he wants—a reaction. But he won't get it. "I'm bored, Kane. Be a good little soldier for your daddy and get to the point."

"You want me to be your enemy so bad? *Fine.*" He moves quickly, jolting forward as his hand snaps out and grips my jaw hard. I don't bother fighting against his hold that's likely bruising my skin, but instead lift my chin, letting my eyelids lower in said boredom. He doesn't let my expression deter him.

"I know you more than I wanted to. So much so, I've found myself in a rather..." Ezekiel trails off, his gaze lowering to my throat, then to the tops of my corset. But instead of continuing down, his eyes stay locked on the space where my heart is. My body burns in response, his boldness somehow making me both angry and intrigued.

"Fucked-up situation," he finishes.

"Ah, well, let me thank my cunt for saving me," I say facetiously. "Tell me, Kane. Does your father know you were fucking the enemy? Would you be punished if he found out?"

He drops his hand, his head tilting in amusement as he backs away. I blink rapidly, ignoring the tingle working through my veins as he smirks. "Who do you think told me to do so? Thought it would be the fastest way to get what I needed."

His words burn a hole into my ribs, and my lungs squeeze, the air becoming impossibly thin. He's lashing out, matching my condescending tone with his own form of defense. "You're a liar."

He moves back into my space until we're inches apart, something I'd wanted so he'd be close enough I could knee him in the groin. Only now, I can't quite get my body to cooperate with my mind. Instead, I stay perfectly still, my breath coming in pants, while my limbs remain still as if I'm paralyzed.

Kane lowers his now frozen green eyes to mine. "How would you know, Boss? All the while I was watching you, learning about you, memorizing you, had you ever wondered about me?"

I swallow, the sour taste of my secret obsession burning on the way down. When weren't my thoughts riddled with anything but Kane? From the moment Maddy brought him into my office, I felt the pull. When his background report came in, I poured my attention over it, scanning the pages again and again, wondering if there was something I'd missed the first time.

There was no corner of his background I didn't know. His love of libraries when he was younger. The fights he'd gotten into because of a sister with a heart too big for her own good. His 4.0 GPA in high school, yet he didn't even attempt to go to college and instead stayed in Sherwood Valley, accepting cash jobs.

It still doesn't add up. Seeing him now, knowing who his father is. In fact, it makes the entire situation more of a conundrum. Why would he need to work when he was training to take over for his father, who is the second richest person in Washington?

Why would he live in the slums and drive that death trap of a car? Why wouldn't he be the face of the family like Phineas?

None of it makes...

Then it hits me in the chest, jolting me as far upright as my restraints allow. A fire erupts in my limbs as the pieces fit together. "He's planned this since your birth."

I say it more to myself than to him, but his smirk confirms it. "*Mo chailín cliste.*"

"He raised you away from the life so no one would know he had a son. A son he could have at his disposal later." Hot bile burns my throat as I work it out.

I remember asking my mother about the Murphy family. How he could traffic young girls when he had a wife. Did he not see her in the vacant eyes of the women?

"His marriage was arranged. A deal made to give him more connections in the east. The wife." My mother's face softens, her hand lifting to brush my curls away from my face. "She couldn't bear children. From what I've heard, she's nothing more than a bag of bones and bruises."

Perhaps Kane is an offspring from an affair. One Phineas kept in his pocket until he saw good use for him.

Imagining him and his father speaking about me, and how he could infiltrate my home sends a vicious ache through me. One deep in my core that seizes my heart in a constricting vise.

I was a job. A way in. Nothing more than an iron gate he was meant to unlock. And no matter what I thought was there, lingering between us, it was nothing more than a facade. He can put on a front about how he had no choice, but now I think that's a lie too. He's manipulating my emotions. My thoughts. My focus.

A common form of exploitation used to break a captive down. That's all I am, after all. His feat. His trophy. Nothing more than the prisoner of his great victory.

"I hate you." The hushed whisper sounds small—juvenile, and while I mean the three little words, I loathe that he was able to coax them out of me.

Hating him means he meant enough to me. That I allowed him to take residence in my life and hold value.

Hating him means I am not the ghost and heartless woman I've trained myself to be.

"Say it again." His voice snaps me from my self-inflicted pity party, drawing my attention to the fact that he is one big breath away from my face.

"What?" I blink away spots suddenly encroaching my vision.

He huffs from his nose, the warm air coasting over my face. "Say it again."

"No," I say defiantly, lifting my chin to meet his hardened gaze.

Ezekiel's brows pinch together, and for a moment an emotion similar to pain flashes through his eyes. It's fleeting, though, disappearing quicker than it came, then his voice drops. "Say it. I want to hear it."

"I think I've made it perfectly clear I've never cared much about what you want."

"Hmm, tell me another lie. They sound so pretty when they come from your lips." Strong fingers slide down my jaw, and when I snatch my face away, he chuckles.

The sound is low and makes me bare my teeth like an animal. "Get away from me, Kane."

The corners of his lips lift. "I've heard you say that before. I wonder if you mean it the way you did the first time you said it."

His eyes darken at the same time the images of me writhing in front of him in the shower flash in my mind. The soft clicks of my barbells hitting into the slick glass as he took everything I had to offer. And I gave it to him. Not because he asked, but because he *took* it.

Something I hadn't realized I needed. But he did. Now, I'm left with the residual anger growing into a dark, twisted version of self-hate. Too many should haves and missed signs on my part.

"Tell me, Boss." His hand finds my throat, squeezing just enough to force my face to his.

I close my eyes, not willing to let him see me anymore. "Leave, Kane."

His hand disappears, but the phantom warmth of him remains as heavy steps signal his retreat. "As you wish."

It isn't until the door closes and I hear nothing but the hum of a nearby generator that I finally open my eyes. I let the emotional whiplash, defeat, anger, resentment, and frustration bubble to the surface.

It's then I do something I haven't done in years.

I scream.

EZEKIEL

AGE 10

CHAPTER FIVE

Pushing my spaghetti around with my fork, I watch as baby Fi slurps up the noodles on her plate. Her small face is covered in marinara sauce, bits of green parsley sticking over and across her cheeks like freckles. I'd gotten distracted with the ending of a chapter from my *Goosebumps* book and put too much of the seasoning in the pan.

Luckily, it doesn't really add any flavor and Fiona doesn't seem bothered. Or maybe it's the dash of sugar I threw in that has her eating wildly with pasta dangling over half her face.

It was a tip I saw once on TV, from those late-night infomercials that try to sell different things while also showing you how to use them. A lady with long blonde hair was explaining how her special spoons could measure, strain, and serve pasta. While she was making the sauce, she tossed in sugar and said it helps cut the acidity of the tomatoes.

Not too sure what it means, but I tried it once and haven't gone back. And considering we have spaghetti once a week—four times, if you count leftover days—I want to make it as perfect as possible. That way Fi doesn't complain and I don't have to use up all the bread in three days by making nothing but sandwiches. My kitchen skills are still pretty limited after all.

I can also make regular things like mac and cheese out of the box and put waffles in the toaster. But that stuff is more expensive and doesn't last as long or make as much as a big pot of spaghetti.

My eyes drift from the noodles dangling from Fiona's nose to my mother. She's sitting on the couch, her head pressed back into the cushions, eyes closed and her feet on the small coffee table. She just got off a double shift and I know she'll probably stay like that until her alarm goes off for work in the morning.

She's had the same routine for three years now. Work, home, sleep. Work, home, sleep. Day in and day out.

Ever since the day we lost baby Bunny, things have changed.

My mother became a stranger and I became a caregiver. I had to learn quickly how to take care of a one-year-old. How to somehow balance my Wednesday night training, hide any cuts and bruises, and make Fi breakfast. Learn what time I need to be up in order to drop her off at the neighbors so I could be on time for school. How to eat on the go, that way I could cut my after-school library trips by moving them to my lunch period, ensuring I'd pick her up before it gets too late.

Then we play until her stomach tells me it's time for dinner. After that, a bath and story before tucking her in for bed.

It isn't until I've cleaned the house, washed the dishes, and scrubbed our clothes in the sink, that Mom usually walks in. Besides Wednesdays, she's coming home later and later, her eyes dimmer and emptier each day.

Still, she always smiles at me, thanks me, then kisses a sleeping Fi on the forehead before taking her own shower and going to bed.

There was a time I used to be angry with her. Mad she seemed to leave me and Fi behind as if we didn't exist, just like Bunny. But as time has gone on, the more I realize she's still hurting.

I wonder if every time she touches her tummy she thinks of her? I know I do when I look at her flat stomach, and because of that, my anger has faded into understanding. Into wanting to do the best I can to keep any more stress from her shoulders. And when I'm old enough to work, I'll take over the bills too. Let her rest at home and enjoy time with Fiona. Maybe then she will have time to heal.

Though I already know her answer, I walk quietly over to her, laying a hand on her shoulder. "You hungry, Mom?"

She mumbles something I can't make out, but shakes her head.

"I'll leave you some in the fridge," I whisper before returning to the table.

I wrangle a squealing Fi out of her strapped seat, tickling the side of her ribs as I carry her to the bathroom. After setting her down, she watches me fill the tub up with soap, pouring in bubbles under the spout until it's almost overflowing.

Once it's ready, I go into the hall and put my back against the wall. I finally got her potty trained a couple of months ago, so now we have a little system. She goes potty, washes her hands, and then gets herself into the tub. Once she's covered in bubbles, I step back inside, sit on the toilet, and tell her funny stories until the suds begin to fade.

Tonight she picks the book *Goodnight Moon* after she waddles into her room, still wrapped in her towel. After we get her pj's on, and she climbs into bed, I get to the last page before her soft snores fill the room. I make a mental note to put the humidifier on before my ride gets here.

Hitting her night-light on, and traveling back to the kitchen,

I notice my mother still in the same position. I keep quiet as I clean everything up, but the knock on the front door shakes the frame and makes her jolt upright.

"It's fine, Mom." I say, putting the top on the humidifier. "It's just my ride."

She nods, her eyes instantly welling with tears. "I love you, Zeky. Please come home to me in one piece."

I hate when she cries. She does it every Wednesday. It's not her fault I have to go with him, and there is nothing she could do to stop it. She knows this as much as I do, yet she still allows herself to carry the guilt. Something else I hope to take away from her one day.

Leaning over the couch, I kiss her temple. "Love you."

Ignoring the second knock on the door, I hook up the humidifier and grab my backpack. Inside, I've got a change of clothes and a first aid kit because, without it, my mom would freak out when I came home.

By the time I reach the door, the bald man is the same shade as Fiona's favorite crayon—Jazzberry Jam. When I shut the door and go to pass him, heading for the dark limo, he guffaws. "You damn sure get that from your father."

"I am nothing like him," I hiss, anger instantly swelling in my chest.

He chuckles, following behind and watching in amusement as I yank open the car door. "You say that, kid, but you two are a spitting image inside."

Comparing me to a man who is vile, disgusting, disturbed, and all the itchy synonyms in between has a fury I've never known sweeping through me. He's dedicated his life to hurting women, while all I do is protect the ones at home. Just because I'm being forced here against my will to endure his training, doesn't mean I'm anything like him.

Or ever will be.

I move before I allow myself to think, swinging my backpack around and knocking the bald guy in the face hard. He yelps like our neighbor's chihuahua and slaps a hand over his face while grabbing a handful of my shirt in the other.

"You *little shit.*"

"I am not my father," I spit, jerking against his hold. "And we are almost the same height. Let me go. *Now.*"

He does as told, shoving me back so forcefully I fall into the limo. "I don't get paid enough to fucking babysit bastards."

After slamming the door closed, he gets into the front seat with the driver. *"Fucking Leanbh. Déan deifir agus scaoil leis ionas gur féidir linn an cailín a thabhairt di."*

I smirk to myself. Phineas has been making me learn the language and even though I don't know a lot yet, I catch on to him calling me a fucking baby.

It's nice knowing I can make him mad and there isn't much he can do.

The single pro in this whole messed-up thing is that only dear old dad can lay a hand on me. But I'm sure that courtesy may wear out eventually, too.

Either way, the bald guy needed to know—I may be the son of a monster, but I'm not one.

When we pull up to the mansion, its windows are all alight with life. Like rats in a sewer, the Murphy soldiers do most of their work at night. I don't know much beyond what I catch in the brief walk from the limo through the foyer and to the back room, but I get the gist.

They make money in strip clubs, drugs, guns, and women.

Lots of women. From my understanding, they are kept in warehouses for a while before being shipped off. Something about the other Mafia family in the state making it harder for them to ship quickly. It's gross to think about another group of people like my father running the other side.

I wonder if they treat their kids to this same type of upbringing. If they have a son who they hit until tears can no longer form from the swollen ducts. Or a daughter they waterboard until she's begging for death to take her.

My stomach rolls at the thought. Thank god Fiona isn't his daughter. I mean, her dad was killed the moment Phineas found out she wasn't his, but he's left her alone. And for that shred of a miracle, I'm grateful.

Inside, the foyer is pretty empty except for two guards standing near the entrance. Guns are slung over their shoulders as they both stare into a phone one is holding. Small moans and slaps of skin seep from the speakers as both men salivate over the video. They don't even notice us passing through.

When we get to my father's office, he's pulling up his trousers while a dark harried woman stands from her knees, wiping the tears and makeup streaks from her cheeks. Her name is Juliet. His wife. The woman who couldn't have children, resulting in Phineas' need to find women who could give him one.

Though she still has to take his abuse, I know she's grateful not to have to watch her own child go through it. Maybe that's why she never looks at me. Because although I'm not hers, I'm a child nonetheless, and she can't stomach what he does to me.

"What happened to your face, Sam?" Phineas asks the man next to me, dismissing his wife with the wave of his hand.

She scurries out, her head down the entire way.

"Your little shit of a kid here hit me with his bag. Fucking zipper or something cut my damn face."

Phineas chuckles, his muddy eyes flashing to me. "Is that so?"

I nod. "Yes, sir."

"Well." Phineas slaps his thick hands together, turning back to Sam. "I'll see to it you never pick him up again. Don't want my second-in-command getting slapped around by my heir."

My father is amused, while Sam looks relieved. All the while, my stomach is tightening because I'm watching Phineas' hands ball into fists at his sides. He's mad I hit Sam. Mad I'm making him find someone else to pick up his secret kid. It leaves room for people to catch wind that he has a son. For his grand scheme to come crashing down.

He told me last year I would be the key to bringing down the last obstacle holding him back from owning the entire state. He also needed me to know that when he felt I was ready, these training sessions would stop. It would become harder to hide me, and I would have to be on standby. Sitting around waiting for *the* call.

It should make me feel at least anxious knowing even when he stops coming to get me that I'm still his to use. Like a cloud always following overhead, not knowing when it will finally split open. But it doesn't. Instead, there is only relief. Happiness. Pure joy from knowing one day, life will be different, even if just for a while.

Caught in thought, I don't notice Sam leave, but definitely notice when Phineas's hand moves.

I jerk back too late and he catches me across the side of my face with an angry blow. The pain is instant, radiating across my jaw and through my ears, making them pop.

"First mistake is touching Sam. The second, daydreaming." His voice is a hot poker in my side.

I shove my own fists into my pockets as I turn back to look at him. If I give him an apology—even though it would be completely fake—I'd be in more trouble. So instead, I straighten my spine and glare into his eyes.

He smirks, his thin lips curling at the corners. "Seems to me you're still thinking like a child. Let's fix that, shall we?"

CHAPTER SIX

He snores like a freight train. A freight train that is running out of steam and is plowing through an overgrown jungle. It's wet, loud, and almost seems as if he might stop altogether. Which wouldn't necessarily be a bad thing, but also probably would.

Zek's plan worked out great for the most part. He told me to find the weakest guard and get his attention. Once I found one and got him to look my way, he developed a crush rather quickly, and in a few days, my not-so-nice stay felt a heck of a lot better.

I'd lied to Zek. I didn't want him to worry, and since I *thought* this whole thing was my fault, I figured it'd be best to keep him in the dark. But the truth is, when I first got here, I was pretty sure I wouldn't make it through the night without a few of the guards visiting my room. They'd put a bag over my head, nearly cutting off my oxygen before leading me through the mansion. I couldn't see anything, but god did I hear *everything*.

The slurs being thrown, I could handle. It was the sound of sloppy wet kisses and obscene noises of them pretending to fuck me that made my skin crawl. Then they physically threw me in a cage they called a room. It was bare of anything except a cot, but luckily I had a window—albeit with thick metal bars—and an attached private bathroom. There was only one roll of toilet paper, but the place was clean and I'm sure that in itself was something I should be highly grateful for.

My entire first day, I literally tucked myself in the corner of the room, staring at the door waiting for someone to come. When no one did, I slept as much as my body would allow, and tried to become invisible, in hopes they would forget I was even there.

But then the next day, Sam paid me a visit.

He tossed me a phone, told me to come up with a good excuse to my small group of friends as to why I'd be MIA for a while, then pushed a couple of buttons to basically disable anything but incoming calls.

At first, the place wasn't terrible. Meals were sparse, but I wasn't bothered in the ways I'd first feared. Time passed slowly, and besides the view of men patrolling outside my window, and food drop-offs, I never saw anyone. But when weeks passed and Zek was barely giving anything useful, that all ended.

Guards stationed outside of my room and suddenly thought it was fun to torment me. To bang at the walls in the middle of the night, jack off right outside the door, and shoot their jizz under the small space. The time between meals got longer and the moments to sleep without interruptions got shorter. The fear I had on my arrival grew tenfold and because of it, I started to get mad.

Mad because I know my brother. I know how good he is at anything he's ever done. How he can work a puzzle like the freaking Riddler and strong-arm anything out of anyone. He's never had any issues with getting me out of situations before and I couldn't understand how this could be any different. What could possibly be taking so long?

I think that's when I realized I couldn't be nice during our calls anymore. My downplay of the situation had him forgetting that I wasn't off in some five-star resort. I'd already planned to be firm with him, but then, Phineas came to see me.

One Week Ago

The clink of the lock sliding flips a switch in my body. My nerves instantly begin to vibrate as I shove myself in the corner, wiping away the sweat already breaking across my hairline. Anytime the door swings open, I'm not sure if it's a half-eaten food delivery or a guard who wants to push me around a bit just for kicks.

But instead of either of those things, an unfamiliar man steps through the threshold. His body is massive, somewhere between a sumo wrestler and a boxer, leaving his suit a little too big for him in some places while tight in others. A short salt-and-pepper beard covers his pale face, while his matching hair is slicked back.

"Hello, Fiona." The man says dully, his dark eyes scanning over my unmade cot and stretched-out shirt and stained jeans. I imagine the smell is also terrible, though I'm immune to it having sat unbathed in here for so long.

He stops a few feet away from my bed and tucks his hands in his pockets. Rolling back on his heels he introduces himself. "My name is Phineas Murphy."

When I don't speak or respond to the name, he frowns. "You don't know who I am?"

I shake my head but quickly open my mouth. "I mean, I

know you're the owner of this mansion. And that you run an illegal organization—"

He laughs. It's full and deep as if I'd made an actual joke. How can someone meant to be so dangerous, sound casual? Like nothing more than a typical car salesman.

Before I have time to ponder the question, he steals my breath with a single sentence. "I'm also Ezekiel's father."

My brows snap together. "I think I'd know if Zek had a father. Especially if it was you."

He shrugs, his nonchalance beginning to unsettle me. "Well, you were just a baby when I had my weekly visits with him, and by the time you were old enough to notice his absence, he started working."

My mind flips to anytime Zek would have done or said anything that indicated he has a father. When we were younger, we were together constantly. It wasn't until he was thirteen he started working, and they were jobs that kept him out late. I guess it's true he could have easily been seeing this man while I was blissfully unaware. But then, does that mean—

"I'm not your father," he answers as if he can read my thoughts. "Killed your papa when you were fresh out of the womb. Didn't need him hanging around. He might have figured things out."

Is it possible to mourn someone you never knew existed? Perhaps not, but I feel the anguish at having the option taken away. My lungs squeeze with the thin air, and suddenly Phineas seems much more sinister than he did moments ago.

"You see, that boy of mine has been on a leash since the moment he was old enough to take a punch. Very few people know who he is, and even fewer know my plan. But I'm going to make you privy because even though he belongs to me, his weakness seems to be keeping him from following my instructions."

He doesn't have to elaborate on what my brother's Achilles heel is because I already know—it's women. Me and my mother specifically. His entire life he's doted on us, raising me and taking care of my mother more than any child should ever have to. Even when he started working, he still made time to play with me in the woods, teach me long division, and cook us dinner. He never let on how tired he was, or if it ever even weighed on him.

And yet, I never once thought to consider it. Not when I put more stress on him from my humanitarian shenanigans, or when I yelled because he wouldn't let me go out with my friends late at night.

A mix of hurt and confusion swirls in my chest. I want to be angry with him for keeping such a secret, but how can I when I know, without even asking, that he hid it to protect me? Knowing myself, I would have tried to find a way to get us out of Sherwood despite my brother's concerns. It probably would have put us in a bigger mess than we're in currently, but then again... "So why the woman in the van?"

He chuckles, making his belly bounce. "An arguably juvenile part of the plan, but important. I told your brother to take you to get ice cream on a street I knew would be pretty vacant on a Tuesday. I had my men leave a van unguarded knowing you'd see it on the way home, and due to your... inquisitive nature, I figured you'd look inside. Happy accident was when your brother left you to your own devices to go grab your mama's medicine."

My brain is reeling, straining, as I attempt to soak in all the information and fit together pieces of a puzzle I didn't even know were missing. Still, it doesn't make complete sense. "But why did you hope I'd let the woman out?"

"So you'd be indebted to us. Like a sort of insurance. See if you knew the real plan, you could tell anyone, and I can't go and kill you because then your brother wouldn't be so easy to keep on his leash," he explains, his tone almost annoyed at the fact my brother cares about me so much. "But keeping a facade, just in case, was important. Onyx has a soft spot for saving women. If she caught Ezekiel but found out why he was doing it, he still stood a chance to bring her to me."

Whatever my face is doing must make him feel the need to elaborate, though he appears downright annoyed. "To save you. Or maybe to drop off his body on my doorstep. The possibilities are endless, really."

I suck in a shallow breath, nausea rolling around in my stomach at the thought of my brother dead. This man isn't Zek's father. He's the devil using his own kin for his agenda. A stupid, convoluted plan at that.

"Now, I'm not here to threaten you, Fiona." He takes a tentative step forward as I scoot back, pressing my back into the corner while he peers down at me. His frame covers the overhead light, draping his face in ominous shadows causing my throat to go dry. "I'm here to threaten your brother. If he doesn't get me something that can get me through those gates in the next seven days, I'll bring him back here. I'll tie him over there to the bottom of your toilet and make him watch as my entire army fucks you on this very cot. His entire life's purpose will vanish in front of his eyes as he sees his sister torn apart from the inside out. Your tears, your cries, your begging. All of it will drive him mad, and even after you're dead and gone, my men will continue until you finally start to rot."

Unable to keep the vomit down any longer, I catapult to the bathroom, hugging the same toilet my brother could be chained to if I can't find a way to make him understand his time is up.

My esophagus burns as bile, and what little I've eaten makes a reappearance, splashing into the porcelain bowl. By the time I've wiped my mouth and flushed the evidence of my fear, Phineas is gone and the phone they gave me is ringing.

Present

I wasn't nice to Zek that day, but it wasn't because I was angry anymore. It was clear and very ironic of our situation, that for once, *I* needed to save *him*.

For the first time in my brother's life, he cared about someone other than me and our mom, and deep down, he knew sacrificing me for a group of people wasn't right. Hell, if it wasn't me, lingering on the precipice of being raped to death in front of him, I'd say fuck Phineas and not to give him shit.

But the sobering fact about self-preservation is that it *is* me, and I don't want to die. Not in that way at least. It makes me selfish, I know, and even if I use the excuse of not wanting my brother to witness my murder, it all boils down to this—I'm terrified.

A plethora of unwelcome and painful emotions flutter through me as I think of the level of fear I experienced over the two days after that. I'd given him forty-eight hours before telling him I'd run out onto the lawn and let them shoot me.

And I meant it.

The more I stewed on our conversation, the more I realized I would much rather take a bullet than the alternative. But when he called me back, he had a plan, and to say it was the most convoluted thing I've ever heard is an understatement.

I glance over at the man I was told to find. He's sprawled across my floral bedsheet, his arms outstretched on either side. His name is Lawrence. Okay guy, if you ignore the fact he works for the evils of the world, and that he sounds like a dying locomotive.

Slipping out of the bed, I tiptoe out of my cracked door and down the short hall. The streetlight outside seeps into the dingy living room window, giving me enough of a glow to locate his phone resting on the couch arm where he left it to charge.

My hands begin to shake as I reach for it, unlocking the screen and tapping on the call button. After a look over my shoulder and confirming with his jumbled groans that he's still sleeping, I dial the number I memorized the second my brother told me it.

It rings five times, and with each one my heart rate increases, anxiety and determination playing tug a war with the weak muscle. On what I assume will be the last ring before the voice mail picks up, someone answers. I hold my breath as I listen for them to speak, pressing my ear to the receiver so hard I make out the faint beeping of a monitor.

"H-hello?"

"Is this Maddy?" I rush out before my throat can close.

"Yes."

"My name is Fiona Kane. My brother is Ezekiel and..." I close my eyes and sit. Zek is depending on me. "He told me to call you about his father, Phineas. Do you have a moment?"

"I'm sorry. I must have misheard you. Did—"

I cringe to myself as I cut her off. From what my brother has told me and from listening to the stories of the guards, this woman is dangerous—completely unhinged. But I don't have time for explanations. "I'm sorry, I must be brief. I was told to call you and only talk to you. He wanted me to let you know that your boss is safe, and he will give you her location in a few days."

"That fucking flitterp—"

The snores from the other room begin to grow softer.

"Again, I'm sorry to be abrupt. I must go but I think you misunderstand what's going on. My brother is trying to *save* her. And I know in no world should I ask this, but for his sake... please don't call this phone back or I won't be able to reach you again."

I tap the red button, say a prayer that this Maddy woman heeds my warning, and stand, pushing open the window to peer out just as Lawrence makes his appearance.

"Fiona?"

Turning around, I give a weak smile. His tall lean frame is only partially visible in the doorway.

"Sorry, I thought I heard something."

He nods, pushing back his thick, dark hair. "You don't have to worry about that. You're safe with me. Come back to bed."

I swallow around my racing heart and push out a sigh before taking a step toward him. Back in the room, he cuddles behind me, framing my body with his, effectively locking me in place.

When the phone doesn't ring and the wet noises of Lawrence's breathing permeate the air, I finally find sleep.

Two days. I gave him two, and he gave me two in return. Only this time, it's not just to save my life or his, but everyone's.

CHAPTER SEVEN

It's hard to keep my mind away from my family when I have no idea what's going on beyond the four walls of my cell. I'm uncertain how many hours it's been since Phineas took me, and even less certain of what could have happened to them when I left. He's made no demands of me thus far, and no one has dared to come see me after Kane left.

There are too many unknowns. And with no leverage, I'm incapable of guaranteeing I'll make it out alive and obtain answers to everything that's plagued my mind since the moment I woke up.

I sigh, adjusting my wrist yet again. My arms are weak from their current position and my eyes are growing too heavy to keep open for much longer. But it's impossible to sleep even if I wanted to. Besides the discomfort of my full bladder, my stomach is a hollow shell, groaning and twisting as it stays empty.

That's when I realize at least one thing that's happening. They're trying to break me down, weaken my body through starvation and isolation. They want me weak and docile so I won't pose a problem when they move me. Where? I can't begin to imagine, but I know from the heavy sounds of a man's boots smacking against the floor, I don't have to wait long to find out.

The metal door unlocks and swings open, revealing Kane holding a long, thick chain.

My heart thumps erratically as I watch the silver catch hints of light from the hall and reflect on the cement. It illuminates the dried blood and gives the illusion that it's freshly spilled.

Kane's suit is still pristine, but it's a different shade, telling me more time has passed than I thought. Loss of time, an effect of dehydration.

He moves inside, and I sneer. "I think I told you to leave."

Kane shrugs, seemingly bored, and takes two more wide steps. "And I think you misunderstand who is in charge here."

I scoff. "Neither of us, I can assure you."

It's a hint to the fact that he's nothing more than a puppet, tied to strings his father controls. Judging from the tic in his jaw and narrowed brows, I know I hit my mark.

He doesn't like to be controlled—this much I already understand from our encounters—but his disdain is much deeper than meets the eye. It forces me to wonder about his youth. He grew up away from prying eyes, that much I know, but how *was* his upbringing?

Images of Kilo and the twins flood my memory. Blood, bruises, and broken spirits. My boys were nothing but ghosts of themselves until finally, they had a fresh foundation to build themselves back up. Their training was created upon a strong base, and because of that, they healed much of their trauma.

I don't imagine Phineas' training was anything like that. If it was, Kane wouldn't react the way he does. No, I bet Kane endured nothing but meaningless torture. Wounds inflicted to do nothing more than build tolerance. Scars that tell stories of pain and not healing. For a brief moment, I feel sorry for the man in front of me.

My hate doesn't diminish, but the pity I have for him grows. If he'd have been my parents' child, there is no doubt in my mind he would be unstoppable—a formidable force who would have brought Phineas's reckoning long ago.

"Are you ready?" The chains sway in his oversized hand as he nears me.

"For what?" I keep my voice level, moving my eyes over his frame until they meet his gaze. It's low, dark, and full of challenge.

"It's a yes or no, *mo bhanríon.*"

"How about fuck you?"

He smirks, his dimple peeking through his light stubble. "I wouldn't be opposed, though I'm not sure that's what you mean."

Kane reaches out for my hands and the moment his fingers brush against my raw wrist, I jerk violently. The rough pads of his skin feel like fire, sending shock waves of pain down my forearms.

"I'm not going to hurt you," he snaps, grabbing the chain holding me up.

A feeble laugh falls from my mouth and it grows louder as Kane's brows furrow. A deep line creases between his eyes as he examines my face. It's such an insult of a statement, yet the hurt look curving his lip downward makes it unbelievably funny. It isn't just the irony of our entire situation, but the very real idea that he believes his words.

"Onyx."

My name is sobering, drying my overflowing river of laughter in less than a second. He's only ever said it twice. Once when the explosion happened, and now. I swallow around the incredulous notion he may actually be serious.

I steel my voice and shake off the knot of emotion trying to swell in my chest. This man is nothing but a liar, and to consider trusting him means death. I refuse to leave this earth without taking the men responsible for my torment with me. "Enough with your games. Take me where you need to and then leave me."

Kane's jaw flexes as he steps closer, his woodsy scent invading my nostrils. The heat from his body envelops mine and though I want nothing more than to close my eyes and deny him access to them, I tilt my face up to his in a challenge. I can't back down.

A nerve in his neck pulses. "Tell me you hate me."

I do. You took everything from me and I let you.

I want to kill the man in front of me more than I want my next breath, but the unbearable notion that, even as my enemy, he still feels something, coats me in more doubt. Doubt I've never had to worry about before him, and it's because of that, I hate myself more. I feel... weak.

It must be the lack of food and water that has my internal ramblings anything less than murderous. But the deep ache in my heart tells me there's something much more to it.

By the time I realize a lone tear has escaped the corner of my eye, Kane sweeps it away before it's halfway down my cheek. "I wish you knew. Understood."

Finally, my resentment of him, us, and everything that's transpired over the course of the last ten years, bubbles to the surface, forcing me to look away. I find a stain of blood splatter and focus on it as Kane unhooks my cuffs and locks me onto the new, thicker chain.

The pain is hot at first, the skin tender despite my constant adjustments and keeping my weight from bearing down too much. But as the blood rushes into the limbs, tingles that feel like electricity radiate through my arms, and I have to bite into my cheek to keep quiet.

To my surprise, he doesn't hold on to my new restraints but instead, checks that they're secure and tucks his hands into his pockets, along with the key. Then he turns toward the door, expecting me to follow behind.

He knows I'm too feeble at this point to pose a real threat, and that irritates my soul. Between Antonio and Trigger, I've always been taught to shield any discomfort, vulnerability, or fatigue, no matter how great. Yet here I am, nothing more than a weak pile of bones and flesh without even the dignity to put up a fight.

The last bit of energy I have surges to the forefront, and without a rational thought, I lunge.

Even with the additional weight of the chains, I manage to wrap my arms around his neck, and use all my body weight to pull it taut against his windpipe. His muscles tense beneath me, and I jerk to the side just before his elbow juts back.

Hoisting myself up, I lock my legs around him and tug harder on the metal. Kane loses his balance and takes a wide step back. One hand latches on to the outside of my thigh while the other reaches for the metal digging into his neck.

"Come now, Kane. I thought you'd be into breath play."

He doesn't respond but instead lashes back and forth. Not wildly, as if to harm me but enough to shake me off. Pair that with his tight hold around on my leg to keep me steady, and now I'm fuming with anger. He's trying to prove that even while I'm trying to kill him like some rabid dog on my last wind, he won't hurt me.

A fire erupts in my veins, and I squeeze all my limbs, contracting around him.

I am not some damsel in distress.

I am not someone who needs to be protected.

I am beyond death.

I am the end.

His end. Just like I will be his father's.

Another pull of the chains and I feel it. The small crack and dip of muscle. Just a little more and—

"Enough," is all he says before my back meets the hard cement wall.

It isn't enough to damage my spine but it does hit the perfect nerve that forces me to loosen my hold. In that brief second, he's able to slip from beneath me and spin around, pinning me to the wall with only the chains wedged between us.

His breathing is ragged, much like mine, and the fire in his eyes is unmistakable as they sweep over my face. I loathe the sweat sparkling across his brow, and the way the green storms in his iris swirl. How he refuses to cause me harm and how somewhere deep inside that makes me *want* to trust him.

I bare my teeth, shoving the intrusive thoughts back into their depths. "When all is said and done, your head will make a pretty post near my garden."

He smirks. "At least you still think I'm pretty."

"Oh, I think a lot of things about you, Kane. But what I wonder the most..." I let my gaze drop, slowly and methodically. "Is if you're a screamer."

His lips stretch farther upward but then disappear completely. It's as though he had a witty comeback but it was quickly replaced by something darker. "I'm afraid that's one thing you won't get the pleasure of hearing from me."

Kane withdraws from my body, and I'm immediately surrounded by the cool air. Goose bumps prickle along my bare arms before he yanks the chain and wraps it around his hand twice.

I almost mention how I *have* heard him scream. The same

instance he used my name for the first time. My ears were full of high-pitched ringing and the sounds of faraway men yelling, but still, his voice penetrated the noise. The fear. The urgency. It was clear as day when he screamed my name. It was that very thing that planted the mustard seed in my chest. The seed of hope and admiration. Of loyalty and understanding.

Of feelings I've denied myself since my parents' death.

It was planted in the freshly dug soil that he'd managed to find, but thankfully it hadn't grown roots and was easily ripped out the moment Phineas opened his mouth.

CHAPTER EIGHT

I allow Kane to lead me from my current cell but assure myself it's only because it's in the hope he brings me somewhere with a toilet.

In the hall, things aren't much different. Pipes trail along the ceilings and besides the concrete and industrial fluorescent lights, there aren't any indicators as to where I am other than it's one of Murphy's many warehouses. Streaks of blood, both new and old, stain the floors, leading us like a red carpet around a corner and to a steel door at the end of the hall.

Kane turns the knob and pushes it open with ease. Much to my relief, there is a metal toilet similar to the one you'd see in a jail in the corner. In the middle, there are two half loops about eighteen inches apart which are welded in the ground. A chain flows through either end, attached to wide cuffs that instantly remind me of Ryan Reynolds when he was a captive in the third *Blade* movie.

My face snaps to him, anger swelling in my sternum at the realization. "You're not tying me to my knees, Kane."

The irony that I'd be essentially kneeling to anyone who walks in the room drives into my core. Despite the emotional tug of war I have regarding Kane, my dignity will *not* be questioned.

"You don't have a choice. It's here or back in the other, strung up like a rag doll with no way to piss or sleep."

"Lock me in here as is."

"And have you ready to ambush anyone who opens the door?"

"You should be grateful, I'd rid you of weak soldiers."

He sighs, walking into the small space and tugging my chains with slight force. I feign as if I'm not resisting, but I am. Only now, my strength has truly worn out and it takes my entire effort just to slow my pace against his lackluster pull. My joints have already begun to stiffen, and I'm struggling to keep my balance.

Lifting up the new restraint, he clasps it on my right wrist, above the thin cuffs. When he bends to grab the other, I act quickly, throwing my elbow out and connecting with the hard cartilage of his nose.

His grunt of disapproval is more annoyed than pained, and despite the bright blood dripping from his nose, he clasps the other in place, effectively making me hunch over.

I snarl, my voice lowering to almost an animalistic growl. "I can't wait to kill you."

He unlocks the smaller cuffs from my wrist, taking the thin chain with it before looking up at me. His eyes are tired, filled with a guilt I refuse to acknowledge anymore. "Honestly, neither can I."

Instead of being surprised by his words, I find myself vexed at the hypocrisy. There was a time he told me to feel my demons eat me alive so I could become the rightful queen to properly lead my kingdom. Yet he himself has been living knowing he'd welcome death than to continue on.

That's the thing about life. Only the strong survive because the alternative is so much easier.

Kane runs a hand over my bruised wrist once before gathering my old restraints and leaving, locking the door behind him.

After the awkward maneuver of relieving myself in the cold metal toilet, I cross my legs and lean forward, propping myself on my hands. Sleep takes me in seconds.

It's dark, void of anything coherent, but riddled with screams. Screams of over a dozen voices I can pinpoint. Voices I stopped hearing when Kane arrived.

One is Kilo when he was fighting the pain of detox. Another is Shi on the third day in the woods as she was torturing the man who took her soul. Mine, when I begged my driver to take me back to where my parents lay slain on the sidewalk. Of Maddy and Antonio. Of victims pleading for their meaningless lives. Of the women I couldn't save.

And then, all at once, they fade into nothing, leaving only one.

"I wish you knew. Understood. I'm not going to hurt you."

"This is your kingdom. There's no disputing that. But when we're here, like this? You're mine."

"Until a bullet stops me."

Then, as if the opening to a play, a curtain draws back and I watch as me and Kane sit together at a blackjack table in one of my casinos. We had gone to inspect some of the recent inflation but while there, he was able to identify a counter. Even with training that took me years to master, his ability to do it in moments intrigued me. Made me curious as to what else he may be able to notice, or if he himself had once counted cards, making it easy for him to spot one. So much is still unknown about my guard and I wanted to know more than what the few pages of his background check told me.

I watch from above as we venture to the floor, both accepting a house cocktail from a passing waitress. We sit in silence as the pretty dealer shuffles cards and places our chips in the middle of the table to make our wager. When she deals our hands, Kane leans over, his shoulder brushing lightly against mine to get my attention. I remember how intimate it felt. Almost as though we were longtime friends sharing a secret.

"Why are you asking me what to do?" I watch myself hiss.

His eyebrows furrow as he tilts his head. "Why not? It's not me against you. It's us against the dealer."

At the time, I thought it was such a silly thing to say. But knowing he wanted my advice, I couldn't help but make a suggestion when the dealer asked if he'd like to "hit" or "stand". Kane has a seventeen. It's a good hand, much better than the other five players, and a lot better than my ten. But the twitch on the dealer's mouth told me hers was even better.

I motion toward her. "Hit."

Kane taps the table without hesitation, without throwing me a questioning look or even pondering over the high chances of his loss. Instead, he blindly trusts my call.

I watch as she flips over a four of spades.

Blackjack.

He grins as the dealer moves on to me. "Good call."

Still in awe, I tap for her to give me another card. "Why did you trust my call?"

"Because you truly believed it was the right one to make. And even if I lost, you'd still have a chance."

I shake my head. "But what if I was leading you to lose?"

He shrugs. "Sometimes you have to trust what you can't

see. Take a leap of faith and hope that your partner knows something that you don't."

The king of hearts is flipped over on my deck. And after I motion to "stand", the dealer reveals her nineteen.

A hard knock jostles me from my dream. Only when I peel my eyes open in a dreary daze, I realize it isn't a knock.

"It's time, son. She can eat later." Phineas' voice seeps under the door causing all the tiny muscles throughout my neck to tense.

"It's been almost three days. She needs water." Kane.

"Two and a half. Why do you seem so concerned about her well-being?"

"If she dies, you won't get what you want."

A robust laugh echoes around me and my stomach rolls. "I'll get what I want with her, dead or alive. It will just be a fair amount bloodier with the latter."

The door finally swings open and both men walk inside. Phineas doesn't look much different than he did the other day, still donning an untailored suit while his son's slacks are pressed and starched. Kane has done away with his jacket and instead wears a crisp white button-down, rolled halfway up his forearms. In one hand, he holds a bowl of what looks to be fruit, and a bottle of water in the other.

My mouth gets drier at the sight but somehow I'm able to rein in the quiver working at my lip. I've been without food before. Five days was the longest stretch my uncle pushed me to, but never past two without fluids.

Phineas follows my line of sight to the bottle in Kane's hand and chuckles, holding his palm open. Kane's jaw clenches, but he gives his father the water.

"Now, Onyx, I think it's time we have a little chat." Phineas crouches down, leveling himself with me, since I have yet to lift my head.

My breath is labored now, the effort to continue sucking in air almost too much in itself. It burns the lining and stings my esophagus, but still, I remain steady.

He takes my eye contact as an adequate cue to continue and dangles the bottle between his legs. I force my gaze to remain on his, though the swish of liquid splashing against the plastic is so loud I have to strain to hear him.

"I want the ports."

Of course he does. Having the ports means he can ship women and other contraband across the Pacific. I blink lazily, and luckily, he gets the idea.

"See, I know you might want to say no, but I have a deal you won't be able to pass up."

When my lips part, I realize I must have been asleep for far longer than it felt. The flesh cracks and pain radiates across them. "Kill me, Phineas. You won't get the ports."

He shakes his head, twisting open the bottle. I clamp my jaw shut, a failed attempt to feel the pain elsewhere, but my head pulses as the bottle's top clatters to the concrete beneath me. With my adrenaline spent, and my body near collapse, I can't even muster enough energy to reach for it.

"I'm sure you're well aware, but at a certain point in time, the body begins to deteriorate rapidly. Your mistake was using what stored energy you had on killing my guards and choking my son."

My eyes flit to Kane who isn't standing as casual as he has been the other times I've seen him. Right now, he's only a few feet from his father and his entire body is tense as he shifts on the balls of his feet. It's then I notice the dark bruise around the column of his throat. An odd pattern consistent with a chain.

"Now, it's only a matter of time before you pass out, and soon after that, those organs of yours will shut down and you'll meet a much nicer fate than your parents."

He smirks in my periphery, and my eyes snap back, boring into him with all the hate I can muster into one glare. What would be fury, is muddled, low in comparison to the darkness encroaching in the corners of my vision. I *need* the water.

"I know that if you die, your property is then under the ownership of that girl of yours, Madeline. And I don't wish to do business with her."

Because she'd kill you.

"I also know your suppliers are incredibly loyal and will see your death as a reason to move their own people in rather than work with me."

True on all accounts. My parents were big about creating a relationship with everyone we traded and worked with. No one crossed them because they didn't want to. They were compensated well and taken care of outside of only imports. Something I continue to do long after their death.

"But to see the queen bow before me?" Phineas lets out a guffaw mixed with congestion. "It'd be the perfect message. It would let them see death as a mercy."

"You've bested me, Phineas. I'm locked on my knees. What else do you want?"

"For you to sign over everything to me."

My laugh is nothing more than a feeble wheeze but he gets the message.

"Tell me this, Onyx. Do you think that family of yours is guarding Hearts right now? Or are they looking to get you back?"

Realization and confirmation that they are alive is both tremendous and fleeting before terror sweeps through. They most likely are pulling extra guards from everywhere to find me, leaving all our establishments vulnerable, especially Hearts. The thought steals my breath.

The corner of his lips curl as he watches it play across my

face. "Halfway to death's door and you still get my point. I'm having the paperwork drawn up right now. You'll be signing it no later than tomorrow night."

"I won't." I close my eyes briefly as I envision the women I'm sentencing to death with my words. But giving him everything means thousands more will be lost.

"You will." He swishes the water around again garnering my attention.

I shake my head and make a declaration he'll understand despite my delirium. "Humpty Dumpty sat on a wall."

His eyes flare as he stands. When I keep my gaze on the floor he steps back a foot before tipping the water over and letting some spill out on the floor. My stomach and heart squeeze in unison but I take a shuddering breath and calm my nerves.

"Humpty Dumpty had a great fall."

Another tip of the bottle and this time a quarter of its contents spill out.

"All the king's horses and all the king's men..."

Half the water soaks into the dry concrete.

"Couldn't put Humpty together again."

Phineas drops the bottle on the floor before turning his back and leaving without another word, the red hue of frustration creeping up his neck.

The door slams shut at the same moment I finally tumble, leaning over on my side and internally brace myself to hit the hard floor, but instead meet warm arms.

Kane hovers over me, gripping me around the back and cradling my head. He doesn't say anything as he moves my body around to get comfortable and leans over to grab the discarded water. I'm not sure how much is left, but the moment it meets my lips, it doesn't matter. The first bit seems to soak into my dry lips and tongue while the second actually goes into my throat. The third is when my body finds strength and grips onto Kane's arms like a vise, urging him to pour faster.

"Slower, or you'll throw it up."

I grunt my disapproval but let him take his time tipping the rest in. When it's gone, he tosses it to the side and readjusts, pulling another bottle from his pocket. It's small, similar to the ones my mother would put in the mini-fridge in my room to limit midnight snacking.

After finishing this one, I gather enough energy to pull myself upright and out of his arms. He doesn't argue but instead gets to his feet and picks up the bowl of fruit. It seems as if he tossed it in an attempt to catch me before I fell and half of the fruit is scattered across the floor.

He brings the bowl in front of me, and I reach a shaking hand out to grab one of the sliced cubes of pink fruit. I take my time chewing it before realizing it's watermelon and reaching for another. Slowly, my trembling limbs begin to stabilize and my vision clears. I'm able to grab at the food with a steady hand and discern the various fruits he brought. When the bowl is empty, Kane picks up the spoiled fruit and empty bottles, and turns for the door.

Whether it's because I'm still delusional or just honestly grateful, I push the words out of my mouth, ignoring my pounding heart. "Thank you."

He pauses for a moment and I ready myself for the cutting reply. But instead, he continues walking. "I'll be back with breakfast."

Then he shuts the door.

Maddy

CHAPTER NINE

"Do you think she's really coming?" I ask as I pace the room for the hundred and sixth time.

Pacing keeps me going—keeps my mind from imploding, from falling through a hole made of nothing but broken shards of glass and manic echoes of laughter.

With every step I drive it away, prolonging the inevitable as I listen to Kilo's steady heartbeat and Shi's hushed whispers. But just as my foot lifts off the ground and the worry ebbs, it comes crashing back to shore the moment I stop.

Onyx.

Z.

Sister.

Harlow.

My sweet Harley.

"Madeline. She's coming," Shi reassures me yet again as she brushes Kilo's hair away from his face.

She offers him another sip of water which he accepts gingerly.

He woke up this morning just after the boys called to give us an update on the estate's repairs. I've never seen his eyes so clear. So still. Even now as he watches me sulk back and forth, his gaze follows a smooth path left to right.

He hasn't verbally communicated, which doctors seem to think is normal for now. Waking up after a surgery that took both legs can be rather *traumatizing*, they said. So as long as he communicates with the occasional head nod, and his vitals stay good, they aren't worried.

Hearing that hasn't really eased my mind how it should, but it seems to have done the trick for the rest of the family. The twins have been able to find extra guards who can be on standby at the estate, ready to grab materials for the builders so they can work straight through into the night. Cat, and the collection of maids, were able to clean up the butler and other bodies from the yard while also cleaning the inside to look as if nothing had ever happened.

Shi's already made funeral arrangements for the few men we lost, while the others who were present during the attack have all been discharged and sent to Hearts for extra protection.

Onyx trained us to go on if she were to ever be... indisposed, and I know she'll be proud of what the others have done, but me? I'm unraveling. Tearing at the seams. Grasping at anything to keep me from ripping the city up, brick by fucking brick, until I've torn out every throat of every Murphy in the state.

See, out of all of us, Onyx included, I'm the maddest. The one who laughs as I gouge someone's eyes out and later uses them as martini olives. The person who you'd think has a simple switch in her mind that goes from here to there in a second flat. But really, it's much more complex.

My mind is made on an unsturdy foundation. I'm the house at the end of a dock, in the middle of the sea, with only two by fours as my support. Everything looks certifiably dangerous but is actually perfectly balanced. It's a wonder how it all stays put, but it does. Until it doesn't.

One of my support beams is missing, and without it, it's only a matter of time.

Ticktock.

Ticktock.

In tune with Kilo's monitor, the clock ticks. It's only because he's awake and the constant sounds beeping steadily that I haven't crumbled into the seas raging beneath.

"Mad Maddy, she's here." One of my runners sticks his blond head inside the door and motions behind him with a swollen thumb. "She's alone, unarmed. No one followed."

I nod, hopping over to Kilo's bed and sit on the edge. I hear Shi make a disapproving sound in her throat but I ignore it. The man is literally only using two-thirds of the bed, he can spare the end.

"Let her in," I tell him, drawing my dagger from my right boot.

As I wait for the girl to enter, I play with it in my hand. It was once something I did to intimidate but has somehow become a grounding mechanism.

The door opens again, and this time a frail girl steps inside. Immediately I see the resemblance she has to her brother—dark hair, tan skin, gems for eyes. Her sweater is oversized, hanging off one of her delicate shoulders, but the dinginess of the hem says she's been wearing it longer than she should be.

Her timid eyes flash around the room, bouncing from me to Shi, then stop at Kilo.

"You." I hear the soft whisper of Kilo's cracked voice. So *now* he can speak.

Turning my head enough for him to know I'm addressing him, I ask for elaboration. "You know this one?"

In my periphery, he nods. "She's the one who let the girls out."

"Girls?" Shi inquires.

"My comrade here isn't in the best state to do any explanation, so please, Fiona, fill us in."

The girl's throat bobs with a hard swallow. "Yes, of course. May I sit?"

I tilt my head to the side, curiosity lifting my brows. It's unlike most people to want to sit down in a room when they're alone. Most of them want to have a clear shot to the door in case things go south. She must know it doesn't matter either way.

"Of course," Shi says, leaving Kilo's side for the first time today and moving one of the uncomfortable hospital chairs toward her.

Fiona nods her thanks and sits, crossing her legs at the ankle.

"How old are you?" I can't help but ask. She's so small. So unbroken. I don't remember ever looking like her, not even before I was swept away by the Murphys.

"Nineteen. I'll be twenty next week." She tucks a stray lock of hair behind her ear and lets her eyes flash behind me to Kilo. "Is he going to be okay?"

I shrug, leaning forward, twisting the knife counterclockwise. "Let's talk about these 'girls.'"

Fiona chews on her bottom lip, her gaze moving between my hands, Kilo, and the standard round clock hanging above his bed. "Okay. But then I must hurry and tell you what I came for because I only have an hour."

My eyes widen as I stretch my arms out. "By all means. *Start.*"

She swallows again, then begins. She tells us about the night she went out with Z and saw a van, let out women, and later found out they were property of the Murphy's. She then goes on to explain how she was taken by them for the debt and Z was instructed to come work for Onyx as a bodyguard in order to tunnel secrets back to Phineas. But he wasn't doing such a great job because the big guy paid her a visit and spilled the beans on being Z's daddy. Told her he'd have his army rape her while he watched.

The more she talks, the angrier I become. Angry, because I should have looked deeper into Z. Livid, because I led him to Onyx myself. Hurt, because I cared about him. *Trusted* him. And pissed, because I thought he'd be the one to save her. Not kill her.

My limbs are shaking by the time she finishes her story, and before I know what I'm doing, white dots decorate my sight and propel my feet forward. I'm behind the small girl and have her throat pressed against my blade before she gets her scream out.

Kilo sits straighter, the arm not riddled with tubes outstretched toward me. "Maddy."

"Tell me, Fiona." I nuzzle my face in her neck before skimming my nose along the column until I reach her ear. She smells like fresh strawberries. "Tell me why I shouldn't use you like Phineas did, huh? Keep you locked away and have your brother return our queen for your life?"

"Because I'm only insurance to them," she squeaks, her entire body vibrating the chair as she trembles against my tight hold. "They don't fully trust my brother, so they still have a guard watching me."

"Why wouldn't Phineas trust his own son?" Shi asks, stepping forward.

When Fiona doesn't respond, I nick her neck. It's not enough to do any real damage but it does draw a nice amount of blood. Surprisingly, the girl only sucks in a sharp breath. "Because my brother wasn't the one that gave them the access codes to the estate."

"What?" all three of us say in unison.

I feel my blade move slightly as she begins to shake her head but stops herself. "Zek is Phineas's son by blood but the vile man had no hand in raising him. He lived with me and our mother. I could tell he didn't want to turn you guys in. He was willing to risk me for—"

"I didn't ask that. Nor do I give a single iota of a fuck. Who was the one who gave Phineas the codes?" I interject.

"I don't know an exact name, but my brother wasn't the first one they used. He was the last resort."

My gaze flashes to Shi. The guard Z caught couldn't have been the one. They would have come shortly after his death.

We have so many guards. So many people working for us. Some have been at the estate as long as Onyx's parents. The new ones, aside from Z, are all placed at the businesses until they build up enough trust to be moved anywhere near the estate.

It's possible Phineas had the codes for a while and waited for the perfect time. He did just start buying real estate in neutral areas.

"What did Ezekiel want you to tell us?" Shi reroutes the conversation.

She sighs. "He told me to find Maddy and tell her that Onyx is alive, and that he has her location."

"Which is where?" I hiss, drawing my knife flush against her throat. I want to feel the relief cooling my burning veins but I also know this girl could be lying. If Onyx is dead, the land and all assets fall to me and Shi. This could be just another trap to kill us.

"He said he'd call me with the location in three days."

"Liar!"

"I'm not. Through all this, I have nothing to gain and everything to lose. If it's not you with this dagger at my neck, it's a

Murphy with a gun at my head. I owe it to my brother to do this."

"That seems a tad far fetched, child." Shi leans on the edge of Kilo's bed and folds her arms over her chest, her classic wide smile curling her lips. "Even if I *did* believe this wasn't some convoluted game to kill us, your brother lied to you. Why do you feel the need to repay him?"

She shakes her head, this time ignoring the metal pressed against her. "He raised me. He's saved me more times than I can count. I know he didn't tell me about his father because he wanted to protect me."

"I wouldn't be so sure. Look at you now, little mouse. All alone with three wolves." I capture her earlobe between my teeth and bite down, her shivers vibrate against me. "Did he think sending you here would be safe?"

"He said that you don't hurt women," she squeaks.

I laugh out loud, scaring the frail girl and making her jump. "Your brother lied."

"Maddy." Kilo's voice fills the room. "Let her go."

"Why the fuck would I do that? She could be the only way we get Boss back."

"Or you could get her killed!" he snaps.

My eyes flare. Never has Kilo *ever* raised his voice. Not only that, but he's not the *rational* one. The majority of the time I've known him, he's been functionally high, but never really had much thought. So *naturally*, now would be the time he'd start.

I release the girl and round the chair before kneeling in front of her. I dip my finger through the small pool of blood at the base of her neck and smear it over the faint freckles decorating the tops of her cheeks. Her thick lashes flutter and I grin. "You have seventy-two hours. If we don't hear from you by then, I'm calling the number you begged me not to, and we'll be paying a visit to your mother's house. Do you understand?"

She nods, her small shivers becoming more visible. "I do."

I point to the door with my dagger. "Now go on, little mouse, before I ignore *my* brother in the bed over there. You know, the one *your* brother almost got killed, and filet you like a fucking fish."

Her eyes flit to Kilo once more before she nods and stands. I don't watch her go but instead turn my heated gaze to Kilo. "Explain. *Now.*"

His silver irises disappear as his lids drift closed. "I trust her."

"You don't even know the girl, Kilo!" I'm screaming now, rage swelling in my body too fast to stop. I latch on to the rails of his bed and shake them. "We trusted Z and look where that got us!"

"Regardless, killing the girl would do nothing but put us in the dark." Shi shuffles next to Kilo and lowers her voice. "We're going to get her back."

She can try to deny it, but I hear the doubt. The fear. It intertwines with her words and paints them in a vibrant shade only a true killer can pick up on. And I see it. Just as I saw it when Fiona spoke. It seems as if she doesn't know much more than we do.

But for now, it will have to do.

Three days.

If I don't have Onyx back in the next three days, the entire city will burn.

CHAPTER TEN

In no world did I ever think Kane would bring me breakfast again. Not in this life, at least. But after a soft knock and a quick fumble of the door handle, he walks in with two plates in his hands, proving me wrong.

Wearing a similar outfit as yesterday, it's easy to make out the full-sized water bottles poking out of his tailored suit pants. He uses his freshly polished loafer to close the door behind him, before casually sitting down on the floor and leaning his back against it.

Smart, considering it's the only spot I can't reach with my new chains. Their short length allows me enough room to perch my ass on the nearby toilet and to stretch out my legs, but that's it. Shame, since I only need about a three-inch reach in order to kill a man.

"Which one?" Kane asks, lifting both the dishes.

I scoff. "You think I'll take breakfast from you? I'm sure it's poisoned."

His nostrils flare twice. "Not only have I told you I won't hurt you, but I proved it to you by feeding you yesterday."

"So I'm alive to see your father's plan come to fruition? No need to play coy anymore. We both know who you really are." I ignore the obvious hurt that flashes over his face, causing his shoulders to drop slightly.

"You don't know anything about me. Not really."

"Enlighten me then," I challenge, letting my gaze drift to the full plates in his grasp.

Both hold two over-medium eggs, three slices of slightly charred bacon, and a cluster of berries. *My usual.* Swallowing around the burn piercing through the back of my throat, I peer up at him.

He lifts the breakfast slightly. "Eat with me and I'll tell you."

"And if I choose not to eat?"

He shrugs, places the paper plates on the concrete, and pops one of the blueberries in his mouth. "Then you don't eat."

Kane doesn't elaborate. Nor does he goad about how foolish it is to pass up food considering I'm not sure how much I'll be offered. But also, if he decided to poison the food, there's a lot worse things I could feel than death.

I know, because I've done it before. There was a man we caught one time who was stalking my casino dealers on their way home before assaulting and robbing them. Maddy held him down while I spoon-fed him a cake that had him leaking from every possible hole and screaming for death.

Such horrible things can come from beautiful plants.

"When I was a kid, the only breakfast I knew how to make was frozen waffles." Kane picks up a strawberry this time. "One box didn't last long enough though, and they were too expensive, so I learned how to make eggs. Those are much smaller and easier to steal, you see."

He slides me the plate he's been nabbing fruit from, stopping a few inches away from my chains. On closer look, the eggs have been cut, which makes it easy for me to scoop them up with the bacon.

No fork means no tool to pick a lock or stab someone in the jugular.

How annoyingly astute of him.

"We didn't get many channels on the TV, but late at night, I'd stay up and watch the infomercials that'd come on. The ones that go on for hours and always feature some type of Tupperware." He grabs a piece of bacon now. It's perfectly browned and crispy, and the edges are slightly charred.

My stomach cramps, filling the small space with evidence of my hunger. He does me the courtesy of pretending not to hear it, which only vexes me more.

"Anyway, they taught me there are a dozen ways to make an egg, and with how nutrient-dense they are, I decided it would become an everyday meal addition. My baby sister didn't care for them too much at first. She usually played with them and ended up throwing them across the damn room. But eventually, I found out she only likes egg whites. Not scrambled, but over easy. Then she wanted the yellow taken out. It was like performing surgery every morning."

He uses his bacon to scoop up some of his eggs and takes a bite. When he glances back at me, something foreign crosses his eyes. Something too close to uncertainty to make any sense.

"Why didn't your father buy you food?" I ask, finally taking the bait. I tell myself it's not because I want to know more about Kane, but about his relationship with Phineas.

He scoops up more eggs, but this time chews slowly. When he swallows, he pulls both water bottles from his pocket. He rolls one to me, which stops the moment it meets one of the metal loops holding me in place. "My payment for serving my father was that my mother and sister continued breathing."

"And what type of service did you provide?"

He doesn't answer right away, and when I think he won't at all, he sighs. "When I was six? Keeping my mouth shut while he knocked me around a bit and extending the time I could hold my breath when locked in tight spaces. When I was nine? Learning to evade two fists while taking two others. At twelve, it was being waterboarded. Fourteen, learning not to show emotions when women fucked me until I had nothing left."

The warmth drains from my face as his story soaks in. As I previously suspected, he wasn't trained to lead. His father wanted to strip him of his humanity. Of his empathy and hope. Kane's fate was to become scum just like his father. Nothing more.

"Yeah, my dear old dad would force a little pill down my throat, then have me chained to a chair while his newest shipment had to fuck his son to prove they were worth selling and not killing. If I didn't come, I'd have to sit and watch their throats get sliced up the middle."

Hot bile burns up my esophagus. My stomach churns around nothing and for a moment, I think I'll be vomiting stomach acid over my untouched plate.

Kane's been nothing but a tool since his birth. Something to be used in the most disturbing ways with no control whatsoever. In reality, he never stood a chance of escaping Phineas.

Of escaping me.

"Then came twenty-five." Kane stands and snaps his empty paper plate in half. "I know it's hard but try to get some rest. No one will bother you."

With my mind currently battling for some hint of sanity, I don't offer a reply, and he doesn't wait for one. He turns, opens the door, and latches it closed behind him, leaving me with the heavy air settling in the space.

I hate him, I tell myself, shaking the creeping doubt from taking a stronger hold. His upbringing or the reason behind it doesn't lessen what I feel. What I *need* to feel.

Thirty times I repeat it, but each time, I mean it a little less.

We were born in the same world on opposite sides, and in shoes… I don't allow myself to finish the sentence because it will create another vulnerable spot I can't afford.

And that's not something he deserves.

Not when his weakness for one person destroyed something my family took decades to build. When he allowed that *one* life to replace hundreds.

Trepidation squeezes my lungs at the reminder of my family's whereabouts. They aren't weak by any means, and I know they're alive, but in what state? The blood I saw before they knocked me out didn't just belong to the butler. Kilo's state is one of many that wears on my soul.

I exhale a shaky breath and pluck a blueberry from the plate. It's wet, I assume from being recently washed, and doesn't smell of anything telling.

Before I talk myself out of it, I snap it in my mouth and chew. The flavor instantly bursts across my tongue, the tangy sweetness igniting my taste buds making my entire mouth tingle. I surmise the watermelon didn't have much of a taste because I was barely functioning. But now, it's taking an absurd amount of strength not to devour the entire plate in one breath.

Begrudgingly, I finish my breakfast slowly. It's nothing like Russ's dishes but it does the job. When I'm done, I suck the first water bottle down completely, just in case someone else pays me a visit and takes it away. Then I flip on my stomach, flinching slightly as the cold floor connects with the small sliver of skin exposed below my corset.

I stretch my legs as far as I can, arching my foot until my toe taps against it—the bottle Kane left behind.

True to Kane's word, no one else comes to see me. I'm alone for the remainder of what I assume is the day to stew in the mess he's left. The vile imagery, the constant wondering, the back and forth. I don't *want* to understand him. I don't *want* to feel sorry for him. But somewhere deep inside, I'm beginning to.

I meditate, sip water, and relieve myself in intervals to bide my time. I need to be well-rested and keep an empty bladder in case they move me and I don't get the chance to for a while. When fatigue begins to creep into my limbs, I fold my legs and lean over on a fist.

By the time I wake to the rattle of the door, my mind feels clearer, almost as if I've gotten a full eight hours.

Kane enters and does the same thing he did yesterday, gliding down the door and sliding me a plate of breakfast. I mimic our encounter by not touching it, and instead, watch as he eats from his own plate.

"How are you feeling?" His deep voice is full of genuine concern, but I force my mind to ignore it.

"You don't deserve to know."

He opens his water bottle and takes a swig. "Perhaps I don't."

We sit in silence as he finishes his food. My anger toward him is now tainted with something I refuse to confront, and I know that if we continue to talk, things will only become hazier than they already are.

Since my parents' death, everything has become black or white. Neutral parties could no longer stay idle but had to pick a side. Any of my employees caught in bed with anyone known to work with the Murphys became a liability. A loose end. A snake in the grass, no matter if they were innocent or not.

Which means a lot of people have died. And never once have I batted an eye.

Never once have I questioned my choices. The decisions I've made for my family.

I am the necessary evil to end all evil, and up until a few weeks ago, I have *never* swayed.

Yet the man in front of me has brought to question what I would do if he had one foot on white and one foot on black and the line was no longer clear. He's mixed the colors together, leaving the space in which he stands a muddled hue of gray.

"I'm sorry."

Kane's simple phrase catches me so off guard I don't have enough time to hide the shock that snaps my brows together and parts my lips. "I must have heard you incor—"

He shakes his head before racking a hand through his thick locks. "No, you didn't. I have a deep understanding of how what I have to say will fall on deaf ears, but if I don't say it..."

Kane rises to his feet, drawing out the two water bottles from his pockets and taking a step toward me. My blood surges in my ears as he nears, my pulse the only audible sound as he drops both of them near my hands.

He's so close I could touch him. I could reach toward him and yank him down, render him unconscious, and steal the key from his pocket. It wouldn't be easy, but possible.

So why are my hands still in my lap? Why is my pulse thrumming in my neck? Why do I want to hear what he has to say?

He steps back, alleviating my mind of its internal questioning, and sighs. "I never wanted to help Phineas. Before I knew his grand scheme, I wanted no part of it. And that was before I even knew it had anything to do with you. But when I met you? All of you–"

He draws in another deep breath, and it's then that I notice the shadows under his eyes. Just like the growing scruff on his face, the dark circles are growing more profound each time I see him.

"Phineas had offered something I couldn't refuse. Something I'd have killed half this city to get. I went to you with an end goal in mind. Hell, I figured you and my father were different threads of the same blanket. I never expected to care about you. I never thought I'd risk everything on the small fragment of hope that you'd hear me out rather than kill me. But in the end, I decided the chance was worth it. Because *you're* worth it."

A sharp pain radiates across my jaw as my molars crack under my tight clamp. This is a game. He's playing games. He can't...

I can't *believe* him.

I *can't* believe him.

The burn at the edges of my eyes threatens to show him just how much his words affect me. How I want so fucking badly to trust the man that has brought me peace. Who stopped the screaming.

My eyes flash to him with the intent to say something. *Anything*. But nothing comes to the surface.

Instead of responding he nods, collects the two empty water bottles and plate from yesterday, and turns to leave.

But before he shuts the door, the only words I can find tumble past my lips. "What did he offer you, Kane?"

He hesitates, but only briefly. When the heavy metal door swings closed, I hear his fading whisper. "*Saoirse.*"

CHAPTER ELEVEN

Time. Most people feel as though they don't have enough. Some wish it away, looking forward to the future, while others dwell in the past and become stuck in its muck, unable to move forward. But when you're left in a room with no windows and a locked door, leaving you with the mere *idea* of time, what happens?

Reality and fantasy mesh, memories, and hopes intertwine. Thoughts become voices which turn into questions. Into doubts.

I've been trained for this. Put in a room with nothing but my mind to keep me company. It's where I honed and shaped my rage into purpose. I developed a goal, a plan, and ran through countless scenarios that could hinder me from success.

Never did I account for a man. No, not any man. For Ezekiel.

He is the puzzle I have yet to crack. An entity I thought I had figured out from the very beginning.

See, the thing about being a predator means that you can sense others. And what's even more important is knowing when they are stronger than you.

Kane is.

Because of that, my bullet was always meant to be his end —*before* he realized what he was capable of.

Yet somehow, the man has managed to make me feel in control of a situation in which I am a mere captive. His words don't seem meaningless, but genuine. Still, I can't do anything with his pretty words. They won't change what's happened, or how this will end.

Like I summoned him, whether with my thoughts or timed stomach growl, the handle turns and the heavy metal door swings open.

I pull my arms high over my head, the muscles and tendons drawing tight as I stretch the constricted ligaments. "Don't you have an..." My voice trails as I watch the man who is *not* Kane, appear on the threshold. His long, dingy brown hair is slicked back into a haphazard bun, his face clean of any stubble, and his suit a wrinkled mess.

His dark eyes scan over the empty plate and water before narrowing on me. The fine hairs on my neck stand, but I ignore the slight chill and straighten my back, lifting my chin. My gaze becomes low, and I school my features into relaxed boredom.

Even in my position, I refuse to appear anything less than dangerous.

"So you're the infamous Onyx Embros."

It's not a question and I don't respond. Instead, I read him in the moment of silence. One of his hands is on a gun tucked by his hip, while the other still rests on the doorknob. He hasn't fully entered the room and his ears have twitched twice, telling me he's listening for something. As if on cue, two faint knocks echo down the hall.

This brings a disgusting smirk to the man's face, his eyes lighting up and creasing in the corners. It's then he enters and pushes the door to a near close.

"Funny. I thought you'd look different. I mean, don't get me wrong, you're hot as fuck, but there's something missing."

He takes two wide steps toward me and bends down, tapping on his chin as if really trying to formulate a thought. After another second, he looks back down at the empty bottles and huffs. "That bastard walks around like he owns this place. Ain't been here but a few months and already he thinks he calls the shots."

"Someone must make him feel as though he does," I reply, watching his knuckles bloom white as he tightens his grip on his gun.

"The new recruits. They don't have the nuts to do some of the... testing."

I realize quickly what he's referring to. It seems as if testing women is a common occurrence with the entire army. My stomach clenches. I can't wait to kill them all.

"That's what it is, huh? He must have tested you and decided you were too good to share." The guard moves closer, his eyes locked on my mouth. "Yeah, and that's what's missing. My cock down your throat."

He rises, drawing his gun and directing it at my temple. "On your knees, slut."

My upper lip curls. "No. Also, do women a favor and broaden your vocabulary. That word died as an insult long ago."

"On. Your. Fucking. Knees." He moves his aim to my chest.

I'm not sure what I'm more irritated by. The fact that if these chains weren't holding me down, I'd have already cut out his throat. Or the fact that Kane has just appeared behind him and is about to do it for me.

I raise a brow, forcing my eyes on the filth in front of me so as to not make him realize what's about to happen. "I don't get on my knees for any man."

He cocks the gun, his face red and angry as he shifts his weight on the heels of his feet. He's impatient and rightfully so considering he was clearly sneaking in the first place. But how he didn't hear Kane enter nor feel his overwhelming presence is beyond me. *Imbecile.*

"Then think of me as your Go—"

His speech turns into garbles as a knife pierces through the back of his neck and out the front. Immediately, his eyes widen and his lashes blink rapidly, the shock and pain of seeing his own blood splattered over my face squeezing his features.

Kane's eyes are near black, his pupils so wide the green is a mere outline. A vein I've never noticed pulses in the middle of his forehead—a forehead that is already decorated in blood.

"I thought I made myself perfectly fucking clear that no one was to step foot down this fucking hallway." Kane yanks the knife from the guard's neck and we both watch as his hand finds the gaping hole.

His back hits the wall and as though he just remembered he was holding a weapon, he points it at Kane.

Annoyed, Kane sighs and draws his own gun from behind him and puts a bullet directly in the middle of his eyes. I'm thankful for the silencer on the end, but annoyance still nips at my skin.

"I could have handled that."

He smirks, his dimple prominent even through his stubble. "Oh yeah? Tell me, *mo chailín cliste.* How would you have managed such a feat?"

I roll my eyes, ignoring the heat curling low in my stomach. "I may still do the same to you."

"Look at me when you lie to me, Boss."

He closes the space, snatching the chains from the floor. He draws them tight, forcing my hands to slap against the concrete to prevent myself from falling forward. I swallow around the knot and peer up into his raging irises. Even like this, when I want nothing more than to pluck them from his skull, they still manage to steal my breath.

My heart picks up its pace, banging into my chest. Perhaps it's because he killed someone, or that we're both bloody and breathing far too hard, but it puts my mind back to the time we'd finished off Manny in my basement. When he took control of my body and I shattered around his hand.

As though he can read my thoughts, his lips lift higher. "Tell me you hate me."

"Let go of my chains so I can show you."

His face ebbs closer, so close I can smell the mix of spearmint and cooper mingling near his mouth. "Ever the donna."

"The queen." My voice is a heated whisper.

He shakes his head. "Not yet. Tell me, if you could kill me right now, how would you do it?"

Kane's hooded gaze roves over my face, his mouth less than an inch from mine now.

"Fire."

Closer. "You want me to suffer."

My chin flicks down half an inch. "Yes."

"Because I make you feel?"

"You make me feel anger."

"What else?" His lips are brushing against mine now. The light pressure sends tremors down my body.

"Annoyed and distracted."

"What about desperate?"

My sternum constricts, and my lids disobey my order to stay still and instead flutter, speaking my truth even when I lie. "No."

He *hmms*, his deep tremor vibrating my entire chest. "Let me show you how you make *me* feel."

Kane's hands leave the chains and thread through my hair, holding either side of my head firmly in place. There's one second between the moment he pauses and I can see the war waging across his face to the next where his lips crush mine.

Unlike the others we've shared, it's fueled by emotions. Emotions we wouldn't dare utter out loud but are present, nonetheless.

Frustration. For wanting each other despite everything telling us we shouldn't.

Hatred. For putting us in the situation where we feel as if we're sacrificing our own needs to meet the other's.

Longing. Something I don't think either of us has ever experienced in such a suffocating way.

His tongue licks along the seam of mine and when I grant him access, he takes full control. While his hands grip harder, mine find purchase, using his back and arms to hold on. He's too lost in taking everything he can to realize what's happened.

For a moment, I wonder what it would be like not to do it. To allow this to play out and see just where his head is. Where his heart is. But I know better. This thing we have was always meant to expire in the flames that have flickered idly, waiting to consume me after my plan is complete.

It's too bad though. We could have been something.

The sound of his own gun clicking pauses Kane's mouth. He breaks them away from my lips and smiles softly as his eyes slowly peel open. "Until a bullet stops me."

Ignoring the burn in the back of my throat and the glossy haze over my eyes, I whisper. "Stand up."

We rise together, the key I snuck from his pocket falling to the ground with the cuffs I unlocked. Keeping the gun at his head, I motion to the closed door behind him. "How many?"

"Seven. The two that planned to have their way with you are dead, so five. When you leave here, make a right. There are two at the front door. Don't worry about the ones at the back. They won't be able to get through in time for you to take the last one out that's guarding my car. The driver won't need much convincing to take you home."

My breathing quickens. "Where am I?"

"Outskirts, near the border. It's a lot of Murphy ground you'll need to go through to get to your side, and without the guards checking in on their half-hour time, it won't take long for them to know. Hurry."

I smirk. "My first day here, you said I was your enemy. What happened to that?"

Kane's face grows somber, his gaze falling to the gun in my hand then back at me. "No matter what I said in the heat of the moment, you were never my enemy." He blows out a steady breath. "You were always going to be my end. Not the other way around."

Goddammit.

I grab his neck with my empty hand and yank him toward me, smashing my lips to his one last time. My heart squeezes when he lets me take control this time. His hands find my hips but the hold on them is loose.

My grip tightens on both his throat and the handle as I move my mouth against him, soaking in everything I'll never get the chance to feel again.

How it's possible to hate and want someone so much, I'll never understand, but the gut-wrenching pull I feel in my soul *is* something I never want to experience again.

A slow clap of hands rips us apart and toward the source of the sound. Five men are on either side of him, guns raised and trained at my temple.

"Believe me now, son?" Phineas drops his hand, shoving them in his pockets as he motions toward me. "I told you, you can feed her, take care of her, show her you care. But in the end, she's still a wild animal and will bite your head off the first chance she gets."

The five men move as one, fanning out on either side of me. I could kill Phineas right now. One shot to end it all. But the moment I do, Sam, the man responsible for executing my parents like animals in the street, walks free. My veins erupt into fire, the realization that I'm still so far from succeeding eating my insides like a thousand parasites.

I lift both my hands, letting Kane's gun loop around and dangle from my finger. "Only time I think I'll ever agree with you, Phineas. You should listen to your old man, Kane."

A guard that looks two seconds away from pissing himself moves forward and slips the weapon from my hand, passing it to a silent Kane. He accepts it before placing it behind him in his belt, his face almost somber as he avoids eye contact with me.

With guns still trained on me, he bends and grabs my chains, but Phineas stops him by tossing a pair of cuffs.

"We have to go. Seems as if this place might have been compromised and my lawyer isn't done getting the meeting together."

My eyes flash to Kane. He rolls his right sleeve up his arm, seemingly unbothered, but I see the twitch in his jaw. "Where are we going?"

Phineas grants Kane and I a smile before turning around. "Home."

Ezekiel

Age 14

Chapter Twelve

"What did you do this time, Fi?" I massage the back of my neck as I look down at the same wide puppy-dog eyes she gives me at least three times a week.

Honestly, I don't know where the hell my sister got this tender bone in her body that puts her in all these damn situations, but it's really begun to annoy me. She's only eight for crying out loud, but every time she does shit, half of it's against the law.

I mean, it was cute at first. She stole everyone's trash cans on our street a few months ago and took out all the recyclables. But then a week or two later, she started stealing cans of cat food to feed stray kittens in the alley. The situation has only gotten worse, so when she randomly asked me to go to Petco, I should have known better. When she asked to go talk to the man about lizards, I should have seen the red flags.

Maybe I did, and my mind was busy. I didn't take into full account what was happening. Or maybe I want her to continue to be good even when we're surrounded by nothing but bad. Either way, when she pulls five small clear bags from behind her back bearing fish, I can't help but smile.

"Really? And how do you think we can take care of these?"

She shakes her little head. "They're saltwater fish. I figured we could go down to the docks and set them free."

I sigh. "The ports are not the safest place in the world, Fi."

"Pleeeeeease, Zeky."

Pursing my lips, I stare down at her pouted ones. Her eyes are rounded with the telltale sheen of alligator tears ready and waiting for activation. So unnecessary.

"Fine." I barely get the word out before she squeals, jumping up and down.

"Alright, alright. Calm down before you give them shaken fish syndrome or something. Haven't you seen that part in Nemo?"

We turn in tandem, walking toward the bus stop when she laughs. "That's a cartoon, silly."

I shrug. "It's still a thing."

Her face pinches as she considers what I'm saying. In the end, though, she decides to play it safe and holds the bags to her chest while we wait for the next bus all the way to the ports.

Surprisingly, one of the docks is clear of any guards and we manage to make it to the end without any interference. Still, I know better and understand that this is the territory of my father's enemy. They shouldn't be too far away and it's best we be quick and quiet.

I pat a humming Fi and point to the edge. "Hurry on, I'll stay here and make sure no wild bears come to steal them for lunch."

At first, her brows curve as she considers just how serious I am. But before she gets lost in that head of hers, I wink.

She giggles. "Okay."

She skips to the edge, setting the fish down in a row before flopping on her butt.

Everything's calm for a few minutes as she struggles with

the rubber band. But when she finally snaps it off the bag and carefully pours the first fish into the serene water, I hear the footsteps.

It's only one pair and the slow stride of the person tells me they aren't in a rush, or inherently wanting to scare me. After another few seconds, a man appears next to me, and although I don't turn to look at him, I know he's loaded. The suit visible in my periphery is pressed, his cologne smells expensive, and the watch sparkling on his wrist is damn near blinding.

"I have to say, you are one lucky kid."

Lucky. *Hmph.* First time in my life I've ever even heard the term when directed at me.

I shrug and keep my eyes on my sister who lets out the second fish. "Oh, yeah? How so?"

"Well, first of all, you're on private property. Second, there are two dozen men here that almost emptied a clip in your back."

"But they didn't," I state the obvious, unbothered by the fact I'm being slightly rude to someone clearly important to my well-being.

I'm not sure if it's the fact death is a dream to me now, or that I honestly no longer have the energy to try, but tonight, I'm all out of fucks. The Embros family has a reputation. They wouldn't hurt my sister, and honestly, they'd probably send her someplace way better than here, so for once, I'm not worried.

Or maybe it was what I had to endure twelve hours ago. Vomit, blood, cum, and tears flip through my mind, and hot, burning bile rises in my throat making me burp.

The man sighs, thankfully sensing the fact that I'm missing a few crayons from my box, and not that I'm *meaning* to be a total asshole. "You're a big kid. Damn near look grown and my men thought you stole the little girl."

This makes me laugh. "Anyone that steals my sister will bring her right back, apologies and all."

"That so?"

"Yeah. You see those fish over there?"

I point to Fi, who's taking a long time releasing the third fish. She's lost in between sudden sobs and her speeches of goodbye to even realize I'm a few meters back having a conversation with a stranger—something she'd surely scold me about later.

The man nods. "Hard not to. What is she doing exactly?"

Running a hand through my hair, I sigh. "This girl stole saltwater fish from Petco because 'they don't deserve to live in a small box where people hit the glass.' And now she's setting them free."

This causes the man to laugh. It's high and friendly and I can't help but turn to look at him. I've never heard a man laugh before. At least not one that wasn't followed with the back of a hand slamming into my face.

He's got dark hair and black eyes. They look like the expensive jewelry stones you see on late-night QVC. I think the shade is onyx.

When he stops laughing, he glances back at my sister. "My daughter is similar. Even with all the bad I do, she thinks I'm some sort of Batman. Almost fourteen years old and she still looks at me like a superhero."

"My sister will be this world's first superhero." I cover a yawn and watch as she moves on to the fourth fish. Two more and we can make the long journey home.

A quick peek at the man's watch tells me that Mom will be expecting us in an hour. We'll need to leave soon if we're going to make it even close to being on time.

"Then you better protect her." The man's voice is lower now, more serious.

"I am. Believe me."

"Says the boy that brings her to a private port with guarded men."

"Men we were able to get past without so much as a second glance," I counter, letting my eyes peer at him from the corner.

He smiles and nods. "Yeah. Guess I'll have to fix that, huh?"

"Just so long as my sister can come release her fish anytime." I turn and hold out my hand expectantly. One thing I've learned from Phineas that may actually be useful—act as if the deal is done and it will be. Something about fake confidence or some shit.

The man takes my hand and shakes firmly. "Anytime. Tell them Dante said it was okay."

"Will do. Thank you."

He gives me one last smirk before dropping his hand and turning back around. "You know, when the weight of the world calls for your humanity, it's the ones we love that keep it bound to us. Even when we want nothing more than for it to swallow us whole. Take care, kid."

Dante lifts two fingers, and I'm able to make out the telltale click of safeties moving back into place. Even with him gone, his words remain like an ominous whisper. It's as though he knows just how much I want everything to end. For the ground to open and take me from everything. But as he said, it's because of Fiona and my mother that I latch on to the edges, digging my fingers into the dirt and waiting for the storm to pass.

Another three minutes go by until Fi waves goodbye to her last fish and finally stands, her empty bags clutched in one small fist. Her steps are slow and sad and even though my heart dies a little every Wednesday, it still aches to see her small face so fallen.

"Hey, chin up. You did a good thing." Ninety percent chance those colorful fish were eaten by something big, brown, and ugly, but there's no way in hell I'm going to tell her that.

She tries to smile, her two new front teeth peeking from her poked-out lip. "I know. It was still sad saying goodbye though."

I place my hand softly on the back of her head before drawing her into my chest for a bear hug. "How about we stop at Sue's and see if she's got some ice cream sandwiches? Those always seem to cheer you up."

Fiona nods against my stomach before giving me one last squeeze. "Thank you, Zeky."

"Aye, don't worry about it."

We release each other at the same time and walk hand in hand down the long dock until we get to the road and catch our bus home. On the way, we talk about a new little girl in her class and I learn how she always has the prettiest hair and the brightest bows. I make a mental note to watch a video or two on French braids.

When the bus pulls up to our stop, we have fifteen minutes to spare. We reach our neighbor, Sue's house, first and that's when it hits me. A burning heaviness in the bottom of my stomach. A sick type of dread settling over me.

I clear my throat, pasting on a fake smile when Sue opens the door. But it's no use. She's been around too long and knows me too well.

Her light brows furrow. "What's wrong?"

Fiona looks from her to me, and I widen my grin. "Oh, nothing. But can Fi bother you for an ice cream sandwich?"

"Of co—"

"Why aren't you having one?" Fiona's green eyes widen as she looks up at me.

"I'll be right back. I just want to let Mom know we are back, okay?"

Sue rests a hand on Fi's shoulder and nods. "Come on inside, honey, your brother will be right back."

Fiona hesitates, her gaze flashing from Sue to me and then back again. She's keen for her age or maybe she felt the pit in her stomach too and isn't sure what it is. Thankfully, Sue persuades her.

"I have a new kind. Cookies and cream."

Fi forms a small O with her lips and finally allows Sue to lead her inside. "Hurry up, Zeky."

When the door closes, I take off running, jumping over the stray toys in the yard, the stump I have yet to dig out of the ground, and the few steps up to our door. As I reach for the handle, a vicious chill runs through my spine, and a heavy thunk falls into my gut.

I remember this feeling. I felt it a year ago when I was thirteen and found my mother comatose on the floor. She'd OD'd.

Shortly after, I started working to pick up the slack to allow her to take more days off.

My hands shake but I manage to open the door. Inside, darkness greets me, and only the sound of raspy draws of breath fills the air.

"Mom?"

At first, there isn't an answer and my stomach twists. I reach for the lamp and flip it on. On the worn coffee table is an empty bottle of wine, and dropped a few feet away are empty beer bottles. My mother is hunched over on the floor, legs crossed, her elbows digging into her knees with her hands covering her face.

"Mom." I say it more forcefully as I approach her.

If anyone can understand the shit that makes people want to escape into a bottle or under the influence of something stronger, it'd be me. But knowing Fiona would be home right now and would see her...

Annoyance flickers in my chest. Her mind has been poisoned. Her spirit broken. And if I'm being honest, I hate that Fi and I aren't enough to make her at least try. I hate that I'm constantly being forced to endure the worst types of abuse but told not to lose my humanity because there are people who are depending on me.

What about me?

What about the fact that my entire life has been taken and I have to be the one to suck it up?

I swallow around the burn and force my anger back into its hole. Comparing grief and hurt isn't fair. I know this. All I can do now is do my best to keep Fiona away from it all. It means lying to her about the entirely different life I live outside of these walls, but at this point, it's necessary. If I can't keep Fiona's childhood intact, no piece of advice will be enough to keep me from succumbing to it all.

Wrapping a loose hand around her upper arm, I tug softly. "Let's get you to bed, Mom. I'll clean this up."

She shakes her head profusely, her cries growing louder. I purse my lips but sit next to her, draping my arm over her shoulder.

I try to shush her but it makes matters worse. She begins mumbling something to herself, and even straining I can't make out what she's saying.

"I can't hear you."

"You have to promise me you'll get her back, Zek. Please!" Her desperate shrieks pierce into my body and latch around my heart.

"Who, Mom?"

When she responds, I can't quite understand and pull her closer into my arms. I sit on the floor and begin rocking her slowly, brushing her hair with my hand. "Just take a breath. Slow down and tell me who."

She does the best she can to listen and takes two shuddering breaths. But when she repeats herself, no part of me is ready for the visceral shot to the chest. "Bunny."

I squeeze my eyes closed, willing the swelling pain to subside. It's been so long since I've thought about her. About the loss. "She's not alive, Mom, remember? She was stillborn."

My mother jerks away from me as though I've hit her and aggressively wipes tears away from her face. "No. She wasn't. Her father has her. *Your* father has her."

That doesn't—no. Phineas has Bunny? How does that make any sense? An odd veil of annoyance settles over me. She's drunk and I know I shouldn't put too much stock in her words but I ask anyway. "What are you talking about?"

"He *took* her. He took my baby so we wouldn't leave." Her sobs return, the booze doing a wonderful job of keeping her from being able to hold on to one emotion for long. "He lets me see her on Wednesday nights. Only when you leave. He told me that as long as we live in Washington and stay quiet about you, he'll let me see her. But I wasn't—oh god. I wasn't supposed to tell you, Ezekiel. I wasn't supposed to tell you."

The room spins as she grabs at my chest and begins begging for my silence. She doesn't need to. She should know I would never do anything to hurt her. But now knowing I've let down the sister I didn't even know existed?

No, she's drunk and doesn't know what the hell she's saying. Maybe it's her way of coping, or maybe she's just that fucked up. Either way, it's not possible.

Annoyed, I firmly wrap my fingers around her wrists and detach them from my shirt. I stand slowly and take a step away, wincing when my mother's hand smacks against the hard floor.

"I have to get Fiona," I tell her, turning to pick up the empty bottles on the ground. It only takes a few minutes to fix the mess she made but when I'm done, I turn to my mother. "Please go lie down, Mom. I don't want Fi to see you like this."

She shakes her head, her loose curls waving in front of her face.

My voice drops. "Mom. Get up."

"Not until you promise you won't say anything to your—"

"I won't say anything to Phineas." I sigh, running a hand through my hair. "Now please, go lie down. I'll be there in a few."

Reluctantly, she nods and does as she's told. When the door clicks closed behind her, I light a candle in the kitchen and turn on a lamp before going to grab Fi.

As my feet crunch on the grass beneath me, I think of the man from the docks.

"It's the ones we love that keep us bound to it."

I hope that's always true for me, because deep down, somewhere in the depth of everything I know, something tells me my humanity won't last. And all I can hope is that by then, Batman comes to kill me.

CHAPTER THIRTEEN

"You're not bringing the rocket launcher, Madeline." I toss her a side-eye in the back seat of the cruiser, but she merely laughs.

"I am. As soon as I see her pretty head clear of the path, I'm letting loose." She twirls a stray red curl around her finger and for the first time in a week, she appears like the old Maddy.

We all are a little more at ease knowing this entire thing will come to an end shortly. Ezekiel's sister called an hour ago and gave us the address of the warehouse they're keeping Onyx. We left immediately.

My boys shut down the businesses for the day, leaving a few guards at each post, but the majority of our army has been called out, gathering at the estate to gear up and ride out. Our main plan is extraction. Get Onyx and get out.

Killing Murphy guards is a bonus. Grabbing Ezekiel is a hope. We still don't know what side he's on, or if this entire thing is a setup, but I've refined my skills at being able to get a good read on people. And for Ezekiel to trust us with sending his sister to see us alone with the information she did? I want to give him the benefit of the doubt.

I'm certain we all do. Even in the few short months with us, he was becoming part of the family. Another member that seems vital to our operation. Not with killing Phineas but keeping Onyx going after the fallout.

Now, I don't know what will happen.

"Must you always be so dramatic?" Brushing my hair over an exposed shoulder, I turn to look out the front window as we pull up to the new gate. It underwent construction the day after the incident thanks to the boys and only took two days to finish with all hands on deck.

It's an incredibly thick sheet of steel, held in place by more steel. It's about thirteen feet high, and goes four feet into the ground, slotted in place by a metal foundation. It connects seamlessly to the gate that surrounds the entire property and covers the only forest-free entrance. The rest of the gate disappears on either side and extends deep into the woods that most of our guards are terrified to enter.

Trigger clicks the button and allows the driver's side window to roll down. He reaches out and presses his hand against a screen covered in thick bulletproof glass. Like in a movie, a green light comes to life and scans his hand. It dings once and then a digital keypad appears. He types in a code and after a moment a heavy clunk resonates in the air as the lock draws back and the gate opens.

We pull inside and drive up the half-mile path until Embros estate comes into view. The front has a large black plastic sheet covering the hole which used to be the front door. The builders have demolished the wrecked brick, installed the replacement frame as well as applied the outside wrap, but even with this many people working, it will still be another week until it's finished.

Trigger parks the car toward the back kitchen entrance. "Trick and I will have everyone ready in three minutes. Grab what you need and meet us back here."

We all nod in unison and get out, filing into the house and going our respective ways. Maddy hums a song as she skips past Russ and Cat arguing in the kitchen. A welcomed norm in the recent chaotic events.

"He doesn't have much longer, Russ. Give the man his steak." Cat pulls on her long cigarette stick and motions to me with her chin. "Tell him to make me a damn rare steak, Shire."

"That old geezer isn't dying till he knows his niece is safe. I am not making the man something that's going to make him feel worse." Russ ignores the smoke Cat blows directly in his face.

I give Cat a sympathetic smile before leaving them to their never-ending argument and into the foyer. It's surprising how much they've been able to clean in the short amount of time. Besides the gaping hole, the floor has been cleared of rubble and the damaged parts have already been replaced.

I glide up the stairs, my heart squeezing in my chest as I reach the landing. Besides the initial visit home to clean up and grab clothes, I hadn't allowed myself to really acknowledge the two empty rooms.

My sanity won't let me look to the right, but the closed door in front of me is another story. Pushing my boot into it, it swings open with ease, displaying a room that is pristine in every way. The bed is made, the floor is clean, and the dresser is clear of any belongings.

From the looks of it, it appears to be nothing but a guest room. Something so untouched no one would think that less than a week ago, Ezekiel was here. I wonder if Cat cleaned it.

Or if perhaps he knew they were coming and he wouldn't be here anymore.

A terrible burn begins at the back of my throat. I clear it twice but it only expands, moving into my nose and to the edge of my eyes. The warm tears fall before I can stop them.

I failed her.

I told her not to kill him. That maybe he would be the key to setting her free. But I was wrong.

Wiping my face clean, I sniff and straighten my spine, but as I shift to go, a small white rectangle catches my eye. It's been thrown haphazardly on the pillow and has slid down halfway under the duvet.

After a quick look over my shoulder, I force my feet inside, snatching the envelope and hurrying to my room. I throw it on my dresser and quickly change before meeting everyone back downstairs.

We load up and pull off with three dozen cars following close behind. All the while I'm gazing out of the window with one image in my mind. The script on the outside of the envelope.

Onyx.

Somehow Trick convinced Trigger he should drive, and to say he's getting in the spirit, is an understatement. His fingers grip into my upper thigh as the loud music blasts from the speakers and causes the seats to vibrate beneath us. Maddy sings the lyrics with her entire chest, pounding on the roof above her. And from behind me, Trigger massages my neck with one hand, his eyes interchanging between his phone in the other and the screen embedded in the seat.

The drive will take about thirty minutes and with the number of people with us, it's only a matter of time before Phineas catches word we are coming and moves her. It's the very reason we've created four different ways to meet up with them. We are taking the street directly toward the warehouse, while other guards are cutting other streets off, forcing Murphy's path should they leave before we get there.

Trick's fingers dig into my thigh as he presses harder on the gas. I close my eyes and sink farther into the seat. Just a few more minutes.

It only seems as if one song has finished before it cuts off altogether. My eyes snap open to see the dozens of warehouses lined in a perfect row on the street. The sun is at its highest, directly over the barren white building, giving a perfect view of the empty roads.

My pulse beats sluggishly, and my ears fill with an incessant buzzing.

No one is here.

No cars are parked in front of any of the buildings.

There's nothing. Just us.

How are we too late?

Trick pulls over in front of the address Fiona gave Maddy. "Stay here. This could all be some sort of trap."

Tigger shakes his head. "None of these warehouses have garages. I doubt they would all just be waiting inside to ambush us the moment we answered the door. How would they get away?"

"In our cars. We'd be dead," Maddy points out.

I shake my head. "This isn't a movie. They'd have to have all been dropped off here. Why go through all the trouble? Doesn't make sense. We're too late."

Trick smashes his free hand on the dash, making my lashes flutter. He's been so emotional the past few days and not even I have been able to calm him. Our entire relationship has been built upon him and Trigger caring for me and bringing me back from the edge. It's only now I've begun to realize I haven't done the same for them.

A thick knot forms in my throat as I turn to Trick and place a hand on his jaw. He closes his eyes and leans into my touch. "Shi."

"What is it?" I ask, my voice a mere whisper. We're all handling the situation in our own ways, that much is obvious, but his rage is so far from his normal reactions, I need to understand the deeper meaning behind it.

His eyes peel open slowly, and inside they are hues of ice and sea, battling for dominance on either side of the crater that is his pupil. His confliction and anguish is so evident, it's palpable. My entire heart squeezes in my chest.

"Tell me."

"If I can't protect her—" He doesn't finish and instead rips out of my hand and out his door, slamming it behind him. He draws his gun and signals the cars behind us for other guards to join him.

Trigger leans over the seat and presses a soft kiss to my temple. "He thinks if we can't protect her, we won't be able to protect you."

"But that's not true!" It's been years since I've raised my voice, but my lungs are so tight I can hardly breathe. "Trick must know that's not the case."

"And why not?" Maddy shouts. "Boss had all of us, and we didn't do a damn thing to stop any of this." She starts to open the door but stops at the sounds of birds chirping from her jeans.

She rips her phone from her pocket and slams a finger on the screen, placing it on speaker.

"They knew you were coming. They moved her." Fiona's soft whispers come through the small phone.

"How?" Trigger asks, leaning past me to honk the horn in a rhythmic tone.

Trick and the boys hear it and stop their movement.

"They have people watching your estate. They saw you leave and called it in. They were gone before you even got out of the neutral zone."

"And why weren't we told sooner?" I ask, holding my hands out to Trick, who reenters the car.

"I had to wait until the guard stationed with me was busy so I could use his phone. If he finds out, I'm dead."

Maddy's screams are piercing as she slams a fist against the door. "Fuck!"

"Mad—" She tosses the phone on the dash before jumping from the car, not waiting for the girl to finish.

"Where are they taking her?" Trick asks, his focus, along with Trigger and me, on Maddy who has her rocket launcher over her shoulder and aims at a building.

"To the mansion."

"Phineas'?" I ask. It's rhetorical but the girl squeaks a quiet yes.

"He has everyone there. They are waiting for you all to come. My brother has a plan."

"Tell me why the fuck we should trust him?" Trick roars.

But before the girl can get out her words, Maddy's launcher explodes in the quiet air, and the small missile hits its target—the farthest building in the back. The entire thing crumbles, falling over in seconds.

"I have to go. Please. Just give us more time." Fiona's voice is barely audible over Maddy's demolition.

We don't get to ask anything else because the phone disconnects.

More time.

The most dangerous thing to give when every second that passes isn't guaranteed.

CHAPTER FOURTEEN

Phineas' phone rings for the seventh time, but yet again, he ignores it. Instead, his eyes stay focused on Kane. There's been a heavy tension ever since we were loaded into the limo, but no one has said anything.

Unlike Phineas, though, Kane is relaxed. His arm is strewn across the back of the seats, one leg resting on top of the other's knee. If it wasn't for the blood splatter decorating his clothes and jaw, I would argue that I've never seen him more bored.

But upon further inspection, there's a ticcing in his throat that tells a different story. It could be this wasn't something he was expecting, or perhaps my delivery of a kiss rather than a bullet threw him off. Either way, the steady beating under his flesh informs me his wheels are turning, a new plan formulating.

I adjust the cuffs, ignoring the guards beside Phineas raising their guns at my sudden movement. Rolling my eyes, I hold up my hands. "I would have killed you already if I wanted to, boys. No need to get so anxious."

Phineas's eyes flash to me, but I know his words are meant for his son. "Are you tired of playing with her yet?"

"Not quite," Kane answers, though he keeps his gaze directed out the window.

"You told me she wouldn't cause much trouble and it would be easier than dealing with that Maddy woman."

"And what trouble has she caused?"

"She's killed four of my men."

"Hmm, not accurate. I killed two. She killed one. And your G.I. Joe over there killed the other." Kane finally lets his head loll toward his father.

The amount of arrogance surrounding him is new to me. He's always had a cocky edge, but this is something different entirely. "It was to be expected. You have Washington's most dangerous woman. Did you not suspect the weakest men you have would be dealt with during her arrival?"

"Watch your tongue with me, boy."

Kane drops his leg and leans forward, perching himself on his hands that he rests on his knees. The darkness I've only just *really* seen comes to the forefront, and even I lean slightly backward. His father and the other guards feel it too, moving in tandem as they shift their weight in their seats.

"I am merely a creation of what you made, *father*." He spits the last word with venom. "Does it not please you to see me take the role you trained me for?"

Phineas switches to Irish, probably under the assumption I don't understand him. But as an enemy I'd have to deal with at some point, it was one of the first languages my parents made me learn. "You said you wanted out. That was the agreement. Let you and your kin go."

Kane shrugs. "Without Onyx, there is an entire territory that will be up for grabs."

Phineas' face blooms a light pink, frustration clearly getting the better of him. "It will be mine."

"And you think you'll be able to handle the entire state? All of her businesses? The guards that were loyal to only her?"

A nerve in his father's jaw tics. "Loyalty means nothing when it comes to extra zeros."

Kane shakes his head. "Not with her men. I've been working alongside them. They hate you. They will band together and find a way to kill you even if it means total chaos in the streets."

"So what do you suggest, son?" Phineas booms, his temper showing through.

Though all my attention is focused on the conversation, I feign ignorance by keeping my eyes on the guards. I wink at the one who almost killed me my first day and blow a kiss at the other. I sit back and smile at their confused gazes at one another.

Kane sighs. "I'll take over her territory. I'll give the men the option to join, leave town, or die. Slowly, after a few years of reform, we'll start to add in Murphys to the other side."

My pulse races through my ears, a heat unfurling in my limbs. I want to reach out and break Kane's nose, but I also don't want them to know I understand them.

Phineas sucks his teeth. "That will take too long. I may as well leave this slut to run it."

Kane clenches his jaw and drops his hand. This demeanor is new territory for me, but I'd be lying if I didn't say it wasn't rather intriguing. I've yet to figure out his angle, what he really wants, but his mix of indifference and annoyance is beginning to shine through and tell me all I need to know.

"It's the most cost-efficient way to combine the territories. If you do it too quickly, too many will die in the process. Then you have to consider law enforcement. They will come looking to collect on any damages done to the city. Then you'll have to worry about new recruits. There will be a time when you have no money and not enough gun power to fight off any neighboring families who decide to take advantage."

Like I said before, if Kane had been the son of my parents, he'd be unstoppable. No doubt in my mind.

Phineas works his jaw back and forth, his eyes flashing to me. "So have her sign it over to you then. Is that what you're suggesting?"

Kane nods once.

"I thought you didn't want this life. You asked me for your freedom in return for giving her to me."

I hold my breath, waiting for his answer. But instead of an explanation, Kane lazily shrugs one shoulder. "I think it's too late for that."

"And how do I know you aren't really working for her? I did walk in on you two seconds away from fucking on Lenny's corpse."

Kane chuckles, switching back to English. "She's my whore for the time being. Nothing more."

Whether he's putting on a front or if this is the real thing, I'm not sure, but my anger overflows and I move quickly, slamming my head into Kane's with a force that makes me dizzy. He spits blood on the floor, wiping away the residual on his nose while smiling at me and holding up a hand to the guards who've yet again, unnecessarily raised their guns.

"Doesn't seem like she thinks of herself as yours," one of the guards says, a smirk on his face.

Kane ignores him and keeps his gaze on me. "Oh, she's mine. At least for the next few days. You'd do well to remember that or you'll end up like Lenny."

Phineas grunts. His lack of response and all-around submission toward his son is not only surprising, but bothersome. Just before the guard, Lenny, made an advance, he mentioned something about the "bastard walking around like he owned the place." Which means Kane is much more prominent in the Murphy family than he lets on.

Just another reason why I shouldn't trust him.

I should have pulled the fucking trigger.

"Kane." Phineas gets his son's attention before continuing to speak in his native tongue. "You're smart. Smarter than me, even. But that doesn't mean I'm stupid. When she signs the papers, you put a bullet between her eyes or I'll put one in both of your heads. No more playing house. Do you understand?"

Kane tilts his head and finally breaks eye contact. "*Tá.*"

The phone rings again, but the melody is different, which must mean something because this time, Phineas actually takes the phone from his pocket. "What?"

"They blew up five warehouses." The voice is not only loud enough for me to hear him, but for me to recognize.

That voice.

Every muscle in my body seizes and my breathing stops altogether. I'm fourteen again, hiding in a limo and begging my mother to let me help. To let me save them.

"You can have some dignity and get out on your own. Or we can blindly shoot into the limo before tearing your bleeding corpses out anyway. You decide, Embros."

Sam is on the other line. I know it with every fiber of my being, and suddenly, my goal is right back in front of me. It isn't obscure and hanging on a limb I'm still wondering how I'll reach. No, I've been led right back to it and there's no better time than now.

"Yes. Lucian says Alexi has him doing a few things and he can't finish the paperwork till the end of this week," Phineas grumbles into the receiver, his gaze pinned on Kane who is folding up a sleeve that came loose.

"Hmm. Yes." He switches to Irish. "We're taking her to the mansion. Every guard who isn't on duty needs to be on standby and send a message to the Embros estate that if they cross over into my territory, I'm putting her head on my mailbox, Ports be damned."

Phineas mumbles a few other meaningless things before hanging up and returning his phone to his pocket. A tepid calm works into my nerves, hearing his words. My soldiers are bold, but only my family would do something as drastic as blowing up warehouses. I could bet my life it was Maddy who started it. She's been looking for a reason to use her launcher.

The limo turns down an empty street, lined with tall trees on either side. We reach a small guard booth where three men stand with guns leaning into their shoulders. Such a simple concept. If one really wanted to breach the gates they could merely take out the guys and push the simple button on the control panel inside. It's something I've considered but without knowing what lies beyond the gate, posed too great a risk to chance.

One of the soldiers nods to the limo before allowing us to pass. I take note of the hallowed grounds, the tall, manicured trees, the small duplex I'm sure is the grounds members' living quarters, and the massive home. From my point of view, I can make out five floors of the mansion.

But then, everything else fades into the background. On the grand marble steps, next to the large iron doors, is a face I never thought I'd see again.

Maddy's girlfriend.

Harlow paces back and forth, the loose brown waves not contained in her haphazard bun whipping around in the wind. Her pale skin has splotches of red where she's continually wiped tears.

One of the guards grumbles under his breath as we pull to a stop, but quickly clears his throat when Phineas shoots him a threatening gaze.

My eyes find Kane, and in a moment I'm able to see he too is confused by her presence. I begin to wonder if this will be an entirely new puzzle or one that will make this entire situation that much clearer.

Phineas files out first, followed by the two guards. Kane shifts from the seat, but my voice gives him pause. "I am no one's whore."

He turns, a smirk painting his facc, and I fight the urge not to thrust my head into his nose this time. "Oh, *mo chailín cliste*, but you are."

Without another word, he exits the limo with me close behind, another remark playing at my lips. Before I can utter anything though, Harlow comes into view. Phineas barely makes it to the top of the steps before she grabs onto his lapel, fresh tears streaming down her pale face.

"I did what you said. I gave you the damn codes. Let her go!"

Anger snaps in my chest while panic swells in my gut. I want to pay attention to the first thing that fell from her mouth, but the latter takes precedence. *Let who go?*

"I still need her," Phineas answers.

Harlow's head shakes back and forth frantically. "No, no. Y-you said if I-I. Oh god. You lied to me, *again.* I hurt my Maddy and for what?"

Snot and tears continue to stream down her face and at the same time red dots infiltrate my vision at the realization. Her Maddy. *My* Maddy. The utter fucking audacity for her to open her mouth and say those words is staggering.

Not only that, but it was her. *Her.*

My mind works faster than I can keep up, new questions and more anger clouding my thoughts—my judgment.

I feign complacency and follow Kane up the stairs. Phineas brushes Harlow's hands away but isn't overly aggressive, which has me slotting the pieces together. She doesn't just work for him—she *means* something to him.

Instead of waiting, I advance quickly, interlocking my fingers and latching them around her neck. All the men move together, guns clicking as they direct them toward me, and Phineas urgently barks to his son, but none of it matters as I tug on her earlobe with my teeth.

"The next time you see me, Harlow, it will be the *last* thing you see."

Her body vibrates against mine, the evident fear shaking her from head to toe. When I release her, I grant her a wink before lifting my bare foot and kicking her in the dead center of her chest.

Harlow flings backward, her body colliding with Kane, who grips the outside of her arms to keep them steady. With her next to him, I nearly wince at my blindness.

There's always been something familiar about the girl, and now I see it. Her resemblance to him.

And he doesn't even know.

Phineas grumbles, shoving his thick hands in his pockets. "Women. Such weak, fucking playthings. You though. Tighten your bitch's leash, Ezekiel. She's doing too much."

After ensuring Harlow is physically well, he releases her and scowls at his father. "She won't cause you much trouble from my room."

"Your room?" he scoffs, and though a sarcastic smile curls his lips, I see the trepidation creasing his eyes. "Are you mad? She'll go to the cellar like *every* unwelcome guest in my home. Consider yourself lucky I don't punish her for her actions thus far."

I bark out laughter, ignoring Kane's look of disapproval. "Handcuffed and all, you wouldn't be able to land a finger on me, Murphy."

"So sure are you, girl? Can't wait to shove that mouthful of—"

"Except you won't." Kane steps forward and grabs me firmly by the elbow. "Your word was that no one would touch her, yet I had to kill two guards who chose to disrespect those direct orders. Once you have a leash on your men, we can discuss her living arrangements."

He doesn't wait for a response from Phineas and instead, guides me inside.

CHAPTER FIFTEEN

It's been three hours since we left the Murphy's warehouses. The buildings are nothing more than piles of concrete and burned plastic now, riddled with our expectations of thinking this was over. Instead, we return to the estate empty-handed, with only tension pulling at our seams.

We've done our best to continue our duties, as we know it's what Onyx would deem most important. So in the little time we've been back, we've conducted a few brief meetings, organized money drops and weapons exchanges, as well as our shipments for the week.

The sun is finally setting on the horizon and the boys are packed up to make a delivery when an alarm dings across all our phones. We pull them out simultaneously to a display of the new camera installed at the front gate. On the screen is a kid, no more than fifteen staring at us. His brown hair is scraggly, and with the combination of dark shadows beneath his eyes and the open sores, it's apparent he's not well.

My eyes flash to Trigger who presses the button on his phone that gives him two way communication. "Can I help you?"

The kid's eyes widen slightly before he straightens, brushing off the visible dirt from his torn jazz T-shirt. "Uh-hh, yeah. I'm looking for the one they call Mad Maddy."

I sigh, and Trick laughs. Madeline adopted the name when she took over the drug distribution. Only the men that work directly under her refer to her as such, but I've always found it rather insulting. Maddy, on the other hand, uses it to her advantage, leaving her own calling cards of sorts to anyone who may try to cross her.

Trigger taps the button to speak again. "She's indisposed right now. Is there something I can do for you?"

The boy chews on his bottom lip as though he wasn't prepared to talk to anyone besides her. After a few more moments of deliberating, he speaks up. "Can you like, ya know, call her or something? I was told to talk to only her. Or the girl with pink-and-purple hair. Is she there?"

My twin's gaze snaps to me. Trick immediately shakes his head but I hold up a hand. "We're talking through a phone, love."

His eyes fall, a deep crease forming in the middle of his brows. "I know, kitten, but I just—"

I place a soft hand on his shoulder, and he visibly relaxes, blowing out a deep sigh. Both he and Trigger have been on edge, handling the loss in different ways, but doing one thing the same—carrying all the fault. Truth is, it's no one's.

We were all on high alert *every* moment of *every* day. We did what we were supposed to and took all the proper precautions. There was no evidence that Ezekiel would do what he did—which is still debatable in itself. The letter I found may provide a little more clarity on that front.

I nod to Trigger who presses down on the button. "Yeah, she's right here."

The boy sucks in through his nose before wiping at it, clearly thinking of his recompense for delivering his message.

"Hello. This is Shi." I step closer to the phone. "You have something to tell me?"

"Yeah-yeah. Mr. Murphy needed me to tell you and your people that if he sees you cross into his territory again, he's going to put Miss Embros's head on his—" He stops, his brows scrunching.

My pulse escalates, the blood rushing through my head so fast, I'm almost dizzy. I don't want him to finish his sentence, but I also need him to. I have to hear the threat doled out in its entirety to determine who the threat is coming from—Phineas or Ezekiel.

Trigger speaks up. "Geo, it's fine. Fall back and remain on standby."

The kid looks around and I realize now why he stopped. The other guards must have gotten the alert too and are now at the gate. He holds up his hands to the men off screen to show he's unarmed. "I-I-I don't want no trouble. Just had to tell the lady something. I'm leaving."

"Wait!" The words rush out before he has a chance to run off. "Is that all?"

His eyes flit from the camera to the guards then back again before he shakes his head.

"What else?" I prompt, ignoring the bite of my nails cutting into my palm.

"Mr. Murphy says when his son's finished with her, she'll go to the highest bidder."

As though he knew his words would be his execution, he takes off down the road that will eventually lead him to the main street.

Hot bile surges into my throat. I don't have a weak stomach

by any means, but knowing the threats are no longer empty and directed at the woman who saved hundreds from the same fate makes me nauseous.

I latch a hand onto the banister, sliding my phone back into my pocket. "No one tell Maddy till she comes back."

The boys nod in agreement, but their anger has grown exponentially in a matter of minutes. They both have balled fists at their sides, grimaces pulling their lips into tight lines. Trick's leg is shaking impatiently while Trigger is working his jaw back and forth.

"Since when do we let filth threaten us?" Trick finally asks.

"Since they have *her*," Trigger answers. "We just have to wait."

"For what?"

"The girl," I say for Trigger. "I still believe Ezekiel is on our side."

"He's Phineas' son, babe." Trick's brows curve upward. He doesn't want to tell me I'm out of my mind for believing that, but he doesn't have the keen sense I do. He didn't see what I saw. Not to mention, Ezekiel let his sister walk right into the lion's den. He wouldn't have done that if he thought we'd hurt her.

I need to read the letter to be sure, even if only to validate my suspicion.

"He could be a child of circumstance. Perhaps he hates Phineas as much as anyone with a brain." I pat a hand on his shoulder before standing on my tippy-toes to press a kiss on his temple.

He leans down, meeting me halfway. I see the doubt glimmering in his eyes, but he trusts me. "Okay. I'll wait till Maddy gets home and we'll talk and work out a plan."

Trigger nods. "I think we should move soon though. If we

don't hear from Ezekiel's sister in a few days, we go. She could be telling the truth, but she could also be stalling us."

We all agree, and I excuse myself as we wait for Maddy. My feet tremble as I try to take the steps gracefully, an attempt not to display the distress working through my core. When I reach my bedroom, I slip the letter from its hiding place and turn it over, running my thumb over where he wrote her name.

My fingers trace over the edge of the envelope, the foreign war raging in my mind if I should peer into a letter not meant for me and into the working of what was blooming between them.

It was clear Onyx and Ezekiel were creating something with each other. Bridging a connection between two very broken souls. They weren't set out to heal one another, or to fill the other with purpose. It was deeper.

They were the other's light. A beacon on the shore so that no matter what they faced out at sea, they would always find the way home. And in each other, they were finding peace.

I saw it every time they were in the same room together. It was in the way Onyx's shoulders relaxed and her lips curled more often. In the subtle ways Ezekiel lost the edge from the pain he wears so palpably on his skin. Pain so blatant, it was suffocating.

It's a necessity in the world in which we live, being made men and women. Having an anchor to hold us steady even when we'll be lost to the waves. A buoy to latch on to when we're sure we'll drown.

That's what they were finding in each other even if they didn't recognize it quite yet. And I'm never wrong—about anything—and I feel it in the depths of my core that this letter proves it.

I rip the delicate envelope open and take out the two pieces of paper. With one last look over my shoulder, I read.

Is it too cliché for me to start this letter with "if you're reading this, I'm dead"? I assume so, but in reality it's true, and if I'm being completely honest with myself, I'm writing this knowing it will be read after my death. It's been a known factor since I was given this job and solidified the moment my mouth touched yours.

I didn't expect to care. I didn't expect to find myself feeling more at home here than I have anywhere else my entire life. And I sure as hell didn't expect you.

Somehow, Onyx, you have ingrained yourself in me these past couple of months. You made me reconsider things I deemed as fact. A deep hatred I can never even begin to encompass has been injected into me since I was old enough to formulate a thought. I had these preconceived notions of what the Mafia is and does, especially to members, children included. But you, Onyx, you changed things.

My thinking, my reservations, my assumptions, my doubts. You exposed me to a piece of advice I'd long forgotten.

See, there was a man I met years ago, when I was barely hanging on and everything was getting to be more than I could mentally handle. I'll never forget the way he looked at my sister as she let her stolen Petco fish out to sea. It was a look I'd never seen before. One of compassion and empathy. Something I didn't think a made man had the ability to even do.

He'd said, "When the weight of the world calls for your humanity, it's the ones we love that keep it bound to us."

I was a kid then, barely a teen. But I had already lived through five lifetimes and my time to leave this earth felt long overdue. So, if I'm being transparent, hearing him say it in that particular time in my life really pissed me off. It was yet another person drilling into me that I needed to suck it up and continue to suffer, no matter how great, for the people around me.

I didn't understand the gravity of what he said. Not until you.

I can sit here and explain to you how I never wanted this life, and how I only did this because my family's lives were at stake, but I don't think any apology or explanation would be enough. They wouldn't even begin to scratch the surface of what I owe you. So instead, this letter is meant for you to know that, without a shadow of a doubt, what we had was real.

Those feelings of fear, anxiousness, worry, and trepidation, I felt them too. They are what I imagine the beginning of something unforgettable feels like. The emotions one goes through before they fall deep into the abyss of another person without a care in the world of how they'll get out because they never want to.

What was between us was what those standing on the edge feel right before they let go and give in.

I hope you get to feel this again one day. And I hope you allow yourself to fall.

Perhaps in the next life.

-Kane.

I read it one more time before folding it up and sliding it back inside. Three days, Ezekiel. I hope that's enough. Because if we reach her before then, no amount of my objections will stop my family from killing you.

CHAPTER SIXTEEN

Inside the Murphy mansion, guards loiter at every corner. Each one turns as I enter, their prior conversation long forgotten as they lay their eyes on me. Onyx Embros. The one that should have been slaughtered with her parents, but instead haunts them, killing them off like the vermin they are.

How can they not stop to witness something so delicious? The ghost is caught, shackled in cuffs, barefoot, and wearing the same bloody clothes from the attack on the Embros estate, displaying the evidence of their victory.

They are all soaking in the glory.

I want to feel some way about it, whether it's disgust, rage, defeat. But I don't. My mind is drowning in doubt and confusion, unable to latch on to anything except the burn of Kane's fingertips on my flesh.

Since the realization of who he is, everything has been easy. Straightforward. Kane is the son of Phineas. Given the job of infiltrating my home, my family, and me.

I need Kane to be the enemy. *My* enemy. Because without certainty, there is chaos. It's fraying my edges and breaking the foundation on which I've stood my entire life.

What is reality?

What's real?

Who's to say when the lines are blurred and the circumstances are too strong to ignore? He didn't betray me in the way I thought, and now, I can barely grasp onto the already waning anger.

Dozens of eyes trail Kane and me until we reach the stairs. Phineas' barked order can be heard as we ascend. "Three outside of the door at all times, two at the stairs."

Beside me, Kane scoffs, something light playing in his eyes I can't make out. Then again, I can't understand half the things he's doing anymore. Who he is now, completely eludes me.

I'm quiet as we climb, turning at each small landing. After the third floor, the steps become industrial, nothing more than concrete and black iron rails. We come to a stop on the final floor, five stories up, and turn down the long hall. Kane passes two doors on the right before opening the lone one on the left.

Inside, the room is the size of a small studio apartment. Wide floor-to-ceiling windows line the far wall. A large bed covered in white bedding sits on one side, accompanied by a long dresser, riddled with personal belongings and a small library in the corner. Two doors rest on either side of the bed that I assume lead to a closet and bathroom. On the opposite side of his room is a small round table, counter space, and a slender fridge.

Something tugs in my chest as I walk inside. "Much better setup here than at the estate."

He doesn't respond and continues to stand in the doorway, watching as I lower myself on a chair at the table. He's silent for a moment, almost as if he's waiting for something, and just before I comment on it, guards appear in the hall.

He turns and speaks to them too quietly for me to hear.

When he's done, they disappear and he finally enters, closing and locking the door behind him.

Now it's my turn to stare as he strides to his dresser and begins taking off his cuff links and watch. "Can I ask you something?"

I hold up my cuffed wrists. "If you unlock them."

He smirks, undoing the buttons on his dress shirt. "Not just yet."

"Then I probably won't answer."

Kane peels the shirt from his body annoyingly slow, exposing his taut muscles and inked skin. It's only now that I realize I've never really looked at the images.

A large tree stretches from his ribs to his collarbone and across the expanse of his chest. The branches are long and twisty, some bare, some sparse, and others abundant with leaves. The bark on the tree has intricate detail, the layers peeling away in some places to show both decay and strength. A script flows up one side.

Believe the impossible is possible or perish in your doubt.

My eyes flick to his, the air thinner than it was moments ago.

He tilts his head, stepping around his bed and moving toward me. "Would you like to take a shower?"

Though I'd like nothing more than to shower, I long to do something I've rejected since the beginning. "Perhaps we should talk."

His brows lift. "About?"

"Your plan."

This makes him smirk. "And what plan do you think I have?"

I shake my head. "Don't insult me, Kane."

He shrugs. "That's not my intention."

"And what is your intention?" My voice is louder now, frustration squeezing me around my center. Even fixing my lips to ask is hard enough, beating around the bush makes it near infuriating.

His eyes flicker down before they find mine again. "To save you."

My face snaps away from him as I stand, my gaze settling on the guards outside the window, patrolling the grounds. From this high up, they aren't much bigger than roaches, but like the pest, there is an abundance. I wonder vaguely if Phineas had the ground security increased with the anticipation of my family making a move.

But honestly, none of it matters. Whether they come or not, I will find a way to destroy this pathetic place. "I don't need to be saved."

"So you've said."

I grind my teeth. "And yet, I don't think you quite understand."

"I understand fine." He shifts on his heels, starting for one of the doors without another word.

This only infuriates me more, and I propel my feet forward, following behind him into what turns out to be the bathroom. "Don't walk away from me."

He guffaws. "How the tables have turned."

I ignore his reference as my eyes narrow. "This is not a game, Kane. When all is said and done, we will be nothing more than common enemies, which will only end with one of us dying."

After turning on the water, he straightens, hooking his fingers into the waistband of my slacks and yanking me flush against him. My hands inadvertently brush against the hardness in his pants. I bite on the inside of my cheek, hoping the pain will override the sudden clench in my core. Annoyance flutters through me as well, the idea that even through all this, my body still responds so easily to him.

His eyes flicker over my face. "If I'm being honest with you, I never planned on living to see the outside of your estate."

My brows dip. "You thought I'd find you out?"

Kane shakes his head. "I was planning on telling you the night everything happened."

He was going to tell me? A knot forms in my throat.

"I would have killed you," my voice is barely above a whisper, realization settling over me. We're doomed regardless, whether it was then, now, or in three years when he's taken over for Phineas and decides he wants to finish his father's crusade.

"Yeah, I know. But I had hope."

"Then you were foolish." Agitation works its way into my bloodstream, joining the plethora of other emotions already wreaking havoc on my system.

"Perhaps I still am." Kane's eyes search mine, the crease between his brows growing deeper the longer he does. "It's time to shower."

He withdraws himself from my space and leans against the sink, taking his shoes off.

"I'm not taking a shower with you."

He doesn't look up as he peels off his socks. "But you are."

"Do not tempt me with violence, Kane."

Scoffing, he stands, yanking down his pants and briefs in one swoop. I ignore the slap of his erection against his thigh. "We've done that before. I do believe I won."

"Because I made the mistake of wanting you then," I hiss, twisting to leave. "I *let* you take me."

"Come now, Boss. Do I need to put my fingers in that delicious cunt of yours to prove how much you *still* want me?" He jerks on the back of my pants, forcing me to twirl around.

Frustration wins, though I'm unwilling to admit it's because he's right, and instead, I blame everything else on the day as I lift a balled fist. I attempt to swing at him, but he catches it in one hand and draws me close with the other.

"I just want to fucking bathe you. Why must you make it so difficult?"

I rear my head back to slam it into his, but he moves quicker, taking the hand that was holding my pants and threading it into my hair, yanking it back.

"Why are you fighting me?"

"Because I have to." I spit the words before I have a chance to stop them. My breathing quickens, the steam from the shower making the air thinner.

"Because you'll feel weak if you allow me to take care of you?"

I shake my head and his hands fall away. "My strength is not determined by you bathing me."

"What then?"

"It doesn't matter." I try to backtrack, not wanting to disclose anything more than I already have. Too much has happened, and every time he opens his mouth, bits of my resolve chip away. In hopes of sweeping it away, I unhook my own slacks and let them fall and pool around my feet.

Kane sighs. "You'd rather take a shower with me, then tell me what's in here." He points at my chest and I wince. "You think that caring about someone makes you weak."

"What would give you the impression I care about you?" I try to keep an edge to my words but they don't sound nearly as biting as I'd like.

"You love lying to me, *mo bhanríon.*"

"I am not your queen, Kane."

One corner of his lips curls. It's slow and reflective. "My

captive, my whore, my queen. You're all these things. But most importantly, you are *mine.*"

With that, he rips the thin panties from my hips and unthreads my corset, pushing it from my frame and onto the floor with the rest of my clothes. "I'm merely waiting for you to realize it."

He opens the glass door and holds out a hand, letting me step into the shower. When he follows behind, he immediately dives under the heavy stream, pulling me back against his chest. He turns us around, tugging the ends of my hair until I take heed and let my head fall back.

I don't bother holding in the moan as the hot water delves into my tangled roots, and pelts into the tight muscles of my back. Instead, for just a moment, I allow myself to relax. Even if it's for the duration of this shower only, I decide to let go and pretend that in this short time, the world isn't crumbling around me. That I'm not in cuffs, in the belly of the beast, surrounded by the enemy.

That Kane and I would manage to survive past the end of this war.

"Weakness is not a reason. It's an excuse."

Kane is not my weakness, but the feelings of vulnerability he stirs are frightening. They force me to acknowledge that at one point, I was at the mercy of others. And I lost them.

This is different. I know in the end I will lose him. But instead of wanting to stop whatever this is, I want to *drown* in it.

Strong hands surge into my hair, and his fingers begin to massage my scalp. A familiar scent fills the air, and I will my eyes to stay closed, refusing to acknowledge the visceral ache under my rib cage at the fact that he has my brand of shampoo in his shower.

He takes his time, washing my hair twice before applying a

liberal amount of conditioner. He then slowly draws me out of the water, letting it soak into my ends as he grabs a black loofah.

I watch in silence as he works the soap into a mountain of bubbles. So far, I've been merely observing, but when he reaches for my neck, my entire body tightens. My stomach clenches as he presses against me to maneuver around to wash my shoulders.

My heart thrums in my chest, matching the frantic beat of his. He's so calm on the outside, but inside, I think he's just as lost as I am in the waves of what we've created.

When he moves back, all pretense of him simply bathing me disintegrates in the flame of his eyes. They are hooded, needy, and trailing fire down my skin as they drop lower.

My nerves tingle as his gaze returns to mine while simultaneously swiping the loofah over my breasts. His free hand moves up, twisting the metal barbells and tugging them back and forth through my pebbed nipples. I let my head loll to the side, the sensation too intoxicating to ignore.

Kane's lips part as he glides the loofah down farther, stopping at my cuffs.

"Up." His command is a husky bark.

I want to stay no. To fight for control like we've always done. But then the invasive thought of surrender suffocates me. The idea of what it would feel like to allow him to *truly* take everything.

Too bad he hasn't earned it.

"No," I say simply.

He smirks. "Are you sure?"

I raise a brow, a challenge creasing my eyes. "Finish cleaning me, Kane."

He tsks, clearly amused. Then, everything happens too quickly for me to stop. He pushes me to one side of the tall shower and jerks my arms above my head. He's too strong to fight against, but I try regardless, attempting to yank my arms down, but they don't budge.

A click echoes above me, and I realize he's latched me to something. I try to look up, but he grabs my jaw, forcing me to look at him. "Why must you make everything so difficult when it's all you want?"

I smirk. "And what is it you think I want?"

His free hand snakes between my clenched thighs and swipes through my slick cunt.

"Fuckkkk," he groans at the same moment I think it, burrowing his face in the crook of my neck. "You want *me*."

I attempt a laugh, but it comes out as a heady moan instead. I feel him smile against my neck before biting the flesh. The pain is temporary, melting into pleasure as he licks the spot.

"Tell me you don't." He strokes up the length of my pussy, stopping at my clit. He applies pressure as he circles it. "Come on, Boss. Lie to me."

My voice is a raspy mess, strained under the tight winding of my nerves. "I want you to bathe me."

"Liar," he hisses, making another pass. My body clenches, a heavy sigh falling from my lips, exposing my truth. He coasts his other hand up my stomach and tugs on a barbell. "Every time you lie to me, there will be some sort of punishment. Maybe then you'll be honest with me."

"Kane." It's a warning. But he doesn't heed it and instead passes over my nerves again. There's nothing but pure molten fire in his gaze as he watches the battle on my face.

"How about you tell me what you want, Onyx?"

My name on his lips is my undoing. There's something about the complete and total want dripping in the syllables that cuts through me. I arch my chest, pressing myself into him, and moaning when my leg meets his hard length.

"Hmmm." He pushes his dick closer, letting it dig into my thigh. His thumb moves faster, flicking over my clit so quickly a tight ball begins to form low in my core. "I see. Well, unfortunately, it's not something you're going to get."

My eyes snap to his, the haze of arousal mixing with frustration as I take in his dark gaze.

He shakes his head, the wet ends of his hair dripping water down the bridge of his nose and onto his lips. "No, the next time I fuck you, it's going to be after you beg for it."

One of his thick fingers dives into my pussy and my core clenches around the intrusion. "After your body is trembling and on the verge of utter fucking collapse from hysteria and want."

He adds a second finger before pumping in and out, and his thumb continues its assault on my throbbing clit. "When you think you can't go another second without my cock inside that tight little cunt."

The budding heat expands, and my nerves tingle as he works every single one in tandem. Before I can force the impending orgasm back, he licks a path up my neck and down my jaw until he reaches my lips. "That's when I'll fuck you, *mo bhanríon*."

Another pass and I combust, visions of me actually begging Kane so damn delicious I can think of nothing else. As though he can see the scene playing in my head, he doesn't stop fucking me with his fingers, drawing it out to the point my knees begin to quiver.

"That's my girl. Give me everything," he coaxes in my ear as he runs his nose along the column of my neck, causing me to shiver.

It isn't until my walls stop pulsing that he finally wanes, withdrawing his hand and hooking it around my waist to keep me steady. I hoped after the release, I'd feel better—have some type of relief—but it isn't the case. My core is still tight, my heart still pounding, and my body still leans into him.

I need to put distance between us. Between the fact that I'm a captive, being both held and protected by my captor. I need a minute to breathe without drinking him in. I just need... "Space."

Kane's eyes flicker between mine before he nods and unlatches my hands from what I realize now was a hook. I want to ask what it's for but remain quiet as he backs me into the water again.

He finishes washing us both, careful to make quick passes over my sensitive flesh and tight nipples. I bite into my lip as he takes a brush from his hanging shower basket and takes his time, brushing through my locks. When he's done, he lets the water run over my hair, rinsing the conditioner.

My mind runs a mile a minute as we exit the shower. I want to know what he's thinking. I want to sit down and rationalize everything that's happened thus far. I want to fucking understand without the preconceived notions, fears, and doubts clouding every thought that crosses my mind.

I want him to tell me *everything*.

But I'm not given the chance, because once we're back in his room, he unlocks my cuffs and hands me a pair of his pajamas. "There's too many guards positioned outside. Please don't chance it by trying to leave. Fruit, dry snacks, and plenty of drinks are in the eating area. You're welcome to all of it."

He turns and dresses himself as I slide on the oversized sleepwear. I decide on wearing only the shirt since it reaches to right above my knees and sit on the edge of the bed as he cleans up the discarded clothes.

When he's done, he nears me, stopping a foot away. He examines my knotted fingers, but instead of saying anything, he only sighs and bends to kiss my temple. My chest tightens as I let my eyes flutter closed for one second.

"I'll give you your space and only return when I have a solid plan. You'll be safe in here till then. Please trust that."

My lips part to object but then I snap them back shut. This is what I asked for. It's what I want. Yet the empty churn in my gut says something else entirely.

Still, I manage a curt nod.

He purses his lips, the disappointment evident in the green swirls of his irises. But he doesn't argue and walks to the door.

With every step he takes, an odd sensation swells in my chest—something I can't place until I feel a warm tear tumble down my cheek. That's when I realize it's a deep-seated sadness, an understanding that what he's doing right now will be a blessing to see when this is over.

Because I think we both know, in reality, one of us won't live to see the day after this all ends.

CHAPTER SEVENTEEN

It's almost midnight.

I should've heard from Zek already. When we spoke yesterday, he told me he was coming up with a plan. He swears he has one, even though he won't utter a word of it to me, and said I just need to trust him.

Asking me to trust him so blindly under my current conditions is a lot. But I'm going to try—for now, at least—because I know he has my well-being at heart. Plus, I understand not wanting someone like me to know the details. I'm not what you'd consider well-equipped to handle any type of torture, so if it came down to it, I'd probably sing like a songbird. I mean, maybe. There's also a very high chance I'll run like hell before being caught.

That's how I handle most of the situations I get myself in when pulling my usual stunts, and it's how I ended up back home with Lawrence.

Zek told me to find a guard to flirt with, and I found one. Then he made a deal with Sam, telling him he'd give up the access codes once I was home safe. Like my brother figured, Sam wasn't buying it, not without some insurance, at least. He assigned a guard to babysit me in case my brother was bullshitting. And of course the one who got volunteered for house arrest duty, was Lawrence.

The original plan was for me to come home, knock his ass out with the bat my brother kept in his room, grab Mom, and run. I was nervous as hell, but since Lawrence has a little thing for me, it was supposed to make him put his guard down. But my worries didn't matter in the end because when we arrived, Mom wasn't there. Not only that, but somehow Phineas got the codes and ended up with Onyx and Zek anyway.

Now, I'm a sitting duck, waiting for either the Maddy woman to show up or for the Murphys to order Lawrence to kill me.

My eyes flit to the clock on my phone that Sam disabled. Lawrence was called away a couple hours ago, and since then, I've been pacing, doing dishes, reorganizing the bathroom, and sweeping the front porch as I wait. For what? I'm not completely sure, but the silence is becoming deafening and waiting in limbo is becoming torture.

Frustration has me slamming the glass plates into the cabinets a little harder than necessary.

Does Zek not care that the freaking Embros family is going to come for me if they haven't heard anything? Is he not worried that it's been a week and Mom is still freaking nowhere? Can't say I'm anything other than mad, because the one freaking time I need the woman to come through, she does what she excels at, and disappears. If I knew Zek wouldn't be completely crushed, I think I would have left a long time ago.

Maybe.

I latch on to the sink, doing the best I can to steady my breathing, but it's no use. The air grows thinner the harder I suck in, and the only noise I can hear is the rush of blood through my ears and the pace of my throbbing heart.

Clutching at my chest, I stumble to the living room, dropping onto the worn couch.

Breathe.

I think of the room with the cot, Phineas sneering as he told me what his army would do to me.

Breathe.

I envision what my brother must have gone through every time he went to see that disgusting man.

"Breathe."

I think of my—

My face snaps up at the voice that isn't mine, my eyes wide while my lungs stop working completely.

Maddy leans against the TV, the same blade from the hospital twirling in her hand. Her wild red curls drape over her face, a heavy contrast against her pale skin and black clothes. Her legs are crossed over one another and it's then I see her muddied boots, stained with blood, telling me a story I'm definitely not ready to read.

"Y-you said I had th-three—"

"And I could have sworn you said you had a guard watching you. I've been here over an hour and haven't seen a single soul." She points the tip of the blade at me. "You lied to me, little mouse."

I shake my head profusely, holding a hand to my chest as if it will somehow keep in both my vomit and raging heart. "I didn't. I swear. He left a couple of hours ago. He didn't tell-l-l —" A fit of hiccups erupts from my throat, burning my esophagus as they stream out one after the other. The pain sears through me, and I feel my eyes well with tears, I somehow push back.

"Don't die before I can kill you, brat." I barely make out her words before a cup of water is shoved to my mouth.

I do my best to drink it, fighting through the strong contractions in my throat. I down the entire glass before they finally subside, and my eyes return to her. She's closer now, sitting with her legs crossed, perching on the edge of my coffee table.

"Let's try this again without you choking to death, shall we? How about we begin with simple yes or no questions?"

I swallow again, wincing when the little saliva pushes down. "Yes."

"Good girl," she coos, brushing my hair behind my ear. My lashes flutter, my growing fear squeezing my insides. "Do you know where your guard is?"

I shake my head.

Maddy smirks, wiping either side of her blade against her jeans. "Use your words, little mouse. Have you talked to Z today?"

"No."

"Yesterday?"

"Yes."

She straightens. "Does he have a plan?"

I start to shrug but find my voice. "He does, but he won't tell me."

"Why?"

"I think..." I trail off, the instant familiar burn of tears radiating across my eyes. "He may worry I'll let it slip or something."

Maddy's head tilts, her eyes narrowing as she examines my face. "Why would you let something slip? And to whom?"

This time I lift a shoulder.

"Have you considered that maybe he *doesn't* have a plan and doesn't want you freaking out? You seem the type to go manic."

I soak in her words, ignoring the warm tears falling over the rim. Him not having a plan *would* make me worry, considering there's a ticking time bomb over my head with the woman who's sitting across from me, still gripping a knife.

"Maybe. Or maybe he doesn't think he can trust me. I still haven't been able to do the one thing he asked and find our mom."

Snapping my mouth shut, I bite back a groan. But Maddy laughs, high and wild. "I see what you mean about letting things slip. And your mother? I'm confused. She's at Embros Hearts."

My heart stutters. "I don't understand."

She sighs, her brows curving inward as she explains it as if I'm supposed to already know. "Onyx had me come get her after we showed Z what Hearts was. Your mom agreed immediately, packed a few items and went with me the same night. I guess I didn't get a chance to tell Z because—"

Maddy stops midsentence, leaning back, and biting her lip briefly before her eyes flash to the front window. "Where's a good place to hide?"

"What?" I straighten, panic gripping my throat as I follow her gaze to the flash of headlights pulling up in front of our house.

Shooting to my feet, I use my shirt to clean my face. I don't get enough time to process anything she just said, nor the fact that Phineas and Zek are both walking up the unkept broken sidewalk to the door, before a blur of red hair vanishes down the hall.

"Who were you talking to?"

I swirl around on my heels to see Lawrence closing the back door. He's not in the jeans he left in but a three-piece suit with a heavy-looking gun over his shoulder. Honestly, I could find out aliens are real and it still wouldn't both surprise and confuse me like today has.

I shake my head. "No one."

His dark brows furrow as he brushes by me and glances down the hall. *Shit.*

"I-I-why are they here?" I motion to the door, my voice much higher than it needs to be.

Whatever suspicion he had vanishes and he squares his shoulder, sweeping lint off his lapel. "Some shit went down. The goons from Embros blew up the place where they were keeping Onyx."

Before I can ask what the hell he's talking about, Zek opens the front door, his eyes immediately flashing from me to Lawrence and back again. His gaze drops over the length of my body three times before he's satisfied enough to enter and lean against the wall, making way for Phineas.

Like before, Phineas' outward appearance doesn't seem threatening whatsoever, but I know better now. He's the devil reincarnated in a car salesman's skin. His eyes survey the living room, a look of disgust curling his lips.

My fists ball at my sides, the sudden urge to be a smart-ass despite the clear danger settling over me. How dare he look at the house he forced my brother to grow up in and contort his face to look repulsed?

"How did they know where we were keeping Onyx?" Phineas asks.

I do exactly what Zek told me to do if I was ever asked and look at Lawrence as if I know the question isn't for me. This makes his arrogant face fall for a half a second.

"He's talking to you." Lawrence points.

My brows snap together and I glance at a waiting Phineas. It's a face I perfected long ago whenever the police came around and wanted to know my whereabouts during the last grocery store robbery of dog food. "I'm sorry, am I supposed to know?"

Phineas shrugs and motions to his guard noncommittally.

"Lawrence here tells me you frequently display suspicious behavior."

I don't look back at Lawrence or ask for examples of said behavior—that's what the guilty do. Instead, I turn the conversation.

"How much can he really notice when he leaves me for hours on end?"

Lawrence immediately takes a step toward me, Zek pushes off the wall, and Phineas chuckles.

"Is that so?"

"No, sir. I would never leave her. I've been here all week. This slut is just trying to save her ass."

So much for being a decent guy. "You literally just came back after being gone for two hours. I'm sure his tracks are still fresh." I say the words before I consider how *many* tracks they'll find if they actually look. I'm not sure how Maddy got in, and one quick look around will prove I don't even own a pair of boots.

Luckily, I don't have to worry, because Lawrence fumbles over himself. "No. I was taking a walk. I patrolled the perimeter like you asked, Boss. This fucking bitch is trying to push it off on me."

The burn is instant, the tight grasp of Lawrence's hand in my hair, yanking it from the scalp. I hiss out in pain, but the click and sudden warmth of my brother encompassing me lessens the exploding fear swelling in my sternum.

Lawrence's hand disappears and I move behind Zek, using his back as a shield. My breath is coming out in pants and it's then I realize I've put myself right in front of Phineas.

"Hello, little one. Nice to see you again."

His words drip with a poison so visceral I feel it physically trickle down my skin and seep into my bloodstream. Nausea rolls in my stomach.

"Phineas, get your kid. I didn't fucking do anything. That fucking stupid ass whore—"

The sound of Lawrence's phone ringing shut him up. His phone never rings. It's a rule of some kind that they only communicate over text.

Phineas cocks his head, his eyes flashing to Lawrence above my head. My brother shifts out of the way, but he keeps his gun pointed at him while pressing me against his back. He's shifted to where I'm halfway in the hallway and able to notice the red hair in my periphery.

My heart thrums, my pulse vibrating as sweat breaks across my brow. I let my gaze flicker to her in time to see her wink, a phone pressed to her ear before vanishing back into the room at the end—my mother's.

"Answer the phone, Lawrence." It's an order from Zek. I've never heard his voice so deep, so intimidating. He's never even raised his voice at me after all the trouble I've gotten us in.

"*Now.*" His deep rumble vibrates his back and I jolt.

"He-llo?" I can't see him, but fear is clear.

"Hey, Luy-Luy. I enjoyed dinner, but you promised to call when you got home to tell me where they moved my boss. I kept my word when I was giving you the best head of your life, so—"

"May I ask who's calling?" Phineas asks, taking a few steps forward, and I can't help but peek around Zek's shoulder.

Lawrence is trembling, his head whipping back and forth. "No sir, I don't know who—"

"Shut up," Zek snaps. God, if he would have spoken to me with this much bass in his voice, I probably would have never done another thing wrong in my life.

"Umm. This is a little awkward. Name's Maddy. My friends call me Mad." She giggles. "I was calling for Lawrence. Is he busy or something?"

Phineas face morphs into something dark and furious. "Mad Maddy, is it?"

"Yep." She pops the P. "That's me."

"And Lawrence was going to tell you where Onyx Embros is?"

"Well, yeah. Like he did the first time."

Phineas snatches the phone and clicks the end button. Lawrence flinches and begins babbling, snot and tears streaming from his face. "Boss, I swear, I swear I didn't. I've never talked to—"

A hard slap comes down across Lawrence's face, blood splattering on our old couch. Phineas straightens before yanking the gun from Lawrence's shoulder and shoving it at Zek. "Let's take him back with us. Figure out what else he's been keeping from us."

My brother nods before stepping forward and leaving me to latch on to the wall, my nails digging into the hard texture. He ignores Lawrence's raised hands and hits him across the face with the butt of his gun. Lawrence falls face first.

"It was lovely seeing you again, Fiona." Phineas nods his head toward me with a smirk curling one side of his lips.

Zek hoists an unconscious Lawrence over his shoulder and walks past me. "I'll call you in a few."

His voice is barely a whisper but I nod, watching as they leave me and load up back in the car. It isn't until their car has long disappeared, and I've scrubbed the fabric clean of Lawrence blood, that my phone finally rings.

EZEKIEL

AGE 17

CHAPTER EIGHTEEN

I imagined that my sister being gone for a week would be a blessing. I figured I'd be able to pick up a couple extra shifts and maybe get a few days off from having to hide her recent transgressions. Maybe that's too strong of a word for an eleven-year-old.

She's more like a Robin Hood.

For animals.

I miss her. I hope she's enjoying art camp. Talented little shit won first place in her elementary art exhibition with an abstract heart she made. It was complete with ventricles, tissue, and anatomically correct veins in a crazy mix of colors. It was cool, and I would have been pissed if she *hadn't* won. But when I found out she'd be gone for an entire week, I knew not being able to see her after a night with Phineas would suck.

What an understatement.

Somehow, he found out she'd be gone for six days, and let me know the moment I walked through the door that I'd be calling this place home the entire time.

Phineas has always been a total dick—expected, and by now, a little underwhelming even—but lately something's been up his ass, making him worse. More dangerous.

My first day, he tied my ass up and taught me about isolation. It wasn't too bad considering up until now, it'd only lasted ten hours before I was sent back home. And while I'm certain it helped me build some type of endurance, nothing could have prepared me for *two and a half* fucking days.

No food, no water, no visits from anyone.

I'm sure at some point I began to go crazy, seeing and hearing things that were impossible. The dream—or perhaps hallucination—which stands out the most is the chessboard. It was imprinted on the floor, and was never ending, extending as far as I could possibly see. There were trees and buildings sprouting out of the board making the black and white blocks appear as though they were nothing more than grass. Chess pieces at least seven feet tall stood all across, engaging in conversations. They paid me little mind until Phineas approached, wearing an all-white suit.

"Come here, boy." He grabbed me by my collar, drawing me close. All the white pieces around him turned, their faces all pointed at us. "It's time for you to do my bidding."

I opened my mouth to speak but nothing came out, and when I tried to reach up, I realized I had no hands. That's when I looked down.

My body was nothing more than a porcelain-white pawn piece. My heart didn't hammer, my mind didn't race. Nothing happened because I was nothing. Nothing more than the pawn he always saw me as.

He shifted my body and rotated me around before pointing off in the distance toward a blanket of trees. They went high into the sky, the tops invisible to see, while the trunks were so thick they nearly touched one another. No light could penetrate it, casting the forest in dark, ominous shadows.

"I need you to go there, boy. You see, over there, to the right?"

I followed his finger to the edge of the woods, just before the only visible entrance, and saw her. A girl, not much older than I am, with long black hair stood there. Her light-blue dress stood out against her beautiful tan, amber skin. From my angle I wasn't able to see her face but I knew, and still know, how beautiful it was. There was an aura about her, and I wanted to see her.

"Yes, you see her. Now, I need you to capture her for me. Once you do that, I can set a match to her forest."

Shock, anger, sadness. Those are all the things I wanted to feel but couldn't. Nothing was happening inside me but understanding. Understanding that Phineas's long sought-out goal to make me feel empty and without emotions was beginning to pay off.

Slowly my humanity was being chipped away and I was beginning to realize no matter what, I'd capture the girl.

All I could hope was maybe, somewhere deep inside, I was doing it so that she wouldn't burn as well.

My dream ended with this thought before I woke up on a cot with fluids in my arm, next to twenty other men.

I'm on day five now, sitting in a long room on the fifth floor with the same guys, give or take. A few left and never came back, being replaced with new faces. The majority of them are teenagers like me, while others are a few years older.

My father has been known to grab the young for their easily corruptible minds, or those in debt.

They're all recruits, like what I'm pretending to be, and have to be properly trained. Before we start speaking to one another, I can already tell by the bruises and busted lips, most of them will run drugs or weapons, but I can see a few of them will be in charge of the women.

They have a look in their eyes so similar to the one I did when my father had me "quality test" the first shipment of women. The men with a conscience feel guilt, disgust with themselves, and sorrow.

But unlike me, they don't bear the marks of restraints. Which means they did it without being held down. Without being force-fed drugs to keep their dicks going like a fucking battery rabbit.

If I ever get the freedom I seek, all of the men who test, or run the women, will die. Every last one.

"What's your name?" A boy with wild red curls nudges me on the leg.

He's been here a day, and while he's covered in the same bruises as the others, he has a sort of happiness about him that doesn't fit the narrative. Almost as if he enjoys whatever he goes through.

"Zek."

He grins and holds out a hand. He's missing a top incisor on his left side and his top tooth is cracked. "Name's Oliver. Friends call me Olly."

I hesitate for a moment before finally shaking his hand. "And why are you smiling?"

Oliver shrugs, dropping his arm and crossing his legs. "Hmm, people say I'm a wee bit mad."

"So you're smiling because you're crazy?"

He laughs. It's high and manic, causing everyone else's head to turn toward him. He either doesn't notice or doesn't care. "My reality is merely different from yours, but truthfully, I'm certain I was born with my sensors in the wrong spot. Pain is pleasure, annoyances are hilarious, and frustration is a delightful puzzle."

My brows rise. "Is that so?"

Oliver nods, but something crosses his bright-brown eyes I can't make out.

For the two days with them, I've stayed quiet. Observant. Watching and listening to everyone and separating the weak from the strong, the evil from the stupid. It's probably what Phineas intended, wanting me to go through the same treatment as the others, learn about his guards, why he chooses them, and so on. Though until now, I haven't talked to any of them.

It's mainly because I'm tired, hungry, and angry as hell, but Oliver has piqued my curiosity. There's something about him he's doing a good job of hiding.

I lift my knees and lean forward, resting my arms on them. "So is that why you came to work for the Murphy family? Because of your sensors?"

One side of his mouth hitches up. "Perhaps."

I nod.

After a beat of silence, he clears his throat. "And you?"

"Paying my debt to the universe."

"Ah, so not by choice then?"

I suck in a deep breath and immediately regret it. Even with the attached bathroom the men's two-week stay is only granted with one fresh set of clothes a week, leaving them rancid on the days in between.

"No, Oliver. I would say by fate."

A frown shifts his face into the grumpy cat meme. "That's even worse. There is no escaping fate, lad."

This gets a grunted laugh out of me. "Yeah, tell me about it."

He shifts in his spot before leaning forward and resting one hand on his knee. One of his long, gaunt fingers taps against the scruff of his chin. He does this for an awkward amount of time until his fiery gaze flashes back to me. "You know, something I learned a long time ago from my kid sister? She said even if the road has already been paved, and your future is set. You can always venture off the path and have fun before meeting your end."

A sudden burn blooms at the back of my throat. Being told from the age of six that I'm nothing more than a tool for my father took the joy out of my childhood. It stripped the tender moments into strained memories, tainting them with the reality that I'm on borrowed time until beckoned by my owner. By the one who is both the creator of my misery and the end to it all.

What would it even mean to wander off the path he set for me? To allow myself to truly enjoy my sister's laughs? Soak in the sun as I walk to the library? Allow myself the luxury of not staring at the clock and wonder when my time will finally come?

Of not *wishing* my time would come?

The duration of my stay is spent watching the guards. Against my better judgment, I talk to a few, and get to know their stories. Why they're here and how most wish they didn't have to be. None of them say this outright of course, but it's the desperation painting their every word and the defeat weighing heavy on their shoulders that give them away.

Small relationships are built among myself and the few, and soon there is an understanding that develops between us. A pact of sorts to have people we can trust and confide in. With too much idle time to my thoughts, they keep drifting back to a topic I've long buried, too afraid it might be true. Somehow, though, I muster up the courage to ask if any of them have ever seen a young girl who may look like Phineas' daughter.

When each of them tell me no, it eases the tight knot I've had since Mom told me about Bunny still being alive, and suddenly my heart aches more for my mother. I hate that she has to make up a false narrative rather than accepting that sometimes, life just fucking sucks.

The rest of the week isn't as bad with the newfound friendships. While I'm sure it was never my father's intention, it does make me question what was.

I never do figure out the answer. But when I'm dropped off on the sidewalk in front of my house, I recall what Oliver said.

It's true, fate is impossible to escape, but it doesn't mean I can't do something to enjoy this fucked-up life sentence in the meantime.

All I can hope is that whatever fun I end up finding doesn't make me wish for the impossible.

CHAPTER NINETEEN

Three Weeks Ago

After allowing Kane the pleasure of winning at the blackjack table in my casino, we exit out of the back. It felt juvenile and strange with Kane whispering in my ear to sneak away from my guards, but I couldn't ignore the heavy thumping behind my rib cage urging me to give in to the moment.

A moment I never got in my youth.

Granted, the boys and I got into more shenanigans than I can possibly remember, but the thrill of sneaking away in the midst of a cold war with a lover is far more exhilarating.

The air is brisk, accompanied by a clear night sky and a full moon above. It lights up the alley in a beautiful hue reminding me of old black-and-white detective movies.

Leaning one shoulder onto the brick, my low eyes find Kane standing casually with his hands tucked in his pockets. He's good at pretending to be laid back even when every muscle in his body is tight with anxiety. I wonder if he realizes he's always on his toes, waiting for something to happen, or if it's a natural response to having things happen frequently.

He motions behind me, his gaze right below my knee. I know before he even asks what he's referring to. "What's with the cat?"

A familiar pang resonates across my chest, both the reminder and the significance of the small animal coming to the forefront.

Instead of lowering the guard I have to work harder to keep up when he's around, I feign ignorance. "What cat?"

He smirks, the damned dimple in his cheek dropping a heaviness in my stomach. "Ah, so it means something to you."

"What could an alley cat possibly mean to me?"

Kane sucks his teeth and shrugs. "I mean, the obvious similarities you both share."

"If you think a parentless cat means something to me because I lost mine, so help me, Kane, not even a thousand orgasms are worth letting you keep your tongue."

He laughs, deep and hearty. When he stops, he takes a step toward me. "Quite the pessimist. No, Boss, I'm referring to the distance."

My brows draw together as I let curiosity get the best of me and turn to see the brown stray. She's her normal distance away —close enough to see the green-and-gold glitter in her eyes, but far enough I wouldn't be able to take a step without her scurrying away.

I shift back to Kane. "She's curious, but cautious. Not a bad trait to have when you live on the streets."

"She knows she'd live a good life with you but she's too stubborn to allow herself to get too close."

"Also a smart thing to do if she wants to live."

"What is life, if lived alone?" he counters.

I chew on the inside of my lip, dread closing around my

throat. I already know the answer. Without my family, no amount of miracles could have saved me. I wanted revenge, even that of the reckless variety, and would've easily given my life to blow up the Murphy estate after my parents' death.

Kane eliminates the space between us, tugging my lip free and filling my lungs with his warm scent. It calms my racing pulse, relaxing my shoulders I wasn't aware were tight.

He tips my chin up, our mouths mere inches apart. "If you won't tell me what she means to you, will you tell me *about* her?"

The man has an uncomfortable way of drawing me out despite the alarms ringing in my head. But if I'm honest, the normally blaring sounds are mere faraway beeps when he's near, just like the screams.

Kane clears his throat, forcing my attention to his question still lingering between us.

I roll my eyes, but the urge to tell someone about the moment in my life when I let my guard down, only to be shown why I don't, hangs heavy in the air. I want him to understand that, despite whatever dangerous thing has blossomed between us, it only ends one way.

"Ever since I can remember, this alley has been accompanied by one particular cat. It was husky and had massive jowls only a true predator could have. He always stayed in the distance, never coming within five yards of the entrance. My father didn't let me go near him either, always saying if he was polite enough to warn us with his constant distance, we needed to respect it. Still, every time we went, I'd look for him, waving and leaving a treat I had convinced my father to let me buy anytime we'd go to a store."

"Such a softy." Kane whispers, his breath ghosting along my collarbone. His gaze is no longer on mine but instead following a path down my throat.

I force a steady breath and continue despite the desire to make a rebuttal to his comment. "A few years passed before one day, he was no longer standing at the corner alone but with a smaller cat. This one was thin and pure white despite living on the street. She looked much meaner than the male and for once, my desire to approach him was forgotten."

Kane scoffs, his face now in my neck. He's purposely keeping his body from touching mine while my focus is lost between storytelling and pressing my back into the wall. He won't win this.

"Interesting thing about felines," he murmurs, "is their ability to look down on you, even when homeless and starving."

"Very true, but the same can be said about a man."

I can't see him, but I know he's smiling. "You must have the worst track record with men in the world."

"It seems."

"Even now?" His face moves back up to mine, his arms on either side of my head, effectively caging me in. But I don't feel as if I'm his captive. More like he's protecting me.

Even though he's my bodyguard, the notion vexes me, but also does something else I refuse to acknowledge.

I push the swelling emotion from my chest, forcing my eyes away from the deep greens of his, and swallow. "Fast forward a couple months and kittens were seen around."

A sigh whooshes out of me as I move to the next part. "Shortly after my parents passed, my uncle accompanied me to the casinos. It was my first time being here without my father and it didn't go over so well. I was still so angry. I hadn't properly channeled it into purpose yet. I ran out of the casino, in the middle of collection, onto this backstreet."

Kane's face shifts, the darkness in his eyes lighten to concern, the corners creasing as his brows furrow. I know he must be picturing me as the pitiful teenage girl who lost her parents, stumbling into an alley in tears.

The sad truth is, no matter how weak he's envisioning me then, it doesn't hold a candle to what I actually was.

My stomach twists at the memory of what I used to be. *Pathetic*.

"And what happened?" Kane prompts, his voice so incredibly gentle I find myself annoyed with his sympathy.

"One of the only kittens left, that brown one, was there that night. Alone, just under the streetlight over there." I motion with my chin to the tall pole on the right. "I collapsed against the wall, with so many emotions ripping through me, it was as if I was being ripped apart."

I clear the surging burn in my throat, tilting my face up to Kane. "She came to me. Crawled right into my lap. I was so shocked, the other things suddenly didn't matter. All I could focus on was her. How soft her fur was, how pretty her eyes were. But as soon as the door swung open, she bolted from my lap, using my body as her catapult."

I drop my suit jacket on the right side, revealing the faint silver scar up my shoulder. "My moment of weakness, and her moment of trust meant nothing when a possible threat appeared."

Genuinely hoping he understands me, I steel my voice, straightening my jacket, and willing the growing pain back into its rightful place. I'm not sure what I imagined it'd feel like to say this out loud but I didn't expect this.

He's too trusting of me, too sure that I won't put a bullet between his eyes if I need to. But, at the same time, I'm letting him make me weak. Showing him things no one else has dared to look at, and giving him access to parts of me no one's ever been allowed near.

We're doomed. Both of us. I should kill him now. Rid

myself of the impending trouble that he'll inevitably bring upon me.

But as if he can read the doubts streaming across my mind, his strong hand catches my jaw. "Get out of your head and stay with me. Here. Right now, in this moment."

The gold flecks in his eyes shimmer as he searches mine. It makes my stomach flutter with irritation and want. But I don't get the opportunity to say anything because he closes the small space to my nose and presses a tender kiss on the tip.

It steals the breath from my lungs. Something so soft and tender is a distant memory to me, and now, it invades my every sense.

I want to pull away, to slap him for making my heart thud so viciously, my chest ache so deeply. But every limb is too heavy to move. Too slow to react. It must only last for a half of a second, but it feels like eternity in his bubble before he finally pulls himself away.

"Thank you for sharing that with me." He turns from my body, allowing the cool breeze to sweep across my burning flesh. I shiver against the brick as I watch him gesture to the limo. "And thank you for tonight. It was a pleasure getting to see you, Boss."

See me. His choice of words is purposeful, and I hate what it means. Hate that I like it.

Hate that in the end, I found what my parents always wanted me to have but won't be able to keep.

Present

When I peel my eyes open, it isn't the lack of Kane's body

next to mine, nor the moon spilling through the curtains and illuminating the dark grain in the hardwood floor, I find interesting. It's the steady and soft hum paired with a constant vibration coming from a ball of brown fur. It's curled into a tight ball, pressed into my thigh, and even through the thick duvet, my skin is warm from its body heat.

My first instinct is to shove the intruder onto the floor and prepare for an attack but then the reality of what it is—or I should say, *who* it is—flushes over me like cold water.

He brought me the cat from the alley. The same one who left a scar on my damn shoulder. Part of me wonders if it's some sick joke, intended to display exactly how alone I really am now, but I know the truth. He wants me to feel. To embrace the pain and acknowledge the hurt.

I still don't understand why he's so hell bent on me succumbing to the flames of my demons. Why he wants so badly for me to be reborn from the ashes.

Perhaps he merely wants me weak so he can swoop in and save me from myself.

Or maybe he wants you to let go and move forward. Truly *move forward.*

The intrinsic thought settles in the air, making it thick to inhale. Thankfully, I'm not given any time to suffocate on its meaning because a faint knock at the door steals my attention.

It's too gentle to be Phineas or a guard, and knowing Kane, he'd let himself in. So I take my time, slipping from the bed in a way that doesn't disturb my guest who has probably never in her life had the luxury of a warm bed.

True to my assumption, she doesn't move, but her breathing slows. Part of me wonders if she is awake and waiting—listening as I did when I first realized I was captive. Another brush of knuckles at the door draws my attention.

I pad across the room, careful to step quietly over the cold wood floor. When I step near, I hear the fast, stuttered breathing of my visitor, Harlow.

"Miss Embros?" Her whisper is more hushed than necessary. It's riddled with fear and tears.

I vaguely consider how much she'll scream when I slit her inner thighs. When I yank her tongue from her jaw and pluck her pretty brown eyes from her skull.

"I know you're there, please say something."

"What? Would you like me to tell you all the ways I'm going to torture you?" My voice is low and sultry. I want her to know how good it feels to picture ripping someone apart for the mess I've found myself in.

Someone to take my rage.

I only hope Madeline understands why I need to kill Harlow more than she'll want to.

"I had no choice."

Rolling my eyes, I trace the molding along the doorframe. "Such a tried-and-true excuse for our mistakes."

"It wasn't a mistake. I—"

"Rather bold of you to come to me and tell me that killing my entire family wasn't a mistake."

"No one is dead. I mean, a few of your guards but your family..." She trails off and I can't deny the visceral response my body has to her words.

Without any idea of what's happening outside, I have no idea if they're still alive. For all I know, they could have died five minutes ago. I've been hesitant to ask Kane, too afraid that if he confirmed any of their deaths, I'd succumb to everything. Knowing I saved them all those years ago, just to damn them for my mistakes.

But also knowing that they're alive has lessened my anger. Made me too docile. Much to my regret, Kane was right when he said I needed the rage to fuel me.

Harlow sighs. "I didn't think I'd fall in love with her. I didn't want to. But it was her or my mother. You have to understand. Somewhere deep inside, you must know I didn't want her to die. It killed me to give him everything."

"Does Kane know Phineas is your father?"

She sniffs. "No."

"Did you know he was your brother?"

"Not until recently. Phineas was very angry at me, saying how both his children were in the house yet neither of us were able to do anything right."

I can sense the disappointment in her voice. There's a part of her that wants his approval. It poses the question if he had more of a hand raising her than he did his son. "And your mother. Did your sacrifice save her?"

More sniffles and the light thud of her leaning into the door answers my question before she does. "No. She's been missing since the attack."

I huff. Perhaps that's why Kane has chosen to stay instead of taking the so-called freedom his father offered him. He must know there is no such thing with a man like Phineas. He will hold Kane until the very end.

Moments pass before Harlow sighs and her weight leaves the wood.

"To answer you, Harlow. Yes. I understand why you did it. I would have done the same for mine." I press my forehead into the door, the wistful memory of my mother before her image was forever tainted in blood flashing before my eyes. "But I'd also be prepared to die for that choice."

She doesn't respond, and when her retreating steps fade into nothing, I turn to my bed to find the brown fur ball lying on her crossed paws. Those green eyes of hers bore into me with the same reservations they always have. But when I take a step toward her, she doesn't move.

Another step. Nothing.

I crawl into bed, not disturbing her space as I fall onto my pillow. She curls back into the ball, only this time, she leaves a small space between us.

The feline must know I'm prepared. She won't be able to hurt me this time without losing her own life in the process.

Smart girl.

CHAPTER TWENTY

I'm exiting the shower when I hear the door open. The heavy, steady steps indicate it's Kane. A vexing mix of joy and annoyance surges through me as I lean into the open doorway and spot him bent over, scratching behind the ears of the cat.

"Funny how you give her a warm bed and she seems to forget her guard. I could kill her in a second and she wouldn't be the wiser."

He shrugs, glancing at me in his periphery. "Perhaps. Or maybe she knows she's safe."

"In one night?" I raise a questioning brow. "Seems foolish."

Kane rubs her one last time before rising. His suit is all black, including his button-down. A small gold chain hangs from his lapel and clips to his jacket pocket. He exudes danger, and drips lust. The perfect lethal weapon.

He slips one hand into his pocket, while the other gestures to me. "Yet here you are, unchained, and didn't ambush me the moment I walked through the door."

My eyes narrow as he takes a slow, calculated step toward me. "Because thus far, I'm somehow still relatively safe.

Besides, rushing from here will do nothing but guarantee my death and your father's next breath. Can't have that."

Kane smirks. "Or maybe you know you're safe with me."

"You?" I scoff. "The man responsible for my current situation?"

"We've already discussed this. I am not your enemy. Never was. And I'm currently trying to get you out of here."

"While also planning to take over the family."

Unlike the surprise I thought he'd have once he realized I understood what he and his father discussed, he merely shakes his head. "Yes, I am planning to take over the family. *My* family."

My heart stalls in my chest, the room losing clarity as I soak in what his words mean. I've been well aware since the beginning how this would play out. The possibility of him doing what he's saying. But hearing the words solidifies it.

I swallow around the burn. "You are my enemy."

Again, he shakes his head. "Don't. You know as well as I do, once Phineas and Sam are dead, someone will take over. If you tried, there would be nothing but bloodshed. There are people here that have been conditioned for years to hate you and see you as the enemy. There are also very sick men employed by my father who enjoy the human trafficking part of it. If you took it away, they would come for you, and any of the other guards that join you."

Disgust churns my empty stomach. "So you'd continue to steal wom—"

"Don't insult me. My affection for women goes beyond you and my family. I'd take over and give those opposed the opportunity to get out."

It's hard to ignore what he said. The confession of sorts that I mean something to him. It makes me feel sane. Like this constant tug of war in my heart and brain isn't exclusive to only me.

When my words come out, they're broken and strained. "Why wouldn't they do the same to you? Kill you and take over?"

His annoyingly smug grin tells me he didn't hear anything I've said and instead is focusing on the very real show of emotions I let slip.

I take a step back, holding a hand lazily in front of me. "I am not a weak woman. I will not succumb to pretty words and an equally pretty face. Focus on what I'm asking, Kane."

His head tilts to the side, his dark brows furrowing. "How does knowing how I feel about you make you weak?" He steps forward and I take another step back. "Or is it because you feel something for me?"

"My cunt feels something for you," I snap, not liking the direction the conversation is going.

"Because she's already admitted she belongs to me."

"I belong to no—"

"Yes, I know what you think." He waves me off. "But why do you have this misconception that caring for me makes you any less of the insanely strong woman you are?"

My lip finds its way between my teeth. My mother loved my father with the power of the sun, and it was true, never once did I consider her weaker for it. She commanded an army of men, including Dad, and she never backed down from a heated discussion.

But it was also the love they shared that made them weaker as a unit.

"Why did you bring me the cat?"

Kane stops his advance. "I didn't want you to be lonely up here."

This makes a bubble of laughter escape my mouth. "Who's the liar now?"

"It's true," he protests, and the hint of a blush coasts over the bridge of his nose, giving me pause. "And when you told me the story about her, I kind of felt like she could symbolize hope."

"Hope?"

He nods. "Maybe the idea that things between us could go back to then. To when you trusted me. To when you were standing on the edge of falling off the deep end."

"What?" My heart squeezes in my chest. "I don't love you, Kane."

"No but look at me and tell me what we had wasn't something skirting the line. Something so close, we would have fallen in so deep there was no way either of us would have gotten out."

I close my eyes against the ache, shuffling backward until my back hits the wall. "I didn't—*don't* feel anything for you."

"Look at me when you lie to me, Onyx."

My lids snap open, but my voice displays how unsure I am of anything. "We were using each other. I was a job, and you were only there to make me come. Nothing more."

"Bullshit," he bites, eliminating the space between us. The heat from his body envelops mine, relaxing every tight muscle. "You would have killed me the second you started to have doubts about me, but you didn't. And I know for a fucking fact, it's not just because of this."

He cups my pussy under the towel and I nearly buckle from the sudden contact. My nerves are already tingling, the tension and confessions poisoning my blood with desperate want.

When Kane withdraws his hand, I bite into my lip to keep from groaning my objection. "Yes, it was."

"Well, it wasn't for me," he breathes, his nose brushing against my cheek. There's a desperation to his voice singing to my inherent desire to experience what he's talking about. The very thing I've rejected time and time again, too scared to grab in fear of having it ripped away.

I try to steady my voice, to make it sound convincing, but for the first time, I hope he can hear the lie marring my words. "Kane, when this is over, there is no us. You will be the leader of a family I'm at war with. You will be nothing more than competition."

"Then if I can't change your mind, let me have you until it's done. Until Phineas and Sam are dead and all that's left is the original line which separated our sides." He pulls back and sears me with a hooded gaze. One of trepidation and anger. Of hunger. "Be mine."

A gaggle of goose bumps spread across my exposed flesh. I want to give in. I want to allow him to reign over everything until I can no longer think, obsess, or debate on what's right and what's wrong.

To lose myself in the euphoria and bliss Kane has always taken me to when we're together, tangled in each other and using the other's air as our own.

"Yes." I barely hear my own word over the pounding of my heart, but it doesn't matter because Kane hears it clearly.

His hand lashes out, gripping around my throat and drawing me into a punishing kiss. It's angry and ravenous, stealing my ability to breathe or focus on anything other than him. Kane's tongue slips through my sealed lips, taking control as it tangles with mine.

My towel falls as I wrap my arms around his neck, pressing my body into the hardness of his. We fit together as perfectly as any two humans can, and it's with that gut-wrenching fact alone that I allow myself to get lost in him. To close my eyes and let myself move with him rather than against him.

His hand disappears from my neck and moves around my back. The other cups behind my thigh, lifting me from my feet, and forcing me to latch my legs around his waist.

I moan into his kiss, the feel of his erection digging into my exposed center making my entire core clench.

Kane backs us away from the wall, breaking away from my mouth to nip and lick his way down the column of my throat while walking us across the room. Heat unfurls through my body like tendrils, wrapping around my muscles and seizing everything tight. I grind against him, the sudden need to have him inside me robbing me of any logic.

"My needy girl," he huffs before tossing me onto the bed.

I fall with a small oof, fire burning in my eyes at both the boldness of his act and irritation at the loss. It doesn't last long though, because the molten lava dripping from his gaze as he roves over my body lights me up from the inside. Tingles shoot down my spine, my clit pulsing in anticipation.

"Tell me you want me, *mo bhanríon*."

"Is it not obvious, Kane?" Between the quick rise and fall of my chest, my pinched brows, or the knocking of my knees locked together, I'm not sure how he can't see it.

His voice lowers. "I want to hear you say it."

Unlike our other push and pull, or fight for dominance, this is different. It's honesty. Vulnerability. And if this is the last time we're together, I want to give him this.

The air grows thick as I sit up, grabbing his collar in my fist. "I want to forget who we are, and only feel what we do to each other."

I press a kiss to his lips, relishing the way they mold to mine. "I want reality to blur and time to cease to exist."

My hands find his buttons, and I begin the tedious job of

slowly unhooking each one. When the dark ink, sprawling across his chest is fully exposed, I return my gaze to his. His pulse throbs in his neck, his lips are parted and wet from our kiss. The space between us is near stifling with our desire.

"I want *you*."

He moves fast, pressing me back into the mattress and capturing both my wrists in one of his large hands. "Knees up. Don't move. I need to taste what's mine."

I smirk through my fan of lashes and nod. "As you wish."

Without another word, he leans forward and captures one of my pebbled nipples in his mouth. He bites down hard, making me hiss and buck beneath him.

Kane's only response is his warm tongue darting out and soothing over the ache as his grip tightens around me. He moves to my other breast and nips the mounded flesh before working his way down.

It takes more restraint than I care to admit to remain still during his slow assault over my nerves, and even more so when his hands disappear. Everything is tingling and clenching, the build already starting before he's between my legs.

I moan into a nearby pillow, arching my back as he nears the place I need him most.

He tsks. "You said you wanted time to stop. You need to be patient while I give you that."

My heart rate increases, the pounding in my ribs nearly bruising now.

He kisses down my thigh, taking his time until he reaches the tip of my toes. He moves over to the other leg, repeating the same soft process until he's finally at my center. Still, he doesn't connect and right as I open my mouth to coax his next move, he swipes a finger through my soaked slit. I jolt under his touch, the sudden act sending a tremor down my spine.

He brings his index finger up to my lips, slipping inside.

"Suck," he commands, and I respond immediately. Sucking the digit into my mouth with such force he groans against my thigh. The taste of my desire on his fingers has my head becoming fuzzy, fueling the wetness between my thighs.

"Do you see how fucking good you taste? Why I need to have my tongue on you so badly?" He yanks his finger from my mouth with a vicious pop, and inserts it into my pussy.

My walls quiver at both the intrusion and at his words. He draws it out slowly and then adds another, stroking against my walls with a delicious amount of pressure.

"Tell me," he asks, his voice a husky rasp as his fingers twist inside me. "Will you miss this?"

The air thins, squeezing my lungs. The combination of his fingers fucking me and the realization of what he's asking warring in my chest.

When I don't answer, his head lowers as he murmurs, "I will."

Then his tongue slips inside me.

CHAPTER TWENTY-ONE

I've had the pleasure of Kane's mouth on my cunt a couple of times now, but it never felt like this.

His tongue joins his fingers, all three of them fucking me in tandem as I writhe beneath him. The combination of my emotions and arousal heightens every pulsing nerve. I need to distract myself from what he's forcing me to recognize. From what he wants me to do about it.

I comb my fingers through his thick hair before latching on and tugging him up. "Look at me, Kane. I want to see your face while you feast on me."

A hint of a smile crosses his eyes before they darken again. He slides his tongue out and up, stopping at my throbbing clit. His voice is gruff. "Are you sure you can handle me staring at you like this?"

A challenge. *Cute.*

Propping myself on my elbows, I lower my lids to my casual, bored expression. "Get on with it before I do the job myself."

Kane shakes his head slightly, his nose passing over my tight nerves twice. The jolt of pleasure is maddening, and it takes too much restraint to stop my lashes from fluttering.

"Tell me what else you want." He laps at my clit once, and I suck in a harsh breath. His eyes are brimming with arrogance and premature victory. Then I remember what he'd said.

"The next time I fuck you, it's going to be after you beg for it."

He wants me delirious. Out of my head. To give rather than to have him take.

I sigh and swallow around the truth playing at my lips. "I want your tongue massaging my clit and your fingers fucking my cunt."

Kane smirks as if I said exactly what he intended. As if he's won. But rather than the quick retort I expect, he sucks my clit into his mouth and drives his fingers back inside of me.

My head lolls to the side and rests against my shoulder as he works my pussy. Continuing to do as told, his eyes never leave mine. With every hard curl of his digits or pass of his tongue, it's harder to keep up the facade that my insides aren't crumbling around him.

He laps at my slit as though he'll never eat again, and the feral image of him losing himself between my thighs is my undoing. Heat curls tight in my core, my limbs trembling with the overwhelming sensations, while my walls flutter against him.

But then, as if plunged into ice, it all stops. The warmth of Kane's mouth disappears while the fullness of his fingers vanishes. My body nearly convulses with his loss, and I realize I must have closed my eyes because now I must peel them open to find Kane. He's standing a foot from the bed, with his hand that was inside of me now inches away from his mouth.

A fire blooms in my gut both from anger and arousal as I watch him inhale the length of his fingers. He sucks one in his mouth, closes his eyes, and lets out a guttural groan as the muscles in his jaw clench.

"Thought you said you were going to look at me while I licked that pretty pussy of yours? Can't handle it after all?"

A pain shoots through my mouth as my molars grind together. He thinks he can win this game of ours, and he's sorely mistaken. When it comes to Kane, I've been big on threats, but haven't followed through yet. Guess now is the time.

I lean all my weight on one of my elbows and let my other hand trail down my stomach. My eyes stay pinned on Kane whose gaze has hardened, following the path of my walking fingers.

When I reach my throbbing clit, I roll my thumb over it and let out a heady moan. Again, the pleasure ripples through me and forces my head to the side, but this time, I continue to stare at Kane as I pass over the nerves again.

His nostrils flare as I work my thumb in circles, his eyes growing so dark the color nearly vanishes under his pupils. It only fuels the fire coiling deep in my stomach, and I move faster, chasing the high of his gaze, and the heat of his palpable anger.

"Move your fucking hand, *mo bhanríon*. That's *mine*." His words are strained through his clenched teeth. The tone alone makes my nipples draw tight, and I slide a finger through my slit to play at my entrance.

I lock onto his face, watching his pulse thrum in his neck, his hands ball at his sides, and the pure agony of watching what he thought was an empty threat, unfurl in front of his eyes. It's intoxicating. A level of challenge and ownership I've never quite experienced before.

It's exhilarating and heady. Mind-blowingly sexy.

"Move. Your fucking. Hand." He takes a step forward, stopping when his thighs hit the end of the bed. He isn't looking at me, but my fingers as they work. In, out, circle, again and again.

My breath is coming in pants, my head is beginning to swim, and I'm not sure what I want more in this moment. For Kane to rip my hand away and replace it with his, or to continue and explode with his hooded gaze on my drenched cunt.

Kane's hands shoot out, grabbing both of my knees and yanking me to the end. But rather than shove my hand to the side, he undoes his trousers, letting his cock spring free of its confines. It's incredibly hard, precum glistening at the tip as he wraps a large hand around it.

My nerves singe at the sight, my cunt clenching around nothing, reminding me to return my fingers back to my throbbing center. When I do, Kane smirks and uses his free hand to swipe through my pussy.

I jolt. "What are you—"

My words get caught as he uses my arousal as lubricant, and begins stroking his dick in long, languid strokes. With him mere inches from me, the act stirs up something dark and delicious, and suddenly I want him inside me more than I ever have.

Kane's brows furrow as if something is wrong before pushing my hand out of the way. Before words can form, he leans forward slightly and spits on my pussy.

I start to sit up but stop when he drags the head of his cock through my slit, gathering both his saliva and my arousal. A heavy moan falls freely from my mouth, an entirely new feeling blossoming low in my belly.

But then when he pulls back, I nearly convulse, the loss of him making my head spin in the worst way. I want him back, diving inside of me and relieving us both of the torment. But when he begins to stroke himself again in a faster motion, I bite into the side of my mouth to keep the plea from slipping out. I won't beg.

I can't.

"Don't get shy now, my needy girl." Even if I wasn't looking at him, I would be able to hear the arrogant smirk on his face.

I let out an annoyed huff, but return my hand, a new determination filling my chest. But Kane must know I'm on the precipice of giving in to him because he begins growling whispered commands.

"Slide two fingers inside and curl them."

"I don't need to be taught how to—"

"I want you to fuck yourself how I would. Lie back."

I smirk, though it isn't as confident as his. I hadn't realized until now how much I missed his touch, how much I *crave* it. And imagining it's him touching me is far more enticing, especially with his eyes on me. So while I won't give in to his desire for me to beg, I do oblige this, telling myself it's for my benefit only.

When my back falls into the bed, he growls another command. "That's a good girl. Now play with those tight nipples of yours."

Again, I do as told, but only because my breasts are heavy and tingling with the need to be touched. I rotate my thumb, pressing harder as I interchange between tugging my barbells and pinching the tender skin.

It's all too much, the sensations and heat combined with the tension begging to break. Moans fall freely now as I watch Kane and I work ourselves a mere breath away from each other. Heat expands as his own grunts fill the air, sweat drips between the valley of my breasts and down the side of his temple.

It's too hard not to give in. Not to enter in a bubble with him and just be.

"Your pussy is so damn pretty." His voice is nothing but a growl, a deep want lining every word. "So fucking perfect."

His hand trails fire up one of my legs as it moves over my

flesh. My fingers move faster, fucking myself with abandon as he massages his way to the apex of my thighs. He's so close to my center, my nerves sting with anticipation. It's the not knowing if he'll give in and take me that pushes me closer to the edge.

"Just like that, *mo chailín deas.*" His fingers dig harder into me. "Come for me, Boss."

As if he controls my body, the telling tingle spans out, spreading through my limbs like lightning as my orgasm begins to peak. Kane lets out a harsh curse, releasing my thigh and shoving two fingers inside of me. He pumps them in and out aggressively while I continue to curl mine and too soon I'm catapulting over the edge and into the abyss, his name a strangled cry as I fall apart.

The surge ripples through me, stealing my ability to think as my body shakes and my heart barrels into my rib cage. The warmth of Kane's release finds my inner thigh, as his hand continues to fuck me and prolong the orgasm still contracting my every muscle.

It isn't until I'm almost quivering from the aftershocks that he eases his movements and pulls away from me.

My breath is barely steady before I grin. "Couldn't help yourself, it seems."

Kane strips the shirt from over his head, revealing his inked chest, and wipes up his mess. He smirks when I flinch slightly as he passes over my sensitive skin. "I always thought your threats were empty and seeing them play out was a little harder than I imagined."

"Is that so?" I sit up, watching as he discards his soiled shirt.

"Perhaps I'm too greedy when it comes to you. I said your orgasms belong to me and I meant it."

This coaxes a snort from me. "I see. And speaking of

threats, you don't truly wish to follow through with yours, considering we have very limited time together, do you?"

He huffs before holding out a hand to me. I narrow my eyes but take it, and let him lead me back into the bathroom. "I told you, the only way I fuck that cunt of yours is if you beg for it. I meant that too."

"Spare me the semantics. You're not that stubborn." I set a hand on my hip and examine him as he turns on the water to the tub.

He's quiet as he holds his hand under the water, his back moving slowly up and down with his steady breath. The silence is long, and the tension filtering in is becoming thicker the more time passes, but he doesn't seem to mind as he waits. When he's satisfied with a temperature, he secures the stopper and stands, turning toward the sink.

My lips itch to break the stillness, but my determination for him to do it is stronger. I can't help but wonder though, with what little time left we have left together, one would assume he wouldn't will it away so carelessly. I know my favorite part of our encounters is when we're tangled in one another, breathless and connected. Releasing control while sharing the rare moments where we feel pleasure when all there's been is pain.

All of it was almost too precious to waste on his impossible desire to hear me beg.

Kane finds what he's looking for—a bottle with a white label and purple script. He returns to the tub and pours some out under the stream of water, and the intense smell of lavender soothes my aching body almost immediately.

He returns the bottle before tugging my hand from my hip and ushering me into the tub. I remain quiet but move stiffly, my disdain obvious as I enter the water. Though the moment my calves submerge in the warmth, I nearly melt, sliding the rest of the way down with a fake disgruntled expression pinching my face.

Kane, with all his irritatingly all-knowing demeanor, smirks and shakes his head as he files behind me. The tub is wide, but I doubt his large frame will actually fit until he proves my internal thoughts wrong, and it does.

We sit in the thick silence, only it morphs into something much more tender as he wraps an arm around my waist. His free hand dips into the water momentarily before he pulls it out and drips water down my chest.

I watch as the droplets make small rivers down my breasts before disappearing back into the soapy water, enjoying the moment I now understand is peace.

Such a rare thing to possess in our world.

For a second, I let myself really settle in his arms, my body molds to his too perfectly, but I allow the pleasure to overtake me. My eyes flutter closed and my breathing evens out, my lungs soaking in the calming fragrance that flows from the water.

"What's your favorite color?" he asks, surprising me with what he decides to break the silence with.

I guffaw and turn to face him, but he presses down on my stomach to hold me in place.

"Tell me." His voice is warm in my ear, and the low timbre sprouts goose bumps along the flesh not submerged. "When you said I was stubborn, I wanted to laugh. Tell you to turn over your shoulder and look in the mirror. But then, something else crossed my mind. I only know *of* Onyx Embros, Queen of the Embros family and a mere ghost before she cuts out her enemies' hearts. I know of your untold strength and leadership. Your fearless heart and cunning mind."

His free hand strokes my hair until I lean back into his shoulder. My body is both tight with trepidation and complacent in the safety of his hold. I've no idea where he's headed but I can't deny hearing how Kane perceives me is anything other than alluring.

"I know the armor you show the world, the one you need to, in order to thrive. But I want to know more. The things people deem as meaningless but are the small pieces that make up who we are."

"Why?" Apprehension works heavy through my bloodstream. The instant defense embedded in my flesh stands at full attention. "Unless you plan to write a biography or use what you learn to somehow take over—"

"I will *never* hurt you." His voice is strained as it comes through clenched jaws. "And how you imagine I'll use your favorite color as a way to convince your men into a coup is far too impressive. Even for me."

I bite the inside of my cheek to keep from smiling, though I tell myself it's from his latter comment and not his constant reassurance to my well-being. Clearing my throat, I readjust between his thighs, ignoring his slight erection prodding my back.

While I still have my reservations and think it odd that he'd rather spend time discussing minuscule subjects than losing himself inside of me, I oblige.

For a cost. "And what will I receive for this very private information?"

He doesn't hesitate. "What would you like?"

"To know what's happening out there. To be privy of the plan you've somehow concocted to, as you say, 'save me.'"

He brushes his knuckles over the shell of my ear, sending shivers through me. My body's response to this man is becoming too visceral—too needy—to be healthy. Another moment passes before he pushes out a heavy breath that causes stray hairs to tickle my neck.

"As you wish. A piece of information in exchange for answers to my questions."

I consider his proposition. If he only asks for mundane information that won't provide him any leverage, I don't see the harm in entertaining him. There is also my curiosity to factor in as well. No one has ever asked me my favorite color and it would be dishonest to say I'm not enticed as to what else he wants to know.

"Black. And before you assume, it's not because of my name, nor what appears to be my constant state of mourning."

"Are you in mourning?"

I nod against his shoulder, peering up at him through a fan of lashes. His gaze is focused on where his fingers are splayed across my stomach and it's only now that I realize my own hand is on top of his. It feels natural to lie with him like this. Like our world isn't on the verge of exploding into flames around us and stealing one of us away.

And it *will* take one of us. We won't both make it out alive.

Why does that fact bother me so much now? Why does it make my chest tight with the idea of killing Kane, when I've thought of little more since we first met? I continue to say I knew he'd be trouble, but the more time passes, the more I come to the conclusion that while yes, he would be my ruin, it wouldn't be at the doing of another.

It would be at the expense of ourselves.

Like Romeo and Juliet. Two families that would never be more than enemies, and a connection impossible to create. The only way to escape such a fate—such madness—is death.

"What makes you happy? Brings you quiet in a world of chaos?"

I sigh, still staring at my hand. "I won't know peace until I have your father's head in my garden. Then, perhaps, I'll know the answer to that."

He nods, never moving his eyes from my hand as well. "Do people find peace with vengeance? Or is it with acceptance?"

A thick knot lodges in my throat, but I force it down as I give a weak shrug. "I shall soon find out. Now for my question. Tell me, how is my family?"

CHAPTER TWENTY-TWO

I brace myself after finally asking the question that's been at the edge of my thoughts since I woke up. Even though I know they're alive, I don't know in what state they're in, if they're aware I'm alive, or anything that's happening in a place I have meticulously looked after since fourteen. The muscles in my neck seem absurdly tight, and suddenly, a weight I've ignored thus far bears down, nearly crushing me.

Perhaps I've waited this long in fear that I may act brazenly and get myself killed before seeing justice through. If I knew someone was hurt, or dead, I'd burn this mansion to the ground without caring who's inside.

I've spent a decade preparing them to continue on without me. But the notion of them having to do it *while* worrying about my life was never something I planned for, because the biggest of their problems was to be dead.

Now, as I lie in a warm bath with the man who I thought condemned us to hell, I realize he holds the key to my sanity. Or damnation.

It's all dependent on what he says next.

Kane doesn't prolong the sudden agony encroaching,

squeezing me tighter as if he can sense I need reassurance. I don't like that it calms me.

"Trick and Trigger have overseen the estate's repairs and repositioned your men. Casinos and bars have been shut down temporarily, and more people have been sent to guard neutral territory and Hearts."

A heavy, relieved sigh rushes through my nose. Hearts. I knew they'd protect it, but the confirmation was needed more than I realized.

"Shi is with Kilo most days, taking care of things remotely from his room. He's recovering in the hospital after a double amputation, but he's due to be discharged soon, and from what I understand, Trick has already created some type of prosthetic legs for him."

My heart pinches. Kilo. He'd been trying to tell me something before the explosion happened. I watched as he worked it out in his head, slotting together the pieces before finally getting them in place. That's when I looked up the stairs and saw Kane.

There was such a heaviness in the moment and in retrospect it is clear what it was...

I should have found a way to protect Kilo. While there was no reason to believe Phineas was making a move, guilt wears over my soul.

He'll recover. I say it five times over as the images of what was left of his legs try to creep in the corners of my vision.

"And Maddy?" My voice cracks when I say her name.

"As mad as ever. She helped us out of a bind the other night and I'm having the plans sent to her tomorrow."

"Plans?" I start to turn, but he tsks in my ear and presses down.

"For another answer."

I scoff, but quickly nod, eager to know more important details in exchange for his.

"Something you hate."

"Besides Murphys?"

"Yes."

Rolling my eyes, I lean back into his shoulder. This one's easy. "A sunny day, being called an outdated slur, and sugar in my spaghetti."

Kane stiffens beneath me when I mention that last bit. This time, I ignore his attempts to keep me against him and turn to face him. "You put sugar in your pasta, Kane?"

He shrugs. "Maybe. But also, how can you blame me? I was barely double digits by the time I began cooking."

"You're a grown man now. Rectify that please."

"Sure. I'll make you some."

This actually makes me chuckle. "If it's anything like your bacon, I may have to pass."

"It's kept you alive, has it not?"

"Debatable," I guffaw, shifting back to lean against him. "Your plan. Tell me."

He blows out a heavy breath. "I'll only tell you one part at a time so that this isn't over too quickly."

"You didn't do that with the last question. Don't change the agreement now."

Kane nips at the shell of my ear. "Because that was about your family. They are not some bargaining chip for information."

"Yet the plan that's meant to save me is?" I bite, ignoring the flutter in my stomach.

"Maybe a little. So choose your questions carefully."

"I can't believe I am letting you do this."

I feel him smile against my neck as he runs his nose along the column. I shudder despite the warmth surrounding me.

"Because you like answering questions no one has ever dared to ask."

Ignoring the truth in his words, I mull over my question and attempt to keep my body from its traitorous shivering as he continues to nuzzle against me. "When will everything happen?"

"Tomorrow afternoon."

I jolt upright, but am yanked back so forcefully hard, water splashes over the side of the tub. "And you haven't told Madeline? How do you expect her to move an army so quickly?"

"You don't think she can?"

His words sober me quickly and I slam my teeth closed, a sharp pain shooting across my jaw. "Well, yes, but still, Kane. When will you tell her? What—"

"What's something you miss doing?"

"Wh—I—" A growl vibrates my chest as I throw my hands up. "Kane, I need you to prioritize what's most important."

"It's asking a lot, believe me, I know. But I need you to trust me, Onyx."

I try to speak, to tell him how impossible that would be even without the pretense of everything that's already transpired between us, but he shakes his head. There's a plea in his green eyes I can't ignore. It's a deep, honest vulnerability I've only ever seen once.

It was when my mother asked me to stay put under the seats of our limo. When she asked me to avenge their deaths, just before allowing herself to be slaughtered in the street.

I swallow around the burn and nod slightly. Even if I can't trust him, I can listen to him.

"Within the first thirty seconds of meeting you, I knew this wouldn't be easy. That knowing you even beyond your name would put it all in jeopardy. My family, my freedom. My end."

His voice deepens, and despite the growing ache in my

chest, I remain quiet, waiting for him to work through his words. "I want to know everything about the woman I'm giving up everything for. Even the most minuscule of details that I can think of as I sit on top of the rubble and reign, king of the ruins, and smile." Kane shifts, stroking my hair again. "Please, Boss. Can you give me that?"

A prickle stings deep behind my eyes as I nod yet again. I clear my throat and tell him what it is I miss the most.

"My parents. I miss painting my mom's toes and helping my father balance a budget. Running through the estate and hiding from the boys." The burning ache expands, creeping down my face and into my chest. Thinking and speaking of them so freely feel as though I'm resurfacing long-forgotten happiness that's been buried beneath the anger and hatred.

"I miss helping my mother trim the stupid roses that I later fertilized with my father's latest victim. Oh, and the art. I once thought myself an artist and painted the most horrendous mural on my mother's shed, and it stayed up long after her passing. It was Madeline who told me the truth."

I feel my cheeks rise as a smile takes over my face. But oddly, now that I've begun recalling memories I haven't thought about in years, I can't help but continue. It's as if a door has swung open, and the contents within are spilling out.

"Teasing the new guards and watching my mother and father from the top of the stairs as they danced in the foyer under the chandelier. Sitting on the kitchen counter and watching them bake. They couldn't keep their hands off one another longer than a few minutes."

"Quite the lovebirds."

I huff. "They were. And until recently, I once thought their love was what made them weak."

"But you see otherwise now?" Kane slides his hand under

mine before spreading his digits and letting my fingers fall between his.

The act is so intimate, so tender. It's unlike anything I've ever done and the foreign emotion fluttering through me is conflicting. It's somewhere between contentment and apprehension, and it only takes a moment longer before I analyze what this is.

It's how deep feelings are forged. Not the superficial ones that result in mere anger or the disappointment that comes with even the smallest betrayal. But ones that could burn cities to bare ashes.

I've given him too much already.

I stand from the bath and grab a towel hanging over the side. He watches quietly as I wrap it around my chest and lean against the sink. I only hope he can't hear the heavy pounding of my heart against my rib cage as I narrow my eyes in a false authoritative glare.

"Enough, Kane. Tell me everything."

I can see the disappointment cross over his features. The downward tilt in his lips and the tic in his jaw. But he doesn't argue and instead stands, grabbing his own towel.

"As you wish, *mo bhanríon*."

CHAPTER TWENTY-THREE

I'm not generally a nervous person—I've done far too many illegal activities for that—but the way my heart is pulsing in my *nose*, matching the fast bounce of my leg, you'd think I was standing trial for murder.

But it isn't me who will soon face the music of all my past sins. It's the Murphys. From Phineas himself to every guard who opposes Zek's ascension.

This is it.

The sound of an approaching motor makes me jolt to my feet. I watch as the sleek, dark car pulls around the front and rolls to a stop in front of the house. Its windows are tinted in a way that looks as if it's been painted black, ensuring anyone inside is completely hidden under its veil.

I rub my slick hands over my jeans twice, double-checking the back door is still wide open. I trust my brother when he says no one else will be coming by but having stayed with the scum of the earth for a couple of months, I know better. Being there taught me how sneaky they are and how their ability to stab someone in the back the second they turn around is child's play. They could have easily killed him and are now coming to clean up the loose ends.

No. Zek would find a way from the afterlife to protect me. It's him. He'd figure out how.

The minute I take a steadying breath, the driver's side door opens, and my brother steps out. The rest of my pent-up tension relaxes at once, a wave of calm taking over. There have been many times now that Zek has gotten me out of sticky situations, and every time I saw him, the feeling has been the same.

It's one of complete trust and knowing that with him, everything is going to be okay even when it seems impossible.

I open the door before he makes it up the broken porch steps and engulf him in a hug the second his foot crosses the threshold. It's the first chance I've had to do it since everything happened, and when his arms wrap around my back, an overwhelming tidal wave of emotions hits me all at once.

A strangled cry erupts past my lips as I squeeze him, losing the composure I wasn't even aware was unraveling. My life. His life. Our mom. All of it—everything—has been on the line since the day he was born. He was made to grow up before he went to first grade and has spent every waking moment protecting us. Providing for us. Saving us.

Here I was, thinking by some fucked-up default that my brother had an obligation to get me out of messes I made. And I even had the audacity to be upset with him for scolding me afterward. For asking me to help more around the house and not sneak out on the weekend to go to some high school parties. I screamed at him when he told me I couldn't date someone on the "bad side" of town and slammed doors in his face when he said he had to pick up yet another shift and couldn't come to my art displays.

I was selfish.

An idiot.

A shit sister, who couldn't stop and think for one second

that he might have had stuff going on too. That there was more than just my side of our story.

"I-I'm so so sorry Zeky. I-I—" My shoulders shake as I push out the world's crappiest apology. "I'm the worst. I should—"

"Shh. Take a breath. Calm down." He rubs up and down my upper arms. "You have nothing to apologize for. First off, you were a kid for most of your tantrums, and you didn't know anything that was happening. I completely sympathize with you."

Another sob breaks through, and he hugs me again. Maybe I needed him to comfort me, or maybe acknowledging all the extremely fucked-up shit that's happening is what does it, but either way, I fall apart.

I think of everything, both past and present. My heart aches for what he went through. What he shielded me from. What my mother felt when she realized she couldn't protect us. Then I think of our futures and how it's all about to change. I have no idea if it will be good or absolutely devastating.

It could be seconds, or minutes, but I let myself cry and let my brother hold me through it. It isn't until I sigh with a full breath that he speaks again.

"I should have told you. If I would have explained, you would have understood. I just thought what I was doing would be the best way to protect you."

I shake my head against his chest. "No. You did right, Zek." I release him and make out his sullen features through my tear-ridden vision. "I would have forced your hand and tried to convince you that we could run. We would all be dead without you."

He strokes my hair away from my face before a small, sad smile pulls up one side of his lip. "You're right on both accounts. You could have me believing we got away scot-free until they came knocking on our door."

I huff out a bitter laugh. "Thank you."

"Don't thank me, Fi. I've fucked up in so many ways, I can't even begin to explain." Zek gestures to the couch with his head and we both sit. He threads his fingers through his hair before leaning over and propping his forearms on his knees. "I didn't want to hurt her. I didn't want to hurt any of them. And knowing I was saving you but condemning so much more than them was really fucking with me."

My heart squeezes. It stings to hear the truth outright, but it's not in a hurtful way. More like an "I understand, but it also sucks" kind of way. Still, I don't want him to feel bad about it.

I nudge him in the shoulder. "You got that soft spot from me."

"Oh, that's for sure. Without you, I would have been lost a long time ago. No telling who I'd be."

"Still you. I don't believe for one second you would have turned out anything like him."

He scoffs. "You're saying that to someone who let you be locked up while I fell for the woman I was supposed to capture."

I jolt back, a hand pressed to my chest, a wide smile taking over my mouth. "Okay, first off, I kind of lied about my living conditions so you wouldn't freak out. But wait, did I just hear you right? You *fell* for her?"

Zek sighs again and drops his head. "No. I mean—"

He scrubs his hands down his face, his brows tightly drawn together as he takes a thick swallow. I can see the moment he decides to say it—to be honest with himself and me. "Yeah. I did. It was impossible not to."

He sighs, his shoulders dropping with the confession. "But it doesn't matter anymore."

"Why?"

He shakes his head. "Just doesn't. What matters now is

moving forward, and for you and me"—he gestures between us —"everything's about to change. And I need you to know that either way, you have options."

"What do you mean?"

Zek sighs and leans back into the worn couch. "It means after tomorrow I can withdraw a shit ton of money and send you to the UK to study art, or travel around the world. You don't need to stick around. I don't *want* you to."

My heart stalls in my chest, and my stomach rolls. What he's saying—*implying*—can only mean one thing. "You're staying and taking over for him."

"Yes."

I jump to my feet, ignoring the shivers already running down my spine. "You can't! You're not like him, Zek. Why would you want to continue to do the vile things he's done?"

My voice is trembling, but when Zek peers up at me, I see the hurt and trepidation cross over him. The way he looks completely defeated. Then I realize.

He doesn't have a choice.

"I wanted to leave. But Onyx showed me things that made me understand I can't do what I'm about to do and then go. There would be chaos, death, and then someone else would take over and continue to do the things I could have stopped."

He takes a breath and stands, tucking one hand in his pocket. "Because of Phineas, I used to think all Mafia families were the same. I figured they all did terrible shit, and didn't give a fuck who they hurt in the process. But I know better now and I owe it to so many people to do this."

I shake my head, refusing to believe that he wants to lead such a corrupt and disgusting family. "You don't owe anything to anyone."

When Zek sighs this time, I know I'm fighting a losing battle. His mind is made up, and he's only letting me know and giving me the option to go. I let out another sob, nodding as I pull him back into another hug. "Tell me what I need to do to help."

He leans his head on top of mine. "I need you to make one last call."

If she tries to kill me. At least I'm at a hospital. There's no way I don't at least make it a few feet inside before collapsing on the tile a bloody mess and being rescued, right? Though, it's also possible she could own the hospital and tell them not to intervene.

Can the Mafia own hospitals?

I mean, even if they do, I'm pretty sure the doctors *have* to save me. They took an oath for crying out loud. My brain hurts from the back and forth, contradicting rational thought with possibilities, but that's what she makes me do—question everything.

If someone would have told me about this Maddy person last year, I'd probably think they're insane. But after living briefly on one side and hearing the stories, to being threatened by her with a knife? Then later stalked and saved by her too?

If I'm being honest, I don't think anyone knows just how out of her head the woman really is. This only brings me back to my answer that yes, she absolutely could murder me in front of a hospital.

Calm down.

I force myself to take a breath. Not having my brother to rely on in these situations is beginning to give me a horrible dose of paranoia, and I decide here and now to never dip my toe in anything even *remotely* illegal ever again. And I'd like to at least make it to take my first shot as a legal adult one day.

"Ya know, Kilo fussed at me about calling you a mouse." The sudden voice nearly jolts my soul from my body.

I spin around, heart careening in my chest to find a mess of red curls, and a smug smirk painted on Maddy's face. She's leaning against the brick wall, one leg propped up and her pale arms crossed in front of her chest. Her ability to look somehow friendly and absolutely murderous is a true talent.

"But he said if anything, you're like a dormouse. Sleeping in the middle of a war raging around you, so unconscious to the fact the city is inches away from being torn to the ground. Sounds like blissful ignorance to me, but ya know. Tomato, tomáto."

I suck in a sharp breath, pressing all my weight on the balls of my feet to steady me as she kicks off the wall and takes two broad steps toward me. I imagine her to be something like a bear, sniffing for fear. If I move too quickly or if she decides to make me a snack, I'm a goner. Goose bumps prickle my skin with every pass of her amber eyes until finally, her lips lift higher on one end.

"So what has the little dormouse come to tell me?"

It takes two attempts at clearing my throat enough to be able to speak. "My brother said it's time to tell you the plan."

The only warning I have is the slight flare of Maddy's eyes before her hand shoots out and grips my forearm. I yelp, but don't dare try to resist and instead let her twirl me around and lead me into the hospital.

Women and men move around the hospital in their various colors of scrubs. None of them seem to care, or even notice, that a woman is dragging another—albeit willingly—through the halls.

A shiver runs through me as I consider how maybe the Mafia really can own hospitals.

She passes the elevators and continues to an access stairwell. When we enter, she drops my hand.

"You have until we get to Kilo's floor to spill it all. Best start now, *Fiona*."

The hairs rise with the threat sprinkled on every syllable of my name. But when she takes her first step, the words somehow find me as if I'm an auctioneer.

"Long story short, my brother has been planning a coup since he was sixteen. He always knew we wouldn't make it out and decided to get to know the guards. Around forty percent of them belong to Zek. Their loyalty, that is. They will be stationed at the west side of the building tomorrow during the meeting."

"Meeting?" Maddy's five steps ahead of me and I'm grateful considering the look of daggers she shoots over her shoulder.

I nod. "I should have started with that. Sorry. Tomorrow is the day everything happens—"

Her shoulders visibly tighten as she continues to climb and now I want to stab my brother for thinking this woman is above shoving me down a flight of hospital stairs.

"They are having a meeting to have Onyx sign all her real estate, business, ports, everything, over to him. A lawyer will be present, but no one else."

"Bastard wants people to think she did it on her own. Less of a fuss when people willingly bend the knee."

This confuses me. "How does that make sense when all of you can just tell everyone the truth?"

I can't see it, but I can hear the strain from her clenched jaw. "We'll all be dead the second she signs. I'm sure he's got men ready to attack us before the ink is dry."

"Oh. Then it makes sense why my brother said you need to be in position tonight and not to wait until the morning."

She spins around, and it's then I realize how out of breath I am. I grab onto the rails and take a second to let my heart rate steady. "Sorry. I'm all over the place. I guess you were right about being asleep. It's like I've been plunged into this whole new world and shoved more information into my mouth than I have time to digest. And now I'm word vomiting to a woman who will kill me the second I mess up."

A large whoosh of air releases from my lungs as I find Maddy's narrow gaze on me. She's still for way longer than what's comfortable, and soon I start shifting my weight on the balls of my feet as I wait.

Then, out of completely nowhere, she laughs. Full-on belly laughter echoes around the concrete space and rings near deafeningly in my ear. My hand tightens around the rail while my eyes scan over any possible exits that I can reach before she finally snaps.

But as suddenly as her laughter started, it stops. She takes a deep breath and pushes her curls away from her face. "Alright. There's a meeting happening tomorrow with Onyx, and we need to find a way to cross over and be at the west side of the Murphy's mansion by tonight. Correct?"

I nod.

"And I'm assuming there will be a place we can cross over into their territory without being seen?"

Again, I nod. "Yes, I have the roads you'll need to take that are free of soldiers. They don't expect you to leave, considering their threats. So, they are moving most of their men to a neutral area to be ready for when you cross tomorrow."

"And why do they think we'll find out about Onyx's meeting?"

"They said word would spread fast when people see Lucian." I'm not sure of his importance, but I've never seen my brother so uncomfortable talking about someone else. Judging from the look on Maddy's face with her wide eyes and fast blinks, I'd say she does.

"How the fuck did Phineas get Lucian to do his dirty work?"

I shrug. Not only because I have no clue, but I don't even know who the guy is. "I'm to give you a contact number for a man named Oliver. Zek said to call him at six tonight, and he'll get you squared away with where to enter the mansion grounds."

Maddy takes a moment, though I'm not sure if it's to ponder on what I've told her or if she's still worried about the lawyer. A few more beats pass before she finally works whatever it is out. "And if this whole ploy is just a way to kill us?"

"I thought about what I'd say if you asked that. I even asked my brother. He said there is nothing he can say to make you trust him, but that's what he's asking."

She scoffs, turning back and continuing up the stairs. "He's been asking way too fucking much of me lately, and it always results in little payoff for me. And people wonder why I favor women."

I follow behind her the rest of the way and exit through the metal door leading to the floor where I first met them all. We walk into Kilo's room, who looks much better than he did when I first saw him.

He's sitting up, his white hair tousled as if he'd run his hand through it more than a few times, and his eyes are moving quickly over documents sprawled across the lap tray in front of him.

When he hears us enter, his eyes flash up, the bright blues appear like lightning they move so fast. They flit to me and I suck in an audible breath.

He's so insanely gorgeous, it's jarring. His gaze stays trained on me, and the longer they do, the thinner the air gets.

Finally, Maddy speaks, "Need a favor, Ki."

He continues to hold our stare but answers her. "Anything."

She motions to me with her head before pulling something dark from beneath her dark-green blazer and tosses it at him. When he catches it, we both break eye contact and stare at the gun he's now holding.

My heart thumps loudly in my chest, and my palms instantly become clammy. I don't react fast enough before Maddy has a vise grip on my upper arm and jerks me to Kilo's side. "I need you to watch her for the next twelve hours. If you don't hear from me, put a bullet in her head."

My mouth opens twice like a fish, but nothing comes out, the shock and fear tangling my vocal cords.

This makes Maddy laugh as she produces cuffs from her back pocket. When I asked her to meet, she must have planned to take me this time.

Shit.

I shriek when the cold metal touches my wrist. "I swear I'm telling the truth. My brother wouldn't set you up."

Kilo watches in silence as Maddy secures me to his bed rail.

"If that's true, then you'll be free to go in a little bit. Not a thing to worry about. Watch some TV or something with Kilo. He needs the company."

"But I-I can't—"

"You can and you will, little mouse." She takes two quick steps back before kicking a chair hard in my direction. After that, she flings something silver at Kilo who catches it in one hand. "I do hope I get to see you again though. Preferably breathing."

Ezekiel

Chapter Twenty-Four

Puzzle Pieces

Eight Weeks Ago

THE CALL

There was something I heard on TV one time. It was one of those organizational shows that talks about throwing stuff out rather than hoarding. It said if it doesn't bring you joy, toss it.

Don't like that sweater your grandma made? Trash it.

Hate looking at that picture on the fridge your kid spent all week in art making? Crumple it up.

Look in the mirror and can't find anything about yourself that makes you happy? Well, the point is clear.

Getting rid of shit, materialistic or not, is such an easy concept when you don't consider anything beyond your own selfish desires. I never knew my grandmother, but I'm pretty sure her seeing the sweater she worked hard to create would bring *her* joy. I don't have a kid, but I could never bring myself to throw away Fi's masterpieces because when she went to the fridge to get a snack, her face would light up at seeing her work on display.

And me? Well, I have people who are counting on me to suck up my own disparities with myself and continue on.

But I'd be lying if I said I wasn't tired. Because I am. So. Fucking. Tired.

I don't have it the worst of the worst, I know that. I'm dirt poor, but I still have a roof over my head and don't go a day without food. I'm the son of the biggest asshole murderer in the state who has abused and used me in almost every shape and form, but I'm still breathing, and my sister is safe. My future isn't mine right now, but I refuse to believe it never will be.

Somehow, despite all the shit, I still have hope. Hope for the impossible.

For my freedom.

And tonight, it's exactly what I'm asking for.

The call's finally come. The day I've waited on since I was six years old and I learned that the reason why Johnny got a PlayStation for Christmas and I got socks was because Santa was how deep our parents' pockets were.

Phineas is ready to cash in his biggest secret and I've never been more ready. He's sent a car to pick me up and I've done nothing else but think of how to tell him. How to demand that this is it. That after I do this final thing, he has to let me and my family go, and never fucking calls on me again.

When the car pulls up to the west side of the mansion, I'm nearly shaking in anticipation. My nerves are trembling as I step out onto the gravel. My feet crunch on the small stones as I cross over and pass a few guards pacing near the back door.

I nod to the one who makes eye contact with me. He's one of those I've gotten to know over the past few years. One that would gladly agree to mutiny if I ever decided to start one.

It's crossed my mind once or twice. To kill the fucker and take over, just to spite him. But I don't want this life. It's nothing but sick-ass men dealing drugs, weapons, and women to other sick-ass men. I'd end up killing everyone and burning this place to the ground.

Right now, all I want is to leave and never look back. Nothing can change that.

I find Phineas at his desk, per usual. His piece of shit second-in-command is standing next to him, rubbing the scar I left him down his face. His eyes flash to me as I enter and he huffs, "About time."

"Considering you sent a car to pick me up, I'd say I'm right on time, fuckwad." I smirk at his sneer and turn to Phineas, who is ignoring us both and smiling at his computer screen.

"It's finally time, son."

I grimace at his use of the word "son" and tuck my hands into my pockets. "Last job?"

Phineas' smile fades slowly as he looks at me. He doesn't have any plans to resign from his throne, but he also doesn't have an heir to pass things down to, which will pose a problem for him later. He'll get old, easy to overthrow, and with no family left, all his work will have been for someone else.

Part of me wishes I could be around to see it happen.

He gives a curt nod. "A deal's a deal."

"Funny," I scoff, pursing my lips. "I don't remember agreeing to a deal."

"You didn't want that pretty little sister of yours killed or sold, so if I remember correctly, there *was* a yes. I think it was somewhere in between those piss-ridden pants and snot-filled sobs."

My fists tighten at my sides.

Six. I was six. Most kids are learning their fucking alphabet at six, and I was being asked to exchange my baby sister's life for mine. I feel it when my heart starts beating too fast and the heat rises up my neck.

I won't let him get me worked up. This is it. My leash is so loose now, I can almost wriggle free.

Three steadying breaths later, I push out the words. "After this is done, my family and I are gone. You'll pad my account and I'll never hear from you again."

Sam's brows rise and Phineas guffaws before he sees that I'm more than serious. He narrows his eyes and steeples his fingers. We sit like this for a few minutes before he smiles. It's full and happy, and, even as a grown man, it sends an uncomfortable feeling oozing down my spine.

"Alright, kid. I'll grant you the freedom you want. But you gotta live long enough to see it."

Before I can wonder what he means, he tells me. He explains in vivid detail exactly how I'll die and how any freedom is merely an illusion. How, no matter what I thought, I'll be his tool till I take my last breath. And by the sound of it, it won't be too much longer from now.

He speaks in varying volumes when he tells me the story of Onyx Embros. The woman who runs the other half of the state and owns what should have been his ten years ago. He lists the number of men she's killed, the women she's stolen, and the money she's lost him. The more he talks the more he makes her seem like the villain and only confirms my ever-growing suspicion that all Mafia dons are repulsive human beings.

Then when he's all done, he instructs me to visit a new ice cream shop he's thinking of buying.

THE MISSING SISTER

The body hits the ground before I take my next step.

"Where the fuck is he?" Red fills the corners of my vision as I stride through the foyer, ignoring the harsh curses of a maid complaining about cleaning up the blood now seeping across the floor.

One of the guards I've become familiar with points straight to where I'm headed, though I only make it two more steps before the office doors swing open.

Phineas appears, his face ever the rosy hue as he buttons the middle of his jacket. He eyes me briefly before scanning the mess I made at his front door with the fucker that told me what a great ass my sister has.

"Was that necessary?" Phineas says, so fucking calmly, so nonchalant, it's as though he's not asking me about killing his guard.

"Where is my sister?" I grit through clenched teeth.

Phineas seems so much smaller to me than he used to. Where he's weak, I'm strong. Where he's a complete fucking imbecile, I'm keen. To think I was once scared of him only fuels the raging fire in my gut.

"Think of it as insurance," he says, his gaze flashing back to me.

I take another step forward, fury burning through my veins, causing me to shake. If he's hurt her, I'll kill every fucker in this building.

"She's fine." Phineas holds a hand up, still so full of arrogance as if he knows I'm all bark and no bite.

He likes that he's made me this way. Volatile. Angry. Quick

to lose my temper. He enjoys watching me unravel, taking out my anger on others when it should be directed at him. But even more so, he loves knowing that I won't move a fucking muscle against him if it means my sister or mother is at stake.

My jaw aches as I clamp my teeth down and focus on the bite of my gun clenched in my hand.

"I've been able to squeeze most of that mushy shit from your heart, but your love of women is still a bit of a nuisance for me. Considering most of the people over at Embros have pussies, it's only natural you'll need to fall into one to get information."

"I'm not there to fuck anyone. I can easily get the shit you need from a guard."

Phineas shrugs and steps back into his office, forcing me to follow behind. "Perhaps, but you never know. I don't need you going over there and falling into some bitch's cunt and becoming a liability."

White clouds my vision as I watch him walk to his desk. "If you touch one fucking hair—"

"Save the threats for someone who you have leverage over, son. I thought I taught you that. She's fine and living in Murphy luxury. I'll make sure you get to talk to her when you actually get inside the Embros estate. Until then, I suggest you work fast."

Every instinct in my body is humming for me to end it all right now. To shoot the fucker in the head and kill every single piece of shit out there until I find her.

But one thing I don't allow myself to be is a complete fool, especially when it comes to my father. Sam is probably watching to make sure I leave without a fuss, and if I were to have a tantrum, Fiona would be dead before I made it to her.

I run my tongue over my teeth and step forward, tapping my gun on the edge of his desk. "I'll play your game for now.

But if she's hurt in any way, no threat will suffice for what I'll do to you."

Without giving him a chance to give his signature smug smile, I turn and leave, doing the best I can to quell the simmering anger still rolling in my gut. I brush past a collection of men who are helping haul off the piece of shit I killed before pushing through the front doors.

The cool night air greets me, but does little to calm my skin, which feels like it's on fire. She wasn't supposed to be involved in any of this. I was already irate with myself for taking her to the ice cream shop.

I shouldn't have taken her. I should—suddenly it becomes glaringly clear how much I'm already regretting. How much I should have done but didn't. From here on out I need to plan thoughtfully, and act meticulously. I cannot allow for any more distractions or mistakes.

Everything is on the line, and now, my sister, the only one keeping me bound to my humanity, is somewhere I can't protect her.

As if the universe wanted to collect another debt, the telling smell of tobacco enters my lungs. A quick glance to the right and I find a familiar face, hidden in the dark.

Oliver rests against one side of the wall. He's among the very few in this place I've come to call a friend. He's tried to convince me on more than one occasion to take over for my father and has even gone so far as to find dozens of others that would join the cause, should I ever decide as much.

With everyone busy discussing the mess I left indoors, he's alone. Still, he keeps his voice low. "Sorry about your sister, mate. Fucking animals act like they've never seen a woman before."

I bare my teeth. "Did they touch her?"

He shakes his head, though it does nothing to relieve my

anger. "No, lad. But I'm sure the vile catcalls they threw at her were disturbing, to say the least."

Hot bile burns my esophagus. "Any of your so-called friends?"

Oliver has befriended plenty of other guards, and claims that, like him, they're here because they have no other options. Still, I have my reservations about trusting anyone who ended up with my father.

Again, he shakes his head. "Not a one. Are you ready to meet them?"

"Can they protect Fiona?"

"Aye."

Premature hope blooms in my chest. "Then yes. I'm ready."

Four Days Ago

THE CAPTIVE

By the time I come to, my head is throbbing. The spot where the soon-to-be-dead guard hit me, is sore, and the metal taste of blood lingers in my mouth. I press a hand to my temple and grimace when I find a cut slicing open my eyebrow.

I wipe my hand on my jeans and note I'm inside a heavily tinted jeep, surrounded by the smell of copper and burnt wood. Through slitted eyes, I find Phineas on the opposite side of me, lounged across the leather seats with a wide grin etched on his face. He's staring down at his phone, typing a message out as his shoulders bounce in silent laughter.

Bastard. Got what he wanted after all, and I haven't the slightest fucking idea how.

My eyes open wider as I follow a soft, lemon scent to my right and find an unconscious Onyx.

A deep ache radiates across my chest as I rake over her frame for injuries. Her dark locks are loosely held in place, remnants of debris sticking out in various places. Besides what appear to be superficial cuts and a small bruise forming on her jaw, she seems to be fine.

Still, the visual of her like this boils my insides. My veins physically hurt with every pulse of my racing heart.

How I've let every woman in my life down, despite how hard I try to protect them, is a rip in my soul. A visceral wound so profound, I know I won't survive it if I don't find a way to make it right.

"Tell me, son, how was she in bed?" Phineas' voice doesn't jar me, nor deter my eyes from Onyx, but it does spark new anger in my chest.

He speaks in his Gaelic tongue, which tells me he doesn't want the driver, nor the guard in the passenger seat, to overhear our conversation.

I don't answer him immediately. My rage is too thick to hide, and I don't need to give him any more leverage over me than he already has. Instead, I let my gaze drift from her and to the guard occupying the passenger seat.

"Is that who hit me?" I say in English, and watch as the man stiffens, making the mistake of peering over his shoulder.

"Don't take your anger out on the boy. He was just doing his job. Something *you* were supposed to be doing before you let a piece of ass get in the way." Phineas tucks his phone in his pocket and rests his ankle on the opposite knee. "I'm not surprised you fucked her. Hell, I thought it would be a good idea. But I didn't think you'd prolong your poor sister's stay with me."

Fiona.

Fuck. Before I went downstairs, I had made arrangements with Sam. I told him to return Fiona to our house, and I'd give him what he wanted. He only agreed to my terms on the condition that a guard would go with her.

Oliver sent one that wasn't a friend but also not a complete fucking scumbag who would rape her if given the chance.

But with everything that's happened, I don't know if she's still there.

"She's still at your house. I have no use for her currently and constantly having to watch my men drool over a chance to fuck her was becoming a nuisance."

The sharp bite of my nails in my palms is a fairly good indicator of how little his words calm me.

My eyes flash to Onyx and I entertain the need to speak in Gaelic. "Where are we going?"

Phineas guffaws. "Why should I trust you? You've done nothing for months to indicate as such."

"Blueprints, guard numbers, locations. That—"

"Bread crumbs, boy. You gave me just enough to satiate me. To make me think you were doing your job. But I'm not stupid. You were stalling. Biding your time until you figured a way to save them all. That's your MO, after all. Saving pathetic, weak women."

"Onyx doesn't need to be saved. Nor was I giving you bread crumbs." Anger swells in my chest and though I attempt to keep my voice level, the deep drop in my timbre betrays me. "I was going to give Sam the access codes to the estate gates, as well as the security system, once I knew Fiona was out of your reach."

This makes Phineas grin, and my stomach curdles. "She, nor you, will ever be out of my reach. You'll do well to remember that. Especially after obtaining this freedom you begged to have."

I clamp my jaw shut, ignoring the pain of my molars smashing together. If I hadn't entertained the thought of killing this man before, it's all I want to do now. It'd be such an easy feat to overthrow him and burn his legacy to the ground. I'd reign over the ashes and be king of the ruins.

"Let me explain how you will redeem yourself and earn what you seek." Phineas clears his throat and nods to Onyx. "Since you've been fucking her, I'm sure it will be easier for you to keep her in line. Keep her complacent and docile until everything is done."

"This woman doesn't know what complacency is. She will wake up and kill half your men within the first five minutes." I hear how proud I am saying that, and, in the moment, I don't care if he hears it too.

"Yes, I figured as much. We'll starve her for a bit. Weaken her. You'll be the one to move her, should the time arise. Hopefully, the paperwork will be done before the end of the week, and I will be rid of her and that entire family once and for all."

"Paperwork?"

He nods, slipping his phone from his pocket once more. "She'll sign over everything to me."

"She won't sign anything."

Phineas eyes me for a moment, tilting his head in thought as he passes a look from me to her and back again. "I need you to find a way to make her trust you again. Tell her the sob story about not having a choice and you did it to save your sister. Make her feel bad for you. Then, I don't care how you do it, but convince her to sign ownership over."

"How in the hell do you propose I do that?"

He shrugs. "I don't know. Fuck her some more? Tell her you'll kill me. There's no limit to how many things you can hold over a person, so I don't really care. That's your mistake to fix. You figure it out. And once you do, an obscene amount of money is yours. Then you and your little family can flee. For the time being."

He's such an idiotic man. Money, one of the many things *he's* held over my head, would guarantee he'd never see us again.

Once the cash is pulled, new identities can be assigned. There will be no trail of our existence, and no way he could ever get to us. I know because I made sure no matter what, Fiona and my mother would be able to escape even if I didn't make it out alive.

Still, I entertain his foolishness. "And the point of letting us escape if you plan to haul me right back here?"

"I may not. Who's to say? But be grateful I don't just kill you." Phineas sits back and gives his full attention to his phone, not knowing he's made the funniest joke I've ever heard.

The rest of the time, I watch Onyx sleep and begin formulating my next steps. There are so many loose ends, and not enough time, but one thing I know for certain is this woman will not lose.

Yesterday

THE TRUTH

In all the books I've read, I always try to figure out the mystery before it's revealed. Try to solve how the protagonist will overcome the monster, killer, or ghost that plagues them.

In each one, they all had to overcome their own obstacles before they could actually do anything. It was a necessity, or else, whenever they tried to do something, they were reckless and ended up putting themselves in a worse situation.

Though I only read it in fiction, I connected with the need to overcome my inner demons. I hated the Mafia. I hated what they stood for. What they did and didn't do, and how they were able to rest peacefully at night while people suffered at their hands. My deep-seated hatred for both that and my father made me blind to anything else.

I developed preconceived notions about everything. Men needed to protect women. The Mafia only cared about money and destruction. Those addicted to drugs would find it impossible to start over.

Then I met Onyx and her family and realized just how wrong I was.

Women don't need to be saved. They are more than capable of doing it themselves. It's men's responsibility to not put them in harm's way to begin with.

While the Mafia as an entity, is morally corrupt, so is any form of government. The only difference is, you see the mob in its raw, bloody form, while politicians go the extra mile to hide behind the facade of whitened teeth and a patriotic pin on their lapels. Not only that, but Onyx has shown me how the mob is capable of both saving and giving back to the community just as much as they deal in weapons and run casinos.

My mother was the dimming light that convinced me that people would rather give up, than start over. But Trick and Trigger, along with the women at Hearts, showed me that no one is the same. Every survivor is different and has a path unique to them. Rehabilitation is possible for those that want it, and even more so for those who have others that will stay by their side through all the hard work required.

All I've known is hate, lies, greed, and hell.

But now I want to feel salvation. I want to see the rivers run red as my redemption leaks from the head of my father. I want to watch the blood turn cold as the lifelong tyrant who has reigned over my existence for far too long, takes his last breath.

My journey has taken a turn, and no longer will I seek freedom. Now, I will have what was always meant to be mine, sitting idle as it waits to be claimed.

There is only one thing left to do before I ensure everything comes to pass.

When I enter my father's office, he and Sam are relaxed at his desk, sipping dark liquid from a glass. It's a celebratory drink and a premature one at that.

They turn in tandem and gaze at me before Phineas raises his glass. "To the son who has finally decided to become a man."

Sam's smile is forced, the edges of his lips twitching as he fights to keep them curved. "I'm looking forward to seeing how you prove yourself over the Embros army."

I don't acknowledge his comment and instead, look at Phineas. He downs the rest of his drink before wiping the dribble on his chin with the back of his hand. "I've thought long and hard about your proposal. With the amount of money I'll make from having the ports open, I've decided to grant you a year's time to make the integration complete."

Sam sucks his teeth and takes back his drink. "I told him that was a mighty *generous* offer."

Again, I don't trouble myself with forming a response. I came here for one thing. The thing that has plagued my mind since I heard it. I tried to put the idea to rest. Told myself it was the ramblings of a drunk, emotionally drained mother. I hoped it was a story she created to deal with her grief, her loss. And with Oliver telling me he never saw anyone that fit the description of what I assumed Bunny would look like, I buried the thought.

But seeing that girl outside. There was something about

her. Her eyes aren't green like me and Fi's. Her hair isn't nearly as dark either. But I know siblings don't always look alike. I know the girl can't be a day over eighteen, which puts her at about the right age. Her height and frame are similar to my mother's as well.

I didn't see her much when I was at Embros' estate, and I never thought to make the connection before. But now, having spent the time to truly look at her, combined with the fact she works for him, I know. And it's time I rid myself of this last piece of selfishness and take responsibility for not trying to save her.

I swallow the lump that's formed in my throat and push out the words. "That girl. The one I just caught when Onyx kicked her. Who is she?"

Sam laughs out loud, and this time I don't ignore him. I put all my weight behind my punch, hitting him square in the jaw and knocking him off of his upholstered seat. He hits the wooden floor with a loud *thwack* and the sound loosens some of my apprehension.

"Jesus Christ. This feud between you two is getting rather tiresome, don't you think?" Phineas slams his newly filled glass on his desk, his brows furrowing as he watches Sam scramble to his feet.

"Your second-in-command needs to show a bit of respect."

"How about you do something to earn it? All you've ever been is his errand boy and punching bag." Sam steadies himself, one hand on the desk while the other rubs his jaw. A deep red creeps up his neck and spreads across his bald head.

"Sounds like you and I are the same then." I draw my gun, aiming it directly at his throat. He talks so much shit, I'd enjoy watching him choke on his own blood.

"You're taking your anger out on him, boy. Put that gun

down before you end up owing me a debt even your sisters' cunts can't repay."

My face snaps to him, fury burning bright through my limbs. I'm shaking, I can feel it—trembling as I soak in his plural use of the word. "My mother never had a stillborn."

It's not a question but Phineas answers anyway, "I've said it before. You can never have enough leverage. And your mother threatened to take you away too many times. Keeping her broke didn't matter. I knew getting her hooked on a few drugs might not do it. I needed something stronger. I realized I could have two surprise elements that Embros had no idea about, should I ever need to use them."

His words swirl in my gut, and I feel it the moment nausea turns into something more. I have to force it down twice as I work through all the times I was angry with my mother for forcing me to do her job. To raise Fi and pay the bills when she could no longer leave the house. Really she was fighting this man all by herself, doing her best to keep us all alive.

"What did you use to threaten Harlow to give you everything?"

Sam smirks, and I consider pulling the trigger more than I ever have. "Pretty obvious, is it not?"

Fiona told me our mother was safe at Embros Hearts, but Harlow wouldn't know that. She was in the same boat as me, just trying to save her family. My eyes flash to Phineas as I put my gun down. "Where is Harlow now?"

This makes Phineas visibly upset. His brows draw down and his face blooms pink. "Gone. On the run. But I'll find her right after I deal with Onyx. Priorities, you know?"

And just like that, Phineas has sealed his fate. None of the women I set out to protect are within his grasp, which leaves him open to everything I have planned.

Sam pours them both new glasses before sitting back down,

a grimace now decorating his face. "If you're done with this family quarrel, we have a contract to go over."

Phineas eyes me carefully before nodding. "Women are poisonous. They will kill you and do it slowly if you aren't mindful, son. Remember that the next time you fall into one."

I nod to my father's drink before turning to leave. "As is a bottle of good whiskey."

CHAPTER TWENTY-FIVE

I had to force myself to sleep after Kane left, and since I've been awake, it's been torture. I've spent nearly the entire day with the images of what transpired between us, playing on repeat, while also thinking of his plan and all the ways it could go wrong. It's somehow simple, yet convoluted, and I'm almost certain it won't work out how he envisions it.

But no matter what I try to convince myself, I trust him. Trust that he means well and by giving me his father, he will forfeit any chance of freedom he longed for. He will be forced to rule over a family he never wanted and will need to convince his army to change their practices or suffer the same fate as Phineas.

As much as I want to, I can't foresee the former happening as much as the latter.

The Murphy family has been allowed to poison their people for too long. They have ingrained the idea of what is acceptable and it will take too much work to purge them of it. They will rebel. Riot. Kill.

I give credit where it's due, but I believe Kane will be in over his head. He won't be able to change it all, and in turn, he'll let some of their practices continue. As long as the trafficking stops though, I'll find contentment because honestly, I don't *want* to kill him.

The irony of this entire thing is that Kane, my enemy, has grown on me. Not just the idea of peace he brought me when I first met him, but something different—something deeper—has taken root.

I thought I rid myself of the seed he implanted in my chest but it turns out, it has already begun to grow, burying itself into places I can't reach. And its ability to thrive in complete darkness is both astounding and alluring.

For the first time since my parents' demise, he makes me wish for the impossible. Makes me long for the prospect of him and I being something after this. That somehow, we could combine the families under one umbrella and I would finally see what life is like after vengeance.

After I know peace.

The small tuft of brown fur unfurls from her tight ball and stretches along the length of my thigh. The cat's small mouth opens as wide as it can as she yawns, and I stare in slight fascination at the tiny little blade-like shapes on her tongue. I've always been intrigued by how they look like hundreds of micro claws.

I scratch behind the feline's right ear, to which she grants me a vibrating purr of approval. This makes me smirk. "Even though we've had our quarrels, you're not so bad. A warm bed and a little scratch in the right place and you've turned into quite the docile animal."

As soon as I say it, I laugh out loud. Kane brought me from the cold cement floor to this room, then scratched me in all the right places. And look what I've become.

Still, if I were to make the wrong move, I have no doubt in my mind that she would try to kill me.

I hope Kane knows to expect nothing less from me as well.

A quick rap on the door draws both of our attention. Kane opens it slowly, his eyes flashing to me on his bed. The quick curl of his lips makes mine do the same and for a moment, I forget the trepidation rolling in my stomach.

But the moment Kane nods to someone I can't see, it returns, forcing me to my feet. He accepts a bundle of clothes from the person and slides inside, closing the door behind him.

He's dressed in a black fitted suit, his face shaven and his hair freshly cut. The once angry red mark slicing through his brow has begun to heal, and I can't deny the slight appeal it adds to his already handsome face.

"Are you ready?" Kane holds out the clothes to me, and leans in, pressing a soft kiss to my mouth.

It almost feels natural for him to greet me this way, and I have to actively stamp out the wave of tingles that shoot through me.

I nod. "More than ready. Is my family here?"

"They are. West side, just inside the woods, waiting for my call. There's still about a half hour until I'm supposed to bring you down."

"The contract?"

"Everything goes to me, not Phineas."

My heart thrums hard in my chest. This is where I have to truly trust him. Two weeks ago, I would have assumed this was a ploy to make it easier for me to sign things over, but now? I believe Kane wants this to end. I believe he hates his father, if not equally, more than I do, and wants to see him and his vile men dead. So for now, I'm trusting him.

Accepting the clothes from his hands, I dress quickly. I slip off the shirt and put on the matching set of lace underwear. When popping off the tags to the brand-new black slacks and button-down, I grin to myself. They fit like a glove.

"Know my size, do you, Kane?"

He smirks and holds up a pair of black heels. "I do."

I bite the inside of my cheek to keep from smiling and slide the shoes on. Again, they fit perfectly.

Kane watches in silence as I retwist my hair into a tight bun, his eyes raking over my body in a way that makes my core tighten. When I'm done, he releases a heavy sigh.

"Considering I could die today, I'm kind of wishing you gave in and begged a little last night. I would have taken just one 'please'. Even a whispered one."

This time I can't hamper the huge smile that spreads across my face. "You won't die today."

I realize after I say it, just how much I mean it. When Kane dies, it will either be from the reaper coming to collect an old man or a bullet from me. No one else.

He grabs my chin with his thumb and forefinger. The flicker of heat that was brewing earlier is now a rush of fire, my desire for both him and the finality of today waging war in my chest.

His brows furrow as he attempts to read whatever's being displayed on my face and for the first time, I let him. I want him to know how I feel. How he *makes* me feel.

"I need you to know something," his voice is rough. "I need you to understand how much I want this to make it."

"This," I whisper, tilting my chin up and brushing my lips against his. "Is impossible."

Using his free hand, he grasps mine and brings it up to his chest. It's where his tattoo of a tree and the script is. "Why can't it be? We would be something incredible."

I swallow around the surge of dread swelling in my throat. It's the first time one of us has acknowledged what brews between us, and knowing it can't be, even though we want it to, is torment.

"I'm going to kill your father."

The crease between his brows grows more profound. "He deserves the fate coming to him."

"We are enemies."

"By whose standard?"

This gives me pause. He is the son of the man who ordered my family to be killed. Who tried to kill me. The man who's killed and hurt hundreds of women—

"I am not my father." Kane releases my face and grabs me by the hips, yanking me flush against him.

I press my hands into his chest, a surge of emotions swelling in my chest making it harder to breathe.

"This would never work."

"We could make it work."

"Why are you doing this, Kane?" I snap, heat rising up my neck.

"Because I want you." He bites, gripping me tighter. "I want your smart mind and keen sense of humor. I want your fight and dominance. I want to be there when you realize you're just as strong without the shield you carry around. I—"

Kane slams his mouth against mine so hard that I have to grip his shoulders to keep my balance. His hands wrap around my waist, somehow drawing me closer, and with my mind reeling from what he's confessed, I allow him to take control.

He kisses me with a passion I've never experienced before. It's raw, angry, and desperate. It's filled with words and promises, riddled with apologies and secrets we've yet to tell. It's everything I didn't know I was capable of, but everything I want.

Regaining balance, I kiss him back with just as much fervor, my nails digging through his jacket and finding purchase. He hisses into my mouth before clamping onto my bottom lip. I gasp and Kane takes full advantage, sliding his tongue over the tender flesh and into my mouth.

He leads the kiss, but I push my mouth harder against his, shoving his jacket from his shoulders before locking my fingers into his thick hair. My blood surges into my ear, the whooshing sound making my head dizzy.

I turn us and shove him against the wall. My pussy clenches around nothing when he grunts, his eyes flaring before he reclaims my mouth. It's somehow needier now, the lust taking complete control of both of us.

His hands snake up my sides and while one finds the middle of my back, the other finds my throat. He squeezes both in tandem before pushing me back and turning us around so that it's my spine that connects with the wall.

"Tell me." Kane runs his nose along the column of my neck before capturing my ear between his teeth. "What does my precious little whore want me to do to her?"

His words swirl low in my stomach before settling between my thighs. My body is on fire with need, the desire to feel him too great for me to care when I utter what we both want, "I want you to fuck me as if this is our last time."

He draws back far enough to look me in my eyes. A nerve in his jaw tics and I see it the moment he wants to say something, but I stop him with a hard, drawn-out kiss. This time when we break apart, we're both panting. His erection digs into my thigh, while my nipples are so hard, they ache.

"*Please,* Kane." It's barely above a whisper, but it's good enough for him.

A grin spreads over his face, his gaze becoming hooded with promise. "As you wish."

After that, it becomes a fight over who can tear off whose clothes first, our fingers grabbing at anything and tugging each other free.

Our chests heave as the last bit of clothes is shed, and he grabs me around the waist before tossing me on the bed. I suppress a giggle as the small cat bounces from the bed and disappears into the bathroom.

Kane stands near the end of the bed, his hand loosely wrapped around his dick. He strokes it lazily as his gaze roves over me. It burns a path along my skin as he takes in every curve and dimple. It's intoxicating the way he's soaking me in, almost as though he's memorizing every part of me.

My breath hitches when he comes to a stop, his eyes trained on where I want him most. He runs his tongue along his bottom lip before smirking. "We have time."

He drops down, grabbing around my thighs and yanking me to the end of the bed. His fingers dig into my flesh as he takes a deep inhale, and the groan that comes out of his mouth makes my insides quiver. "This is *mine,* Onyx. Even after this. If any man dares to come close to you, they're dead."

The arousal that shoots up my core at his words pales the moment Kane's mouth is on my cunt.

He completely devours me, sliding his tongue down and in, before focusing only on my throbbing clit. I buck beneath him, the sudden pressure and feel of him almost too overwhelming.

His fingers grip me tighter, the promise of a bruise lingering under his fingertips. I thread my fingers through his hair and jerk his face back. "I told you to fuck me, Kane."

Before I realize what's happened, a pop rings out, followed by a sharp pain radiating over my slit, where he slapped me. "I like it when you're needy."

My nostrils flare but Kane ignores my death stare. Instead, he sits down next to me and yanks me on top of him. I barely have my hands on his shoulder before his cock impales me, driving so deep I bite into the curve of his neck to keep from calling out.

Kane shakes me off as he lifts my hips and slams me back

down. "Absolutely not, *mo bhanríon,* I want everyone to hear me fucking you. They need to know the ghost belongs to *me.*"

He grips me by the throat again and presses me backward. His other hand steadies my waist as he guides me up and down. The angle grants him a full view of my body while allowing me to see him sliding in and out of me.

"Attagirl. Take all of me."

My head falls back as I bounce, my hands holding on to his knees to help me meet his thrust head-on. The pressure is already building, the tingles beginning to form as he drives into me again and again. He tightens his hand around my neck, thrusting up so hard, my head becomes dizzy.

His grunts mingle with my moans as sweat drips down the valley of my breasts. Kane leans in, drawing me back upright as he licks up the wetness and then circles around one nipple.

I latch around his neck, pushing my breast farther into his mouth. He bites down forcing a cry to slip past my lips. This makes him chuckle before his arms wrap around my back and he lifts me completely off of him.

My pussy aches at the loss. "Kane."

It's meant to be a warning but does the opposite of what I intend and he smiles. "Miss me already?"

"I miss that muscle between your legs."

He guffaws. "Good."

As quickly as he plucked me from his body, he flips me over. He yanks me toward him by my hips and hoists my ass in the air, forcing me to my knees. My fingers dig into the sheets as I arch my back, my nerves vibrating with anticipation.

He grabs a nearby pillow and shoves it beneath my waist, all the while his other calloused hand rubs along my outer thigh until his fingers sink into the flesh of my ass.

I moan when he lines his head up with my entrance, probing it so teasingly I almost whimper.

"You know what I think, Boss?"

Before I can make a remark, he rams into me hard, and I scream out, pressing my hands into the mattress to push myself back up.

Kane helps me, the hand not holding my hips yanking my bun down. He wraps my hair around his hand and pulls, forcing my head up. The pain is delicious, mixed with the fullness of his cock filling me to the hilt.

He drags himself out slowly. "I think that there's no way this pussy wasn't *made* for me."

He slams back in, this time keeping me in place briefly before pulling out. "I think *you* were made for me."

My body convulses around his words, and the heat begins to unfurl in my core. As though he can sense my nearing orgasm, he picks up his tempo, fucking me relentlessly. Each time his hips meet mine, it sends a vibration straight through to my throbbing clit.

I snake one hand down to relieve the mounting pressure, but just as I reach between my thighs, Kane releases my hair and forces me down. I start to use my arms to lift myself back up, but then I feel it. The new position allows him to drive into a spot that nearly takes my breath away.

My moans grow into needy whimpers and soon I'm biting into sheets to keep from screaming out.

"That's it, Boss. Come for me, just like this. Then I'll take care of that greedy little clit."

It only takes him slamming into me a few more times before the orgasm rips through me. It's a tidal wave of tingles and heat that seizes every muscle and charges every nerve. He continues to fuck me through each contraction, and when he comes, I'm still pulsing around him.

Spent, Kane collapses next to me, his chest heaving up and down, sweat dripping down his temple. My hand itches with the need to push back the hair that's fallen over his forehead, but it feels so intimate that I stop myself.

This is our last time together.

The thought sits heavy in my stomach and at the same moment as if he can read the internal struggle on my face, Kane strokes a finger along the length of my jaw. My eyes close of their own accord and I lean into his touch. After another breath, I prop my weight on my elbow and reach out. He watches quietly as I lift my hand and move toward him, threading my fingers through his thick hair, and pushing it back into place.

Both of his dimples make an appearance as he gives me a boyish grin, and even I can't resist mirroring his smile. The green in his eyes seems to shine even in the dim room as his eyes rake over my face.

"When you smile—"

I lower my gaze. "Don't."

"Don't what?"

"Ruin this moment by saying I should smile more."

He blows air from his nose and grips my chin to look at him. "I like that you don't smile."

My brows furrow and he grins.

"I love how reserved you are. How most think you're quiet, but really you're observant—reading everybody in the room, knowing their next move the moment they make it. You categorize everything, think with a sound mind, and always plan meticulously. You save your emotions. And when I get you mad or make you smile, it's an achievement I know I've truly earned."

I ignore my heart thrumming in my chest and the ache settling between my thighs. "So you enjoy frustrating me?"

"A little. But my favorite—" He drops his hands and traces idle lines down to my nipples. Goose bumps sprout over my exposed flesh as I watch him work his way past my waist and over my hips. "Is making you unravel."

I smirk and enjoy the way his eyes move to my mouth. "Speaking of which, clean up your mess."

"I don't know. I rather like knowing you'll be walking around with my cum dripping down your thigh."

I lift a brow and he chuckles. It's deep and throaty, traveling straight into my core. I wasn't aware just how much I liked such minuscule things about him, but I do. Before I considered him my temporary peace. A break from the internal chaos. Slowly, though, things have changed. Morphed into something deeper.

It makes me wish we didn't have to end when everything else does. That somehow we could both make it through this and find each other on the other side.

"Stay with me. Right here. Just for a little longer."

"Kane," I breathe, suddenly feeling the burn radiate across my chest. It's a familiar ache and I understand what it is almost immediately.

It's loss.

I know I'll lose him in my need for vengeance. I'll lose hope for what comes after I find justice.

And there's nothing either of us can do to change that because while I didn't start this feud, I *will* finish it.

"Hey, look at me," Kane's husky voice draws my attention.

He presses against one side of my hip, coaxing me to my back, before moving on top of me. He kisses my lips gently before peppering more across my jaw and down the column of my neck.

I ignore the rising heat and make a fairly weak attempt to push him off. "What are you doing?"

He's at my breast now, adding small bites as he works his

way to my nipples. I arch into him when his warm mouth sucks one into his mouth, my heady moans fill the air.

"Kane."

He releases my breast and continues on his path down. "You told me to clean you up."

"With a towel. We have places to be. Men to kill."

He chuckles, the vibration so close to my clit I whimper. "My watch says they aren't expecting us for another ten minutes. Didn't you say to fuck you like this is our last time? That includes kissing this delicious cunt of yours goodbye, too."

Something in my chest cracks, but he doesn't allow me to feel it for long because his tongue glides over my slit.

A sharp hiss escapes from my clenched teeth as he does it again, running the flat of his tongue over my pussy as though he's licking the melting side of a popsicle.

My clit throbs, the nerves fraying from the lack of friction. "*Up*, Kane."

"*Hmmm*. Is that desperation I hear?"

I buck beneath him. "If you'd like to watch me do the job myself again, all you needed to do was ask."

A sharp pain shoots up my cunt and all my muscles squeeze in tandem. He just bit me.

"Close that fucking mouth of yours and let me enjoy my last meal."

My heart squeezes, but I nod, allowing my head to fall back. "Speak to me like that again, and I slice that tongue from *your* mouth."

I feel him smile against me. "Yes, ma'am."

Then he consumes me.

His mouth works over my clit with a ferocity I've never felt before. It's urgent and hungry, and full of need. The desperation Kane spoke of earlier is evident in the way he licks me, and all too soon my mind is spinning from dizziness.

His fingers dig into the flesh of my thighs as he spreads me wider, focusing solely on my nerves.

I grab onto the sheets, tearing them closer to me as Kane's tongue flicks over my clit faster than I thought possible. The orgasm builds quickly, and while part of me wants to combust, the other wants to prolong this moment, to drag it out until the very last second.

My walls clench around nothing while heat expands until my legs begin to quiver. This only fuels Kane's torturous pace. "Kane, I—"

He tightens his grasp, the hold now painfully tight. I release the sheets with one hand and grab hold of his hair, yanking him into me harder.

He fights my grip, pulling his head back slightly, and my eyes instinctively snap toward his. The deep hues of green with the embedded flecks of gold threaten to steal my breath as they tempt me to dive into them. From the tips of my hair to the soles of my feet. I feel *him*—his presence, his dominance—everything, everywhere. And I realize just how badly I'll miss this.

Miss *him*.

Tears burn the delicate flesh of my lids as I lose my grip and collapse backward. Another few passes and I combust, everything exploding in my center and sending electricity outward. The orgasm rips through me all while he continues to suck my tender clit in his mouth.

Shock waves ripple through me until I'm nearly shaking, and it's only then that Kane lifts his head. He eyes me for a minute in silence, both of us breathing too hard to say anything, but we don't need to. The look of somberness passes over as reality settles in.

It's him who finally breaks eye contact and stands, running his thumb along his bottom lip. "We taste *so* fucking good together."

I bite into the inside of my cheek. "Is that so?"

"It is." He nods slowly, drawing his lip between his teeth. "And I think you're all clean now, Boss."

This garners a small curve of one side of my lips. "I'd have to agree."

He holds a hand out to help me stand. "Did Onyx Embros just agree with me on something?"

I roll my eyes as I hurry with retying my hair. "Spare me the semantics."

He opens his mouth but is cut off by a knock at the door and a muffled voice coming through the cracks. "Five minutes, mate."

Kane doesn't respond but instead grabs me by my waist and draws me to him. He presses a soft kiss to my nose before brushing a stray hair back into my bun. "Whatever happens down there, I need you to know something. No matter how we came to be, you made this life worth it."

I swallow around the sudden lump lodged in my throat and nod. "As did you, Kane."

He smiles and delivers a sharp slap on my ass. "Now let's go make a mess."

CHAPTER TWENTY-SIX

By the time we're both dressed and suitable to leave, the butterflies and euphoria of our last moments together have faded into the background. In their place, adrenaline moves in, thrumming through my chest and tightening every muscle.

I've waited ten years for this. The moment I destroy the man who ordered my parents' death but was too cowardly to pull the trigger himself. The things I'm going to do to him will pale in comparison to every other scum I've had the pleasure of killing.

Phineas's death will be long and excruciating. It will take days and only end when his head rolls on the floor while his heart takes its last beat in my hand.

And then there's Sam.

The executor.

He's the one responsible for taking them away, stripping me of loving parents, and dousing me in rage. He robbed me of sunny days and replaced them with cloudy skies.

He stole my peace and filled me with screams.

I almost didn't make it, and for that, his debt will be great.

So much so, I'm not even sure his flesh, bones, and every drop of his blood will be enough to pay for it.

Kane opens the door to three guards standing idly in the hall. All of them are without the gold-chained brooch on their lapels, indicating they all side with Kane. The one with wild red curls turns and a burn flickers behind my rib cage.

I miss Maddy. My *family*.

"Good evening Ms. Embros. Nice to meet ya." He beams, displaying a full set of bright-white teeth.

I give him a curt nod in return.

Kane smirks, holding his hand out to the redhead who gives him a pair of cuffs. My eyes narrow and my hackles rise, automatically triggering my fight reflex. A quick look at the men and I begin calculating how quick I could kill each one.

He isn't going to hurt you.

I quell my doubt and hold out my wrists, allowing him to attach the cuffs. The cold metal is jarring against his warm hands, and I tense beneath him.

Kane lowers his head as he snaps the first one closed. "I've got you, *mo bhanríon*."

Again, I nod, even though letting him restrain me makes my nerves vibrate with trepidation. After he closes the other cuff, he lowers my hands gently, brushing his thumb along my wrist.

The touch is soft and timid. It feels like a goodbye. Like it's the last time we'll ever touch one another. The way that thought makes my stomach churn is too unsettling to mull over.

Two of the men gather behind me while Kane and the red-haired man stand on either side of me. We walk in silence the opposite way I came upon my arrival, and at the very end of the hall, there's a small elevator. Kane presses the button and it opens immediately, revealing an empty cabin.

It's too small for all of us, and when I move to take a step inside, Kane tugs lightly on my elbow. "Only three at a time. We'll let them go, then us."

I nod and step back, watching as the guards who were behind me file inside and the doors slide shut. After the soft whoosh of the elevator indicates it's begun its descent, the red-haired man speaks. "Everyone's in place."

"Thank you, Oliver."

He beams. "It's my pleasure. I've been waiting for this day for a long time." He turns to me. "Guess I should thank you for changing his mind, lass."

My brows pinch together for a moment and he must realize I'm unsure of what he means because his eyes shift nervously to Kane. "I'm sorry. Did I misspeak?"

Kane shakes his head. "No, it's alright."

"What does he mean?" I ask.

He presses the button on the wall again before looking at me. "My original plan was to leave. Get my sister and mom and get the hell out of here."

That much I already knew. "And now?"

"I didn't want to leave you with the fallout of what we're doing. And I didn't want more people to die than needed to." His gaze drops for a moment before flashing back up to me. There's a profound sadness in them now, riddled with guilt. "I owe it to the women I couldn't save to make it right. To those women at Hearts."

He runs his thumb along my jaw. "To you."

It's almost too hard to ignore the simultaneous lightness in my chest and the heaviness in my stomach. This man has found a way to both wreak chaos on my nervous system while quelling my inner storm.

I used to think I wanted him for the peace he brought, but now, with my endgame so near, I wonder if I'll just long for *him*.

Clearing my throat, I rid myself of the emotion trying to clog it. “So you’ll take over the family?”

Again, it’s something I assumed but hadn’t asked outright. Perhaps because I still held out hope—for what, I’m not certain—but there was a piece of me that wanted to believe the impossible.

“Yes. I don’t want the wrong person to try and step up. It could put more people at risk.”

“I see. And will you keep running the same businesses as your father?”

A nerve in Kane’s jaw pulses. “I understand your need for assurance, so I’ll be forthright. No. Things will change.”

An air of that earlier hope moves in. “Which includes?”

He smirks, his dimple making a brief appearance. “Whatever helps me keep you the longest.”

Oliver chuckles, clapping Kane on his shoulder. “Never met a more murderous Romeo in my life. He’s like a giant teddy bear that wields a knife.”

“Or a gun,” I agree.

Kane shakes his head, the corners of his lips twitching with a smile. “I hope you both consider me the same after this evening.”

A thick silence moves over us as we wait for the elevator to reappear, a renewed focus on what’s about to happen.

I don’t get nervous, nor worried, but with so much out of my control, I need to be particularly cautious—observant.

We file into the small elevator and ride it the short way down to the bottom floor. When the doors slide open, the guards who were with us upstairs, retake their positions behind me when we step out into the back of a long hallway.

The clatter of nearby pans and muffled curses of a frustrated chef indicate we’re near the kitchen. My chest burns.

Don’t think of them. Focus.

I inhale a deep breath and push the images of Russ and Cat from my mind. I'll see them soon, and when I do, I'll have the two men we've all wanted for a decade in my hands.

We enter the foyer, which is riddled with soldiers, most of which are wearing the chain and brooch, which means I'll be killing them soon. I take in each one as we stride across the foyer.

There are some with sneers, others with confident smiles, and some that seem as if they couldn't care less. None appear to have more than two guns, and about a dozen of the men have them in fastened holsters. Easy targets since they'll be the slowest to draw their weapons.

My eyes scan over the twenty men, and I notice Sam is nowhere to be found. Kane told me he'd be in the lobby to stand over these men, and the fact he isn't present makes me more cautious.

He's not lying to you.

I take a breath, and as if Kane knows exactly what I'm thinking, he gazes over at Oliver. They exchange a brief look, and Oliver nods. "I'll make sure he's around."

The muscles in my neck unwind a fraction as we turn down a hall and stop at two doors. A man with a long, dark braid stands near the door. He greets Kane, and a quick glance at his lapel tells me he's working with him.

I'm ushered inside the space, which is nothing more than a typical boardroom. A long oak table sits in the middle, surrounded by black leather chairs. Like mine, it seats twelve, accommodating the department heads, and any guests. Tonight, however, only one person sits at the far end of the table.

Like others have heard about me, I've heard of him. Only now that I'm seeing him in person, I don't think the rumors did him justice.

Lucian Hyun.

On paper, he was an everyday lawyer that handled business affairs. Over the past two years though, he's changed gears and is now an up-and-coming prosecutor in the east, with a winning record that seems improbable. He's in the news quite often, usually for putting away another drug dealer or arms trader, and the threats that follow behind him are growing.

Only those that make the threats often wind up in the Savannah River.

My assumption was because in the shadows, he works for Alexi Babin. A notoriously vicious don running the entire state of South Carolina. But now, as I walk to the seat across from him, I know exactly how all those men have found their footing at the bottom of the river.

He stands as Kane pulls out my chair, putting his hands behind his back while nodding a solemn hello. When I sit, he does as well, allowing me a moment to observe him while the others take their places.

The air around Lucian is unlike any other I've ever encountered. It's calm and collected while also feeling incredibly dangerous. A quick look at his surface will show just a handsome man in a navy suit, with a layer of stubble on his sharp jaw and a professional haircut. But someone like me—someone who has killed as much as she's saved—knows that he will never be able to wash off all the blood that stains his hands.

My eyes flit to Lucian's fingers as he drums lightly on the table. It's a light thrum as the pads hit the wood, but it's the flash of silver that catches my eye.

It's a coin of sorts, a little larger than a half-dollar, and his ability to wind it through his fingers as if it's merely an extension of him is impressive. My eyes follow the path and it isn't until the door behind him opens that I glance up.

His dark eyes meet mine briefly before he beguiles me with an inquisitive expression.

For the first time since my capture, I feel as if I've met a match. Should Lucian be overseeing the transfer of power because he works *with* Phineas, he'll be the first we need to kill, or he'll kill us.

Fortunately enough, I don't have to worry for long before Phineas and a few others enter, and everything else in the room no longer matters.

My heart rate increases, fluttering in my chest so quickly, it's nearly vibrating. My spine straightens, my muscles tense, and a giddiness I've never known bubbles to the surface.

This is it. I'm so close now I can almost taste the sweetness of my vengeance.

A quick assessment of the other soon-to-be-dead bodies in the room and I have to bite into my cheek from laughing.

I'm unsure if it's because Phineas is that blind, or perhaps that arrogant, but he's only accompanied by three guards and a man in an ill-fitting suit. My guess is that he deals with Phineas's money.

Phineas takes a seat at the head of the table, a wide smile planted on his face. I wonder briefly if I should glue his lips in the same expression after I rip his head from his shoulders.

"I'm so glad you could finally make it, Lucian. I nearly considered telling Alexi I'd use my favor for something else." Phineas chuckles.

"Yes, well, I'm sure he would have told you that his business comes before yours, and that patience is a virtue." Lucian breaks his gaze on me and opens his file. "After he ripped your tongue out, of course."

A delicious shiver runs down my spine. Not only because I no longer have to worry about this man being a problem in ten minutes, but the professional dialect in which he delivered his threat.

Phineas purses his lips before chewing on them. He wants to make a remark but must know better because he merely shakes it off with a guffaw. "That Alexi is something else, alright. Now, on to business."

Lucian stands, unclipping a pen from his jacket pocket and slipping it into one of my cuffed hands. "There are a few different contracts here you'll need to sign. I'll explain each one in detail if need be and answer any questions you may have." His eyes flash to my restraints. "Or if it's easier, I can just point where to sign. The first few are standard real estate contracts, the next are assets, and the last one is forfeiture of your array of businesses. Are you ready?"

I nod. "Yes."

Lucian gives his own nod in return before pushing forward the first paper. While he explains the document, I survey my periphery. Phineas is on his phone, no doubt sending a celebratory text, while his accountant types furiously on his computer. Every few seconds, he checks something with his phone's calculator before shaking his head and doing it again. The few guards that entered with Phineas are like statues, their gazes pinned on Lucian's back as if they too feel the unseen power radiating off him.

Kane remains silent next to me, rubbing his thumb and forefinger together in small circles.

"Alright, if you're ready, sign here." Lucian points to a line near the end of the seventh page.

As if Phineas has only just realized I'm present, he finally glances up at me. I hold eye contact with him momentarily, and a flare of fire rolls in my stomach when he smirks.

He thinks he's won, and the moment I shift the pen to write, his lips stretch into a wide smile.

Perhaps I'll pull his teeth one by one first. I mean, the possibilities will be endless.

The next few minutes go by in nearly the same manner. I'm read a synopsis of the page, I sign, the accountant types, and Phineas smiles. It goes on like this for over a dozen signatures and double that in initials.

But when Lucian files away the documents and grabs the last folder, everything in the room shifts. To the average person, nothing's changed, but to people like me, it's all different. Kane's guards are tense now, the moment they've been waiting for minutes away. While Kane has stopped moving completely, only exchanging very quick glances around the table at each person. He's cataloging, making sure everyone is where they need to be. My nerves start to dance, certainty sinking into my bones and fueling my racing heart.

Unsurprisingly, Lucian has caught on to the change as well. His eyes bounce from Kane to me as he examines our body language and explains the last document. It's the release of Hearts and all my casinos.

Naturally, Phineas is clueless and near giddy as he looks at Kane. "Get us a drink, son, then kiss your little whore there goodbye."

My muscles involuntarily tense as Kane rises slowly. He pushes in his chair and rounds the long table to a small bar at the end. I can't help but watch from the corner of my eyes as he pours two glasses half full of liquor before walking back to his father.

Lucian points to a line, and I notice he's breathing slower.

I sign.

Kane passes behind the lawyer and I catch a glimpse of the tumblers in his hands.

The air thins. *He wouldn't.*

Lucian points to a smaller line. I think he's told me to initial it, but with the blood rushing through my ears, I'm not certain.

I initial.

Kane sets the glass in front of his father. Lifting his own in a false cheer. *He's not.*

My throat turns to fire.

Phineas is *mine*. He belongs to *me*. Kane can't take this from me. *He can't.*

"Last signature, Miss Embros." Lucian points to another line.

This time, I don't sign, because I can't see. Red has all but taken my vision, and before I can utter a word, I'm too late.

Phineas has already picked up the glass.

EZEKIEL

CHAPTER TWENTY-SEVEN

One thing I love so much about Onyx is her ability to figure out a puzzle before she's even seen half of the picture. She reads people as though they wear their stories on their chest, and her intuition is one of the strongest I've ever encountered. I knew she'd figure out what I was doing the moment I poured the liquor.

I knew she'd see the variation in the color and realize it won't be her who gets to kill Phineas tonight. It will be me.

In doing so, I'm acutely and bitterly aware I'm risking what I've worked really fucking hard to build with Onyx. The possibilities, a future—everything is on the line if she can't understand.

God, I hope she can understand.

The pain, the anger, the sorrow, the deaths. This man owes me *everything* yet can give me absolutely nothing. And while it's taken me time, I've come to peace with all the suffering I've endured by his hand. I've dug into what he's done and pulled out the only frail silver lining that can come from his abuse.

I've become a fierce protector. Both to my family and those I've connected with along the way.

I've learned to take on the burdens of others, no matter how great, dealing with the problems they can no longer shoulder.

Perseverance. Resilience. Empathy. All of it came from the situations he put me through in an attempt to steal the little humanity I desperately clung to.

Still, I never buckled. I prevailed.

And as much as I've absorbed the weight he's placed on me, there's something I still need to find any sort of closure. Something only he can give me when *I* take his life. And once it's done, I'll spend my life trying to make Onyx understand why it needed to be me.

My chest aches as I walk back to her. She's sitting in such a quiet manner it's impossible for anyone else in the room to notice she's actually seething. But I know when my queen is mad, and she is livid.

She keeps her eyes on the paper in front of her as she finally signs the last line, effectively giving me all she has.

Before she lifts the pen from the paper, Phineas takes a swig of his drink. "Kiss your whore goodbye, son. Then a bullet goes between her eyes." My father lifts his glass in the air, a toast he holds while I draw my gun.

My heart hammers in my chest as I look down at her. Everyone else in the room has faded into nothing as I burn under her rising gaze. Her eyes find mine and in them, there's an emotion hidden in her dark depths that cracks my very core.

Hurt.

With it, I realize that no matter what my reasons are, or how I try to make it up to her, she'll never let me in again. I'm stealing something she thinks belongs to her, and nothing I say will convince her of anything different.

I use the reality of it as fuel when my free hand reaches out and grabs her chin in a bruising grip. Use it to justify my selfishness when I lean down and press my lips against hers as hard as I can.

In the kiss, I tell her everything I want to say but know she'll never hear.

Forgive me.

A sharp spike of pain radiates across my lips, driving me to break away. Onyx's chest is heaving up and down, her eyes full of fire and her swollen lips stained in a bright red.

I press a fingertip to my mouth and when I draw my hand back, I find blood.

My angry girl bit me.

Phineas's chuckle reminds me of his presence. "I told you once, I'll tell you again. She can't be house trained." He takes a hard swallow of his drink, emptying the glass in one heavy gulp before standing and buttoning his suit jacket. "Now put your animal down."

A lightness expands in my chest as my pulse begins drumming into my ribs. My eyes flash to Oliver who tosses me my silencer. I catch it above Onyx's head before spinning it onto the barrel of my gun.

When I look back at Onyx, any hurt that was there is now gone, replaced by fury. A nerve in her jaw pulses as she peers through her dark fan of lashes up to me. I thought I was ready for her discontent, for her resentment. But the heaviness in my stomach and the ache radiating through my sternum forces me to come to terms with how much I'm really not.

I don't want her to hate me. I don't want—fuck. I don't know what I want, but this look she's giving me is definitely not it.

"Onyx." It's barely a whisper.

She turns her face, her chin tilted up as if she can no longer be bothered to acknowledge me. "Get it over with, Kane."

Phineas coughs twice but I ignore it. Why I need her to

understand more than I care about giving him my attention is beyond me. But the overwhelming need for her to look at me is more than I can handle.

"Ony—"

"What are you doing, boy?" His question is garbled in another fit of coughs. "Kill her."

Onyx nods. "Time is a thief. Best to get on with it before you miss your opportunity."

I suck in a sharp breath. She's mad, but she wants me to finish what I set out to do. She's allowing me to own the moment I've waited for since I was six. "As you wish."

Three short pops ring out in the air as each of Phineas's guards take a bullet in their foreheads. They fall, one after the other, while my men pull their weapons and aim them at Phineas and his accountant.

My gaze shifts to Lucian who has been quietly observing the exchange while collecting the papers. He has no ties nor business with my father outside of granting him a favor he was owed by Alexi, but what he chooses to do now could pose a huge problem for the future.

Lucian glances at my wide-eyed father, who is now wheezing, one hand clutched to the end of the table while the other claws at his chest. The heavy dose of cyanide is working quickly.

Lucian flips the large coin he was playing with earlier between his fingers before finally looking back at me. The man is unnerving as hell. "I'll see to it that these documents are discarded, but Alexi's debt to the Murphy's is paid."

I nod to him before he turns and exits through the back door. Then I jut my chin toward Oliver, who tosses me a key and a gun. I set both down in front of Onyx, and quickly round the table to my father who is attempting to rise from his chair.

"You fucking idiot! I will kill you!" He just barely gets the words out before he starts coughing again.

The back of my gun comes down hard across his face, the cut that forms from the wide gash on his cheek begins oozing quickly.

He gapes at me, sucking in as much air as his pathetic lungs will allow, but it's clearly not enough, because his wheezing grows more desperate.

I repeat the words he said to Onyx the day he brought her in. When she was bound and hurt but still managed to kill one of his guards. "Tell me how you think you'll manage such a feat, old man?"

His eyes flare right before he tries to stand again. "She will kill you, you stupid fucking boy. None of those men out there will respect you."

This makes me chuckle as I strike him again. This time the force is so hard, blood hits the wall to the side of him. "Funny, because half the men out there already belong to me."

He coughs again, only now the sound is wet. "Impossible."

I step closer, inhaling the air that is now pungent with his blood. "And you will perish in that doubt."

Phineas starts to panic now, flailing around as if someone in the room will move to help him. He latches on to my lapel and tries to stand, only to stumble, flipping the chair over as he hits it on his way down.

A smirk spreads across my face as I watch varying hues of red decorate his cheeks. I slip off my blazer and toss it, along with my gun, onto the long meeting table.

The way I'm choosing to end him may seem as if I'm letting him get off easy. But in fact, suffering at the expense of his own kin, without the ability to do anything but watch it happen, is so much sweeter.

"This is for the six-year-old who wanted to believe that

Santa Claus was real and only wished for a father." I roll one sleeve up slowly.

"For the ten-year-old who only wanted to protect his family." I fold the other sleeve up my forearm.

"The fourteen-year-old who was so tired of being beaten and forced to fuck those women that I used to beg the grim reaper to take me in my sleep." I strip myself of my watch and grab my discarded gun.

"I'm thankful the seventeen-year-old found a friend because while I thought all I wanted was freedom, he knew better."

Heat expands through my body as years of torment flash through my mind, one after the other. My limbs shake as I recall every single occasion I've thought about this—longed for it—but never believed it possible. I was always looking forward to leaving and ridding myself of him entirely, and because of it, I never allowed myself to be selfish. Never allowed myself to take what I want.

And it was Onyx who showed me that sometimes, if you want something, you have to *take* it.

I move forward, my steps weighted as I near him. "My name is Ezekiel Liam Kane. I am the son of Lucy Kane, and the don, Phineas Murphy. I am to tell no one of who I am or where I go on Wednesday nights. I am to wait, watch, and learn."

A hot angry tear slides down my face, and I don't bother wiping the evidence of my rage away. "One day, my father will call on me to do something that will set my mother and *sisters* free."

I hold open my arms as Phineas's eyes grow impossibly wider. He scratches at his throat, drawing small beads of blood where his fingernails nick before finally vomiting. My foot comes down on the side of his head, forcing it to the left to ensure he can't choke to death on his vomit. "I'm not quite done with you yet."

He heaves, regurgitating everything in his stomach before finally sucking in air. When I know he's ready, I yank the handkerchief from his breast pocket and wipe his mouth. "I am a product of your abuse. Of the childhood you stole and replaced with blood. While you take the last few breaths of your feeble existence, there is something I need you to know."

A rush of adrenaline flushes through me as I kneel down and grip him by the collar, yanking him up toward me. I lean in and whisper in Irish, keeping my voice low enough to where only he can hear me speak in his native tongue. "After I take over, and kill the soldiers faithful to you, I'll free every woman you have locked up, whether here or in those clubs of yours. I'll burn your warehouses to the ground and rid the streets of the laced drugs you peddle to teens and single moms. And in the end, your head and heart will be fertilizer for my queen's rosebushes."

My shoulders sag as I release him and listen to the violent thud of his head hitting the floor. His eyes are nearly barren now, and I know his heart is taking its last few beats.

"Now choke on the poison you created." I turn to Oliver and the other two guards. I want the last thing he hears to be me, the new don of the Murphy family, making my first order. "Kill them all, except Sam. He belongs to *her*."

When I glance back down, Phineas' head lolls to the side, and in this small moment, I take my first breath not coated in his venom.

No longer am I his tool living under the constant pressure of his thumb. Never again will I be threatened or used, I am finally in control of my own life. My own choices.

This is freedom.

My body feels indescribably light as I look at Onyx. She's

standing now, rubbing her wrists as she lets her cuffs clatter to the table. “Give me another gun, Kane.”

“So you can kill me?” I smirk, an odd type of relief winding through my body. It’s as though I’ve purged myself of a toxic leech that’d been slowly sucking my life away. I feel light. Joyous, even. “I’m not so sure it’s a good idea, *mo bhanríon*.”

She cuts her eyes at me. “Don’t insult me. One is plenty enough for that. And stop with the facetious nickname.”

I jolt back, surprise and irritation suddenly making an appearance. “What in the hell makes you think me calling you my queen is facetious? Like you don’t control my every thought and emotion? As though I wouldn’t go to the ends of the goddamn earth if you ordered it?”

Onyx’s eyebrows furrow, and her eyes narrow. “You *stole* him from me.”

“He was never yours to begin with.”

Her eyes flare. “He took everything from me.”

“And he paid for it with more than just his death.” My voice is rising now, a fire beginning to brew in my gut. I don’t want to fight her on this, but I’ll defend my decision. “His legacy is mine. You are free. There is nothing killing him yourself would have done for you.”

“Mate, we have to move,” Oliver tries to interject but Onyx ignores him.

“It would have brought me peace!”

I scoff, rounding the table and pushing my gun into her chest. “Nothing will give you peace until you confront the demons in your chest. He’s dead, and I’m giving my life to make sure you never have to look over your shoulder again.”

“I have *never* had to peer over my shoulder, Kane. Unlike yourself, I have never allowed myself to be at anyone’s beck and call, other than my own.” She snatches the gun away and turns toward the door. "When this is done, you'll keep breathing so long as I don't ever lay eyes on you again. Do you understand?"

A deep ache pulses behind my heart, but I won't fight her anymore. Not right now.

I slip my phone from my pocket and dial a number I haven't since I accepted the job of Onyx's bodyguard.

She answers before the first ring ends.

"Ready, Z?"

"Ready."

EZEKIEL

CHAPTER TWENTY-EIGHT

As planned, when the double doors open, there isn't a sudden ambush or rapid fire. The guard outside the doors works for me, meaning any noise he heard, fell on deaf ears. He looks at all of us, one by one, before glancing at the small collection of bodies behind us.

When his gaze reaches me again, he smiles before glancing at his phone. "Lucian went out the back, he's at the gate now. Is he free to go?"

I nod once, my eyes remaining on Onyx. She's quiet, both guns clutched in her hands and an eerie calm circulating around her. The elation of ending Phineas is the only thing keeping my racing mind sane as I watch her shoulders rise and fall with her steady breaths. I want to reach out to her, but I know better.

Whatever I thought–or hoped–could happen after this, died with Phineas.

"Shouldn't they be shooting by now?" a guard in the back whispers.

"When she's ready," Onyx replies, not moving her focus away from the long hall.

Any minute now, they'll spot Maddy and the men, and once they do, there will be mayhem.

I move to stand in front of Onyx but pause when she huffs from her nose. "Is there a problem?"

She keeps her eyes straight ahead. "Not at all. Just a bit exasperated with you thinking I need you to protect me."

I scrub a hand over my face, doing the best I can to keep my voice low and steady. "When they round this corner, they are going to have their guns drawn, ready to shoot anyone that isn't Phineas. They'll be confused by their own men turning on them and by standing here, you'll be right in the line of fire."

"Again. It's vexing that you think anyone would be able to pull a trigger with a bullet through their skull."

I clamp my jaw shut, ignoring the pain of my molars smashing together, and throw my hands up. She wants me to stop doing something that I have done my entire life? Fine. So be it.

The acceptance rips through me like a bolt of lightning, reaching around my spine and yanking me backward.

No. No. You know what? *Fuck that.*

She's mad, I knew she would be. But I'm not going change who this entire fucked up life has shaped me to be because of her anger. I'm protecting her, and she can resent me for it later.

"Kane, mo–"

The first shot rings out. It's muffled through the walls, but loud nonetheless, and the moment of silence that follows is thick and weighted. The only audible sounds are the click of our safeties and our shallow breaths.

My heart is pounding, the blood in my ears a constant whoosh matching my pulse. I'm confident everything will work out in my favor, but the notion of anything happening to Onyx puts me on edge.

I start to glance at her over my shoulder but stop to what

sounds like fireworks, followed by chaos. A concession of gunfire, yelling, feet pounding into the floor, and screams of the maids splinter the air in tandem.

Oliver and I move quickly, sprinting to the end of the hallway and straight into two guards. I shoot the first, and Olly gets the second. They go down on top of each other, forcing us to step over them.

In the foyer, blood and fists are flying everywhere. Weapons are held by some, but most have resorted to a full-out brawl, and it becomes evident some are hashing out old grudges.

Glass shatters around us from stray bullets hitting frames and art pieces. But through the mayhem, just outside the wide open doors, I make out the red curls of a fierce fighter.

Maddy is out on the lawn, hammering her fist into the face of someone who looks as though they've lost consciousness. It's like she can feel our presence, because her face snaps in our direction. A bright red stain is splattered over her entire left side, and it seems as if she's split open her lip, but it stretches into a wide smile when they land on Onyx.

"I got eyes on Boss!" she yells, dropping the comatose guard and stepping over another toward the open doors.

A sudden movement to my right steals my attention. About a half dozen men are flying down the stairs, and none of them belong to me. I push past a group fighting and cut them off as they come down. The first two take quick bullets to the head, but those behind them are able to push through.

A taller man pummels right into me, pushing me back into a pair fighting. I use the back of my gun and slam it down on his spine, and when he jolts back, I bash it across his face.

He falls, but another is right there, weapons drawn and pointed at my chest. A pop rings out and he stumbles, his eyes widening briefly before fluttering closed as he falls.

Oliver shoots two more as I regain my balance. My heart pounds into my chest as I search for Onyx. When I find her, she's only a few yards back, putting bullets into every man's head who's wearing a brooch.

The entire rush of blood that flows south is jarring and intense. Besides our time torturing in Embros estate, I haven't seen her in full form. The way she moves in between the chaotic crowd with such grace–the serene look of indifference on her face as she kills one after the other–is fucking artistic.

Her eyes flash to mine and I can't help the involuntary wink I give her with a smirk. She clenches her teeth before backhanding a man twice her size and kneeing him in the dick as he reaches for her.

He collapses, but another takes his place, charging at Onyx over the cluster of bodies. I lift my gun, but she beats me to it, shooting him directly in the throat. Blood flies outward, droplets spraying over her untouched blouse. The color seeps into the dark fabric, almost disappearing on contact.

Before I can admire the amazing handiwork she doles out to another man approaching her, a hard hit to my jaw pushes my head in the opposite direction. My gaze turns fuzzy, white spots decorating my vision as I turn, shooting almost blindly. But I catch him in the neck. Another shot sends him down.

I whirl around to make sure Onyx handled the guy but don't see her. My pulse races, the heavy thrumming growing harder as I search through the madness.

More men appear at the top of the stairs as well as down the long hallway near the kitchen. I empty my clip into the ones coming down the stairs before bending and grabbing two dropped weapons by dead guards.

"Ezekiel!" My first name from *her* mouth jolts me upright, and I look up in time to find Onyx's gun pointed at me.

Not at me, above me.

Three shots ring out and the heavy thuds of their bodies follow. I stand, turning slightly to see a new collection of dead guards piled on the floor.

I shift back to Onyx, who is nearly covered in blood now. The visual, paired with her rescue, has something in my stomach actually fluttering. "You saved me."

She scoffs, rolling her eyes. "Because only *I* get to kill you."

Why that turns me on, I have no fucking clue, but I take a step toward her and reach out a hand. "Thank you."

She steps away, averting her eyes. "Don't thank me, Kane."

"Onyx, I–I'm not sorry for killing him, but I am sorry for hurting you."

Her eyes narrow, a deep crease forming between her brows. Her mouth parts but she's cut off by one of her twins.

"Boss, we got him." Trigger appears at her side before letting his eyes flash to me. Something indiscernible passes between them, but in the end, he tugs on Onyx's upper arm. "We need to go."

A muscle pulls in my chest as she nods and turns, stepping through the litter of bodies without so much as another word. Her heel pierces into one of the fallen guards who reaches up and grabs her calf.

Intuition lifts my arm, and I squeeze the trigger, shooting a bullet directly into his temple.

The silence becomes overwhelming as my soldiers finish clearing out my father's loyal men and I watch her disappear through the front double doors.

I rub at the ache in my chest with the side of my gun. Every step she takes is weighted, and the inherent need to chase after her is so damn visceral, it's tearing my frayed edges into tattered fringes.

My gaze flashes to Oliver, who nods. "There aren't many left. Go."

I don't hesitate, moving through the thinning crowd and out the front doors. My feet push me down the entry steps two at a time until I'm right behind her.

Maddy, the twins, and Shi are collected in front of her jeep with a group of other guards. All of them wear the marks of fresh wounds, but collectively seem relieved to have what they came for.

Shi is the first one to acknowledge my presence, her eyes shifting from me to Onyx, then back again. Trigger opens the door, and starts to help Shi inside but stops when he notices her demeanor. He turns, following her gaze to me. Soon enough, Maddy and Trick do the same.

All of them stand silent, their faces wearing emotions I can't make out while random gunshots ring out behind me. Oliver is likely having our men go floor by floor now, clearing out anyone who was smart enough to not come down.

My gaze returns to Onyx's back. She's paused, but hasn't yet turned around. "I'd advise you to go back inside, Kane. You've got quite the mess to clean up."

She grabs onto the handle bar to hoist herself up and I step forward, ignoring a few of her men drawing their guns.

"Can you just wait? For just one second." I hate how my voice comes out almost like a plea, but the sudden notion that I'm going to lose her burns across my body.

Her shoulders rise and fall as she releases a heavy sigh. But after a moment, she drops her hand and turns around. Her dark eyes seem to shine under the night sky, glimmering from the stars reflecting in her iris.

In all her fierceness and strength, she's so goddamn beautiful.

"What more do you want from me?"

Her question gives me pause. My brows knit together as I shake my head. "I don't want anything from you, I just–"

"You lied to me." She takes a step forward. "Then you stole. You took something from me that I've waited nearly a decade for. I've done nothing in those ten years but eat, drink, and kill, waiting for the moment I had my gun to his head."

Her voice grows louder as she takes another step. Her hand shakes at her sides, her knuckles blooming white from her grip on her gun. "He was mine!"

Rage flashes through me. "He was *always* mine! Since the moment he backhanded a six year old kid who thought he was Santa."

Onyx jerks back as if I slapped her. She lifts her gun and trains it right over my heart. "You didn't even make him suffer. He got to die with his debt unpaid, and you've left me with *nothing*."

"You have the man who killed your parents."

"I was owed them both!"

Dropping my gun, I scrap my hands up my face and through my hair, tugging on the ends. "Don't do this. *Please*."

"Do what?"

I blow out a large breath, my shoulder sagging as I let my hands fall. "You're forcing this wedge between us. You're so fucking scared of what you feel for me that you're using this as a way to get out."

She guffaws, lifting her free arm up and gesturing around her at the mess of bodies. "I don't have to force anything, Kane. I was a prisoner who did what she needed to do to get out alive."

"You've always been a shitty fucking liar," I breathe.

Onyx's eyes flare and she shakes her gun at me. "You mean nothing to me. And if I ever lay eyes on you again, it will be the last thing you have the pleasure of looking at."

She turns on her heels and returns her grasp onto the railing, but I still can't let her go. I take a step forward.

"Onyx–"

I hear the pop a second before I feel the intense pain. It explodes down my arm and across my chest. The shouts coming from behind me remind me that we were having our dispute amongst everyone and now, all guns are drawn on both sides.

Swallowing around the heavy knot, I lift the arm not damaged with a bullet to stop my men from any retaliation, and look at Onyx.

She's breathing fast, her hand still wrapped around the gun she just shot me with. The determination in her gaze is clear. "You are nothing. No one. And I never want to see you again."

Perhaps it was all just a dream.

A hopeful wish.

Because it's clear now that, in reality, all she feels for me is disdain.

I saw my lip between my teeth as I let the truth sink in. My body deflates, and I nod, doing my best to ignore the hot burn radiating through me.

Until a bullet stops me.

"As you wish, *mo bhanríon.*"

My eyes flash to Shi and Maddy before I turn and leave. It isn't until I'm inside, listening to the sounds of retreating vehicles that I finally sigh.

"I'm sorry."

CHAPTER TWENTY-NINE

I peel the sticky, bloody blouse from my chest as if it's the reason my skin is currently on fire. The fabric drops onto the jeep floor and is soon joined by my slacks. But still, I'm too hot.

Maddy tosses me a small hand towel from the front seat and I use it to scrub my face until it's raw.

"Boss, are you alright?" Maddy asks, turning in the passenger seat to fully face me. "You got a little upset back there. Almost like you're doing that thing you do when you hold stuff in until it explodes."

I bare my teeth. "Do not test me, Madeline."

A calm hand finds my knee, and I nearly lurch from my seat. Shi removes it, holding it up briefly in mock surrender. "Onyx, she's right. You're unraveling."

My eyebrows draw together so hard it hurts. "Unraveling? Tell me, Shire, have you been locked away for days, driven into delirium, before finally having your enemy hand-feed you so you don't succumb to death?"

Her expression turns solemn, regret instantly marring her face, but I don't stop. The words tumble one after another. "Were either of you put on a leash and had your parents' murderer inches from you with no means to kill him? Did you fuck a man who used you over and *over* just for him to turn around and take everything from you?"

"Onyx—"

"No!" I'm shrieking now, and while I have never once raised my voice to scream at my girls, I can't stop myself. I can't hinder my tone from shaking and breaking as I throw a disgusting pity party. Rage and frustration bubble to the surface, and my ribs ache from the pounding of my heart, but I keep going.

"I *felt* something for him. I *trusted* him. I allowed him, and your acceptance of him, to lead me astray. And when I succumbed to his pretty words and talented tongue, he used me again! I was nothing more than a tool. For his freedom? For his new position? For him to be able to kill his father? Perhaps all three. And he got it all. He won everything, and I—"

My fingers fly to my chest, the sudden itch on my skin too strong to ignore. My sharp nails scrape at the delicate flesh, the desire to rid myself of these clothes he bought me too overwhelming. I want to scar the smooth skin he kissed. To feel the pain physically rather than emotionally.

Shi's hands find my shoulders, and when I try to jerk away, she holds me tighter. "Listen to me."

"Let me go," I hiss.

She shakes her head, the loose, black tendrils not matted with blood whipping back and forth. "Listen to me. You know I have experienced *everything* you just did, and not for days, Onyx, but for years. I understand your anger. Your pain. And what you're doing right now is drowning. You're feeling too many things at once, and the pressure is too much for you to bear."

I suck in a breath, but it isn't enough to fill my lungs. Again, I try to shake her off, but she holds steady, forcing me to look at her. Forcing me to not only hear her but *listen* to what she has to say.

"You need to get control, Onyx. Take a second and grab onto something to keep you afloat. You're safe now. The man who ordered your parents' execution is dead, and the man responsible is in the trunk of the car in front of us."

Inhaling her words, I drop my hands from my chest. The skin burns where I clawed into it, but it's no longer itchy. "What—what else has happened?"

She wastes no time filling in the blank spaces. "Hearts' women were moved temporarily, but have already returned home. Deliveries and shipments were scheduled out, and businesses have continued to run as normal until last night. We put all hands on deck to come and get you. But we'll open them back up tomorrow and include a few specials to make up lost profit."

Somehow, my pulse doesn't hurt my veins anymore, and the buzzing in my ears is beginning to fade. "Kilo?"

Shi exchanges a brief look with Maddy before nodding. Maddy leans over the armrest and twirls a stray lock around her finger. "That bastard is fine. He lost part of his legs, but the boys have already had him fitted for some new ones. He's going to be walking around looking like an off-brand *Terminator* soon."

When I take my next breath, the air isn't as stifling and fills my lungs completely. "And Antonio, Cat?"

Maddy laughs, throwing her head back. "That man won't kick the bucket until he knows you're alright. Cat and Russ haven't stopped fighting. They got everything in order and have already arranged funerals for the guards we lost in the ambush, along with Edwards."

I nod, and Shi lowers her hands. Sinking back into the leather seat, my skin begins to cool against it, goose bumps sprouting along my arms. I allow my head to loll to the side and I peer out the window into the passing forest. Everything is a blur of black and green as Trigger speeds through the city.

It feels as if it's been months since I've seen the trees, felt the wind, or smelled the ocean air. And suddenly I realize just how easy it is to miss the little things that I never appreciated before.

We ride in silence for a moment as I attempt to soak in everything that's happened in the last few hours alone. My emotions are unstable, and I've been unjust to my family and their patience. All of them have endured more pain than I have at the hands of the Murphy's, each of them hurt in ways I've never been. To lash out at them was juvenile, just like what I did to *him*.

He protected me, and I hurt him. I was selfish, thinking what I wanted came before him. While I lost my world the day my parents died, Kane has been subjected to his torment since his birth. Forced into a life he could never escape. Meant to be used until his last breath.

A tightness pulls across my chest, a feeling of heaviness moving over me. Thankfully, Shire doesn't let me stew in my newfound guilt for long.

"Feeling out of control is hard. Be kind to yourself." Shi pats me on the knee.

"Yeah," Maddy chirps. "You've just been through the wringer, Boss. It's only natural to be a bit high strung. You can say even I have been a little, uh, volatile since you've been gone."

"Not sure I would say a little." Trigger interjects. "But really, we've all been a bit out of our minds, so don't worry yourself over any outbursts, Boss."

"Agreed." Shi nods.

My stomach twists as Maddy hands me a small bag with a change of clothes.

Now that they've pointed it out directly, it's easy to see my reaction was in response to my lack of control the past week. I had no say in where I was, what I ate, what I did—*anything*. I was just another prisoner of the Murphys—usable until I was disposable.

I slip on the loose black joggers and black tee, thankful we'll be home soon and I can have a proper shower.

As if a flip has switched, visions of Kane and I in the shower flood my mind. His gentle work of cleaning my every curve and crevice after being locked up. His hands in my hair, massaging my scalp. He took care of me in the best ways.

I swallow thickly, a sudden lump forming in my throat.

I shot him.

My shoulders drop, the sickly feeling of guilt returning stronger now as it slides down my spine. I can't recall exactly where I hit Kane, and now I'm worried. "Where did my bullet strike him?"

Trigger answers this time, his eyes creased on the side with a smirk. "Somewhere that didn't do much damage. I think even in your bout of rage, you knew you didn't want to hurt him."

"I shouldn't have done that."

Shi's hand finds my shoulder. "You were angry, caught up in your head. And unfortunately for us, people in our world have a hard time using words to express that anger, and instead, tend to shoot people. And something tells me he understands that."

A warmth swallows my face as I look at Shi. I want her to see the hurt I'm hiding, and how far gone I am. I need her to help me rid myself of this feeling of suffocating despair.

"He used me." It's more of a question than a statement now.

A small smile curls her lips as she shakes her head. "He didn't."

The certainty in her words squeezes around my heart. "How do you know?"

Shi turns and digs into the panel of the door. She pulls out a white envelope with my name written across the front. She's slow to hand it to me, and when my fingers connect with the paper, tingles shoot up my arm.

"What's this?"

"Something you should read when you're ready."

"When I'm ready?" I repeat, my eyes flashing from her to the white rectangle then back again.

She nods. "When you're ready to accept that every story has two sides. Every person has a past. And love doesn't make us weak."

"I don't love him."

Shi purses her lips to one side. "Perhaps not. But if you did, it wouldn't take away from your strength."

I run my finger along the edges of the envelope and bite on the inside of my cheek. It feels like lead in my hands; the contents within so heavy, I know it will pull me under the torrential waters I'm already struggling with if I open it.

So instead, I keep it closed, clutched in my hand. It isn't until we cross into my territory, that I decide not to open it, but to destroy it.

Because if I don't, I know within the depths of my soul that *it* will destroy *me*.

CHAPTER THIRTY

I pace the length of my office for the twenty-seventh time. Since returning to the estate, I've showered, dressed in black tapered slacks and a matching blazer, and adorned it with a long feather necklace. My father and Trick made it for me.

It was one of the first pieces of jewelry they made together that doubled as a weapon, which inspired Trick to make more jewelry.

My fingers trace over the blade idly as I continue to walk, my heels clicking on the marble floor. While waiting on my men to get Sam situated, I've gone over things and found nothing amiss. My family has done an excellent job with cleaning up the destruction the Murphys caused and simultaneously ensured that the casinos and real estate properties have run smoothly.

I was relieved to see it all for myself, and with the leftover time, I've allowed myself a moment to think. To process. To jot down all the different ways I want to kill Sam. At first, I considered making it quick. Perhaps slicing open his stomach and pulling out his innards with the grace of a harpist.

Now, though, because I'm without both Sam *and* Phineas,

I've decided to make it last. To savor every drop of blood he spills, along with every tear and ounce of sweat. I want his screams and his agony. His vomit and then the bile when there's nothing left.

I want him to make false promises as he begs for me to release him. Then later, when he understands I won't, I want the whimpers of a man who thinks I'm finally going to grant him the sweet relief of death, only to realize I'm not.

Kane may pride himself on making peace with his demons, but I have not.

And it won't be until I've had my fill, and Sam's body is cold and without a single iota of blood left, that I'll relent. That I'll allow him his journey to hell.

A shadow growing outside my office doors makes me pause. My breath becomes stilted, the air suddenly thin as the dark blur takes on a familiar silhouette of one of my boys.

Anticipation works through my bloodstream, and I find I'm holding my breath. But then, what should be a singular person, is a wheelchair, followed by Trick.

A fierce burn spreads across both my chest and face as the office doors open, revealing the remnants of a man I haven't seen sit still since childhood. Already, too many things have transpired in the past week, and seeing Kilo like this only chips away at my very carefully constructed composure.

I watch quietly as Trick pushes the chair inside and I absorb my brother's condition. Kilo's white hair is mussed, strands facing every direction as though he just took off a helmet. Superficial cuts that are already fading decorate his arms and parts of his face. There's also a hollowness in his eyes with accompanying shadows, displaying his lack of sleep.

All of these features are nothing we haven't experienced before. Nothing we haven't shaken off and healed with a few shots of rum. Nothing that made me so violently angry my inside vibrated.

No, it isn't any of those things that strip my self-control and make red spots dance across my eyes.

It's that the man whose story would bring even the strongest person to tears, has yet again, been written another shitty chapter.

A thick, white blanket covers his thighs and waist, draping close to the footrests where his feet should be—but aren't. My stomach twists, but I steel my face, doing the best I can to keep my emotions from showing.

"Hey, Boss. I was on my way to tell you we got the cue ball all set up, but then I ran into this guy as the boys were bringing him in. Seems as if he was caught in a compromising pretzel in his hospital bed when they went to discharge him."

Trick rubs Kilo's hair aggressively, ignoring our friend's grunts of displeasure. "I'd hardly say it was a pretzel."

"Her legs were doing some weird thing in the air, Kilo. Let's not play coy."

"She was massaging my thighs!"

Trick scoffs. "With her pussy."

A knot swells in my throat as the boys go back and forth. The anger that raged through me just moments ago dissipates into a simmer.

I haven't seen Kilo coherent since before my parents' murder. He'd relapsed right after, but never took too much to keep him from functioning. Just enough to keep his mind going and going, always looking forward to the next task, so he didn't have enough time to stew in his misery.

Now, without legs, he will be forced to slow down, if not stop, and face the demons he's been running from. I can only hope he survives it when he does.

The realization hits me square in the chest. The epiphany

that in just a few moments, I too will do the exact same thing. Only I haven't been running from my demons, I've been letting them fuel me.

What will happen when the fire finally burns out? Will it consume me? Save me? Release me?

There are so many unknowns when my life has become nothing but vengeance.

Nothing but fulfilling a promise I gave my mother who loved me until her last breath.

Blood is all I've known since that day. Yet, sometimes, there are moments that make me remember. That *force* me to remember—I was someone else before this.

I was someone who laughed, cried, dreamed, wished, *loved.* I was fearless because I had my family, but then, without them, all I knew was fear. I barely survived their deaths, and though my boys held me through the dark, they were no longer invincible either. They all became very human, and suddenly, I was terrified of losing them.

So they became weaknesses, and I had to create a boundary between us that would keep me from growing too close. Every emotion with them needed to be muted. Filtered.

But its moments like these, where Kilo and Trick are laughing despite the terrible things we've all endured, that make me hopeful. That makes me *want* to dream again.

To love again.

"The evidence is clear. What do you think, Boss?" Trick finally turns to me, a wide smile etched on his face. "Was she massaging him with her cunt or fingers?"

My eyes flash to Kilo who is observing me in silence. It sends an unfamiliar tingle down my spine. One I've only ever felt once before.

He examines me even as I look back to Trick and answer. "Was it the nurse or the doctor?"

Trick chuckles. "Neither. It was Zek's sister, Fiona."

"Fiona?"

Trick nods. "Yep. Maddy had Kilo here watching her in case things went south, but looks like he had other things in mind."

My brows lift in surprise. "Where is she now?"

"The Murphy mansion. Or should I say the Kane Mansion?" Trick shakes his head. "That shit sounds weird as hell."

I purse my lips and glance back at Kilo. The banter and silliness are gone from his gaze as he focuses solely on me. Somehow, I know what he wants, and even though I want nothing more than to go visit the man downstairs, I grant Kilo this. He's owed that much.

"I'll take him to his room, Trick. Will you make sure there's sulfuric acid and hydrogen peroxide down there as well?"

Trick nearly giggles before turning to leave. "Oh, yes, ma'am, I sure will! See you down there in a minute."

I wait until the door closes behind him to shift back to Kilo. "How are you feeling?"

"You don't have to do this."

My face jolts backward. "I must not have heard you right."

He holds up a hand. "I'm not saying *at all*, Boss. I'm saying you don't have to go down there right now."

I guffaw. "And when would be a better time to end this, Kilo? Please, tell me."

I can feel my heart racing now, the sudden increase making my veins throb. With the obvious anger radiating from my body, he surprises me again when he merely tilts his head and shrugs. "I'm not sure. But if you do it now, it will be over before it starts. All those emotions still fresh and bubbling to the surface will cause you to rip him apart."

"That would be a mercy, and I can promise you this—that man will *not* know mercy."

"As he shouldn't. But *you* deserve it."

It's hard to swallow around the lump forming in my throat. "I don't."

"And why is that?"

I shrug aggressively, rage and guilt tangling around my spine and setting my soul on fire. "Because I couldn't protect you! I couldn't protect any of you! I've made mistake after mistake and in the end, I couldn't even provide you with the man that caused you the most pain."

"You're human. And why do you think we wanted Phineas? He was *your* crusade for *your* closure."

My brows furrow. "Phineas' death was for all our benefit."

Kilo nods. "Yes, but not a necessity for us. He hurt you, and you needed him dead to move on. We didn't. We found a new home here. In each other. In you. We learned to love again. But you learned you could never do it because that meant it could be taken away."

Fire burns at the back of my throat, and I'm sure my face is one of distraught because Kilo moves his chair forward and puts one of my shaking hands in his. "Finish this. Truly finish it. Let it die with him."

I close my eyes against the burn and nod. No matter if Sam was to die tonight or next week, one thing is certain. "I intend to, my friend."

Every step I take into my basement is both weighted and light. It's a move toward salvation. Toward redemption. Closure and rebirth.

Who I end up being afterward is yet to be seen but I know one thing; I will survive.

Red hair comes into view first. Maddy's leaning against the wall near the bottom of the stairs, twirling her favorite blade as she watches the center of the room. My fierce little warrior. She yields to no man, including Father Time, and will stop at nothing to protect her family.

Next to her is Shi. Ever the reserved, she too is looking at the man in the center.

Shi. My adviser and second-in-command. She has the wisdom of a woman who's lived much longer than her twenty-eight years, and without her, there are many times we would have been lost.

As I reach the bottom, I see my boys. My twins. Total opposites in nearly every way, but together they are passionate. Creative. Ingenious. They are the pillars on which my operation stands.

And in the middle, stands Sam, chained by his wrists and latched to a hook overhead.

Like myself, he's been merely a ghost up until now. The memory of his voice has haunted me. It's plagued me. I haven't gone a day in ten years without hearing it.

But I must say, seeing him again after all this time feels almost disappointing.

He's big. But not as large as he was when I was fourteen. He looks brawny. But not as strong as he did when my parents were kneeling in front of him. He's deadly. But half as much as he was when he cut them down on that pretty day.

I've worked so hard to no longer be the girl from that day. To not allow their deaths to plague me, to not let their screams feed into my nightmares. But standing in front of the man who took everything, I am her. I am her rage. Her loss. I am her savior and her death. After this, she will be no more.

And a queen will take her place.

A smug grin stretches his lips, bringing attention to a long scar on the side of his cheek. "You look so much like that slut mother of yo—"

A harsh crack rings out in the space as the back of my hand connects with his face. I remain impassive as I watch him spit blood on the concrete.

Something between a cough and a laugh seeps from his mouth as he turns to me. "No introductions?"

I tilt my head slightly and hold out a hand. On cue, Trigger places a small scalpel in my palm. "I need you to understand something."

Trick moves behind Sam and rips the shirt from his body.

"I want nothing from you."

Shi steps forward and slips the belt from his loops.

"And there is nothing you can give me."

Maddy giggles as she skips in front of him and uses the blade in her hand to rip his pants down the legs.

"This will not be pleasant. And even when you beg for death..."

I move closer to him, running the small scalpel along his temple and reopening the old scar all the way into the stubble on his face. He hisses as the blood beads quickly, dripping down his cheeks and falling onto the floor.

"He will not come until *I* tell him I'm done."

Chaos

CHAPTER THIRTY-ONE

EZEKIEL

I knew I was going to make a mess. I knew cleanup would take months to truly complete. But I also knew we'd have to work quickly, keeping as much of it under the radar as possible, and get new men in as fast as we could.

What I didn't anticipate was Oliver having already acquired over three dozen new soldiers, training them in one of Phineas's empty warehouses, and then having them on standby.

He told me that when he found out Fiona was brought to the mansion, he held out hope I'd take over after all, and for his wishful thinking and preparation, I'm thankful.

In two short hours, the new men have helped rid the grounds and the mansion of the dead. They've assisted the maids in scouring the floors and reported to Oliver to find out where they would be needed after.

In that same time, my shoulder was patched up, I was able

to hold a meeting with my father's accountant, who is faithful only to money, and contacted Lucian again about transferring ownership of my father's businesses. I now owe the lawyer a favor, but with the dozens of people moving in and out of the mansion, asking me for different decisions, and relying on me for answers that won't get them killed or arrested, I don't mind.

Having spent those weeks watching Onyx, and how she operates, has helped me tremendously in these last two hours. Each new person I speak with poses a different problem—and different attitude—but my calm demeanor stays the same.

Some of the conversations are easier than others. The managers for the strip clubs don't know the extent of the changes I'm going to invoke, but will be here in the morning to go over them. The drug runners are already on their way, and I'm almost certain that after they hear the changes, not all of them will walk out with a pulse. And the men guarding the women in warehouses are none the wiser as Oliver's group heads over to slice open their throats.

I give it about a day or two before the police show up, and with the way the men are working, I don't think it will be a problem. Besides, I'm not sure they'll be too upset that I'm cleaning up my father's wrongdoings.

Not to say I won't continue some of them, but one thing I've learned is that you can still be the lesser evil even when you're knee-deep in hell.

Men will still seek the company of women, so the strip clubs will remain, but dancers will be of legal age and protected from any acts they don't wish to partake in. Those seeking drugs will still be able to buy them. Only now, they must be old enough to legally buy alcohol. I'll also raise the prices, but they won't have to worry about laced drugs anymore.

Now, as for the men that come to collect women they think are nothing more than objects they can own? Well, I anticipate a lot of enemies, but I'm hoping Onyx will help me with that. I know she doesn't want to see me now, but I also know she doesn't want anyone to move in on me and continue to traffic women even more.

In the end, she may still not agree to see me, but perhaps Shi will accept, and we can work together on that front.

My stomach churns as I walk back to my office. I'd be lying if I said I wasn't fucked up about how everything ended with me and Onyx. How fucking hurt I am that she can't see that she wasn't the only one that deserved to kill him.

But really, no matter how much I hoped for the impossible, I already knew the outcome. Worst case, she would kill me; best case, a bullet somewhere on my body.

That's what we promised each other after all.

Until a bullet stops me.

Shooting me there was a message, and no matter how much it rips my heart out, I'll respect it.

Before I turn the knob to open the doors, I feel it. The prickling and hair rising on the back of my neck. I use the hand of my uninjured shoulder to grab my gun and hold it outright as I let the door swing open.

I'm not exactly sure who I'm expecting when the intruder comes into view, but it definitely wasn't her.

"Hello, son."

Onyx

Sweat breaks across Sam's brow, the small droplets joining the blood as it drips down his face.

I like this position he's in. Taller than me, forcing me to look up at him. It makes him feel like he still has some type of power here. Like he can somehow leave this place alive.

I see it in the way his lips subtly curve. How his eyes don't stay trained on me but on his surroundings. Almost as though he's making a plan in his head on what to do and how to escape.

It makes me laugh while also pissing me off, for him to have the gall to think he's anything other than dead.

"Do you know how long I've waited for this, Sam?" I ask, trailing the scalpel down his broad chest. It's surprising he has so much muscle considering he doesn't do anything besides giving orders to the little obedient soldiers beneath him. Then again, you must be strong to hold down the women you rape.

"My guess is every second of your pathetic life." His voice is dull, indifferent.

Cute.

"So then you know how much I've thought about the things I'm going to do to you."

He smirks. "If they're anything like what I did to your headless mother, then I'd say we're in for a good time."

Hot bile shoots up my esophagus, forcing me to clamp my mouth shut to keep it at bay. My fist smashes into his face hard, much harder than it did the first time, and not even the small clink of one of his teeth hitting the floor is enough to calm my racing heart.

I mourned my parents' deaths over two empty holes for seven days. In a way, I liked that they weren't there, because it made it not real. It made it so that there was a possibility the entire thing was nothing more than a horrible dream.

But reality came crashing through my juvenile hopes on that eighth day.

Antonio didn't let me see when my parents' bodies were delivered. He also tried to keep me from seeing the coroner's report. But I saw it.

Cause of death: Decapitation. Postmortem cuts observed. Postmortem sexual assault. Samples taken from vaginal, anal, and oral areas.

They all belonged to one person. I always thought it was Phineas.

"She was just too beautiful. I couldn't help myself. Couldn't let her go to waste, ya know?"

Black creeps into my eyesight as I grab his thick neck. My sharp nails dig into the sides, piercing into his skin with ease. He jerks beneath my hold, and he must try to move his legs because the twins come forward, holding each one in place.

I squeeze my hand tighter, my quiet reserve threatening to break under Sam's smug smirk. It isn't until hues of blue creep up his face that his smile fades and panic makes his eyes flare.

Adrenaline pumps through my system, the pounding of my pulse so loud I almost don't hear Shi approach.

Her hand finds the small of my back and it's then I realize that I'm holding my breath with him. I'm *dying* with him.

"He will not know mercy," she whispers.

I release him and step back, sucking in a sharp breath and relishing the harsh burn of it as it fills my lungs.

Sam spits and coughs, his speech completely incoherent as he tries to shake it off. But the red and purple decorating his neck in a glorious ring informs me he still feels me.

"Tell me, Sam," I say, walking over to my table of tools. They're all laid out in beautiful succession. Each one so similar yet so different, meant to do the same thing but in separate ways. My fingers curl around the slip-joint pliers before I finally turn back to Sam. "Which hand did you use to touch her first?"

My mother crosses and uncrosses her legs again, shifting in her chair as her eyes move around, not settling on anything for too long.

Her hair is freshly washed, pinned into a high bun. Her cheeks are flushed and full, indicating she's gotten plenty of rest and food, and the dress covering her frame makes her look like a Step-ford wife.

Underneath the physical facade, though, I notice the way her shoulders droop and her puffy, red-rimmed eyes. Not to mention that no matter what she's looking at, her gaze keeps drifting to the door. Almost as if she's waiting for the other shoe to drop. It's clear she's more than uncomfortable being in a place that used to belong to the man that once controlled her. A man that stole one of her children, used the other, and threatened the third.

"He's not coming, Mom. He's dead." I sigh, placing one hand on my desk.

She only relaxes a hairbreadth. "Are you sure?"

"I mean, I killed him. So, yeah."

She takes a hard swallow, her lashes blinking rapidly in what I hope to be relief. Her chin juts to my injured shoulder. "Is that from him?"

I shake my head, ignoring the sharp pain in my chest. "No."

Her lip disappears between her teeth as she saws them back and forth. I can tell there's something she wants to say or ask, but with everything that's happened—everything I've seen—in the past few months, I'd be lying if I said I didn't want her to finally be the one to speak up. To be the one to say something. *Anything*.

Protecting her and my sister was second nature, but part of me, the child I never got to be, wishes she would own up to at least some of her shortcomings. To at least take responsibility for me sitting behind this fucking desk.

I suck in a hard breath and shake my head. None of this is her fault. Not Phineas, not her addiction, nor her way of coping. I made the choices that led me here. I made the decision to take over instead of running. To kill instead of saving.

To love instead of hating.

Another ache stretches across my chest and I rub at it, the phantom pain becoming stronger than I can handle at the moment.

I look back to my mother, who is quietly sitting still, her chin pointed toward her chest as she fiddles with the hem of her dress.

"I don't know what's going to happen here, but in a few hours, all of Phineas' money is mine. I'll have enough for you and Fiona to leave and start over wherever you'd like."

Her light eyes seem to glow when she looks back up. "And Bunny?"

Bunny. Harlow.

A new pain gnaws at the back of my heart. The way she just asked about her like I've known all this time. Like my father's death made it safe to speak a name that didn't torment me for years.

"My men are currently looking for her. Seems as if she stole some money from Phineas and ran."

My mother shakes her head, tears almost instantly filling her eyes. "She wouldn't do that. She wouldn't leave me."

I huff, swiping a hand down my face. "You'd be surprised what people you think you know will do when their backs are against the wall."

Her hands clasp the hem of her dress, her nails leaving angry red marks as they scrape against her thigh. "You have to find her, Zek."

"I just said that's what I'm doing, Mom." I steady my voice as I push out the words I know aren't really sincere. "But she's not my responsibility nor my priority right now."

"How could you say such a thing? She's your sister!"

Heat flares in my gut. "A sister I thought was dead. A sister I didn't even know existed, despite your incoherent confession, until I saw her. She's another woman I was unable to save. Another woman who could be dangled in front of me like a toy to force me to do everything in my power to protect her. I'll find her, but it won't be right now."

She jumps to her feet, tears streaming down her face now. "She's my daughter!"

"And he's your son." Fiona's voice makes both of us snap our faces to the door. "And I think a 'thank you' is in order."

I stand without a thought, rounding the corner of my desk, and embracing Fiona in a hug. It's tight, and void of any fear or doubt that I may not see her again.

"Thank you," I whisper in her hair.

"I'm just glad this is over. I need a damn vacation," she says in my chest.

I release her after another moment and look down into her big eyes. "Anywhere."

She pokes out her bottom lip in a pout I haven't seen since she was eight. "Can I take a friend?"

"It depends. Is this friend a—"

"How about we focus on what matters!" my mother shrieks. "Like finding my daughter!"

"Pretty sure he just told you she ran. And if she wants to put herself in harm's way, it's not his responsibility to risk everything—including his life—to find her."

My mother's mouth is wide open as she gapes at Fiona. They've never been close, but Fiona's never dared speak to her this way. Still, the need to reassure her that Harlow will be found weighs heavy, but when I open my mouth Fiona cuts me off again.

"Zek has spent his life protecting us and raising me. You did the bare minimum, only worried about *her* while your other two children suffered, if not more than her, right under your own roof. He was beaten, used, broken, and hurt. I don't even know half of what he had to go through, but I do know one thing—he deserves better than you!"

Our mom tries to interject, a fresh round of tears streaming down her face, but Fiona doesn't let her. "You checked out and he had to step up. The least you can do is acknowledge that. Appreciate that even while he was trying to figure out a way to kill a woman he was head over heels for in order to save us, he still made sure *you* were safe. When he got captured and had to plan a whole coup, he still had to know you were safe!"

Fiona's shaking now, her hands balled into tight fists at her side. I place a hand over her shoulders, squeezing her lightly. It takes a few breaths before she looks up at me, her rage slowly evaporating.

When I turn back to my mother, her defeat and shame are clear. It makes my stomach churn as I examine her downturned mouth and quivering chin. "I...I don't know what to say."

Fiona tries to speak but this time I cut her off with my perfected parent stare. She rolls her eyes but gestures with her hand for me to proceed.

"You don't need to say anything. What's done is done, and no part of me resents you or regrets taking care of either of you. We've all made mistakes, granted some more damning than others, but what matters now is that it's over. Fiona deserves a damn vacation, you deserve a minute to breathe, and Harlow deserves her moment alone. She has to want to be found in order for me to find her, and when I do, you'll be the first to know."

Despite my sister's huff of irritation, I unwrap my hand from her shoulders to hug my mother. Our lives are about to go down very different roads, and I doubt she'll stay around for that, meaning this could be one of the last times I get to hug her.

"Go home. Pack what you want, and in the morning, I'll send you wherever you want to go."

"I'm so sorry, Ezekiel." She sobs into my chest. But the light grasp she has around me tells me she's not sorry for leaving. And that's okay.

"Don't be. Go live the life you never got." I release her and move back around my desk.

Her eyes flit between me and Fiona. "And what about you two?"

I shrug, watching as Fiona flops down in one of the chairs across from me. Something mischievous crosses her features, and the familiar look makes me smile. When my gaze flashes back to my mother, it's as if she's seeing her children—really seeing us—for the first time.

There's a curtain closing on a relationship between us that ended years ago. The mutual understanding that not everything can or should be saved.

I love my mother and believe she loves me. But sometimes love isn't enough, and it's okay to release people. Even your family.

"Take care of yourselves," she says, wiping away the lingering tears staining her cheeks.

I clear my throat, ridding myself of the sudden swell of sadness. "You too, Mom."

It isn't until the door shuts behind her that Fiona finally speaks up. "You're going to pay someone to watch her twenty-four seven, aren't you?"

I nod. "Yeah. Probably."

Onyx

Sam's wails of agony are delicious. Better than I ever thought they could be. Each time I hear the crack of a bone, something in me heals. Each time I open a new vein, a part of me relaxes.

It's been years since I've felt such relief. Such euphoria. It's everything I thought it would be and more, and yet it still isn't enough. There's something missing from it all. Something he's not giving me.

Sweat coats every surface of him now, the pungent smell of blood, piss, and body odor almost overwhelming at this point. But for me, it's the smell of justice. Of vindication.

Every one of his fingers is broken in two spots. He's now missing twelve teeth, all of which are from the back of his mouth, and he's sporting thirteen brand-new cuts over his stomach, thighs, and triceps.

He coughs and the sound is wet, riddled with blood. "I have to give you credit."

I turn, pick up the glass jar of Piranha cocktail, and walk back to him. Shi follows behind, bringing a small standing tray and setting it down where it's out of his reach.

He coughs again. "You're smarter than your father."

"Perhaps you shouldn't mention the man you murdered in front of his daughter," I reply coolly, placing the mixture on the stand. "Instead, maybe you should tell me which body part you'd like to have cut off first."

"Fuck you, Embros."

This makes me smile. I have to admit, his unwavering arrogance is entertaining—inspiring, even. Let's see how long it lasts.

I look at Trick and nod over my shoulder. Immediately he drops the side of Sam he was holding and goes to the corner to grab his cauterization bag. When he returns, I have the sharpest knife from the table, and one thick glove covering my right hand.

"Down, please," I tell Trigger, who's quick to strip Sam of his last article of clothing. His flaccid flap of muscle sits stiffly between his legs and for a moment I think of cutting it down the center. But after finding out he's used the disgusting thing to violate so many, my mother included, I decide it needs to vanish completely.

I grab the vile thing in my hand and yank it toward me, stretching it enough to get my blade across it.

The scream that erupts from Sam's mouth is satisfying, but unlike the other few I've had the pleasure of neutering, he doesn't vomit.

Trick moves quickly, burning the flesh and sealing the wound before too much blood spits out.

This time, he does throw up, the splash of chunks and liquid shooting across the floor with surprising force.

Maddy grunts from her spot on the wall. "I'll go get a mop. Perhaps I can use it to plug him up for the next part."

She bounces off just as I wiggle the small piece of flesh in my hand. "Now for my favorite part."

I position the little stand with the mixture directly in front of Sam. His eyes widen, sweat dripping as though he just took a shower while shivers and goose bumps wreak havoc across his body. I move far enough away to not be splashed, and then wink at Sam before dropping his member into the clear liquid.

The pop and sizzle are near deafening as the cocktail does its job of eating away at its food, turning the liquid an inky black.

Sam's eyes snap shut, a grimace contorting his face as if I'm doing this with it still attached to his body. Shi hands me a vial of peroxide, which I add to the solution, coaxing an even more violent reaction.

It only takes a minute of this before the sad little cock is completely vaporized and the satisfaction that he won't have it, even in his afterlife, seeps into my bones.

"Now, what's next?"

Sam smirks, despite the excruciating pain I know he feels, and peels his eyes open. "Whatever you want, *baby love*."

The name is a visceral shot to my chest. A bullet in my heart spreading burning poison down my limbs. The entire room shrinks, then expands, the air too thin and heavy, while everyone fades into darkness.

"Don't apologize, baby love. That passion, that fierceness you have to protect them, is what will make you a great donna one day."

I don't think about what to do, my body now driving of its own accord as my heart and mind collapse into a raging sea that's been threatening to pull me under for far too long.

"Daddy, please. Please."

My hand clutches around a blade, but how I got it, I don't remember. I lift it and shave off a layer of skin reaching from his elbow to his armpit.

"And you, baby love. You are my heart."

He hisses through clenched teeth, jerking as hard as he can against the boys' hold but still doesn't give me what I want. What I *need*. My hands move up. I pinch one eyelid in my fingers while using the other to slice it clean off.

"You have to stay strong because I need you to finish what we started. And after that, I want you to kill them all. Every last one."

His screams are piercing, the fear that's been missing now abundant in his cries. It's like a balm to my burning soul. It flushes a cool shiver down my spine and sparks a new idea.

"Burning is such a painful way to go."

The memory of Kane and I's conversation somehow emerges in the flood of chaos working through my mind. And in that one second, a decision is made.

I walk back to the table and grin as I find the matches. "How about I give you a bit of a preview of what awaits you?"

Oliver slides another piece of paper in front of me. It's the seventh one since my mother left and I have to say, at some point, I thought I might get to sleep tonight. "And what's this?"

"A list of all the drugs we currently run. You'll need to decide which ones we're keeping and where you want to allocate more funds."

"Who's in charge of the narcotics department?" I sigh, running a hand through my hair and glancing over at Fiona. She's still in the same spot, watching and listening to everything as if she's to be tested about it later.

"Currently being cremated with all the other department heads."

I nearly wheeze. "All of them?"

Oliver nods, "Aye, mate. All except me, and I may be biased but having the head of security still kicking isn't too bad of a tradeoff."

I sigh, wincing when I move too fast and pull on my arm. "That it's not."

We go over things, one by one, until I'm almost cross-eyed. He finally relents and gives a small chuckle. "Gotta say, mate. You've done more work in these few hours than I've seen your old man do in years."

I start to grumble a response but am cut off by my phone vibrating on my desk.

Fiona sits up straighter as she looks down and sees the name flash across my screen. We exchange a brief look before I answer, my heart beating in my throat.

"Maddy?"

"Hey, Z. Whatcha up to?"

I've always liked Maddy but hearing her voice now evokes a deep panic in my core. She has no reason to call me unless something is wrong. Unless some—

"Is Onyx okay?" I rush out.

"Physically? Yeah. But something tells me that she's about to have a slight mental collapse here momentarily."

"Momentarily?" I repeat, grabbing the door handle. It's then I realize I got up without thinking.

"Yeah. She's doing a number on Sammy boy right now and soon enough, that fire is going to burn out."

"She'll probably shoot me when she sees me." As I say the words, I realize how much I don't care if she does. "Hell, Trick or Tigger will probably do it before I get to her."

"Believe me. We already knew how much you cared about her before you knew. Granted, they may give you massive shit, but they won't kill you. Just bring a gift or something, you know?"

I can't help but smile a little. When I look back over at Fiona and Oliver, they both have a similar inquisitive expression on their face.

"Better come quick, Z. I can smell him from here."

She doesn't wait for a response and hangs up, leaving me no time to debate with her on whether I should go or not.

"If you don't hurry the hell up and go, I'm kicking your ass." Fiona's standing now, her arms crossed over her chest.

Oliver rounds my desk and nods. "I have to say I agree with the lass. And I have the perfect gift. It's a bit bloody though, so I suggest wrapping it in a towel."

EZEKIEL

CHAPTER THIRTY-TWO

When I pull up to the gate, I'm greeted with the new security system. I roll the window down and touch the small button on the panel.

My pulse thrums in my neck as I wait for them to answer and when the seconds turn into minutes, a sick feeling of dread drops into my stomach. I push the button again, and this time when the speaker makes a small beep, a bolt of elation prickles my skin.

"About time you got here." It's Shi.

"Is she okay?"

"How are you defining that term?" Trick now.

Irritation singes at my nerves, but I keep my tone steady. "Is she hurt?"

"Would you care?" Trigger.

"I'm here, am I not? Despite her promises to kill me if she ever saw me again." I don't mean to raise my voice, but the runaround I'm getting regarding her well-being is beginning to annoy me.

"Is that him?" I have to strain to hear the faint voice of Maddy. "Are you serious right now, Trigger? Let him in."

I don't get to hear Trigger's response because the gate

buzzes before taking entirely too long to slide open. When it does, I feel my phone vibrate in my pocket. I fish it out as I take the paved road up and around. "Yeah?"

"Sorry about that, Z. Trigger's still a little bitter. Boss isn't in here. She's down past the rose bush mazes by the little pond on the other side of the property."

My mind goes over the blueprint Trick once showed me. It was an area I never really went to as it wasn't one of the places guards were required to patrol. But then, it hits me.

The cemetery.

"I'll park in the back and walk over there."

A heavy huff causes static on her end. "Z. I don't know how she's going to be when you get there, but I hope you give her some grace."

I nod even though Maddy can't see me and hang up, driving a little too fast up the driveway. If Onyx agrees to even talk to me, I plan on giving her more than just grace.

When I get to the side of the estate near the kitchen entrance, I park and bolt from my car. It can't be more than a few minutes away on foot, but the closer I get, the heavier my feet feel. There's a stiffness in the air, an unsettling quiet filling it.

My shoulder burns as I run past the rose bushes and down a slope toward the pond. When it comes into view, the pain subsides into a dull ache, replaced by a vicious burn as I find Onyx on her knees.

She's under a massive oak tree, facing away from me, and toward two large headstones. Clutched in her hands are two bouquets of white roses, stems both long and short, the tips jagged as if ripped from the bushes, and covered in dark-red blood.

The closer I walk, the clearer I'm able to make out the

unsteady rise and fall of her shoulders. They shudder as she breathes, almost as she can't get enough air.

She peers over her shoulder briefly but even in that short second, the moon overhead lights up the streaks of blood painting the side of her face.

Again, the tender muscle encased in my rib cage aches to see her this way. Not because of the gore clear from her time with Sam, but the meaning behind his death. The reality she's coming to terms with.

"Get away from me, Kane." Her voice is a hair below deadly.

I take a step forward. "No."

She rises, turning to face me fully. She's covered in blood from head to toe, her fingers still dripping with the evidence of her justice. And never has she looked so damn *tormented*.

"I don't need you to save me!" she bellows, her eyes widening as I take another step.

"I'm not here to save you."

"Then why?" She runs a hand through her tangled ends, streaking more blood through it. "To collect your fallen soldier?"

I shake my head and take one last step. I'm a foot away now —close enough that she could strike me if she wanted, but far enough away she doesn't feel threatened. I want her to know she's in control even if she doesn't feel like it.

"I expect nothing less than for you to put that fucker six feet under. I'm here to sit with you through the storm. Through the pain."

She laughs. It's bitter and strained, and the sound tugs on my heart. "What pain? Can't you see? I'm done. It's over."

I clench my fists together before shoving them in my pockets to keep from reaching out to her. She can't see what I do. Her edges are frayed, the unknown is finally here, and she is about to be hit with the aftermath. Why else would she be here?

She holds out her hands, as if to display she's perfectly alright. "I'm *fine*."

"You don't have to do that with me, Onyx. You don't have to hold on to this persona of someone who doesn't care. You *never* have to do that."

Her brows pinch together briefly before she takes a hard swallow and steps back, shaking her head. "I told you the next time I saw you, I'd kill you. Was the bullet in your shoulder not a sufficient enough warning?"

"I guess not."

Her lashes flutter. "You're an idiot."

I shrug, drawing my lips downward. "Yeah, probably. But when it comes to you, I've done some pretty idiotic shit, and I haven't regretted a thing thus far, so why not keep going?"

Onyx looks to the ground for a beat, then peers over her shoulder to the graves. For a moment, I think she'll put back on that protective armor she loves to wear, and shrink away, stuffing everything down like she's done this entire time. But when she turns to face me again, tears stream down her face, clearing a path through the blood on her cheeks.

The sight is so unbelievably beautiful and jarring, I don't know how to respond at first. I want to do what I've always done when I see a woman cry and run to hug her. Comfort her. But Onyx is not any woman, and if I touch her, I'm likely to lose a body part. So instead, I stay where I'm at, pressing my weight on my heels to keep from moving, and wait.

She doesn't say anything for a long while. We just stand, and she stares at me with her stunning dark eyes and lets the tears fall one after the other. Another minute passes before her lips part and she takes a sharp breath.

"I'm so sorry," she whispers, and immediately, something deep in my core knows she isn't talking to me.

"I—" She turns, dropping to the soft grass beneath her and staring at the pair of headstones. "I'm so sorry. I tried. I tried to get out. I tried to save you. I wasn't strong enough. *I* wasn't enough."

A burn echoes up my throat, but I force it down. I want to tell her she was a fucking child. That it wasn't her job nor within her ability to protect them, but for them to protect her. That they did what any good parents would do, and she *was* enough. She's always been more than enough. But I don't. And instead, I wait.

Her breathing is labored, and her sobs are coming stronger now.

She squeezes one of the soiled roses in her hand and in the next breath, she screams.

It's deep, guttural, and heart wrenching. It's full of all the things she's held in for over ten years and it spills into the night with such force, it makes the air around me thin.

She smashes the rose against her father's headstone. "You fucking left me! You left me to do all this without you! How did you think I would go on without you? And you?"

Onyx turns her face to look at her mother's headstone, the muscles tensing in her entire back as she screams again. "You were everything! Everything to me, and I hate you for leaving! For ruining me. I killed them for you! Every last one. They're all dead. The driver, the guards, the man who stood on the corner and watched but didn't call the police. All of them!" She sucks in a harsh breath and when she speaks again, her voice is softer.

"I did what you asked, yet peace still eludes me. When will I know peace, Mama? When will I know quiet?"

She drops to her knees, pressing both of her hands into the

ground, digging her sharp nails into the grass, and my heart fucking breaks. Her natural instinct is to fight the pain tearing her to shreds. To try and find a way to push it off. But she's done that for too long, and now it's enveloping her.

Unable to fully control *my* instincts, I step closer, my shadow creeping over her frame. It's long and encapsulating, almost as if the reaper has come to take her away.

Onyx glances over at the ominous darkness, and after a moment, the dam breaks free.

Her entire frame shakes as she cries, the sobs so great she has to take long breaths just to satiate her lungs.

Never have I felt this empathy. This deep-seated sadness that I can do nothing for her but let her *feel*. Feel and overcome. And she has to overcome it.

Because even though she won't let me save her, I'll be damned if she loses this fight.

Onyx

CHAPTER THIRTY-THREE

I was crying a moment ago. A trail of hot tears streaming down my face and burning my skin with its weakness. I was sad, afraid. Hurt.

Some juvenile part of me thought that once I had found justice, all the emotions would vanish. The wounds would heal, and the tight ball of desolation would unfurl and slowly drain from my body with every ounce of blood I spilled.

Instead, a floodgate was opened.

Every downcast feeling on the spectrum overwhelmed me, crashing into me one at a time. My muscles shook, my face burned, my insides twisted, and for a moment, I knew *real* pain. A pain I had long forgotten.

But that moment has passed. The sadness and guilt are gone, and in its place is anger.

No, not anger, but a burning rage.

I don't regret who I am. Who I've become. What I've done.

But I am livid that I allowed my fears that I disguised as caution to rule over me. Over my feelings. It's stolen from me every soft thing my parents tried to implant in my heart and hardened me past redemption.

It has made me selfish where I should be empathetic. Arrogant where I should be humble. Hate, when I should love.

I felt stripped of control after they died, and I decided to do everything in my power to gain that sense of control back. And when I found it, I held on until my muscles were weak, until blood dripped from my tight grasp. Until Kane.

At first, he reminded me what it feels like to live, even for a moment, without misery. Then without control. I fought to keep it, but he took it regardless, showing me that I was capable of letting go.

Despite all the times I've tried to push him away, to uproot the seed of hope he's planted in my chest, he's still here. Growing like an invasive weed. He's forced me to want things I'd never thought I'd want again, and I'm angry because I don't know how to do this.

How to let another person in my life and hope that they don't decide to leave. To allow myself to develop another weakness. To love without fear.

The anger bubbles to the surface, frustration and madness careening up my throat and out into the air. The screams that come ring in my ears, singeing my vocal cords. But I don't stop.

I can't.

I want to rip up the roots of doubt, my hopelessness, guilt, and pure agony. I want all of it to burn in the fire of my screams and leave me void of anything but I want.

They spill from me one after another, and for the first time in my life, I let it go. I let it all go until I'm free. Until I'm weightless.

It could be seconds or perhaps minutes, but soon, my wails fade into soft gasps. The air is too thin now, the wind too cold. My throat burns and my chest aches, and all I want to do is rest. Sleep.

Perhaps I can lie right here for a moment.

Just for a second.

I unclench my hands from the grass and move slowly. My eyes flash to the gray stones over my parents' graves, and I realize I can no longer make out the script on them. Everything is blurry. Spinning.

"Onyx?" I hear Kane, but his voice sounds far away, almost as if he's in a tunnel.

I try to look back at him, but he's not there. There's only darkness.

Maybe he wasn't here at all and it was only a dream.

Though my vision is slowly fading, I feel calm as I reach my hand out and touch my father's headstone. It's then that I feel the warmth at my back. The sweet embrace of a loved one. And then I hear him.

"It can be the sunniest days that bring us the most darkness. And the ones with the blackest skies that we find happiness."

I push out a sigh. Yes, it must have been a dream.

The soft rocking of my body wakes me. I allow my eyes to flutter open slightly, just enough to see Kane's throat between my fan of lashes.

My lids are so heavy, though, I can't open them any further.

But he has me.

I feel safe.

It's the sound of rushing water that stirs me this time. My eyes are closed, but the bright lights of what I assume is my nearby bathroom penetrate the darkness. Strong hands glide over my skin and I move accordingly, lifting my arms and moving my hips, so he can strip me of my clothes.

The rough calluses on his palms leave goose bumps in their wake, and I shiver.

Kane's warmth nearly feels like a blanket as he moves closer, rubbing my jaw with his thumb. "I've got you. Lie back. I promise to have your sheets cleaned."

I don't bother opening my eyes and sink into the mattress, letting him take the rest of my clothes off. When he's done, he places a soft, cotton towel over me. "I'll be right back."

Though no words come out, I must make a disgruntled face because he explains further. "You haven't eaten in close to forty-eight hours, so I'm going to grab you something really quick. I won't be but a minute."

Realization hits me when he leaves, taking the comfort of his presence with him. The last time I ate was the morning *before* our meeting with Phineas. And when I got back home, all I wanted to do was shower and kill Sam.

By now, it's probably close to three in the morning.

As if on cue, my stomach contorts, the pain echoing up my esophagus. Clutching the towel tighter, I turn to my side.

I just need to rest. A few moments longer, and I'll be alright.

This time the sweet, tart smell of pineapple wakes me, accompanied by the bed sinking from Kane's weight. I use entirely too much force to open my eyes. I've never been so exhausted before. It's like I finally let go of something I've been carrying for far too long, and now my body is forcing me to rest. To heal.

Kane repositions me to where I'm pressed into his shoulder and my legs are draped over his thighs. I lay my head just below his collarbone and my hand finds his chest. I don't want him to think I'm weak. That I need him.

"I can handle myself."

He chuckles low, kissing me on the top of my head. "I know, baby. Now eat."

I try my best to ignore the warmth that expands in my chest as he sets the bowl in my lap. I begrudgingly pick up the fork, stab the pineapple chunks, and slowly empty the dish.

It isn't nearly enough to satiate my empty stomach but after a few bites, the room feels a lot more stable. He waits quietly, accepting the empty bowl before handing me a bottle of water, which I also take my time drinking.

"Better?"

I nod.

He gives me a lopsided grin, his dimple making a brief appearance, and snakes his arm under my legs.

"You don't need to carry me. I'm perfectly capable of walking." My words come out labored and fatigued, and it only makes Kane's slightly curved lips grow into a full smile.

"Yeah, I know that too. But this is probably the last time I'll ever get to be this close to you. So, will you please just let me have this last moment?" His other arm wraps around my back. "Is that alright with you?"

A fierce burn replaces the comfortable warmth. The idea that the next time I'll see him will likely be from across a desk at a meeting does something weird to my heart. It's an ache. A clench. Something deep behind the muscle that coerces me to give him exactly what he's asking for.

"But your shoulder."

"A flesh wound." He stands, lifting me close to his chest and turning for the bathroom. "And I ran into Cat while getting your fruit. She's going to take a look at it after I get you squared away."

"Squared away," I repeat.

It's not a question but he elaborates anyway. "I came to make sure you were okay. I'm going to help you get cleaned up and get you some breakfast, then I'll be on my way."

"You risked me shooting you just so you could get me breakfast?"

He smirks, pushing the door open wider with his foot. "And I have a gift. Something like a token of goodwill."

My brows furrow. "You should have started with the gift. Where is it?"

Kane nods toward my bedroom. "Near the dresser."

I twist enough to see a box I hadn't noticed before resting on a towel. It's a brown packing box no bigger than a foot tall, but it's the collection of red on both the bottom and the fabric that catches my eye.

My face snaps back to him. "Is that your father's head?"

"And heart."

My eyes flare and my heart flutters. My mouth opens and closes twice to say something—anything—but I'm cut off by his chuckle.

"I'll assume that means you like it."

"I do," I breathe.

"Good."

He sits on the edge of the tub, repositioning me in his lap as he turns on the faucet. Part of me still wants to push him away, tell him I don't need him to take care of me. But the longer I spend with this man, the more I realize it's not about me *needing* him. I *want* him.

I like that he stood by my side while my screams reached hell. I like that he picked me up and carried me all the way back to the estate. I like that despite my selfishness, our differences, and me shooting him, he's still here.

Not because I'm a job assigned by his father. Not because

he's trying to save his sister and mother. Not because I'm his prisoner.

But because *he* wants to, just like I want him to.

I open my mouth to finally thank him, to tell him the things I should have said a long time ago, but he turns, ushering me inside the wide tub.

The moment the warm water hits my back, everything melts. I lean back under the tall faucet, letting the water cascade over me, pelting into my muscles so hard I nearly groan.

My head lolls to the side as I watch the water turn a deep crimson, splashing into the empty tub before swirling down the drain. I lie like this for a while, watching as the color lightens to a pale pink until I shift, letting the water run over a new part of me, and repeating the cycle.

Kane and I sit in silence, the calm from his presence doing strange things to my heart.

After a few minutes, he stands, grabbing a washcloth, soap, shampoo, and conditioner. At first I think he's being courteous, but then he reclaims his seat on the edge of the tub. He places the things down in a row before grabbing my body wash.

"Kane." My voice is laced in warning, but he ignores me.

"Sit there and be quiet, Onyx."

My eyes narrow at his command as he squeezes the soap on the small cloth, rubbing it together to make thick suds. Almost immediately, the citrus scent fills the room, enveloping us in a smell that I know reminds him of our first time in the shower.

A time when things shifted between us and became so much deeper than him simply being my guard.

A heaviness moves between my thighs, but I force it away, focusing on what he just said. "You have washed me one time too many. I can do it myself."

I hold my hand out expectantly, but he ignores me again. "I'm well aware of what you can and can't do."

"So then hand me the soap."

"No."

"You're acting like a child."

He shrugs. "Well, you haven't kicked me out yet, and considering you threatened to kill me the next time you saw me, I think I'll keep pushing my luck."

"Because I don't want to kill you." The admission slips out without my permission, but I don't bother denying the truth anymore.

He smirks, moving down the side of the tub and grabbing one of my legs. "I know that too."

A spark of irritation flickers through me. "And what else do you know, Kane? Please, enlighten me."

I watch with a straight face as Kane washes my calf with such a delicate touch. I have to fight the urge to tell him he's cleaning nothing with the little pressure he's applying. He slides the cloth up my thigh, moving faster when he reaches close to my cunt, almost as if he doesn't want to touch it.

Kane, the gentleman, through and through.

When he doesn't answer and moves to the next leg, I sigh impatiently. "I don't like waiting."

"Another thing I know."

I huff. "I'm starting to reconsider a few things."

"You're not. If anything, you're learning more and more about how you like being transparent with someone. How you like knowing that you can be vulnerable."

He blows out a deep breath and works the cloth up my stomach, around my breasts, and over my thumping heart. He stops when he gets to my throat, caressing the column with his thumb.

Every nerve in my body is vibrating, a war erupting inside of me on whether to deny or accept his claims.

Would it be so bad to trust again? To give whatever we have a chance?

My heart knows the answer seconds before my mind does, and Kane must read it across my face because he leans in, pressing a soft kiss to my nose. "And if we're being completely honest, you like knowing you're mine."

"Yours," I repeat, breathing in his faint woodsy smell before he draws back.

He nods. "You are. And when you figure that out—when you accept it—you know where I'll be."

My heart swells, and a knot forms in my throat. His patience is one I'll never know, but truly appreciate.

Instead of a response, we both remain quiet, and I let him do what he always does, and wash me clean. When he's all done, it's all I can do to not grab onto his hand and tell him to stay. Tell him to lie with me until I fall asleep.

But that rational side of me that's been in charge rears its head and reminds me of all that's happened in the past week. All that we've been through.

I need to rest. To sleep. Eat a full meal.

So instead of doing what my entire body yearns to do, I accept his outstretched hand and hoist myself from the tub.

He hands me a towel before turning. "I'm going to get your breakfast and get patched up by Cat before I go. Lie down and I'll be back in a bit."

"Thank you."

He shakes his head. "Don't thank me. It's my job to take care of you, *mo bhanríon*."

A smirk curls my lips before I can stop it, but then the tender spot in my chest aches when he turns, leaving me in the bathroom alone.

I stare at the door until goose bumps sprout over my shoulders, the result of cold water dripping from the tips of my hair.

It could be the fatigue, or maybe just the beginning of a new era, but nothing feels the same. My mind, heart, and soul are at war, all of them fighting for dominance as to who should have the last say.

My mind is stubborn. It repeats Antonio's teachings over and over. It tells me to stuff down the need I feel to give in to my heart. To give in to the passion that arises every time I even think of Kane. But my mind is also selfish. It wants me to claim Kane the same way he claims me, even though it doesn't want me to care.

An uninvited image of another woman on his arm turns my entire body hot almost immediately, that foolish heart of mine squeezing with a flare of envy.

My heart. Such a distracting muscle. It hasn't worked quite right in ten years, and after Antonio, I'm not sure how it still works at all. I thought it would take its last beat when I was out there on the grass. In front of their graves, crying. Screaming.

Hoping.

The waves of my life were overwhelming me. Consuming me. Tearing my vessel to shreds with every lash of lightning, and score of wind. In those moments, I sent a silent prayer to my parents that if I was meant to come out of this alive, to let me find a light to lead me back to shore. To somehow calm the raging waters.

And they did.

Ezekiel Kane did.

My eyes flash to the door again.

My soul, my innate being, is made up of the remnants of my mother and father. It's crafted from devotion, commitment, admiration, and love. It burns with the fire to help the helpless and save those who deserve retribution. To condemn those who don't.

Even through my plans for vengeance, I never lost those things. Perhaps they had been snuffed out a bit, placed on the back burner. But never gone completely, no matter how much my uncle tried.

To give him due credit, he taught me many lessons over the years that would result in us getting everything we wanted. He prepared me, and made me into the donna and machine that I am today. But whether it was because we never thought I would survive the other side of that justice, or simply because he didn't think he'd live to see it, we never talked about life after we succeeded.

Life after I found a reason to love. To *want* to love.

My gaze flits to the bloody box near my dresser. Is it mad that I'm smitten with the fact that Kane brought me the head and heart of his father? Perhaps. But I've never proclaimed to have my sanity.

And the man who has brought me back from the brink of death twice now doesn't seem to mind at all.

He doesn't mind any of my faults. He doesn't try to fix them either. He likes to be everything I need when I need it, while also enjoying those very same aspects of me. Kane is my light, my shore to rest, and I refuse to give that up.

I refuse to give him up.

The idea formulates before I step out of my bathroom. I make quick work of dressing and putting up my hair. I grab a new towel and wrap the box up before tucking it beneath my arm and exiting my room. I pass the stairs and go down the long hall, past the long windows that look out over the pool and stop just before my uncle's door.

I don't have my father, nor my mother, and perhaps for that reason, I need his blessing. His release from the chains that tell me I can't do this. That Kane and I can't make it work.

Trepidation works in my bloodstream as I rap my knuckles against the wood.

Antonio coughs twice, the sound somehow a combination of wet and dry. "Come in."

My hand shakes when I lift it to turn the knob. Not because I'm afraid of the man bound to his bed in illness. Nor the idea that he might tell me I shouldn't try to be with Kane.

But because I know that my uncle, the last relic I have to remind me of my father, will soon join him in death.

I push the door open slowly, revealing a man I've avoided since he became bedridden, and a deep-seated heaviness moves over my heart. His gray ends are swept back, away from his sullen face. His thin frame can be made out from the blankets Cat has tucked in around him. And when he opens his eyes, they are no longer the piercing stones I remember them to be, but instead, glazed over gray marbles.

It's hard, abysmal even, seeing such a strong man brought down by his own body. It's cruel really, a death only karma can bring to someone like us.

He examines me for a few seconds before he beckons me inside. I swallow, clearing my throat as I enter, my steps much heavier than they were on my journey here. "Good morning, Uncle."

He gestures to the chair next to his bed with the slight tilt of his face. "Is it morning already?"

I glance at the bedside clock that's pushed too far back for him to see it, and nod. "Yes. It's still early, though. Only four."

Antonio coughs again, his small body seeming to rattle as it jerks.

"Do you want some water?"

He shakes his head. "I'd much rather speak with my niece.

I'm happy to see you back home. I knew you would be, of course, but I did worry about lasting until you did."

The indirect mention of his impending doom spreads a twinge of pain through my extremities. "I'm glad you did. I have something to show you before I use it in the garden."

Antonio's eyes flash to the box in my hands. He nods once and I respond immediately, opening the lid. I tilt it toward him slowly and we both look together, the sight one of pure euphoria.

Of pure relief.

He sinks back into his pillow as I close the box and place it next to the chair. "It is done."

"It is," I reply but the guilt makes me clarify. "It wasn't by my hand, though."

He nods knowingly. "Your guard. His son."

"Yes."

"And he gave you his father's head?"

"Not the most normal way to profess a crush on a girl, even in our world." I try to make light of the tense air, and thankfully Antonio grants me the smallest of grins.

"Normal is an illusion. What is normal for the spider is chaos for the fly. Your idol said that, did she not?"

It's my turn to smile now. "Morticia Addams, a queen if there ever was one."

"*You* are a queen, Onyx."

My face sobers immediately, the telltale sting of tears prickling my eyelids. My uncle has never complimented me, and now that he has, I feel as though I don't deserve it. I shake my head. "I didn't kill him."

"Did you kill Sam?"

"Yes."

"Did you not bring all the others to justice that were there that day?"

"I did."

His face blooms pink, as if his body wants to cough and expel the buildup in his chest, but he refuses to succumb as he speaks. "And you survived. You survived witnessing your parents' brutal demise at a young age. The training of a man who holds no punches, and the grueling reality of what it is to be a female mob boss. Only a select few can claim the same, Onyx."

He tries to sit up and waves me off as I lean forward to help.

"I am amazed by you, Onyx. Of both who you are and how well you've overcome the obstacles against you. You know as well as I do that women are made of exteriors like stones and hearts that never stop growing. The will of a bull and wisdom of an oracle. And you are a fine example of that."

A flurry of emotions swells in my throat, but it's his final words that release my tears to fall down my cheeks.

"I'm proud of you, and I know for damn certain, with every fiber of my being, that Jada and Dante are as well. You've done right by them, Onyx."

My body moves of its own accord, and I lean forward, wrapping my arms around my uncle, and hugging him until he groans in happy protest. It's the first time I've hugged someone since my parents died, and I hadn't realized just how much I missed the simple act.

Every muscle in my body relaxes, the chaos in my mind dwindling to calm. "Thank you."

He pats my back and I pull away, swallowing hard and wiping my face of the residual tears.

"It's been my pleasure to be here. To be able to say I helped shape such an amazing woman. I mean it." Antonio shifts, falling back into his pillow. A fit of coughs spew out and he accepts the water I grab from his bedside table with no qualms this time.

After he slowly empties the bottle, he turns to me, a foreign, playful gleam in his eyes wrinkling the skin in the corners. "Now, for a story."

I arch a brow. "A story?"

He nods stiffly. "Yes. I only get paid visits by that worm of a woman, Cat. So I'd like to hear firsthand what's been happening."

A sharp pang echoes in my chest, guilt still present even though we've made amends. "Caterina is far from a worm. She looks after you."

"Let us agree to disagree on that front. But tell me." He hands me the empty bottle and closes his eyes. "I want to know everything, especially about the man who's made my niece fall head over heels."

This gets a laugh out of me. "I'd hardly say I love the man."

"And here I thought you were past the stages of denial." He peels his eyes open, a more somber expression now pulling down his features slightly. "I was wrong to tell you that love meant weakness. I was so focused on avenging my brother that I wanted to make sure it was all you thought about too. But, Onyx, from your found family that used to drive me up the wall, to this guard, I'm so glad you still found it within you to care. To love. You are so much stronger than even I gave you credit for."

I push out a heavy sigh. The combination of emotions he's evoking from me are fraying any edges I have left intact. So instead of a response, I slide my chair closer and place a hand on top of his.

His skin is cold, despite the thick duvet covering him, and so frail, I make sure my nails don't touch him in fear of scratching him. I lay my head on his shoulder and close my eyes.

It's the only tender moment we've had besides the initial news of my parents. But even then, he only wanted me to feel anger. So, I take advantage of this rare moment and rest with him. We sit like this for a long time, and it isn't until sleep tries to steal me that I finally rise.

"Get some sleep, Uncle. I'll be back to check on you later."

A grin curls his lips. "I'd like that. Maybe then you can tell me about this guard of yours."

I chuckle low as I move the chair back in place. "He isn't my guard anymore. He's the don of the Murphy family now. Our competition."

He shrugs. "Or perhaps it's the dawn of something new. Whatever you decide, I know it will be both what's best for you, and the Embros family."

My heart warms as I nod my thanks, but as I bend and pick up the box with Phineas's head, Antonio sits up straighter, gesturing to it. "What will you do with them? Plant them in the roses?"

I almost start to say yes, but a new idea forms. When I was younger, it was never a secret that I didn't care for the thorny bush. I only ever went to the garden because it was time spent with my mother. After her death, I avoided the white ones, the constant reminder of red dripping from the petal too much for me to bear. Little by little it's become easier, and now, I think it's time for the redemption of the flower that taught me why beautiful and delicate things can also draw blood.

"I think I'll put him down by mom. Plant a new white bush next to her tombstone."

His eyebrows lift. "White?"

I nod. "Yes."

"Maybe you can wheel me down there and I could help

you?"

We both smile. "I'd really like that, Uncle."

A sheen crosses his eyes as he closes them. "If you see that old worm, tell her don't wake me in an hour with breakfast. I think I'll sleep in today."

I laugh low and shake my head as I walk to the doorway. "Sure."

My steps aren't heavy when I travel back down the hall. My chest isn't tight as I drop off the box at my door and walk down the stairs. And for the first time in entirely too long, screams don't fill my head as I wander to the kitchen.

In no way do I think I am completely and miraculously null of my pain. Of my deep grief. But I know this is something new. It's promise and hope blooming in a place I thought void of life.

And it's beautiful.

Cat's voice reaches me in the hall just before it opens to the kitchen. "Why must you be so insufferable? Give the man steak and eggs."

"So he can die of a stroke? Fairly sure that's more painful than what's taking him right now."

"Yes, that would hurt more," Kane agrees with Russ.

Kane.

My heart flutters like a prepubescent teen, and I have to bite into my lip to keep from smiling. *He's still here.* This man is the epitome of mad. And I absolutely love it.

"And who... are you?" Cat bites.

The low roll of Kane's laughter sends goose bumps up my arm and pushes my feet forward. "Ezekiel Liam Kane. Don to the Murphy family."

Cat's eyes flash to me briefly before narrowing in on Kane. "So not the guard you claimed to be. Seems as though you're a little lost, then, *don to the Murphy family.*"

He shrugs, pushing a plate across the bar to the empty seat on his right. "Perhaps. But the danger in staying here is worth the potential ending."

A fierce burn radiates behind my rib cage as his words remind me of the remnants of something I was told so long ago, I thought it lost to memories.

"Anyone can fight for redemption, baby love." My mother wipes away the lone tear streaking down my cheek. "Only those that deserve it will face any obstacle, and if they never lose sight of what they're fighting for, it's always worth giving them a second chance."

In my eyes—in my heart—Kane deserves the same courtesy he's extended to me. He's allowing me to prove that I am more than my parents' deaths, more than revenge, just as he is more than a tool used to do the bidding of others.

We are one and the same, and it's time I accept that as the fortunate miracle it is.

I steady my expression and move behind him. "Is that so?"

Russ chuckles, adding a cup of steaming coffee to the vacant spot, while Cat gives me a mischievous smirk.

Kane glances over his shoulder. "It is. Come to eat with me?"

"No. Simply delivering a message to Cat."

He turns swiftly in his chair, rotating so quickly I barely have time to step back. He's able to catch me around the waist and tug me between his legs. My heart leaps in my throat as I try to move against his tight hold. "Look at me when you lie to me, Boss."

I don't want to smile, to admit just how much of a liar I am when it comes to my feelings for this man. But I think I'm done pretending. At least for today.

I look at the full plate next to him and realize he was

expecting me. It's my usual. He hoped for the impossible, and he got just that.

"I guess. But only because I don't want to insult Russ since he's already made it, and my stomach is still rather empty."

Kane's dimple shows as he smirks and releases me to sit. "Yeah, of course, that's why."

I bite on the inside of my cheek and stay between his legs. "But you can be a good boy and feed it to me."

A row of pearly white peek through his lips, as he draws a thumb down my jaw. "As you wish, *do mhórgacht*."

My heart sings the entire time we eat, laugh, and enjoy Russ and Cat's banter. It isn't until the kitchen is clean and Cat's patching Kane's shoulder, after I told her not to wake Antonio, that I realize it.

All along, I knew Kane was the key to my downfall. To my end. What I didn't understand, but do now, is that through the destruction of what I once was, I am the woman my parents raised me to be.

A woman of passion and respect. Of righteousness and honesty. My hands may forever be stained in the blood of the evil, but my heart is full with the promise and hope of those I've saved.

When I was a child, I always wondered how the Queen of Hearts became the way she was. Why she was so angry. I ran through many ideas. Many speculations. And while I'll never truly have the answer to that question, I do know one thing.

Her blind rage, her perversions of logic, her entire essence wasn't that of a monster. But of someone that was bound to fear. Ruled by it.

And with my family, with Kane, I will never again succumb to the depths of such turmoil. I will never be allowed to perish in my doubt.

With them, I will *always* believe in the impossible.

Ezekiel

EPILOGUE

Three Months Later

"I'll give you Walton Street if you give me Bordon," I say through clenched teeth, my nerves on fire now.

Negotiating with Onyx has become, well, for lack of a better word, excruciating. She drives a hard bargain, and with her stubborn as hell mindset, it often takes us days to come to an agreement on something that should only take us an hour.

Merging the two sides will take time for a plethora of reasons, but most importantly, by doing it slower, we are reducing the risk of any unnecessary altercations within the ranks or possible accusations from nearby families of being a monopoly,

Who knew the Mafia could become a monopoly? I sure as hell didn't.

"Kane. You're not getting Bordon. It's too high traffic for either of us to occupy, and you're well aware of that fact." Onyx tightens her grip on my jaw, forcing my face to the right as she leaves a trail of hot kisses down my throat.

I try to adjust, but the restraints don't give enough leeway, and my wrists scream as I pull against them. But the pain mixes with a surge of blood traveling south, and I groan. "The girls at the club need more traffic. I took away too much of their money with my new rules."

"Keeping your girls happy. I'm not sure if I should be proud or a little jealous." I feel her smile against my chest as she works her way down.

Even though she's messing with me, the thought of Onyx jealous makes my pulse soar, and my dick jerks in response.

"Patience, love," she tsks, moving both her hands down to glide over my naked stomach.

Everywhere she touches turns to fire, and my body aches after having to endure thirty minutes of the constant back and forth. She's touching and teasing all the places with multiple nerve endings, and my cock has never been harder.

"Let's finish talks of new territory later," I say, hating the way the low timbre in my voice conveys my want. This woman always wins when it comes to who caves first.

Her soft lips touch past the V of my hips and when her warm breath cascades over my erection, I can't hold back the groan.

She smiles. It's bright and beautiful and all the things that make me fall in love all over again, but right now, it pisses me off. "What could be more important than *coming* to an agreement?"

A joke. Funny.

"Your mouth on my cock. Your pussy on my face. *So* many things, baby."

"Hmmm," she hums, moving farther down the bed and repositioning herself right between my thighs.

She peers up at me through her thick lashes and my dick fucking weeps at the sight.

"I *need* you, Onyx. Please."

"I never thought the sound of a man begging for my cunt would make me tingle as much as when they beg for death. Perhaps if you did it more, you'd find I can be quite generous."

Her pink tongue makes an appearance as she wets the corner of her mouth and I hold my breath. Why I agreed to be tied to this bed is beyond me, but I know I've never regretted anything more.

"*Please.*" Did I just fucking whimper?

She smiles, triumph clear in her tone. "Tell me exactly what you want. Control my every movement, Kane."

My nostrils flare as I soak in her words. Control without control. This woman is maddening.

"Lick me," I grit through clenched teeth. "Base to tip, then back again. Then I want you to put those perfect lips around my cock and suck until your cheeks hollow out."

She smirks before doing what she's told. "As you wish."

This time when her tongue comes out, it finds the base of my dick, the heat from her mouth making me buck my hips. Onyx gives me a disapproving growl as she moves her hands, digging her nails into both of my thighs.

A sharp hiss escapes me, but the pain quickly morphs into pleasure as her tongue curls around the head, then trails back down. When she comes up again, her lips form a perfect circle before sealing around my cock.

I sink back and my eyes shut, the sensation so damn overwhelming it makes breathing almost impossible.

She glides her mouth down, then up, her tongue flicking and caressing underneath. My head begins swimming, the muscles surrounding my spine tightening every time she allows me to hit the back of her throat.

I want to touch her. To grab her. To fuck her mouth until tears are streaming down her face.

"Onyx," I groan, the heat in my groin already building. She knew what she was doing when she teased me for thirty minutes; I refuse to let her win, and for this to be over so soon.

Still, when I look down at the sight of such a powerful woman with her lips around my cock, I can't help but appreciate how stunning she is. "You're so fucking beautiful."

"Hmm," she hums again, continuing at a pace that's beginning to make my legs shake.

"Give me your pussy. I need to take it. *Now.*" My voice is a command and to my slight surprise, she follows it promptly.

She releases my dick with a wet pop, and slowly—oh so fucking slowly—drops her satin robe to the floor.

Her body is all soft curves and smooth amber skin. Her eyelashes flutter as she looks to me for further instruction. The way she's both dominating me while being submissive to my will is such a turn-on it hurts.

"Up here. On my face," I grit out.

The corner of her lips curls as she climbs on top of me, putting her knees on either side of my face. She hovers over me at first, another ploy to tease me with the perfect view of her glistening pussy.

It's so fucking wet, and all I want to do is sink inside of it.

I groan, shifting beneath her. "*Drop.*"

She chuckles. It's low and breathy, and fuck, if I'm not deep in her cunt in the next five minutes, I'm going to lose it.

The slight slack on my restraints allows me to grab her knees and yank them apart, forcing her delicious pussy on my mouth. She shivers with the contact, making me smile.

I like that despite her passive exterior, her body always tells me what she won't.

My pace is slow at first, the flat of my tongue making long, languid strokes as I coax little whimpers from her. But then she seats herself farther, granting me the ability to suck her swollen clit in my mouth.

She tenses. "Attaboy. Just like that."

Fuck, her heady whispers are going to do me in.

She only allows me to play with the sensitive nerves for a few moments before she lifts slightly, then drops back down. I position myself right at her entrance, my tongue dipping in and out of her as she rides my face.

She does this again and again, her legs starting to shake as she continues to move up and down. "You're such a good boy, Kane. Fucking me with that talented tongue of yours."

That's right, mo bhanrion. Take what you need.

She rocks her hips back and forth now, her moans spilling out one after the other. It fuels my movements, and the lashes of my tongue become fast and torturous.

I feel her try to snake a hand between her thighs and relieve the pressure I know is building, but I nip at her clit, making her suck in a harsh breath.

"Mine," I bark, before going back to work on her pussy.

"Kane..." She trails off and I already know.

My fingers dig into her thighs as she continues fucking my face, trying to find the perfect angle. When she does, she jolts, and her entire body tenses.

"Come on my mouth, baby. Give it to me."

Onyx groans again, pressing herself so close to my mouth she nearly cuts off my breathing. I swear, every time I think this woman can't get any more perfect, she does.

I suck her clit harder and, as if on cue, she comes, leaning her forehead into the arm she has against the wall for support, and screaming her release.

I allow her a moment to come down, but she's panting, shaking, and I'm fairly sure she's still pulsing when I shrug my shoulders and force her to rise. "Now be a good whore and untie me so I can fuck you."

As if I told her a fire was happening, she moves, her hands fumbling with the knot so quickly the rope chafes against me. I couldn't care less, and the moment she frees one hand, I help her get the other loose.

Onyx yelps when I flip her, pushing her onto her stomach, jerking her body to the end of the bed so I can stand between her thighs. I position my hand in the middle of her spine, pressing her farther into the mattress while the other slides down her back and caresses her ass.

It's so soft under my rough hands.

"Give me Bordon Street," I say, rubbing down to her thighs before digging my fingers back up.

She doesn't miss a beat. "No."

A loud pop rings out, along with her hushed curse as I rub the tender spot I just slapped.

After a moment, I move the hand that's been holding her in place and comb my fingers through her long ponytail. She sucks in a breath, likely knowing what I'm about to do as I wrap it around my wrist.

"Give me what I want." She shakes her stubborn little head and I yank her back, forcing her to arch her spine. "Or I'll take it, Onyx."

Still, she doesn't relent. "*No.*"

Keeping her head in place, I draw my hand back and slap her ass again, this time much harder.

My blood soars when she tries to wriggle from beneath me, her moans of pleasure somehow driving my dick harder than it was already.

As if she knows, she pushes back, her wet cunt sliding over my cock and making me gasp.

She wants to play dirty? *Fine.*

I rub the angry handprint I left behind before I move to fist myself. I drag my dick through her slit, and *fuck*, I'm so glad she can't see my face.

"Is this what you want?" I ask, making another pass.

When she tries to make a gesture with her head, I tug on the ends of her hair. "Words, Onyx. Use those pretty words of yours."

"No," she lies, not even bothering to hide the whimper in her voice.

"What did I tell you about doing that? I need my whore to look at me when she lies to me." I make a harder swipe through her wetness, tapping her clit with the head of my cock. "Tell me what you want and it's yours."

She doesn't answer me for a long moment. The only noise in the room is our quick breathing and my racing heart. I give her another second before I release her hair and bend over, shifting my hand around to her delicate throat.

I let my cock go as well, and my fingers find her clit, stroking in lazy circles as I catch her earlobe between my teeth.

"I want you to fuck me, Kane." Onyx widens her legs and allows me better access. "But you won't come until I tell you to. Until I've had my fill."

My fingers falter, my hand losing its tight grip around her neck.

It's a challenge, and she knows I love a good challenge.

Fuck, this woman.

I smirk, euphoria rushing through my veins as I accept. "Yes, ma'am."

In one quick motion, I'm up and have her flipped on her back. I yank her down by her thighs, latching my arms around them as I line up with her entrance.

My eyes flash to hers, and the sight of her hooded gaze is

breathtaking. It's hungry and needy, and I don't bother being sweet as I slam into her. She wants her fill? I'll give it to her.

Onyx cries out, her hands flying over her head to grab on to anything to help her. At least that's what I think until a pillow hits me square in the chest.

"Under me," she commands, her voice damn near lethal.

I do as told, and shove it beneath her, just under her hips. The new angle has both of us groaning in unison as I drive in and out of her.

The silver barbells in her nipples catch the light every time my hips meet hers, and I promise myself to have them between my teeth after she comes again.

In and out. I slam into her with a punishing force, loving the way her body starts to writhe. "Tell me who you belong to."

In. Out. In. Out.

When she doesn't answer, I draw all the way out, and slap her glistening cunt, before plowing back inside.

"You, Ezekiel," she gasps. "I belong to you."

"That's right, *mo chailín deas*. Mine."

My thumb rubs circles on her throbbing clit, and it doesn't take long before I feel her starting to clench. Her legs stiffen and her knuckles bloom white as she fists the sheets.

"Harder, Kane. Fuck me like I'm your whore and not some delicate flower."

"Yes, ma'am." I chuckle, dropping her legs. "Hold them open."

She does as told, forcing her legs far apart as I barrel into her again and again. My own orgasm starts to build, and it takes everything in me to hold it at bay.

My hand not occupied at her clit slides up her stomach, and over her breast, grabbing hold of her throat. I squeeze the soft column and bark my command. "Come for me like the good girl I know you are."

She tries to prolong it, but it was already there, and the moment I say the words, she combusts.

Her cunt grips me as her orgasm rips through her, and the heat flares up my spine. I know better than to think I can deny myself much longer.

She shudders with every pulse, her chest heaving up and down as she tries to catch her breath. I decide to use her state of bliss to my advantage.

"May I come now, *mo bhanríon?*"

I've slowed my pace significantly, drawing out her orgasm while also attempting to calm my racing heart.

Onyx looks at me, a dreamy and satiated gleam in her dark eyes. An ache stretches across my chest. She's so damn gorgeous in every single way, but this look—the one where she knows nothing but bliss and happiness—is my favorite. And knowing it was me that made her feel that way only lights up my soul.

Finally she nods, and I release the breath I was holding.

She yelps when I grasp either side of her hips and flip her, forcing her legs to straddle me as I sit at the edge of the bed. When I pierce into her, she gives another startled cry, and I can't hold back the chuckle.

"You're going to give me another one, Boss."

Her eyes widen and she shivers, but she still tries to come off impassively. "If you can achieve such a feat, I welcome it."

I smirk. I like when she does this. When she pushes me to the brink of my sanity. It makes it all the better when she crumbles.

Keeping my hands firmly on her sides, I lift her, and slam her down. Her hands fly to my back, her nails coercing a hiss from me when they dig into the flesh.

Again I lift her, dropping her harder this time.

She screams out, her head falling to the side, and my eyes

follow the curve of her neck down to the perky nipples of her breasts. I lean forward, the urge too great to ignore, and suck one into my mouth. My tongue slides over the metal, tugging it slightly, before I bite down just enough to make her jolt.

Onyx moans her approval, threading her fingers through my hair and tugging by the root. "Again."

I smile as I move to the other side. "My needy girl."

"Yes," she sighs. "And I need you to close that pretty mouth and fuck me."

This grants her a more forceful bite, which I soothe with my tongue afterward.

She grinds against me, bouncing just enough to keep her fully seated. I release her breast and move up, trailing kisses and soft bites until I reach her mouth.

Her second hand joins the first in my hair, and we kiss as if we need each other to breathe. It's starved and passionate, nothing but tongue, teeth and pure need.

She continues to move back and forth as we take everything we can, and it isn't until I feel her shaking that I relent and pull away.

I return my hold to her hips and start thrusting inside of her like a madman, using her to fuck myself. She grabs onto my shoulders, trying to match my pace and intensity, but the game is over.

I lift and yank her down, and the scream she lets out reverberates down my spine and into my dick. Heat and lightning unfurl, my own orgasm building into something it never has before. My muscles are tense, my body rigid, everything wound so tight it almost hurts.

"God," she moans, and I feel the clench of another climax about to break through her.

"No. Not God." I somehow pound into her harder, my heart slamming into my chest so violently my rib cage aches.

"Tell me." *Thrust.*

"Who." *Thrust.*

"You." *Thrust.*

"Belong to." *Thrust.*

She screams my name as the waves of our orgasms tear through both of us. I continue fucking her, riding it as fire erupts low in my gut. Sparks fill my vision, the room going hazy as I spill everything into her, pain and pleasure ricocheting down my back as she claws into me.

It isn't until she's trembling and whimpering from overstimulation that I finally slow to a stop, easing her gently on the bed.

I shift to lienext to her, my hand trailing down her stomach lazily. Her muscles tighten as my fingers walk closer to her cunt and when I reach it, she grabs my hand.

"You've proved your point, Kane. You'll ruin me."

"Just as you drive me mad." My smile evident in my voice. "And are you saying you can't give me another?"

In Onyx fashion, she narrows her eyes, tossing my hand away. "Give me ten minutes."

"Five."

Her eyes flare. "Eight."

"As you wish, my queen," I say, my pulse still thrumming in my neck.

My chest is so full and light. Who fucking knew that the debt I owed the universe in the first half of my life would lead me to this?

If I would have known, I wouldn't have complained for one damn second.

Onyx's head sinks into the pillow and she boops me on my nose, that look I love so much cemented on her face. "My king."

My heart stutters in my chest, and a similar bliss like the one lighting up Onyx flows through me.

Reluctantly, I force myself from the bed and grab a warm,

wet towel to clean her up. She shudders and squirms as I slide over her clit, and I'm fairly certain she curses when I push some of my cum back into her cunt.

But when I'm done, I crawl back in bed and pull her into the crook of my arm. We stay like this for what could be an hour as I stroke her hair and whisper how incredibly amazing she is. All the while, she accepts my praise with a content smile on her face, telling me that no matter how sweet I am, I'm not getting Bordon.

Never did I think this would be possible. That I would be allowed to live in a reality that feels like a dream.

But that's what she's done to me—merged the two to where I don't know which is which.

Then again, it doesn't matter. She's the queen of my madness, I am the king of her ruin, and this is our wonderland.

THE END

Maddy

EARLIER...

She's so beautiful. Why is she so fucking beautiful? This would be so much easier if she had the personality of a troll. If she wasn't as tormented as me, but still somehow stayed pure through it all.

She doesn't deserve to die.

Not like this.

Not by me.

I twirl the knife in my hand as I watch Harlow enter the corner store. She's got on ripped jeans, a faded House of Blues shirt, and combat boots. It's so unlike the little waitress number I met her in. Her brown hair sways behind her as she walks briskly down the front aisle, right in front of the store's floor-to-ceiling windows.

The guy behind the counter looks up as she enters, but goes back to his gardening magazine, seemingly uninterested in her presence.

That shouldn't bother me. It shouldn't make the nerve in my jaw tic or cause me to tighten my grip on my blade. But I do. Everyone should notice such an unbelievable creature like her.

A creature you're about to skewer.

I shake my head, focusing on the make-believe rattle of my brain instead of the wayward thoughts.

It doesn't matter that she's beautiful. It doesn't matter that she's got the will of a flower growing through a brick wall. It doesn't matter that I love her.

Loved her.

She betrayed my family. Boss. Me.

And she can't live to see tomorrow.

Decision made, I tuck my blade in my back pocket and check both sides of the street again. It's fairly barren this time of the night, with only the occasional skateboarder or late worker passing through.

I cross over and wait in the alley next to the store. It only takes a few minutes before the old-fashioned bell hanging over the door rings and I hear the heavy steps of her boots as she leaves.

Sucking in a breath, I ignore the whooshing of my blood in my ears.

Get your head on straight, Mads. Focus.

A flash of brown hair and a small squeak later, Harlow is up against the alley wall, my hand pressed against her mouth, my blade at her throat. The bag of items she bought is scattered on the floor around us, and her eyes flare when she sees it's me. When she realizes she's caught.

"Hey there, sweet girl. Long time no see."

She squeezes her eyes shut, shaking her head the best she can under my tight hold.

"Are you going to scream or be a good girl?"

Harlow nods once, her eyes fluttering as they fill with tears. The sight is not unfamiliar to me as I've watched them stream down her face plenty of nights I've pushed her past her limits with orgasms. But tonight, it's not from the intense pleasure. Not from extreme bliss. It's from realization.

Her gambled lies have caught up with her, and I have come to collect the debt.

I move my hand that was covering her mouth but keep my knife in place. She sucks in a sharp breath before more lies start to spill out. "Madeline, I swear I had no choice. I would never, ever do anything to hurt you. They had my mother, I couldn't. I'm—"

She stops when I nick her throat, drawing the smallest drop of blood. My heart is beating faster now, the desire to believe her so great I nearly choke as I dole out my threat. "I will finish slicing this delicate little neck of yours if you don't stop talking. I'm not here to talk. I'm here to teach you the consequences of your actions."

Harlow begins to cry now. She tries to reach up and touch me but must think better of it because she drops her hands to her side.

"I didn't think—"

"People that don't think,shouldn't speak, sweet girl." I run my blade along her collarbone and watch the goose bumps trail up her arm.

"Madeline, plea—"

"Don't." My eyes flash back to her and I hate the way my stomach curdles at how wrong this feels.

How I know without a shadow of a doubt that she didn't want to hurt me. But it doesn't matter. She has to pay for what she's done.

She has to.

I clamp my teeth together, cursing my shaking hand. *Fuck.*

"Here's what we're gonna do. You're going to run. Run as far as you can. And if I find you—" I pause, running my nose along her neck, inhaling her sweet vanilla scent for the last time. "*When* I find you, your head is mine."

She whimpers, and I hate that I'm not sure if it's from the

promise of death, or that she knows we're over. The lover in me hopes it's from the latter, though. I take a wide step back and point with my knife, ignoring the rip tearing my heart to shreds.

"Now. Run, little rabbit."

Harlow chokes on a sob and the pain in my chest rolls down my limbs. But I somehow force my feet to stay in place.

She blinks at me twice before nodding, her voice barely above a whisper. "I'm sorry."

I'm silent as she turns and runs, not stopping once to look back. It isn't until she and her scent are long gone that I finally breathe. "Me too, sweet girl."

The Hatter and the Hare:
A Novella to come

Acknowledgments

AHHHHH! You made it here. Member that's what I said last time? And it was worth it right?! Right!?

Hehe, no but seriously. Thank you so much for falling down the rabbit hole with me and going on this amazing adventure. I've had so many people reach out about short stories surrounding the other members of Wonderland and I'm happy to say it's in the works.

As always, I also want to thank my hubs who made this book possible with wrangling the kids and cooking me yummy meals. To my kids for always walking in when I'm writing the spiciest scenes. And to my incredible alphas and betas.

Lo, Well read, Booktok's Drew. My light. The one I call when the world is on fire. I would say you're my fire extinguisher but it doesn't sound a poetic. But seriously, your patience, your encouragement, your check-ins, your four hour conversations...all of it, every last bit, is what made me believe in the impossible. (Yes, I know it's the theme of this book. Coincidence? I THINK NOT.) There will never be enough words to express my utter, and profound love for you not only as a reader, but a true friend. Thank you, Lo.

Batool Zainab Suleman. SERIOUSLY. I have never, and I mean NEVER had someone push me like you have. There is no way this story would have transformed into what it has without you and I am so incredibly grateful. YOU ARE PHENOMENAL!

Andrea, Lana, Garnet, M.L., Matti.

Thank you so much for all of your help and feedback and helping me craft the finale to this duet!!

Thanks to my amazinggggggg editor, proof readers, and cover designer. Ellie, Rosa, and Cat, I don't know how I got so lucky but y'all are incredible. Please stay with me forever and ever and always. Y'all polish my art to a shine no one else can and without you, **sadness**. Thank you ladies!

Again, thank you to everyone! I can't wait for you to get your hands on the other characters of Wonderland.

But until then...Lucian wanted me to ask you...Head or Tails?

About the Author

Lee Jacquot is a wild-haired bibliophile who writes romances with strong heroines that deserve a happy ever after. When Lee isn't writing or drowning herself in a good book, she's laughing or yelling at one of her husband's practical jokes.

Lee is addicted to cozy pajamas, family games nights, and making tents with her kids. She currently lives in Texas with her husband, and three littles. She lives on coffee and Dean Winchester.

Visit her on Instagram or TikTok to find out about upcoming releases and other fun things! @authorleejacquot

Also by Lee Jacquot

I wrote a couple books before this one! Check them out here!

Holinight Novellas

Christmas on the Thirteenth Floor

The Four Leaf

The Wicked Wonderland Duet

Queen of Madness

King of Ruin

The Emerald Falls Series

The Masks We Wear

The Masks We Break

The Masks We Burn

Printed in Great Britain
by Amazon

86752606R00201